The Graelian Chronicles Book Two

THE LEGACY OF ENID

James Colson

To request permissions, contact the publisher at info@jamescolsonbooks.com.

ISBN: 979-8-9901227-3-4 (Hardback)
ISBN: 979-8-9901227-4-1 (Paperback)

First edition printing 2025

Cover art by Renee Colson
Book design by James Colson
Map design by John Flanagan II & James Colson

James Colson
www.JamesColsonBooks.com

For my parents who taught me to be the best version of myself I could be. Thank you, Dad, for your hard work through the years, sacrificing your time and body to provide for us. Thank you, Mom, for taking care of me — I know I wasn't the easiest child to deal with.

To God be the Glory once again for helping me complete this work.

CONTENTS

ABRIA
ROSEWOOD FOREST
GREAT SEA
NORTHERN CITADEL
NORTHWICK
MYSTIC MORNINGS
FABLED WONDERS
MILSTON
OAKSHADOW
LORELEI
FARNA
CASTLE ABRIA
ABRIAN PLATEAU
LAKEDON
Lake Conchobar
VALLEY MOUNTAINS
Cave of Tera
VALLEY WOODS
LILY OF THE VALLEY
ALWYN POINT
CLERICSFOLD
WHISPERSONG
ALWYN
Kingscrown Rock
Lorelei River
Windale Mountains
GREAT SEA
Kingscrown Bay
IDLEWIND
Windale Desert
ABRIA

Chapter 1

The Fallen

Tiernan opened his eyes. Lying on his back, the battered King found his gaze fixated toward the nighttime sky. Just a few moments ago, he had watched his sister Enid, the Dragonborn Heroine herself, disappear in a brilliant flash of light.

In the seconds before her sacrificial act, the gargantuan sphere of magic below Castle Abria, one that had sat undisturbed for close to a thousand years, had been under siege. The combined forces of Zoran, Kane, and Folas wanted its power for reasons unknown.

After a mighty — and costly — battle, Enid had done *something* using her Dragonborn powers to destroy the sphere and release the contained magic back into the world.

Sister, what did you do? Where are you?

A sinking realization washed over Tiernan. With Enid now gone, no one else could stand beside him to defeat their enemies. *I've failed. So many have died, all of them my fault. Because I was too weak. Manus Midir, the guards, Mom, Dad, Wayland, Enid. I failed, and because of that, they're all dead.*

Tiernan stared at the stars above. Their twinkling lights emitted a soft, solemn glow. Like the flicker of a candle, the continuous and subtle shift in their ambience felt like a memorial, a farewell tribute to those who had died throughout the past year.

Tiernan wet his lips, realizing how cracked and parched they felt. Once the battle began, no one had any time for rest. From the moment they encountered the Elven illusions to his last-ditch effort to secure the ancient relics, Tiernan had fought nonstop. By the end, only adrenaline fueled his muscles.

The jewel. What was the jewel all about? Enid, what did you do? Tiernan swallowed as he pondered its significance. Years ago, on the day of their birth, another jewel had played a role in ensuring Enid survived.

No. Not just survived but reborn. And now that she's gone, what does this *jewel mean?*

Tiernan blinked, accepting that he did not know. That he may never know. The only truth his mind could comprehend was that, as Enid attacked the sphere, she disappeared. The truth that, after a brilliant, blinding explosion of light, the three ancient artifacts fell to the ground. The Mind Shield, Power Ring, and Soul Sword lay in a perfect triangle protecting a new object: a book-sized, red, glass-like stone.

"Kane…" The first words Tiernan spoke in his bruised state echoed his disgust and contempt. Moments after Enid destroyed the sphere, the Divider picked up the jewel to inspect it. Tiernan, in a fit of desperation, knocked him over, running shoulder-first into his opponent's torso. The King didn't know what effect his attack had on the already injured Kane.

Tiernan moved his hands in frantic recall. *The relics!* He couldn't remember if he had grabbed any of them. There were only ticks between his attack on Kane and before the Dark Elf transported him here — wherever here might be.

Below Tiernan's hands, the pliable blades of grass running through his fingers and along his open palm felt as empty as his soul. The spongy soil below the greenery let him know he was at least in a fertile land, not that the agricultural viability of this region mattered right now.

After a moment, he felt metal next to his left hand. Tiernan tried to roll over to it, though his body would not cooperate. To his relief, it didn't take long to figure out which relic he possessed.

"The Mind Shield. Thank Aila." At first, Tiernan didn't know why he invoked the name of the fabled Ailan Huntress. The longer he stared at the sky, the more he made the connection. The rumored legacy of the pre-historic heroine bore an uncanny resemblance to Enid.

Moving on, he tried feeling for the others, not sure if he had grabbed the Power Ring or the Soul Sword in his fall. The teleportation flash was disorienting, a sensation he was neither accustomed to nor one he wished to experience again. In his twenty-one short years of life, Tiernan couldn't recall anything else like it.

First, a bright, blinding flash enveloped him. Next, it was as if he didn't exist, torn from reality and lacking any semblance of consciousness. There was no pain, though no comfort either. A state of nothingness he found almost impossible to describe.

It was fleeting, though, and as soon as it started, it was over. A second flash of light deposited him here.

It all happened so fast. He blinked again, trying to figure out where in Abria the Dark Elf had sent him. Alone in the dark, with only the nighttime sky to keep him company, Tiernan screamed, his anger overtaking his thoughts. The King's wail echoed throughout the nearby surroundings, filling the once peaceful field with rage and despair.

Am I even in Abria? High in the distant sky, he could see the Abriacholae constellation looking over him. Its familiar shape told him he was at least in the same hemisphere of the world, though whether he was still within the borders of the Kingdom or thrown all the way to Lyra, he could not tell.

Tiernan groaned as the pain radiating throughout his body snapped him out of his stargazing haze. "Enid…Sister, why? What happened to you?" After another few ticks on the ground, he decided he had to move, regardless of the discomfort. Tiernan tried to sit up.

Instead, the beaten warrior let out a grunt of pain and fell flat on his back.

"Owww." Every muscle, every bone, every square centimeter of his body ached. He had never felt agony like this before.

Not surprising, all things considered. He took a deep breath and, mustering all the strength that he could, rolled over toward the Mind Shield. He felt its metal on his exposed right kneecap, letting him know this portion of his armor was now missing. Its cold metal texture somehow felt comforting on his bare skin, a reminder of the relic's protective embrace.

Tiernan remained face down for a few moments. He smelled the grass, its cold and damp blades brushing his face. The odor of the dirt below felt like an omen of what lie ahead. *Okay, time to put those push-ups from the first Statuo to use.* Tiernan placed his palms flat on the ground, once again feeling the dew-soaked, malleable grass below them. He dug his fingers into the ground, dark rich dirt embedding itself under his nails. Tiernan made a fist, pulling clumps of sod and soil into them, then stretched his fingers outward once again.

With all his might, the King pushed himself up as he let out an angry and determined battle cry.

Though successful, his body was not pleased. Every nerve in his arms and torso screamed at him, letting Tiernan know this was enough movement. Instead of standing, he sat on his calves. It reminded him of how his best friend, Wayland, had once sat in a similar pose. Closing his eyes, Tiernan rested, much like his now-departed friend had done on that memorable day.

Except, this time, there was no one else nearby to comfort the lonely King.

No friend to encourage him, no trainer to guide him.

He had been the ruler of this realm for less than a week, responsible for the land and everyone who lived in it. The burden of leadership weighed heavily on his mind, and more than anything, Tiernan needed a friend with him right now.

After all, despite his best efforts, he had no idea if he had done anything to protect the Kingdom. It seemed more plausible that he may have just utterly failed every denizen under his guard.

So much for my role as a Protector of Abria, he grumbled to himself.

"Time to move." Tiernan dug deep, finding the strength to push himself up from the ground. Still unsteady on his feet, he surveyed the land. He thought in the far distance, if he closed his eyes and concentrated, he could hear something that sounded like water. To be sure, Tiernan took a deep breath, exhaled, and listened harder, trying to shut out the wind, crickets, and other nighttime noises around him.

Okay, that's in my right ear. Yes, definitely water. The intensity, if he was still in Abria, could only mean he was within walking distance of the great Lorelei River. Tiernan bent over, grabbed the Mind Shield, and scanned the open fields one last time. With no sign of the other relics or the strange red jewel, he turned toward the direction where he could hear the raging flow. With each step, pain radiated throughout the King's body. Walking was going to be a chore, but he had no choice.

Unbeknownst to him, Tiernan's foot brushed another object in the fields. It made a small, almost imperceptible *ting* as his boot made contact with it. It rolled over and, as he continued west, the moon's beams reflected off the small, circular piece of metal. Glistening in the light, the Power Ring rested between long blades of grass, waiting for its destined new owner.

Overhead and out of Tiernan's sight, twisting streams of energy continued to spread across the land. Many were well into the early steps of an unknown journey that would have lasting repercussions for years to come.

Tiernan walked for what felt like days; in reality, it wasn't more than an hour or two. The stars in the sky continued their journey across the horizon as Grael spun on its axis. Tiernan himself had no way of knowing when the sun might rise or how soon he would encounter someone else. By now, he walked with a limp. The King realized his exposed knee was also throbbing, a sign of an unseen injury from the battle.

"There it is." In the distance, he saw the banks of the Lorelei River along with a group of horses drinking from it. As it came closer into view, he felt stupid for not realizing where he had reappeared within the Kingdom.

"Of course. It's so obvious. The plains near Whispersong." The fertile nature of the soil made sense now, and Tiernan reappeared in a grassy field Ahern, the proprietor of Whispersong, had yet to cultivate.

Tiernan had only visited here once, not long after the first Statuo. On the day of the games, he borrowed a horse from the temporary stables at Alwyn. He rode it across the fields, arriving just in time to watch Wayland compete in an equestrian competition. For whatever reason, Tiernan felt an immediate bond with the steed, and upon arriving at his friend's event, claimed the horse as his own, a rare act of asserting his royal position.

He named the horse Chocolate because of the color of her coat and in honor of the stallion from legend that Aila was said to have ridden during her adventures. A few weeks later, he brought the horse here to Whispersong for training. It was in these fields where the then-Prince and Chocolate solidified their bond.

Tiernan winced. If he was right, Chocolate could still be tied up near the entrance to the Cave of Tera, along with the other horses and their supply crates. When he ordered the remnants of his accompanying Royal Guards to take Midir and the others back to Farna, he did not give them specific instructions to take Chocolate with them. It would be up to random chance whether they retrieved his beloved horse or chose another. The thought of the Royal Guards leaving her behind made Tiernan queasy.

After all, if they did not take Chocolate back to Farna, she would surely be hungry by now. Tiernan swallowed, realizing his adversaries may have even hurt Chocolate — or any of the other horses — once they left the underground grotto. Unfortunately, there was nothing he could do at the moment. He shook his head in sadness, blaming himself for taking her to the Cave of Tera as yet another sign of his failed leadership. In an attempt to clear his head, Tiernan readied his aching body for the next task at hand.

"Now to cross the river." Tiernan looked around to inspect his options. As far as he could tell, there were going to be two major possibilities from which he could choose. Neither was appealing.

Option one, he could head north to the bridge near Lily of the Valley. With his injury, it would take a long time to reach that location on foot. Afterward, there would be the added delay of walking to Central Abria. Even on a trotting horse, it took most riders the better part of a day to reach the Cave of Tera from the eastern side of the Kingdom.

The way Tiernan felt, his bruised body would be moving far slower than a trot.

His next best option, he decided, was to take his chances and ford the river. This was risky, as the Lorelei River was still experiencing significant runoff from this past season of Frost. Darkember, and leading into Begynde, had been unseasonably warm. The conditions throughout Abria had been so temperate that the four of them — Enid, Wayland, Eislyn, and Tiernan — opted to celebrate Moon Rise in Lorelei instead of Farna. This weather pattern, not to mention the breadth of the Moon Rise celebrations Lorelei had put on, set everyone's expectations for a mild snowfall this year.

Those assumptions and forecasts couldn't have been more wrong. As if on cue, the first day of Florin arrived with the most snow Tiernan had seen in his life. The recorded snowpack broke all historical records, blanketing the northern communities and burying them under several meters of dense, heavy powder. To everyone's surprise, the unrelenting snow battered Milston and Northwick well into the third week of Windbloom. High in the Milston Mountains, even today in the second week of Flametide, snow continued to melt, fueling the might of the Lorelei River.

He walked up to the banks. The angry sound of the water's movement seemed, paradoxically, peaceful. While torrential and imposing, it felt less full of turmoil than what he felt in his heart.

"I wouldn't do it," said a voice.

Tiernan turned around to see a stable hand sitting on a giant boulder along the river's edge.

"Crossing the Lorelei *without* a steed during this time of year? You know how dangerous that is even if we hadn't had a ton of snowfa—" The man's eyes widened. "Prince Tiernan? What are you doing out here, sir?" He bowed out of instinctive respect.

"Don't," Tiernan said, as he grabbed the man's arms. He didn't want any undeserved pleasantries right now, nor did he feel it necessary to communicate his new status as King. Enid stepping down and the exclusive transfer of power to Tiernan and Eislyn was a relative secret outside of Farna.

In Tiernan's view, there was no need to make the man any more uncomfortable than he already appeared in the presence of royalty. The King shifted the conversation away from titles to the matter at hand. "I need to get back to Farna as quickly as possible. Do you have a horse nearby? I believe Ahern domesticates new herds during this time of year."

The man nodded his head. "There is a small group of horses we've been trying to train not far from here. We built a large fenced-in enclosure for them, but they're many months from being ready."

Tiernan sighed, then rubbed his temples. "Well. An untrained horse crossing these waters is better than nothing. Which way is the enclosure?"

The man pointed southeast toward Idlewind.

"Guess I better get going." Tiernan turned around and began walking.

"Wait, Sir. Here. Take this." The man handed him a small dagger from his satchel. "For protection. I see you have a shield, and an interesting looking one at that, but no weapon. You never know what might be around the corner."

He continued in an even more respectful tone. "And if it's all the same to you, it would honor me if you would allow me to accompany you back to Farna. For extra safety."

Tiernan took the blade from the man and regarded it for a moment. *I don't want to drag anyone else into this, but I'm in no condition to fight. And home is a long way from here.*

Tiernan smiled. "You know, I could use the company. Would you follow me to Clericsfold at least? I have something I must retrieve from the nearby fields, and then you can return the horse I'm borrowing. Sound good?"

The man nodded.

Tiernan raised an eyebrow. "What about your employer?"

"Ahern? Well, yes, it would be honorable to let him know what I'm doing. But I think he'll understand when I explain who I was helping. No one would take issue assisting a member of the royal family."

Tiernan, tired of the royal platitudes, shoved aside the thoughts bubbling to the top and reminded himself that no one could change his lot in life. He coughed, stopped and gazed westward toward Farna, running his hands through his crusty, sweat-dried, dirty hair in deep contemplation. For the first time in his life, Tiernan considered cutting it. *Some kind of style Dad would have liked. Eislyn will know of a good barber.*

If I make it home, that is. Just then, a sickened feeling washed over him. *If Zoran or Kane invade Farna before I can make it home, Eislyn will have to lead our people into battle.* He closed his eyes in a round of self-loathing. *She didn't sign up for this. I've dragged her into this mess, too.*

Tiernan decided he had waited long enough. "Let's go," he said. The two men began walking toward the makeshift enclosure to the south. "By the way, I didn't catch your name."

"Rosk."

Tiernan narrowed his eyebrows as the men walked side by side. "What a curious name. What city are you fro…" Tiernan could not finish his words. Instead, the world around him began spinning.

Rosk reached out to grab him, but was too late.

Tiernan's footing fell out from under him. The last thing he heard was the distant sound of Rosk's voice yelling his name.

Chapter 2

Taking Charge

As the sun rose over the Valley Mountains and woke the communities of Abria from their collective slumber, one member of the royal family had yet to sleep. Queen Eislyn paced back and forth in the throne room, having been here since the explosion in the northern portion of the city rocked this once peaceful community three days ago.

The ten guards with her stood motionless, letting their commander vent her quiet, yet growing, frustration. With the King missing, she was the temporary — and though no one wanted to speak it, possibly official — ruler of Abria. Every passing day reaffirmed this unspoken belief to all of those within the hallowed halls of Castle Abria.

The weight of leadership could not have come at a worse time. Eislyn's thoughts drifted to her unborn child as she paced. Fear gripped her heart. She hoped the stresses of leadership would not affect the development of the life she carried in her body.

Stresses of leadership.

Eislyn stopped her pacing at the mere thought of the phrase, recalling all that had happened since her husband and his sister departed Farna. Of course, there was the requisite waiting period. Traveling to Central Abria took time. At best, it was at least a day's travel, such as when traveling solo on a champion steed. With their supplies and the volume of guards they took with them, Tiernan's journey would have taken longer.

Then, of course, there was the exploration of the mostly unknown underground cavern system. Eislyn rubbed her face with her hands. No one knew how complex the subterranean passageways were, never mind with a group of their size. Assuming they found their enemies somewhere below, there would be a battle.

Eislyn resumed her pacing. The lack of news and communication ate at her soul. Compounded by the still-unexplained explosion that had wrecked portions of Farna, this had been anything but a normal week. The needs of the Kingdom required that she step up, moving beyond a placeholder rule and taking proactive measures to protect Abria.

Out of the corner of her eye, she saw a guard let out an accidental yawn. Across the room, the commander of this unit, a first lieutenant, gave him a reprimanding stare. She chose not to acknowledge the interaction and instead reflected on their presence. Each of them stood spaced evenly along the walls and behind the dual set of thrones carved by her father-in-law ages ago.

Eislyn sighed, feeling sympathy for their plight. Once the ground exploded, she had no choice but to increase security precautions throughout Farna. This included the number of guards with her at all times. This group had been with her for well over a full day without a rest.

It went without saying that the past sixty-seven hours had put everyone in Farna on edge. Nervousness and trepidation encompassed those who served within Castle Abria. No one wanted to admit it, but with recent events, the truth was becoming more and more clear.

Farna was no longer the city of peace as it was known throughout Abria. It had become one embroiled in worry, turmoil, and now even severe hardship. The mood of the populace was a far cry from the harmonious and joyful community of her youth.

And, until the King returned, all they could do was wait.

Wait for the next battle.

Wait for the next explosion.

Or worse, wait for their enemies to invade and summon the end of all they had grown to know and love.

A guard knocked on the wood of the open door, interrupting the Queen's uneasy thoughts. She took a deep breath and closed her eyes. *Please let this be word of my husband. Tiernan, return to me safely. This is your Kingdom. Not mine. I'm not cut out for this.*

Sensing her unease, each of the guards stationed throughout the throne room grabbed their swords as a precaution. The Queen opened her eyes and cleared her throat. She turned around to address them.

"Legate." She nodded to the unnamed deputy. "You have news?" Her voice, firm yet also gentle, masked the fear lying below the surface.

"We do, Your Majesty. Once the…" The legate searched for the word. "…crater, as we've been calling it in the field, appeared and the energy stopped flowing out of it, Commander Titus began sending new scouts down every hour." The guard looked exhausted despite his attempted polished appearance.

Her frustration broke through. "Speak plainly to me, legate. What did you find?" Eislyn wanted more than anything to be kind. Her management style at the Drunken Alligator was always one of equality with her subordinates. It created a mutual respect that made her parent's tavern a desirable place of employment within Farna.

Today, Eislyn didn't know what to do other than maintain military decorum. After all, they were in a state of war. How she managed those under her authority during peacetime, she would have to figure out later.

For someone who had only been a part of the royal family for a little over a month, Eislyn's rise to Commander of the Abrian Royal Army happened just one week ago. She only knew a few of the names of those under her authority, and her normal methods of instilling trust and building rapport would have to take a back seat to a more pressing need.

Keeping Abria safe.

The deputy nodded out of respect to her position. "Yes, my Queen. It took a while. We finally found enough rope to rappel down the chasm. Of course, it took many of us holding those ropes in place to support the guards who rappelled down. It was exhausting work."

Eislyn made a mental note to commission some kind of lever-based system for the future since the chasm was now a permanent feature of the Farna landscape. The Queen empathized with the plight of the guards tasked with holding the ropes in place.

"To your original question, yes, I come bearing news. They explored every meter of the antechamber, connecting caverns, and the nearby tunnels. There was nothing down there, besides the bodies of many fallen soldiers and deceased Elves."

Eislyn swallowed. *Fallen guards, but he didn't mention T or Enid.*

"What about my husband? And the Princess?"

"I'm sorry, Your Highness. We found neither of them, nor did we find their bodies."

Eislyn tried to keep her composure. Tiernan and Enid charged into this battle with only minimal knowledge of the threat they were facing. Anything could have happened. Zoran's power was an unknown variable as well. For all she knew, he vaporized their bodies the moment he saw them. *Why did I let him go?*

Before she could ask more questions, another lieutenant showed up.

"Pardon the intrusion, Your Highness. A group has arrived from the Cave of Tera. And, oddly, a horseback messenger has also arrived from Whispersong. He said he has information on the whereabouts of your husband."

That's ironic timing, she thought. *Could be a trap.* Without thinking, she rubbed her belly. She had told no one besides Tiernan about their coming child. Not even her parents knew. After realizing her accidental motion, she tried to cover it. She turned to the deputy.

"Legate, I could use something from the galley. Small, simple. Bland. I don't remember the last time I ate. Perhaps an Abrian Artisan Strudel."

The deputy snapped to attention. "Yes, my Queen."

As he left, she turned to the new arrival. "Bring the survivors in. Who made it back from the Cave of Tera?"

The officer lowered his head for a moment, then looked her in the eye. "Five. Two from Manus Midir's original expedition, and three from the King's."

"Is Midir among them? And what is their condition?"

He shook his head. "We asked. They said the Manus, even in a weakened state, charged back into the battle but did not return. The two from his expedition are in rough shape. It might be best to take them to the infirmary first. The other three seem exhausted, but alive."

Eislyn wished more than anything Tiernan was here. This mysterious messenger from Whispersong might reveal some vital information. Then again, it could be a hoax like the Shapeshifter incident from last week.

"Do we know *for sure* that the five from the Cave expeditions are, in fact, Graelans?"

The officer started to speak, then pursed his lips.

"The messenger from Whispersong. Anything on him?"

The guard lowered his head without speaking a word.

Of course. And no magical Princess to stop them if they're a foe.

Eislyn realized that she was facing an impossible situation. She wanted to know what had happened. But also, as the Queen, she had to keep herself as safe as possible. For the sake of the Kingdom.

No, not for Abria. For the heir to the throne. Boy or girl, Eislyn allowed the implication that her unborn child would one day sit on the throne to linger in her thoughts so that she could keep it at the front and center of her decisions.

They're my *unborn child, but it goes deeper than that. I have to protect him or her at all costs for the sake of Abria as well.*

She looked at the ten guards, then back at the one in the doorway. *Time to be a leader.* "We have to play it safe. I want a half dozen guards watching the group going to the infirmary. At the first sign of anything suspicious, they are to be…" She took a deep breath. "…dealt with." She paused, intending to let the gravity of the unspoken order sink in.

"Do I make myself clear?" she asked.

"Yes, Your Highness," they answered in unison.

She continued. "The same goes for the other three, though I want the number of guards with them doubled since they're mobile. Once you are reasonably sure they're Graelan, I'll come."

"It will be done," the commanding lieutenant responded.

She raised her hand, finger extended toward the lieutenant. "One more thing. Send the captain of the Abrian Royal Guard to me immediately. We need to increase our security procedures even more and I need to discuss those details. No one should walk around alone. Everyone in Castle Abria must travel in pairs. Dismissed."

The commanding lieutenant motioned to another guard to follow.

Once they left the room, she turned to the other eight. "I hate to do this, but the city is now on lockdown. No visitors from outside of Farna may enter until we can confirm they're Graelan or Graelian."

She sighed, holding back tears as her next command weighed heavy on her heart. "The following edict should be posted at all public gathering places and distributed to each home. Write this down and send to the castle scribes for immediate duplication and dissemination.

"'Until further notice, no one may leave the city of Farna. All citizens are to remain in their homes if at all possible. There should be no social loitering. If your home was destroyed, please move your family to the Drunken Alligator. Volunteers are needed for reconstruction. If you can help, see the Queen's mom, Freya, at the Alligator for assignments.'"

A guard finished taking down her words as the captain of the Royal Guard walked in.

"Ah, yes, Captain Nico. Come." Eislyn motioned toward the open throne room floor. "Did the lieutenant mention anything to you?"

He removed his helmet and put it under his arms. "Only that we were to increase security precautions and to come here right away."

Eislyn turned to a nearby window. With her back to the room, she closed her eyes. "The city of Farna and Castle Abria itself are both on lockdown. The guard with the notepad has a royal edict to disseminate. Travel with him to the scribes and see to it that you familiarize yourself with its contents. We are at war, captain, and we cannot let our guard down for any reason.

"In addition, you are to post additional guards at the entrances and exits of Castle Abria as well as all main entrances to Farna itself. Every common room in this stronghold must be locked. If it isn't critical to castle operations, seal it. If it's open, no less than two guards should be posted at its entrance." She leaned on the windowsill, both to support her exhausted body and with a great, gut-wrenching sadness. "My message must be distributed throughout Farna *with haste.*" Nico and the other guard both nodded and left without saying a word.

Eislyn kept her back to the rest of the room as she opened her eyes. Gazing at the streets below, she watched the people. The view reiterated her lament: the joyous, peaceful aura Farna was known for was gone. With these commands, she had just declared Imperial Law. Though she was no historian, she knew such draconian measures had not been implemented since the rule of King Farris.

Eislyn remained at the window, watching as the visible guards issued commands to each other. Once they understood their orders, several began approaching denizens and pointing in different directions. Eislyn glanced toward the gaping hole in the ground, watching the guards collect the ropes.

For the first time, she dared to look at the Drunken Alligator. One of her former wait staff appeared to be unscrewing the hinges from the doors. In silence, she watched as the man pulled the door off of its frame and carried it out of sight. Another member of her team, a hostess named Regina, motioned for more people to come inside. Eislyn couldn't make out all the details, but it looked as if her parents had removed the tables and replaced them with cots.

The man who took the door down returned, this time holding a tent. He yelled something inside and a few moments later, a pair of men came outside. They pitched the tent, then began carrying out cots.

Eislyn sighed, looking at the crater in the distance, an entire row of homes in ruins near it. Her parents had responded by turning their tavern into a home for displaced citizens.

Over Farna, a cloud moved in front of the sun and obscured its light. Eislyn turned her head in its direction as an ominous feeling washed over her.

Imperial Law. This is just the start of what's coming.

Chapter 3

Those That Are Lost

Tiernan opened his eyes. Or rather, he tried to. No matter how much effort he exerted, he could not focus on what was around him. Likewise, a similar blurriness clouded his mind. The King couldn't think nor could he even comprehend what he was seeing. Tiernan rubbed them, but it didn't help. He massaged his temples, realizing his head was pounding worse than anything he could ever recall.

That may have been relative, though, considering the number of times Zoran used magic to throw Tiernan against the cave walls. Even in his most intense training sessions, he hadn't felt pain like he had in the underground caves.

Tiernan put his hands back down to his sides. Below them, he could feel a padded mattress. He blinked a few times again, desperate to get his eyes to come into focus.

It was a futile effort, so he changed his tactics to trying to sit up. However, his body felt heavy. He tried to push himself off of the mattress, but lacked the strength. With no other options, he called out.

"Hello…?" His voice had a raspy timbre to it, barely louder than a whisper. He waited, but no one walked into the room. So, he tried again.

"Is anyone…" Tiernan coughed. "Is anyone out there?" This time, he could exert a bit more volume out of his weak lungs. In a hallway outside, he heard movement. Whoever it was walked into his room.

"Good afternoon, my liege. Welcome to Whispersong. How are you feeling?" The voice belonged to a woman, though not one Tiernan recognized in his haze. Tiernan realized his hearing was affected too and, with his eyes still unfocused and body unresponsive, he was at their mercy.

"Horrible." He swallowed. "How long have I been here?"

"Three days. Rosk carried you to the nearby enclosure and brought you here on the back of a horse. My husband sent him to Farna using one of our proven horses to inform the castle of your whereabouts. I'm Pernella."

Three days…

"Pernella. I remember you. You brought me something. What was it? Some kind of meal each day when I trained Chocolate here."

Pernella walked over to Tiernan's side and placed her hand on his shoulder. "I remember too. Spiced Veggie Pockets. You said it was one of the best things you ever tasted."

Tiernan turned his head toward her voice and tried to smile. He put his left hand on top of hers. "That's right. Listen, Pernella, do you have any other stable hands? One who could make it to the Cave of Tera quickly?"

"We do, but why?"

Tiernan removed his hand, then closed his eyes to let them rest. No sense in trying to clear them. Whatever ailment had affected his vision wasn't giving up. *Do I tell her what's going on? By now, Rosk should be in Farna. Eislyn surely would have filled him in.*

He coughed to clear his throat. "Because there's far more at stake here. But besides that, I left my horse near the Cave of Tera. Chocolate. I fear for her safety."

"What is at stake?" Another voice, this time belonging to a man, entered the conversation. Tiernan opened his eyes, hoping they might be more cooperative.

Thankfully, they were. He could see the outline of the man's form this time, even if it was still a shadow of a silhouette.

"Prince Tiernan, this is my husband, Ahern. You met him once during your stay here."

Ahern threw up his hand as if to say hello. "Yes, I was away on business for most of the time you were here. I heard many stories. I'm glad we could be of service, both then and now as well. We'll do whatever we can to make your stay here comfortable, Prince Tiernan."

"It's King Tiernan, actually." *Time to break the news.* "A lot has happened over the past few weeks."

"King Tiernan? What happened to Princess Enid?" asked Pernella.

"Last we heard, you and your sister had agreed upon some kind of joint rule," Ahern said.

"If I knew where my sister was, I would tell you. The truth is, I don't know. Chocolate is at the Cave of Tera because Enid and I led an expedition to rescue Manus Midir…"

"The guy from Idlewind?" Ahern asked.

"Yes, from Idlewind. We hoped to rescue him along with defeating a group of…collaborators, I guess."

"And you're the King because?" Pernella asked.

"You heard about the attacks in Alwyn and Idlewind? And that Prince Wayland was killed during them?"

The couple exchanged a look of concern. Ahern moved closer to his wife. "We only heard that Idlewind had been under siege from a beast called Gamelyon. We didn't know about Alwyn, nor that Prince Wayland had been lost," he answered.

"So soon after the wedding…" Pernella lamented.

"The attack happened during the reception. An ancient evil has returned, an entity we now know as Zoran. Our mission to the Cave of Tera was to defeat him." Noticing their confusion, he continued. "Kane from Clericsfold. Folas, a Dark Elf from the

Rosewood Forest. They killed Mom and Dad, awoke this Zoran being, and tried to steal a large repository of magic below Farna.

"Enid stepped down, paving the way for my wife and I to ascend to the throne as the official King and Queen in place of my parents." Tiernan paused, letting the gravity of each sentence sink in.

"And you said you don't know what happened to Enid because…?" Pernella's voice trailed off.

Tiernan closed his eyes again before answering. "Like her husband, she's gone too. Lost in battle against our enemies."

Queen Eislyn walked into the threshold of the war room. It was here that, just two weeks ago, her husband sat with Enid and Midir. Those strategies to defeat Zoran and Kane clearly failed, leaving her in charge. It felt odd to Eislyn to be the one making decisions, pretending to be some grand ruler of Abria when all she ever wanted to be was the wife of the man she fell in love with.

Stop it. You are *the one in charge. The days of running the Alligator are behind you.* Eislyn suddenly found herself thankful for the privacy of her internal monologue. Those under her command and leadership needed to see confidence and authority, not doubt and weakness.

As she surveyed the room, she noticed every guard now stood with another side-by-side. Captain Nico was quick, a characteristic for which Eislyn was grateful. This change, while somewhat redundant, might ensure that no single guard could be compromised without someone else knowing about it.

Around the table sat the three men who had returned from the Cave of Tera. Next to one of them, a nervous horseback rider from Whispersong looked scared witless.

Still on edge and somewhat cautious, Eislyn remained at the doorway entrance. She then addressed the men.

"I hope you don't find our increased security measures offensive. With the events of the past couple of weeks being what they've been, these are practical considerations. Nothing we've done has been intended as an attack on you or your character."

The rider from Whispersong looked even more confused and scared. Something changed within him at her words.

She eyed him and realized what it was. *Graelan emotion.* The look on his face alone made Eislyn feel at ease. *No Shapeshifter could emulate those expressions. I hope anyway.*

A guard spoke up. "After what we saw in the depths below, your caution is warranted, Your Highness."

Eislyn nodded to them. "What is your name?"

"Argyle," he said.

She raised both hands. "Stop. Let's go around the room first. We need some formal introductions. I know it's my job now to know your names, since you're under my command even when the King is here. But since my sister-in-law was your commander until her resignation a week ago, I'm still trying to get caught up.

"So please. Forgive my lack of knowledge and tell me your names."

"Of course. As I said, my name is Argyle, sergeant first class."

"I'm Jabron, lieutenant junior grade."

"My name is Tadgh, sergeant second class."

Everyone looked at the messenger from Whispersong, who sat with a nervous and overwhelmed look on his face.

"We're waiting. Your name, please," Eislyn reminded him.

"Rosk, ma'am. My Queen, I guess? I'm sorry, can someone fill me in on what's going on here? When I left Whispersong, Tiernan was the *Prince.* He never said anything about him being King."

Eislyn felt the hairs on the back of her neck stand up. If his words were the truth, Tiernan was still alive.

And it was true what he said: no one outside of Farna had time to learn of Enid's decision to step down. His confusion made sense.

Unless Shapeshifters have gotten better at deceit. Eislyn felt sick, and wasn't sure if it was the baby or the predicament she was in. She realized she had to push Rosk harder.

"How did you meet my husband, exactly?"

"It was extraordinary. In the far distance, I saw what looked like a flash and something fall to the ground. It was as if a force had snapped him there.

"I kept my distance as the form approached the area where I had been stargazing."

"Why didn't you try to help him?" The Queen's words put the room on high alert. A few guards placed their hands on the handle of their swords, ready to strike.

Rosk noticed. His eyes grew wide, and he stuttered as he explained. "I...I didn't know it was the Prince. I mean the King. Tiernan, ma'am, until I saw him face-to-face. He was preparing to ford the Lorelei River without a horse."

He cleared his throat, regaining his composure. "Besides, consider what I had just witnessed. A man quite literally appeared out of thin air only a month after that beast came out of nowhere and attacked the city to our south. I wasn't sure *what* to think."

Eislyn still felt on edge, but decided that Rosk's story made sense. She nodded to the guards, who were ready to attack. They returned to attention.

"Thanks for believing me. I think. But I don't understand. Why is everyone on edge? All King Tiernan told me was that he left something near the Cave of Tera. He didn't say what it was exactly."

"He probably was referring to his horse, Chocolate," Jabron proposed. He turned to Eislyn. "We brought Chocolate with us. Unfortunately, we had to leave some of the other horses behind. We set them free, hoping they might find food or someone to take them in."

"You let a trained horse run free?" Rosk said with a horrified expression. "If they've been domesticated, it also means they've lost some of their innate—"

Eislyn silenced him with an outstretched hand. Rosk's exasperation and care for the horses confirmed what she needed to know about him.

He was Graelan.

She turned to the others. "What happened in the Cave of Tera?"

Chapter 4

The Riot in Lakedon

Lagen stirred a large pot of soup. He smiled at his wife, a long-haired, petite Elf who stood at the opposite end of the common dining hall. She caught his glance and returned it with a half-hearted, partial upward twist of her lips. Lagen lowered his gaze, knowing what she was thinking without needing her to express the words.

Again. Once again, we're refugees. But this time not from barbarian invaders.

From our very own brethren.

Though no one had an exact count, current estimates were that two hundred of the five hundred-strong Elven population had willingly aligned with Folas along with many others they somehow coerced into helping them. Those specific Elves appeared to be in a daze, as if their stiff, methodical movements were indicative of an unseen power controlling their actions.

Lagen swallowed, remembering one of his dear friends, Soma. One day, while standing side by side, his body turned rigid. His countenance shifted, another force somehow having taken over his body. Soma possessed the power of illusion, a rare gift even among the Elves. Without so much as a cursory glance backward, Soma left the area where he had been working and disappeared into parts unknown of the Rosewood Forest.

Rumor had it Soma later appeared alongside other Folas-aligned Elves, though, try as he might, Lagen had been unable to confirm that for himself. Of course, not long after, it didn't matter.

Once Folas enacted his plan with Kane, the remnants of their once great Elven nation split in two. Some moved to Oakshadow during the Statuo. After the death of King Davien and Queen Kyrie, dozens more fled here to Lakedon while the rest had taken up residence throughout Abria.

The door to Dídean Inn opened. A woman he recognized walked in. Everyone in the community knew Róisín. Her larger-than-life personality was only matched by her biological significance in the Kingdom.

Róisín was the mother of the late Queen.

She and her husband, Lugh, had worked day and night to convert this space into a place of refuge. Dídean Inn had become their home, though not without a sense of sadness. Once a vacation destination to host visitors to Lakedon, it now acted as a sanctuary for Elvenkind. Those unaligned with Folas were no longer welcome in the Rosewood Forest.

No. Not the Rosewood Forest. The Darkwood Forest. Lagen scowled as he recalled this bitter detail. Folas and his followers had renamed their home not long after the King and Queen fell.

Lagen sighed. He tried not to think about that day too often, though it seemed to control his thoughts today. Róisín had returned from the funeral determined. Her daughter's death had transformed the way she viewed the world. No longer content to spend their golden years in slumber, she and Lugh set out with a renewed purpose.

Lagen looked around the hall. Forty-nine. That was the number of his kind fortunate enough to have made their home in Dídean Inn. That included Lagen and his wife. He shook his head to snap himself out of his thoughts.

Lagen tasted the soup in front of him. "It's missing something," he mumbled. "It's almost there. Just needs an extra kick."

But of what?

Lagen looked around the kitchen area and saw a head of garlic. Smiling, he walked over and tore off a clove. Next, he squeezed it tight. A small, steady stream of smoke emerged between his fingers. Then he opened his hand. His palm still appeared red as his compressed Fire Magic caused a bit of skin inflammation. It didn't hurt, since he was immune to the effect.

He sat the garlic on the cutting board and reached for his nearby chef's knife. He chopped the clove with fine precision, catching a whiff of its now-toasted scent. Just as he scooped the pieces onto his knife's edge, a blood-curdling scream filled the air from somewhere outside.

All the refugees in Dídean Inn dropped whatever they had in their hands in response. Lagen's knife fell to the ground, the remnants of his chopped garlic scattering across the floor in a discarded and soon to be forgotten mess. He ran to his wife to embrace her.

"What was that?" she asked with a look of fear spreading across her face.

He smoothed his hand over her hair in a futile attempt to calm her reaction. "It's okay. I'm going to go check it out. Stay here." He kissed her forehead and crept toward the door. The natural skittish tendencies of his kind fought hard against his need to investigate.

After all, his wife was his responsibility, not to mention the other Elves cowering throughout the converted lobby. Lagen saw their faces and understood he had to step up at this moment. He swallowed hard and pushed on the door to open it. The act of walking outside fueled his fear, putting his magic on hyper alert. Though now scared beyond reason, Lagen focused his emotions on the outside, hoping to calm his nerves.

Standing near a tree, a Graelan woman knelt on her hands and knees. Beside her, a boy around ten or eleven years old stood slack-jawed.

"Mom, I'm okay."

"No, no, you're not. This isn't right."

Faster than a moth to a flame, residents of Lakedon crowded around the two of them. Lagen could smell something, almost like the aroma of burning wood. It reminded him of the days of exile, sitting around the campfire trying to stay warm while keeping a watchful eye open for attackers.

Why am I waxing poetic for days long forgotten? Pushing his emotions aside, Lagen strained to see what had caused the commotion. He turned back to his wife through the still-open door, nodded, and made his way down the porch steps and into the open streets of Lakedon.

Before he made it more than a half dozen meters into the village, the unthinkable happened. The boy, now visible, turned around. His hand was open and, as he spun, a wave of red magic burst from his palm. It ignited a nearby tree. Lagen realized there was another small bush ablaze next to the boy's mother, its burning remnants the apparent source of the smell.

Graelans don't have magic, except for the Dragonborn. Lagen stopped moving and observed these interactions with curiosity and caution. Another man, this one much older, walked up and extinguished the flame with his hand. He turned to the mother and her son and smiled.

"It's going to be okay," he said as he knelt down next to her.

"How can you say that? Look at what he did—"

"Yes, and yesterday I froze an entire crop field. It didn't make sense to me either. Please, I can help him. Trust me."

Lagen watched with utter amazement as the man sent a blast of Frost Magic toward the sky. It exploded in a fantastical display of energy, transformed into snow, and spread out across the center of town. As it fell, the snow melted and turned into a light mist that covered the faces of those gazing upward. The crowd reacted in awe before the oddity of this sunk in.

A murmur began spreading from Graelan to Graelan as the man smiled and extended his hand toward the mother.

She stared at it, reluctant to do anything.

"Mom." Her son broke her trance, and she looked up at him. He nodded as his hand burned with his newfound abilities. She swallowed, grabbed the man's hand, and stood to her feet with him.

The man hugged her, then extended his arm toward the boy to bring him closer.

Without question, the youth grabbed the man's hand. "It's going to be okay, Mom."

She gave her son a faint smile just as, in a brilliant and blinding flash, all three disappeared.

The murmuring in the crowd amplified. A woman in the middle of the group spoke up in an angry voice. "Where did they go?" she cried out.

"They teleported. Only Elves can do that," a man said.

"Was that even a man?" another woman asked. She turned around to face Lagen and pointed. "Some Elves can cast illusions. Did you do this? You or one of your people, anyway. You're always causing problems wherever you go."

The crowd turned in his direction. Lagen looked back and forth at their faces. He saw the same thing he had seen centuries ago when the barbarians decimated his people.

Fear. Mistrust. Anger.

Hate.

Step by step, Lagen backed up. As he neared the steps of Dídean Inn, he realized the crowd had continued to advance toward him as well. His left heel made contact with the first step of the porch. It caught him by surprise, and Lagen stumbled backward.

"Thief! Sorcerer!"

"We invited you in and this is how you repay us?"

"Who else have you infected with your schemes?"

Lagen rose back to his feet just as a rock came flying from the back of the group. It missed him by a quarter meter, though it inspired others in the crowd do the same. More rocks flew toward the Inn as the mob grew in both size and anger.

Lagen wished he had teleportation powers. In this moment, he could have transported out of sight and then returned to Dídean Inn to retrieve his wife.

He considered creating a fire barrier between the crowd and himself. He looked around, realizing there was no safe way to protect himself without risking injury to the others — never mind what it might do to the rest of the structures throughout Lakedon.

Another Graelan in the crowd, one with superior aim, threw a rock toward Lagen. This time, it hit him on the shoulder. By now, the other Elves from inside Dídean Inn had walked out on the porch, despite their fear and growing apprehension.

"What's going on?" asked Frist, an Elf with a stocky build reminiscent of his hefty attitude.

Lagen pointed at the burned bush, then motioned his head toward the crowd. "I don't know. I saw a Graelan boy with Fire Magic, and an older male with Frost Magic. Then they both teleported away along with the boy's mother."

More rocks made their way from the approaching crowd toward the porch. Frist stepped forward and cast a Barrier between the front of the building and the mob.

Róisín rushed outside. She looked to the Elves gathered around Lagen. One tended to his wounded shoulder. Frist stood, arms raised, ready to reinforce the Barrier if needed.

"What happened?" Her voice carried with it the same sense of authority and strength her daughter Kyrie had been known for during the latter's reign.

"Something I can't explain. I just saw a Graelan boy with Fire Magic plus a man with both Frost Magic and teleportation powers." Lagen watched Róisín's face. He could see her mind working and assumed he knew what she was thinking.

"Fire and Frost. Like Enid and her husband," she said as a rock hit the Barrier, making a loud thump as it bounced off the invisible shield and landed in the dirt.

Then another. And another. Soon, the crowd hurled a consistent series of rocks toward Dídean Inn. Frist twirled his hands and sent out a layer of magical reinforcement. As some from the crowd walked toward the side of the porch, another Elf with the same powers erected a similar Barrier to stop them.

"We're not safe here," Lagen's wife said.

Róisín nodded in agreement. "No, you're not. How many of you have teleportation powers?"

Four raised their hands. Inside of Dídean Inn, another four shouted various words of affirmation.

Eight of us. That's six or seven each. Assuming they're not low on magic. Lagen shook his head. "That's not enough save everyone."

Determined, Róisín continued. "Of you eight, how many of you attended the Statuo when it was in Farna?" Six raised their hand.

"Okay, you six, I want you to get as many as you can to the capital. Picture whatever you remember from the city and teleport there. When you get to Farna, find my grandchildren, Tiernan and Enid. They'll be able to help."

Another volley of rocks flew toward the porch.

Frist recoiled from the impact. "I can't keep this up," he warned. The other Elf on the other end of the porch echoed the sentiment.

"Let's move! You two," Róisín said, motioning to the other Elves with teleportation powers. "Just go. Take as many as you can to wherever you feel safe in Abria. Just anywhere but here. Go!" Róisín felt a hand on her shoulder. She turned around to see her husband.

"You go with the group heading to Farna."

"Lugh…"

"The Royal Guards are not going to take kindly to a bunch of Elves randomly appearing within the city. But they at least know *you*. I'll stay here with Frist and buy you some time." Lugh tossed an ether to each of the Elves struggling to keep the Barriers active. "That's all I have, fellas. Make it count."

"Where did you get those?" asked his wife.

"I've been saving them for a rainy day. Lucky for us, right? Get out of here. Find the twins."

Before Róisín could protest, an Elf named Serin grabbed her hand along with three others nearby. He snapped his free hand and disappeared.

Lagen stood up. The other five Elves who had been to Farna grabbed the hands of those around them. In an instant, twenty-seven more disappeared.

The two who had not been to Farna remained. Lagen walked up to his wife. "I want you out of here."

She began to protest, but relented after careful consideration. Lagen felt relief as she nodded and grabbed the hand of one of his brethren.

"Where are you taking her?" he asked.

"Well, the Forest isn't safe," the Elf responded. "I'll take her to the beaches to the south by the flaming rock."

Satisfied, Lagen kissed his wife on the forehead, then hugged her. "I'll see you again, my love." He let go and backed up.

With that, the final two with teleportation powers disappeared, along with those they could grab, leaving seven Elves and one Graelan on the porch.

Lugh walked up to the group.

"I'm in this with you," he said to Lagen and the others as someone threw a lit torch over the barrier and onto the roof of the porch.

Chapter 5

A New World

Queen Eislyn did her best to maintain her composure. The details of the battle were bad enough. So many senseless deaths, including the presumed passing of Manus Midir. The revelation that, yes, a large repository of magic had sat undisturbed for untold centuries below Farna.

It was the end that got to her. The uncertainty of those final moments confused the Queen, especially since all current evidence pointed her sister-in-law dying in the final confrontation.

Eislyn turned her attention to the rider from Whispersong. "Okay, we've heard their side of the story. Evil Elves, Zoran, Kane. The disappearances of Manus Midir and Enid. Let's forget about all of that for a moment."

What am I saying? Forget about Enid? How? Even I know she's all that was between us and certain defeat.

Pushing her discomfort aside, she spoke again. "Tell me again about my husband's reappearance in your fields."

Rosk cleared his throat. "It's as I said, my liege. In the distance, I saw an odd flash and a shape fall. I was far enough away that I could tell it was a Graelanoid, but I couldn't tell if it was a Graelan, Elf, or something else.

"They remained on the ground for a while. I kept my distance, cautiously observing their movements. After a while, they stood up and walked in my direction. It took them almost an hour to reach where I was sitting."

"Wait a minute," said one of the guards.

Queen Eislyn turned his direction.

"They were close enough you could tell it was a Graelanoid, yet it took them an hour to reach you?"

"They were not walking fast, lieutenant. Junior grade, if I'm not mistaken."

Eislyn raised her eyebrows as she found it interesting Rosk understood the rank insignia on the Abrian Royal Guard's outfit enough to call them by their proper designation.

Rosk continued. "I would hardly call it walking. Stumbling is more like it. If I was a betting person, I'd have thought they had just left a Drunken Alligator and had a few too many."

Eislyn waved off more protests from the guard. He snapped to attention at her rebuke.

"Continue, Rosk. What happened next?" the Queen asked.

"Once the Prin…I mean, once the King was close enough, and I talked to him, I realized who he was. He mentioned needing to go to the Cave of Tera to retrieve something. I started to walk with him to a pen where we keep horses we're taming. Before we made it there, he collapsed. I then moved him to Whispersong, where Ahern and Pernella said they would care for him. After that, I came straight here on our fastest steed."

Eislyn wanted nothing more than to hop on a horse and take it straight to Whispersong. To be by her husband's side.

Except I have a Kingdom to run right now. At least Tiernan is alive. One minor victory in all of this.

She twisted her hands, rubbing them together in a visual sign of anxiety. "How bad is he?" As the words left her lips, she pulled her hands below the table to hide them from the rest in attendance.

Stay calm. They need you to show strength, not weakness.

"He had not regained consciousness before I left. They administered a few potions to him, but to no avail."

"Did my husband say anything about the Princess before he collapsed?"

Rosk shook his head.

Of course not. "Does no one know what happened to my sister-in-law? Or Manus Midir?" Eislyn let her guard down for a moment, showing a sign of exasperation that was more reserved than reality.

One of the guards from Tiernan and Enid's rescue expedition raised his hand.

"Yes. Jabron, isn't it?"

He nodded. "The Manus was near death from several days of imprisonment *before* we arrived. We had no water, so we gave him a potion. It revived him enough to talk. He said it was vital the twins win. He took one of our swords and then Midir charged back into the battle.

"We followed the King's original orders and brought Jothan and Lucerne back to Farna as the Manus left our sight. We heard an explosion as we made our way through the Cave of Tera."

Eislyn opened her mouth to speak but shut it just as fast. *They should have turned around. But they were following T's orders. Should a guard defy the King's command just to satisfy his wife's curiosity?*

She took a deep breath. "So only the King can fill us in now." The Queen cleared her throat. "We must make preparations to attend to the King and to return him to Farna. I'm open to suggestions."

Rosk raised his hand. "Pernella is no doctor, but she seemed worried that he had internal injuries. She did not feel it wise to transport him here via horseback. The journey would be dangerous, if not fatal."

The Queen let out a faint groan, feeling blocked at every turn. "What if we send our best doctor? Could they tend to him there, nurse him back to health, and then return him to Castle Abria?"

The guards looked at each other, then at Rosk.

No one spoke.

The Queen exploded in a fit of frustration. "*Someone* give me their opinion."

Jabron raised his hand.

"Yes, Jabron. Any suggestion is better than silence."

"While Tadgh, Argyle, and I were being evaluated as to whether or not a Shapeshifter had absorbed us, I saw the patrols and movements of the other guards here in the castle. You've tightened security. I've been asking myself this question over and over again: is it even safe to travel?"

Disbelief overtook the Queen's countenance. "You're telling me you're afraid, lieutenant?"

"No, Your Majesty. I'm thinking about the King's *safety*. What is more dangerous to *him*? If the group heading to Whispersong were somehow overtaken by Shapeshifters, not only would our enemies know where the King rests, but they would also be able to finish the job they started in the Cave of Tera. We could be bringing doom upon him by trying to save him."

Eislyn's earlier disbelief was replaced with rage, though not at the guard.

Instead, it was aimed at their enemies and the impossible predicament in which they now found themselves. She pounded her fist on the table, startling everyone in the room.

Jabron is right. We can't reach T without risking his life.

Her jaw tightened. She began chewing on the inner edge of her lip, thinking about what to do next as an uncontrollable rumbling in her stomach decided for her.

A miner named Janus wiped his sweat-soaked brow. Frustrated, he rose to his feet and walked to his tool cart. He dug through it, looking for a particular pickaxe.

"Where are you?" He moved aside his maul, wedge, and favorite hammer. "Fiend of the Ocean, I left it at the station!" He sighed and rubbed his temples. Though it led to some stress relief, it also left deep black streaks of dirt and grime on his head.

He turned around and yelled. "Does anyone have a diamond-tipped pickaxe?" His voice echoed down the passage in both directions. His companions responded to the negative.

He looked down at his work zone. A large turquoise crystal sparkled in the dim light. Encased and embedded deep in the surrounding stone, he didn't want to leave it here. Unexpected spoils such as these were the property of the miner who excised them. The value of this gem would feed his family well beyond Midfest of next year.

He debated using the tools he had to extract it, though it would take much longer and well into the night. He doubted his lamps would last that long.

Returning to Milston Station would waste time too and, if another miner began excavating the gem, his walk back to retrieve his pickaxe would have served no purpose other than to relinquish his claim on the item.

If only I could teleport like an Elf, he mused to himself. In an act of presumed futility, he snapped his fingers.

Unfortunately, Janus remained in the mines. He made some mental calculations and decided to take his chances by returning to Milston Station. If he hurried, maybe no one would notice his discovery. He turned east and walked toward the exit.

As he passed one of his fellow miners, he smiled. They didn't react, which Janus found odd. His companion usually exuded friendliness, but this time, they seemed oblivious. Janus shrugged and continued on his journey.

Ahead of him, he saw someone he could trust. Torin would guard the gem without question, pretending it was his discovery long enough for Janus to retrieve his pickaxe and return. *I'll even split some of the sale with him as a way of saying thank you.*

"Hey Torin, can I ask you a favor?" he asked with a warm smile.

Torin startled at the sound of his voice. "Who, who is that?" The miner jumped to his feet and held his driving shovel high. "I'm warning you. I *will* attack."

Janus' mouth parted as he stepped back from his friend. "Torin, It's me. Janus."

"I know that voice, but you can't fool me, Elvish fiend! What have you done with my friend?" He started swinging the shovel and grabbed another nearby tool, a rusty crowbar, flipping it around to act as a sword.

"Torin, it's me! I'm right here. In front of you."

"Liar! You no good, thieving sorcerer. I will not fall for your trickery!" Torin jabbed the makeshift weapon forward in an offensive posture, running the sharpened end of the crowbar through Janus' side.

As a miner prone to accidents, Janus knew pain. Nothing could prepare him for the depth of the sensation from a sharp, metal object tearing through his lower torso. He let out a cry of anguish.

Feeling the resistance of whatever the crowbar had pierced, Torin swung the shovel in Janus' direction. It hit him hard on the same side, throwing the man up against the wall of the mine. The crowbar tore from Janus' side and left a deep, bleeding gash along the side of his body.

Janus slumped to the ground, his head and body falling against the wall in a crumpled heap of pain. He blinked in shock, a whirlwind of emotions and sensations spinning through his mind as the blood loss intensified.

Just then, Janus' newfound powers wore off. He reappeared then disappeared, flickering between a Cloak of Invisibility and his normal appearance until becoming fully visible to all once again.

Torin rushed to his side. He fell to his knees and pressed his hand against his friend's wound. As the injury covered his hands in crimson, Torin blinked in rapid succession.

"Janus? It was you after all? How? How were you invisible? I thought only Elves could do that." He cleared his throat. "Help! Someone, anyone, I need help now!"

Janus' gaze locked on the distant exit just above Torin's left shoulder. His mouth fell agape as others surrounded him, though he didn't see anything other than the increasing white glow that overtook his awareness until he exhaled for the last time.

Mira plucked an apple from overhead. One of the last few trees near Northwick, the grove outside her family's farm had been spared from the so-called Great Tree Massacre of 900NE. King Davien's legacy lived on through Northwick, once a wooded region until he cleared the lumber to provide raw materials for the growth in the Valley.

Sure, Davien paid a handsome bounty from his personal funds, enriching the area and reshaping the community. And yes, it now acted as the Kingdom's northernmost shipping port. But with the complete clearing of trees during the construction of Borun Mill and other structures at the Tolith Market, this grove was the only evidence of the city's old way of life.

Not that it mattered to most who lived there. The process of harvesting the forest lumber overhauled the entire eastern Abrian economy. No longer living in Milston's shadow, Northwick had finally broken away from its sister community. Lorelian Mead often departed the docks at Northwick, making its way around the outer edges of Abria to Alwyn, where vendors, resellers, and tavern owners offered it to the western half of the Kingdom.

Beyond that, fishing expeditions were now a commonplace sight despite the rough waters. As anglers ventured deeper into open seas, only the bravest would venture more than a few kilometers beyond the shoreline.

Anything else would invite disaster.

Occasionally, visitors from other parts of the world arrived through Northwick. Lonlin, a farming kingdom not far from eastern Abria, began sending traders with various wares and food supplies. These were rare though, as the rage of the Great Sea made the trip precarious at best.

Despite these problems, Northwick was thriving. Mira's father had helped with those plans two years before she had been born. Thinking about all the changes she heard about over the past few decades, she smiled at her older brother, Marcus. Across the grove, he was busy harvesting apples from another tree. Marcus himself ran the family business, a wholesale company that provided apples to the entire Kingdom.

Often, those same ships carrying Lorelian Mead from Lorelei brought with them apples from their family's grove. It was a two-for-one deal that made transportation costs much cheaper, not to mention more profitable, for their small business.

"It's an early harvest this year," she said, looking for something to say.

"The cooler spring helped these ripen sooner than anticipated." He took a bite of one. "Sweeter than usual. Almost too sweet."

"I'm sure they'll sell well."

"Not good for pies, though," another voice said.

Mira turned around to see a stranger approaching.

"I apologize for the intrusion." He raised both hands as if to show he carried no weapon.

Marcus dropped the apple he had just bit into, picked up a nearby pole pruner to act as a weapon, and rushed to his sister's side. "What do you want?"

"Nothing."

Marcus raised the tool higher.

"Don't come any closer," Mira warned.

The man did not heed her words. Instead, he pulled out a hidden knife from a pocket. "You know how this goes. Give me whatever din you have and I'll leave."

"We don't carry *any* dinage out here. You would know that if you knew anything about our business," Marcus replied.

His soft-spoken voice turned to an angry, deep growl. "Pity. I'm not leaving empty-handed." He raised the knife to rush at the siblings.

Mira raised her hand instinctively. From her open palm, a yellow ball appeared. As the man ran, the ball transformed from a glowing spherical shape into a powerful gust of wind. Mira felt something leave her body and opened her eyes just as the blast emerged from her palm.

Before she or her brother could react, Wind Magic hit the bandit in the upper part of his chest. His head snapped backward as its power threw him high, into a somersault, and far across the field. The man fell hard, cracking his nose on the ground as he landed.

Mira and Marcus froze in place, both in shock and waiting for him to rise to his feet.

He never stood up.

"Mira, what was that? What did you do?"

Mira looked at her hand in fear, quivering as she took a few steps back from her brother.

"Did you…did you just send him away with *Wind Magic*?" her brother asked as his voice shook.

Mira shook her head in confusion and began to cry. Marcus composed himself and pulled his sister close. The siblings hugged each other tight. Marcus put his hand on the back of her head as she sobbed.

"Is he alive?" she asked in a low voice through her tears.

Marcus opened his eyes and turned to look toward the man, still resting in a crumpled position and motionless in the distance.

"I don't know. Come on, let's go and let Mom and Dad know. They'll know what to do."

"What is going on?" she cried out. "What happened to me, Marcus? How did I do that?"

Marcus shook his head as his sister fell apart in his arms.

Chapter 6

Farna

Róisín had only been to Farna a handful of times. The last time was during Wayland's memorial service just a few weeks earlier. Before that, it had been for the funeral for her very own daughter and son-in-law.

Those thoughts — the last that crossed her mind as the Elf grabbed her hand — disappeared in an instant. The sensation of teleportation overwhelmed her mind. It felt like she didn't exist for a moment, almost as if her conscious was ripped away from her only to reappear a moment later.

Let's not do that again, she thought as the area around her came into visual focus. Róisín's stomach dropped. *What happened here?*

The north end of Farna looked like a war zone. Castle Abria itself seemed unaffected, though large swaths of the community laid in tatters. Her group had appeared across the town, closer to the entrance to the castle. Through the open streets and fields of Farna, she could see what looked like a gaping hole in the ground. Structures around it had collapsed, with giant boulders thrown about the surrounding area. Signs of crushed homes were clear, with significant activity around some kind of tavern. *They must have had casualties from this catastrophe.*

Róisín looked at the frightened Elves who arrived with her and tried to comfort them.

Her efforts were in vain as within moments of their appearance, a large contingent of Abrian Royal Guards rushed toward them with swords and spears drawn.

"Let me handle this," Róisín said to her frightened companions. She walked ahead toward the guards, hands raised, palms open. Once they were within earshot, she spoke.

"My name is Róisín. Queen Kyrie was my daught…" Her voice trailed off as the guards surrounded them, weapons corralling them into a tight circle. Róisín took several steps back, feeling her Elven companions compressed against her lower half.

One guard, a bearded Graelan with the stench of alcohol on his breath, addressed the group. "Do not move. Under the order of Queen Eislyn, you are to be quarantined until we can confirm your identity and if you are Graelan." The guard gave the Elves a distrustful eye, letting his disdain show through.

Róisín noticed the intentional slight. "I'm the only Graelan here. These are Elves, but never mind that. What do you mean by our identity? And what is going on here? When did Eislyn become *Queen*? Where are my grandchildren, Tiernan and Enid?"

Róisín's words fell on deaf ears as the guards solidified their offensive positions just as more of their numbers surrounded the refugees.

The guard who had issued the command turned to a third group standing at a distance. He motioned at them with his head. "Inform the Queen that a group of Elven misfits has arrived." His words slurred, a confirmation that he was drunk while on duty. "In addition, with the scoundrels is someone *claiming* to be King Tiernan's grandmother. Tell her majesty we have them contained and can eliminate them at the first sign of trouble."

"Eliminate us?" an Elf asked.

"We should have stayed in Lakedon," Serin muttered under his breath.

Róisín tried to take a step forward but was met with the sharp end of a sword keeping her at bay. She almost pushed the weapon away, but thought better of it. Instead, she protested their predicament the same way she was used to getting her way with the Lakedon Council. "This is preposterous! I demand to see the Queen! I am the mother of Queen Kyrie, mother-in-law to…"

"Save it, lady," the drunken guard said. "We have our orders. You will stay where you are until given permission to move or you will be dealt with." He turned to the third group. "Why haven't you moved yet? Go. Inform the Queen."

"Yes, chief," one of them said before he and two other guards departed.

One of the other guards behind Róisín lowered their voice in a sympathetic tone. "I implore you, please do not take offense to this. I've seen you before and know who you are, but you must understand. Much has happened since the last time you visited Castle Abria. We have no choice but to take precautions."

The Elves, no longer able to contain their motions, cowered in fear, even more than when they had first appeared or heard the ruckus taking shape within Lakedon.

"It's okay," Róisín said, trying to reassure them. "I'm sure we can sort this out in no time." She turned to face the guard. "Can you at least tell me what happened here? That hole, I mean. Why is it here?" She furrowed her brow. "And where is *King* Tiernan?" Her emphasis on his title betrayed her confusion and desire to understand the situation.

The first guard smirked and walked away. Another fell back with him, the two of them conversing.

The sympathetic guard explained. "The chasm is difficult to explain. The ground exploded and a stream of energy, magic, something — we don't know what — erupted through it. By our estimate, the effect lasted for at least an hour. At least thirty-six hundred ticks, maybe more. The damage, as you can see, was severe."

"And this explosion warrants holding us hostage?" another Elf asked, a sense of anger brewing under the surface.

The guard did his best to assuage their worries. "No, it does not. As per the Queen's command, we must confirm none of you are a Shapeshifter."

Róisín looked to the Elves mouthing 'Shapeshifter' as if to ask what they were, only for her question to be met with looks of confusion. After a moment of reflection, Serin's eyes grew wide.

The first guard noticed from across the way and rushed back to the group, weapon drawn. His companion scurried up next to him, as if tethered to each other's side.

Róisín noticed this odd behavior but chose not to acknowledge it for fear of inciting the guard's drunken anger.

"Something you want to say, Elven fiend?" His rage at the diminutive creature surprised even the other guards, though they kept their mouths shut.

All eyes moved to the Elf, including Róisín.

"Serin, it's okay," she said while trying to calm his nerves. "What's a Shapeshifter?"

He swallowed. "I don't know exactly. I overheard Folas mention something called Shapeshifters."

The guard pushed his way through the offensive circle to address the Elf face to face. "Overheard? How? Where? Were you aligned with him? Were you one of the ones in the underground battle? How many of my fellow guards did you kill?"

The guard dropped his sword and grabbed Serin by the tunic, raising him high in the air.

"Stop it!" Róisín twisted her way around the other Elves to confront the guard.

Next to her, two of the other guards decided the drunken outburst had gone too far. "Chief, that's enough!" one of them yelled.

Róisín glimpsed the insignia on that guard's uniform. She couldn't remember the hierarchy, but as her eyes shifted toward the attacking guard, she noticed the former appeared to be more ornate and likely of a higher rank.

"But, lieutenant, this Elf killed our fellow guards." His words slurred again, with dilated pupils and watering eyes an outward sign of his inebriated state.

The lieutenant dropped his sword and grabbed the arms of the lower ranked guard. "I said, that's enough!"

The guard dropped Serin. Róisín steadied him as he fell.

"Chief Quern, you will remove yourself from the field." The lieutenant motioned to the guard who seemed to be tethered to Quern's side earlier. "Sergeant, accompany him back to the barracks. Stay with him until he sobers up."

"Yes, sir." He put his hand on Quern's shoulder, who was now shaking but continuing to stare at Serin, his breath heavy with frustration. "Come on."

Róisín kneeled down to the Elf. "Serin, how did you hear about these Shapeshifters?"

His countenance remained on alert as his voice stuttered with each word. "It was before the big Statuo thing." Serin sighed deep, steadying his breathing. "Folas was eating at one of the nearby tables in the Rosewood Forest where I was sitting. He was mumbling. Something about Kane, Shapeshifters, and other beasts. I don't think Folas knew I overheard anything."

Quern waved him off and turned to leave with the sergeant.

Róisín stood up and met the gaze of the remaining guards. "Satisfied?"

Eislyn walked out of her chamber, her eyes bloodshot and her skin pale. Her four attendants remained in her room, now part of only six in the Kingdom who knew of her condition. Each took a vow of silence, promising not to acknowledge the pregnancy until Tiernan returned — or Eislyn assumed the role as the de facto ruler of Abria for good.

Her guards followed behind, keeping a respectable distance. None of them had any idea why Eislyn insisted on coming here, but stayed within the corridor and on high alert as she ran into her room a few moments earlier. The Queen was thankful they were ignorant men, lost in thought about other matters. Any woman would have recognized the telltale signs of morning sickness right away.

Now that her stomach contents were a part of the castle's waste removal system, she hoped this would be the last pregnancy-induced incident of the day. With a renewed, confident command presence and a hint of grace, Eislyn walked down the flight of stairs from her bedroom to the main atrium of Castle Abria. From there, she turned toward the war room.

No one spoke during their walk through the silent halls, a thankful reprieve from the chaos that had enveloped every meeting and strategy session over the past several days. The sense of apprehension throughout the once bustling fortress was almost palpable, and no one dared say what everyone had been thinking.

This is the new normal.

As the Queen approached the war room, she felt another wave of nausea overtake her far sooner than she had hoped. *Please, child, let me get through this.* She did what she could to push the sensation away and took a nervous step into the once great dining hall.

Standing at attention around the room was a contingent of guards. She nodded, then motioned to the door for them to leave. After they left, she looked at those sitting around the table: an Elf, Tiernan's grandmother, and a battered but conscious guard she had heard was named Jothan, a member of Manus Midir's group and one of their early leads into the Shapeshifter problem.

Eislyn turned to her attending guards. "I wish to be alone. Stand at the door waiting, but I will handle this on my own." The lead guard began to protest, and she raised her hand. "This is an order from your commander and Queen. Do I make myself clear, gentlemen?"

"Yes, Your Highness," they said in unison before taking up defensive positions just outside of the doorway. Eislyn closed the door. She wondered if this was a wise action, both for the guards' sake as well as hers. There would be no one to defend her if the Shapeshifters had compromised one of those around the table. The guards would never let themselves live with the idea that they failed their Queen, delivering her unprotected into the hands of a waiting enemy.

No turning back. I've made my decision. Aila, help me.

She smiled at those seated. "I wish I had something encouraging to say, something that would put your minds at ease. I'm not much for words. That was — is, I mean — Tiernan's strength. I was just a bartender before all of this. I prefer to listen to my customers instead of issuing orders." She pulled out a chair and sat.

"That being said, it's good to see you again, Róisín." The Queen reached out and rubbed the top of her hand. "I wish it were under better circumstances."

"Same. Eislyn, where are the twins? And when did Tiernan become King? What does that mean for Enid?"

"What version of the story do you want? The shorter, but complete one or the longer explanation with many unanswered questions?"

Róisín felt taken back by the Queen's reply. "I guess start with the short version and we can go from there?"

The Queen nodded. "You saw what happened at Alwyn at the wedding with Way. When he..." Eislyn couldn't finish the sentence. The memory of her brother-in-law's death still hurt like an open wound, and discussing his sacrifice felt like rubbing salt into it.

Róisín turned away, tears beginning to stream down her face.

The emotional reaction confirmed what Eislyn needed to know. Róisín was still Róisín, for better or for worse.

"I can only imagine how Enid felt." Róisín let go, releasing her pent-up sadness and own sense of loss in tearful sorrow.

The Queen turned to Jothan and the Elf. "Róisín is Queen Kyrie's mother."

Understanding washed over Jothan.

The Elf nodded.

Eislyn tipped her head toward him. "You already knew that, didn't you? What's your name?"

"Serin, and yes. I did. It was the loss of her daughter, and then of Prince Wayland, that inspired Róisín and her husband to turn one of their properties into a refuge for my people."

"The idea was Lugh's," Róisín explained. "His guilt over the way he treated King Davien overwhelmed him. It had been festering below the surface for a while. In his free time, he had been doing small things at Cabra House, wanting to do some good with it but never saying what he had in mind. I couldn't figure out why he hadn't rented it out to anyone, but let him handle it.

She closed her eyes. "And then we lost them. Our only daughter and her beloved husband." Róisín's face fell into her hands. "Lugh wanted to make it up to Davien, to amend for the years he disparaged him, judged him." Her voice broke. "He never figured out how. The refugees started arriving not long after we returned home that time. When we returned to Lakedon after Wayland's memorial service, we renamed it Dídean Inn and opened our doors to all the Elves living in Lakedon. It means protection, by the way. The name, I mean."

Eislyn let herself smile. *A fitting legacy for Way, always protecting others even after he's gone.*

"Not too long after you left to return home to Lakedon, Enid stepped down as a joint ruler. That meant T became the King by default. And me," Eislyn said as she motioned to her regal outfit, "the Queen.

"All of that happened *after* Manus Midir, the mayor of Idlewind, led an expedition to find our enemies in the Cave of Tera. Jothan," she said as she motioned to the guard, "joined his team. We were attacked by a Shapeshifter in the form of a foot messenger. Enid stepped down, Tiernan became King, and then the two of them took off to the Cave of Tera to end this war."

"So, where are they now?" asked Róisín.

"Tiernan *may* be in Whispersong. No one has any idea what happened to Enid. Only my husband knows, as the messenger from Whispersong was not privy to that information. All we know is that the ground in the north end of Farna exploded, magic erupted through the chasm, and upon exploring the cavern, we found no trace of her." The Queen felt another wave of nausea hit her as she finished speaking. Whether it was the baby or uncertainty for Enid, she was not sure.

"That's the short version?" Róisín asked as she shook her head. "What's the long version entail?"

"Waiting, searching." The Queen motioned in the direction of the Drunken Alligator, though only she knew that was her intention. "Attempts to rebuild. Heightened security. Róisín, we have no idea how to deal with these Shapeshifters. It's why I haven't sent an expedition to retrieve my husband."

Moving past her emotion, Róisín asked the question she had been wondering since she first arrived in Farna. "And what is a Shapeshifter, exactly? I mean, it sounds pretty self-explanatory, but is there more?"

"That's why I asked Jothan to come." Eislyn motioned toward him. "And you, Serin. Anything you can share would be helpful."

"My knowledge of the Shapeshifters is limited, Your Highness," the Elf replied.

"Mine is not." Jothan righted himself in his chair. "I've seen it twice now. Once at Fabled Wonders and once in the underground caves with Midir. Both times it was unpleasant."

"What do you mean?" asked Serin.

Jothan's voice rose in anger as he described the process. "A Shapeshifter doesn't just take the form of someone or something else. It absorbs them. Painfully. The one I saw by Fabled Wonders landed as a raven, assumed its native, ugly winged Graelanoid form, and then attacked a man. Some kind of magical effect. It subdued him with its talons, then pulled him *into* its body before assuming his form.

"I saw it again underground. By then, Midir, the others, and myself had fallen in our fight against Kane and Folas." He gave a side eye to Serin. "Along with the Elves who aligned with them."

Queen Eislyn noticed. "Sergeant, the Elves here in Castle Abria are our guests. They are not aligned with our enemies. Am I clear?"

Unconvinced but willing to defer to the Queen's opinion, Jothan nodded.

Róisín did what she could to shift the direction of the conversation. "So, our welcome when we arrived here? What was that about?"

Eislyn thought about her words in light of the immediate distrust Jothan had showed toward Serin. "The fear within the ranks of the Royal Guard was that a Folas-aligned Elf or Elves could have brought a compromised Graelan — you, Róisín — with them. It was nothing personal or against your Elven brethren,

Serin, and Chief Quern has been demoted for his overreaction in the field. On behalf of the Kingdom, I apologize."

Eislyn rose to her feet and bowed to Serin. "Since the Elves arrived in 479NE, you should have been honored guests of Abria. After all, we're all relatively trapped here in this land, cut off from the rest of Grael. Together. Two peoples enjoying the wonders of our Kingdom.

"At least, that's how it should have been. Whether we've succeeded in that is a matter of discussion for another time. For now, I ask of you to please accept our apologies for any perceived or actual failures."

Eislyn remained with her head bowed until Serin spoke, a single tear running down his face. "Apology accepted. I'm no elder, and to be honest, I don't know where any of them are right now, anyway. Nevertheless, I appreciate your heartfelt words."

Eislyn stood upright, noticed the tear, and then sat in her seat. "This wasn't just about your group. Anyone who enters Farna will be treated the same way until we have a plan. We have no defense against this adversary and the only clue we have as to whether a person is compromised is the way they talk and react. Shapeshifters appear to be unable to mimic Graelian emotions."

Serin raised an eyebrow. "Your use of Graelian versus Graelan was intentional. Am I right?"

The Queen nodded at Róisín. "Your sadness." She pointed at Jothan. "Your anger as you described the absorption process." She looked to Serin. "Your tear, a heart-felt response to Abria's long overdue need to apologize.

"To put it simple, Shapeshifters appear to fail at common emotion. Dogs, bears, birds of the air, it doesn't matter. All living Graelian species have *feelings*. The messenger who attacked us spoke in broken sentences, seemingly detached from his surroundings. How did T put it?" She paused, trying to remember what he had said before leaving for the Cave of Tera. "I think it was something like 'Below. The. Power. Of. Abria. We. Claim. As. Ours.' with its words split between a tick or a click. Cold. Emotionless. Maybe they *do* feel things, but it isn't in the same way as what you or I experience. And none of you have acted in this manner.

"So, we just have to keep pushing until we feel comfortable enough that the person we're talking to has not been compromised."

She turned to Róisín. "And *that's* why we can't risk going to Whispersong to rescue my husband. According to their rider, he's in bad shape. Too sick to transport. But we also can't risk sending a group to him for fear that they could be taken over as well and eliminate him once they arrive."

Eislyn felt her stomach twist. She nodded to Jothan and Serin. "Can the two of you excuse us for a moment?" Both stood up without question and left the room, closing the door behind them.

After waiting a moment to ensure none of the guards entered, Eislyn bolted from her chair to a nearby trashcan full of discarded notes. There, she lost the contents of her stomach for the third time today.

Róisín waited.

Eislyn regained her composure and stood to her feet.

"When are you due?" Róisín asked with a subtle smile.

Chapter 7

No Turning Back

Zoran bellowed in anger. "Never in my centuries on this planet have I ever encountered such incompetence. Such failure! The two of you are—" The reprimand went unfinished as an Elf applied a layer of salve to the Dark Emperor's wound. The sensation caused him to cry out in deep agony. Instinctively, he swiped his hand at the Elf's body and sent the small creature flying.

They hit the wall hard and slumped to the ground. Zoran then stumbled backward, hit the nearest wall, and fell to the ground as well.

Turning his attention from Zoran's reaction to his companion, Folas could not tell if the other Elf was dead or alive.

All the Dark Elf Master knew was that he, too, was in excruciating pain as one of his brethren tended to his wounds. If not for a quick act of magic during the battle, Folas surely would have bled out from Enid's attack. The spot where her axe penetrated his chest throbbed with pain, not to mention the top of his upper back, where the decorative tip of her weapon broke through his skin.

The makeshift infirmary within the incomplete citadel atop the Northern Plateau had never seen this kind of activity. Elves scurried from corner to corner of the room, using what tools, potions, and magic they had to heal their leaders' wounds.

Folas lowered his head. He knew following Kane had been a mistake. The Divider's hubris hadn't brought them an ally.

This was different. Zoran's temper was of a different magnitude, and his disdain for their alliance was almost palpable. The rage of the barbarians during the exile from centuries ago paled in comparison to Zoran's anger. His strength seemed to surpass that of any Orc.

No, a *dozen* Orcs. The power he demonstrated, such as turning Graelans to stone, was beyond any Elven magic. Zoran might appear Graelanoid, but under the surface lay something else far more sinister.

Folas turned to Kane. The gash in the latter's stomach had missed vital organs, but had drained The Divider's strength, especially after Tiernan's final assault.

Across the room, Folas saw the Soul Sword — the only of the three relics of which they retained possession. Propped against the wall as if it were any normal weapon, the Elves in the room seemed oblivious to the power that any one of them could wield if they picked it up and ran with it. For all of their collective efforts to secure the Soul Sword, including killing the King and Queen, here it seemed as unimportant as any other object in the infirmary.

Next to it, an unusual red jewel shimmered in the light. Folas had no idea where it had come from or its significance. Its size seemed forgettable. If a miner stumbled across it, they may have left it embedded in the rock face. Its sudden appearance seemed mysterious on its own. Folas had kept a careful eye on the gem once Zoran had insisted they bring it with them without any explanation.

He coughed hard, then rubbed his head. Recounting and processing these events wore out the Dark Elf. There was a missing piece to the puzzle, one he was determined to understand.

Folas tapped the shoulder of a passing Elf. "Bring me the jewel, Deras."

Zoran's head snapped in Folas' direction, but the pain of movement sent him into another bellowing fit. Folas made note of this as the Elf brought the strange object to him.

"Thanks." She nodded and turned to resume her previous activity. The jewel was warm to the touch, but not so much as to make it uncomfortable to hold. Energy or magic flowed below its hard, opaque surface, though the swirling tendrils moved in such a way that they prevented Folas from seeing its core.

The surface. Folas ran his hands along its top and bottom. The texture of the jewel was smooth, not too dissimilar to an eroded rock from the Great Sea. It wasn't heavy, though somehow Folas could tell it had mass. He placed both hands on the top of it and closed his eyes.

Though obvious to no one but Zoran, Folas' efforts were fruitless. The Dark Elf's attempt to tap into whatever magic flowed through the object, much like he had taken power from the Shapeshifter not too long ago, failed. Instead of a transference, an ethereal force repelled him. The sensation burned through the nerves in his palms and fingertips, causing Folas to throw the object as he cried out in pain.

All eyes turned to the Dark Elf as the jewel fell to the ground. Everyone expected it to shatter. To the room's collective surprise — except for Zoran, who smirked at their ignorance — it landed with a loud *ting* that echoed off of the walls of the unfinished facility. Deras, still close to Folas' bed, picked it up and glanced up at the Dark Elf for instruction.

"Flip it over," Folas said to her with a curt nod.

Deras did as told without question. Folas appreciated her efficiency. As one of those who chose this path, she understood his role as the leader of the rebellion.

The bottom of the jewel showed no signs of damage. Deras flipped it back around and stood to her feet. "What do you think?"

Folas narrowed his eyes and stared deep into the core. Although he couldn't be sure, the center of the jewel appeared to be dimming, as if it had lit up as he tried to absorb it. A blinded Elf, one named Banix, walked up and handed Deras a potion before disappearing back into the citadel.

Deras gave the potion to Folas as she stood nearby, awaiting instructions with the jewel.

Whatever material it's made of is harder than the stone walls of the palace. "Put it back," Folas ordered as he drank the potion. He winced, disliking the flavor.

"It's a special variation. Supposed to help you get some rest, which you need for that to heal," she said, pointing at his chest.

Meanwhile, Kane stirred on his bed. Folas blinked a few times as the concoction took effect. The Dark Elf's eyes clouded as Kane tried to sit up. Instead, the Divider fell backward. The wound in his abdomen prevented any movement using those muscles.

Kane groaned, then looked toward Folas and whispered. "The twins?"

Folas stretched out on the bed and shook his head.

"Zoran?"

Folas motioned to the northern edge of the room where Zoran sat crumpled against the wall with his eyes closed. *Sleep does sound good.* "This was a disaster," he said with a yawn. "The magic is gone. Castle Abria still stands. And now we have to deal with him."

Kane made a sound that resembled a frustrated growl. "He's not who I thought he was. The Archives made Zoran sound like a powerful King. He's strong, sure, but so what?" Kane closed his eyes. "Why did I even bother?"

"You saw what he did to the..." Folas' mind began to drift away. His eyes opened one last time in an attempt to finish the sentence. "...Graelan from Idle..."

The potion took effect as Folas fell into a deep slumber. Kane smirked at the Dark Elf's presumed weakness. "Pathetic."

With his eyes closed, and making no motion, Zoran listened to every word.

Folas' eyes popped open. *How long have I been asleep?* He sat up, this time with ease. He touched his wound. The deep gash where Enid had run him through with her axe was now healed.

No, not quite healed. Folas felt his exposed chest. A giant scar ran from the middle of his torso down to the edge of his abdomen. He sighed, wrapping his arms around his legs and resting his head on his knees as he recalled the battle.

Enid's warrior fierceness surpassed his expectations. A mere Graelan woman. Everyone knew she had magic, but her physical prowess surprised him. The barbarians might have cowered in fear with her rage. He suddenly felt cold, recalling the emotions he felt as he thought he was sure to die from her hand.

The Tall Elf swallowed. He now knew what the squirrel felt that day, when he tortured Voron for the first time and forced the Elf to watch as the critter withered away into nothingness.

Fear.

Then, he understood the rat as it scurried away, sick from his Poison Magic and desperate to find a respite from the growing toxin running throughout its body.

Fear.

Folas' shoulders slumped as he empathized with the guards he tortured in the depths of Castle Abria, burning one alive from the inside out after crushing their bodies with the destructive force of wind and gravity. *What were their names?* Folas shook his head, unable to remember what they had called each other. *Wil-something and Grom?*

It didn't matter. Along with the shop owner, the couple in the field, the first guard, and many more from his reign of terror in the castle, he now understood what each of his victims felt in their final moments, as their life slipped from their body before passing into the beyond.

Fear.

Folas raised his head toward the ceiling and screamed in anger. His obsidian skin, having transformed from a subtle, pale aqua tone to this stained, inky, Ultimus-like color, was a visible symbol of every life he took and no longer felt like his own. As he lowered his head back to his knees, Folas ran his necrotic fingertips along the scar, the only semblance of color on his now permanently transformed body. The scar's gray shade, a remnant of whatever tissues from inside his body had been stitched together, served as a reminder of who he used to be: an unusually Tall Elf named Folas.

Not the Dark Elf Master.

Not an accomplice to a madman.

Just Folas.

A name that once meant 'sincere' in our native tongue. Now, is it marred forever? Will it become synonymous with betrayal?

As the rage boiled in his blood, another horrible thought crossed his mind. Not only was there no way to undo the damage he had done or to reverse his transformation, but he and Kane had willingly unleashed some kind of horrible evil upon Grael, one that saw them as lesser lifeforms and a means to an end.

Evil. Zoran! Folas' head popped up in a flash. There was no sign of Kane, any Elven rebels, the strange jewel, the Soul Sword, or Zoran himself.

Itself? Folas shook off the thought. There was no way to know if Zoran was a Graelan or something else entirely.

Folas' thoughts pecked at his mind like a raven. Every regret, every reflection, every confusion only served to fuel his growing anger. He realized that the silence within the makeshift infirmary was deafening and he had to move, lest he lose what hold he still retained on his sanity.

Folas slid his legs around and let them dangle off the edge of the cot for a moment. As he sat there, he caught a glimpse of himself in the reflection of a nearby weapon. The shadow of his torso from the light of a hanging torch reminded him of something he once said in Castle Abria.

There's no turning back.

He used the palms of his hands to push himself up and onto his feet. He spotted a washbasin in the far corner. Folas walked to it, cupped the water with his hands, and threw water on his face. He remained in a bent over position, letting the water drip back into the bowl. He blinked a few times, then cupped some more water and repeated the motion. Folas grabbed a nearby towel from the wall and wiped his cheeks.

He held it there for a moment.

Please.

In a single word, his thoughts echoed what he hoped deep in his heart was possible. An undoing of the past. A change that might yet set things right.

Folas closed his eyes and pulled back the towel.

Please.

He took a deep breath and held it in, hoping, begging, pleading to that revered Graelan huntress in the sky that the inky stain, the shadow of who he had become, would rub off on the towel.

That he would no longer be the Dark Elf Master.

Just Folas. Sincere. A tall Elf, one that could lead his people back from the path they had embraced without understanding the consequences.

Folas braced for what awaited him, released his breath, and opened his eyes.

Chapter 8

The Growing Darkness

We need to plan our next attack. Our enemies must be regrouping by now. Surely the King will be out for blood. His sister is dead, joining their parents in their shallow, worthless graves." Kane's charged words bounced off the walls in the throne room. Though the space lacked seating, the bones of the room belied its new construction and design.

To an outsider, it rivaled Castle Abria. Or so Kane would say, anyway. Folas shook his head, hearing his compatriot's voice down the hall. Near the entrance stood two Graelans, followers of Kane since departing Clericsfold. They acknowledged the Dark Elf as he approached them, stepping aside to let him into the throne room.

Light shone through the twelve oblong windows facing the east. The mid-morning sun reflected off the stone, a golden-hued mineral harvested from the nearby Milston Mountains. Folas noted the conscious choice to mirror the similar color of Castle Abria in his collaborator's attempt to take over the Kingdom.

"Are you listening to me?" Zoran sat on the floor, his legs crossed and his back to Kane. Folas wondered if he knew this was where the thrones were supposed to sit.

Except that, for the first time, Folas realized there were indentions for only two: one for Kane and the other for himself. Never once had they discussed what role Zoran would play in their new leadership.

Unless there was no plan for Zoran. But what then? What was Kane's intention with the Dark Emperor once we had the Soul Sword and the castle destroyed?

Anger washed over Folas. *Kane didn't think that far ahead. He never planned beyond the next step.*

Folas chastised himself for not seeing it earlier. His rage and frustration at the conditions of the Elven predicament within the Kingdom clouded his judgment. There were parts of their scheme that had no specified outcome, such as what would become of Zoran.

Folas stood at the end of the throne room just within the threshold and watched Kane as he flung the Soul Sword around the room while speaking. He crossed his arms and leaned against the frame.

He treats it like a toy, but it's so much more than he realizes.

"I said, 'Are you listening to me?'" Kane grabbed Zoran's shoulder with his open hand.

Zoran bellowed and used his left arm to swipe Kane away.

Meanwhile, the Soul Sword's appearance shifted, glowing ever so slightly. Folas watched with utter fascination as neither Zoran nor Kane appeared to be aware of the change.

I must take it from both of them. Then, I'll fix this. I'll free my people so we can go home.

"Do not touch me again. Yes, I heard you. I've heard everything you've said since we arrived here." Zoran returned to his sitting position. His voice changed, deepening and echoing as he spoke. "We are in no position to do anything. I must rest. We must rest."

Kane appeared to disagree. "Hold on. You're telling me the mighty Zoran, referred to as a powerful 'Dark Emperor' in the ancient texts, rumored to have controlled vast swaths of Abria itself, is *tired*? That's all you've done since we woke you up.

Weren't your centuries of sleep enough? And now you need more?"

Zoran kept his eyes closed. "Ask your friend standing in the doorway if he has any magic left. Give him an ether from the table and see what happens."

Kane turned around to see Folas, who leaned away from the door and finished walking the rest of the way into the room.

"How long have you been standing there?" Kane asked.

"Long enough. Makes you wonder how he knew I was standing here, doesn't it?"

Zoran answered with the same ominous, baritone voice as a moment earlier. "Do the two of you genuinely believe I can't see *everything* that happens here?"

Folas narrowed his eyes. *Zoran could have caught a glimpse of me as he batted Kane's hand away. This could all be for show to confuse us.*

"What table?" Kane asked. "The ethers, I mean."

Zoran didn't answer, so the two of them looked around the room. Under one of the windows, an Elf-sized table seemed to appear out of nowhere.

Could have been there all along, just hidden by the light, Folas thought.

Frustrated, Kane walked over to it and grabbed one of the ethers. He threw it at Folas who caught with a quick flip of his wrist. He eyed it carefully, wondering where it had come from before pushing it into his right hand and waiting for the power to flow through his body.

When nothing happened, Folas motioned for another. Kane threw it his way and the Dark Elf repeated the process. After it fully absorbed into his palm, he waited.

And waited.

And waited some more.

Nothing. No physical sensation. No power. Folas opened his hand, expecting a ball of magic to appear.

It remained empty.

Folas' eyes grew wide as, for the first time in his life, he was powerless. He patted the pockets of his trousers, feeling for a ring.

Meanwhile, Zoran stood and faced the duo. "Even with a Magic Ring, it won't work."

Folas looked up at the Dark Emperor in a panicked frenzy.

Kane stared at his helpless compatriot. "Why not? What happened to him?"

Zoran's expression shifted from disdain to that of a wizened sage. He took a few steps toward the two and brought his hands behind his back.

"The Dragonborn. *That's* what happened. Try as you will, my Dark Elf. Your powers will be gone for quite some time. And you," he said, addressing Kane, "Throw your sword. I've heard the rumors. Kane's physical strength is legendary throughout this doomed land. There." He pointed to a wood beam. "Throw the Soul Sword like you would throw a dagger."

Kane guffawed and turned away. Folas met his gaze and motioned with his eyes, ever so slightly, that Kane should try. The Divider sighed, readied himself, and took aim. He threw the Soul Sword with his usual force.

And watched in horror as it only traveled three sad meters. Kane fell to his knees, embarrassed at the lack of strength and horrified at its implication.

"What did she do to us?" Folas asked.

"The Dragonborn's legacy is wider ranging than you realize. Even now, what she did is being felt across all Grael. Soon," Zoran said, smirking, "more will come. That boy pretending to be a King will be the least of your worries. The Na'Goh themselves may even decide to interfere. As you Graelans say, 'All bets are off.'"

"Our worries?" asked Kane as he stood to his feet and tried to regain his composure.

Zoran ignored the question. Instead, he walked over to the jewel. Haphazardly discarded among a series of spoils from the battle, the Dark Emperor picked it up.

"This cannot be destroyed, but yet," Zoran said, looking at Kane with thoughtful consideration, "perhaps it can be contained by a caudex."

Folas and Kane exchanged a confused look. Zoran placed the jewel in the exact spot where the Divider's eventual throne would sit. He turned around and, without giving the two of them so much as a passing acknowledgement, left the room.

Kane walked over to Folas. "What's a caudex?"

Folas shrugged, feigning ignorance, though deep down he knew what it meant. *An impenetrable rock.* His eyes moved to the Soul Sword while keeping his face still, hoping his companion wouldn't notice it. *I must obtain the relic for myself.*

Folas sat in the room he claimed as his own many moons ago. Since his Elven brethren constructed this citadel, Folas chose the highest room in the tallest tower. He specifically asked it to face west toward Lyra.

Scattered throughout the room were mementos of his former home in the Darkwood Forest. Some, such as a book from his mother, had been with him for centuries. Others he obtained during his time living as a refugee here in Abria.

He sighed, all of a sudden wondering what was so bad about being a refugee. Anger welled up within him.

Why did I let Kane drag me into this? He tried to remember that fateful encounter in the Rosewood Forest. Folas found himself suddenly thinking of it in the original name instead of the one to which his fellow rebels had renamed it.

Frustrated, he extended his hand toward the window in an attempt to cast some kind of magic. Nothing. He hadn't been able to summon any kind of magic since he teleported the King, wherever he went. For the first time, he understood how truly close to death he had come.

If not for other Elves with teleportation and healing abilities, the three of them would have perished from their wounds in the Cave of Tera. Those accomplices were able to bring their wounded leaders back to the Northern Plateau with the snap of their fingers and begin immediate treatments that saved their lives.

He heard a knock at the door, which startled him out of his pondering. Folas turned to face his visitor.

"Would you like another?" The same female Elf who had helped him in the infirmary was now offering a third ether.

"Deras. Come on in." He motioned to a chair. "I don't know if it will help." She tossed it to him as she sat. Folas pressed the item into his palm, absorbing the concoction. He closed his eyes.

"Well?" A brief, uncomfortable silence passed between them. "Did it work?"

Folas opened his eyes and shook his head. "It's gone. That witch stole my powers somehow. And apparently, once I sent the king to his destination, that was it." He met her gaze. "I'm powerless. I'm as weak as a worthless Abrian Royal Guard." Folas looked at his skin, despising its necrotic, inky appearance.

"Do you still believe you're the Dark Elf *Master*?"

An internal instinct told Folas to guard his words. "What do you think?"

Deras stood and began pacing the room. "I think you've forgotten why you convinced us to align with Kane. I think you've also forgotten why you blinded many from our clan who disagreed with you. Those controlling effects are wearing off. I saw two of our brethren sitting outside in a daze, confused how they got here, but not quite ready to teleport back to the Darkwood Forest. Banix, my assistant, has shown signs of recognition even if he is still obedient to my command.

"They and those of us who believe in our cause need our leader to step up. Otherwise, the ones you've blinded may align with our enemies once your control wears off, and those who willingly joined…well…" She frowned. "They'll be looking for someone else to lead them to victory over Abria."

Deras then turned and walked out of the room, leaving Folas to contemplate his predicament.

Chapter 9

A Queen's Statuo

Eislyn considered whether to answer Róisín's question or to deny the accusation. News of her pregnancy was spreading too fast, and Tiernan should be present for those kinds of announcements. Even more so, he should have the right to tell his own grandmother that she was about to become a great-grandma.

Beyond that, shouldn't my own parents know before anyone else?

"You're not fooling me, dear. I was sick the entire time with Kyrie. It's probably why she was sick all nine months with the twins. I know that look." She sighed. "And I wish I could say I know my grandson well enough that he wouldn't mind you confiding in me. But I don't."

Róisín stood, turned her back to the Queen, and faced the opposite wall. She placed her hands on her hips and raised her head to the ceiling.

"You know that my husband never liked Davien. At least on the surface. Said he wasn't good enough for our daughter." Róisín closed her eyes. "He mellowed, of course, in recent years. The birth of the twins changed something inside of him, but the guilt of those first seventy years never left. He never knew how to build the bridge to repair the damage. That's why we were often absent, at least until—"

"Until they died. And it filled you with even more regret."

Róisín closed her eyes at Eislyn's words. The truth stung more than she wanted to admit.

The stresses of the past several days broke through. Eislyn's verbal accusations intensified as she continued. "Davien was over *ninety* when he died. Ninety, Róisín. I mean, that's young, I know, but it's also plenty of time to make things right. He ruled this Kingdom for almost twenty years. You couldn't find it in your hearts to tear yourself away from your…whatever it is you do. Your lifestyle, to make amends during that time?"

Róisín knew the Queen was right. "If it's any consolation, I adored him. Davien was everything I ever imagined my son-in-law could be. It was Lugh who…oh forget it." She turned to face Eislyn. "What's done is done. Listen, I'm here because we need your help. We had nowhere else to go. The riot in Lakedon threatened both Lugh and me, not to mention the Elves we took in."

Eislyn studied Róisín's words, tossing them around in her head before admitting that, in fairness, no one knew Lugh's current whereabouts. An Elf could have teleported him elsewhere in Abria, or worse, he may have been executed by the mob for protecting a perceived enemy.

The Queen sat back in her seat and refocused herself. Like it or not, Róisín was family. The conversation was veering off in the wrong direction and both of them needed to regroup their thoughts.

Eislyn took a deep breath. "We think the baby will arrive around the end of Frostend," she said with great reluctance.

Róisín's face lit up. "A great grand-baby. Oh Eislyn, Congratulations! I know this hasn't been easy, and this conversation is more than a little uncomfortable. For both of us." She rushed over to Eislyn, kneeled down, and gave her a hug.

The Queen paused, not sure whether to embrace her. After a brief moment, she relented and hugged her husband's grandmother in return. "Thanks."

Róisín let go and returned to her seat.

"This doesn't resolve the issue at hand." Eislyn found it easy to slip back into a leadership conversation. She wasn't sure whether this was because she was growing used to the throne or if her management skills were coming through. Or, as she suspected was truly the case, she was taking her mounting frustration out on Róisín.

"Tiernan. My grandson. We have to get him home." Róisín threw her hands up in the air. "But how?"

Eislyn extended her index finger and tapped on the table three times. "This is his throne, his Kingdom. Not mine," she said, emphasizing each with her hand. "I'm his *support* and always will be, but if I'm being honest, I'd much rather tend tables at the tavern."

"So, what do we do? This threat of the Shapeshifters, as you called them, seems insurmountable. Whispersong is on the other side of the Kingdom. Getting there safely seems impossible. Unless…"

Eislyn angled her head. "You have an idea?"

"Maybe. It depends if you have any ethers on hand."

Tiernan woke up in a coughing fit so intense that it shook him to his very core. The King rolled to his side facing the wall, trying to contain the sensation so as not to wake his hosts, though to no avail. Another round of coughs emerged from his chest, followed by a third and then a fourth. After the last, he spit out blood onto the sheets.

Pernella rushed into his room. By now, Tiernan had rolled to the other side and was leaning up. She glimpsed the blood on the floor and on the sheets. Pernella offered him a drink of water. After swallowing it, he fell back onto the bed forcefully with the room spinning around him.

"Are you okay?" Pernella knew the answer, and Tiernan's silence confirmed her thoughts. She hoped whatever rescue was on its way from Farna by now would be arriving soon. She also couldn't figure out why Rosk had yet to return.

Ahern walked in and handed her a potion. "This is the last one we have," he said as his wife helped the King sit up.

Tiernan drank it and felt some relief from the pain, though reality started sinking in. *Without a doctor, I'm done for. Maybe it's for the best.* He looked at his hosts, his eyes finally seeing them in focus for the first time. "Thank you for your generosity." It took more effort than he expected to speak.

Pernella looked back to Ahern. "What do we do? Rosk hasn't come back yet. Maybe he didn't make it to Farna?"

A thousand thoughts ran through Tiernan's mind. He had only given his hosts a brief overview of the battle. They didn't know about the depth of the waiting evil or the advantages their enemies had over them. Then a hollowing fear gripped his heart.

What if our enemies attacked while I was gone? Farna could be burning *right now. Eislyn, my love. Our unborn baby. All gone because of me.*

Ahern's voice brought the King back to reality. "We'll send another rider. I'll go myself, even." Pernella began to protest, but he cut her off. "Honey, we cannot let the King die here. We must do what we can."

"What about Lorelei?"

The couple turned to the King.

"Lily of the Valley doesn't have an infirmary." Tiernan wondered why his grandfather had never insisted on building one. *A task for another day.* "Lorelei does. They're the biggest city in this region, second only to Farna in all of Abria. They would know what kind of doctor to send."

"What about Idlewind?" asked Pernella.

Ahern ran both hands through his hair. "Idlewind is closer, but we don't know if any of their doctors survived the attack."

The couple looked to the King for his opinion. Too weak to speak, he nodded in agreement and closed his eyes to rest.

"Lorelei is the best course of action. It's further, but with one of our trained horses, I can be there by morning." Ahern walked over to Tiernan's bedside and placed his hand on his shoulder. "I'll leave within two hours. Listen, my liege. I know you've suffered a great deal. Just hold on a little bit longer."

Tiernan opened his eyes and gave Ahern a small nod, then stared at the ceiling, deep in contemplative thought.

Ahern turned to kiss Pernella and headed toward the door. He stopped and turned back to Tiernan. "One more thing."

Tiernan raised his head to Ahern's voice at the door.

"Don't die on me."

Queen Eislyn held the four ethers in her hand with an iron grip. Her guards had scoured the city, talking with every shop owner, weapons dealer, and clothing seller. Graelans had no use for ethers, so finding some within a city with no Elf presence to speak of proved challenging.

The four she held were remnants from a past Statuo, leftover stock that Elven competitors had not purchased. She sat in the war room, waiting in silence.

In trepidation.

In fear.

For this plan to work, certain pieces needed to fall into place the right way. She heard a knock. The guards behind her readied their weapons as she gave the okay for the visitor to enter.

As expected, Róisín walked in flanked by several guards, joined by six Elves with teleportation abilities. The Queen smiled as she welcomed them.

"Thank you for coming. Did the King's grandmother explain the situation we face?" Eislyn hoped referring to Tiernan by his title, as well as Róisín's connection to him, might assuage the Elves' fears.

A series of nods and words of affirmation let her know they were on board.

As each took their seat, Róisín frowned. "So, we have a problem."

Of course, we do. Things can't ever go easy for us. "I'm listening, though I have a hunch I know where this is going."

"None of them have been to Whispersong."

"I hate being right all the time," Eislyn lamented.

"Which means it's going to involve travel by foot in some capacity—" Róisín started to say.

"Or horseback," Serin interjected with a thoughtful expression on his face.

"Yes, or horseback, but we'll get to that," Róisín conceded. She shook her head at him, as if to warn him to keep his mouth shut.

"How close are we talking?" Eislyn asked, noting the interaction between the two.

"Two have been to Lily of the Valley."

Serin and another raised their hand to let the Queen know it was them.

Róisín continued. "Two others to Idlewind."

Those two nodded their heads. Eislyn tightened her lips as she pondered this possibility.

"And the other two have visited no further east than Kingscrown Rock."

Eislyn's tightened lips turned to a full-on bite, and she forced herself to relax her facial muscles. "Okay," she said with a deep breath. "Lily of the Valley might be our best bet. The two of you who have been there, please stay. The rest of you, you're free to go."

The Elves bowed to her as a group, something Eislyn had never seen before. She wondered if her apology to Serin had begun the process of making amends with their people. They walked to the door and knocked on it. The guards let them through and then closed it, though not without a sense of hesitation, per the Queen's command.

Serin spoke. "I have another idea that might work. It's dangerous though."

The Queen leaned forward. "I'm listening."

"Serin," Róisín said, giving him another stern look. "I don't think your—"

"Just hear me out, please. Let the Queen decide. It's her husband and Kingdom that's at stake."

"And my grandson. Don't forget that."

Eislyn admired his boldness. Serin seemed confident and capable, though something in the pit of her stomach knew this was going to be a risky idea.

"Teleporting a horse, as I mentioned a moment ago, would be difficult. It would require all four of your ethers just to make it work. I could take a doctor along with me, but no one else."

He sat forward. "And please understand, Your Highness, that this is just to get there. Once Tiernan, forgive me, the King has recovered, we would need at least one more ether to get *him* home. We don't know what the shop owners in the Valley have in their inventories, possibly none. Depending on what we found, the horse and the doctor could be stuck at Whispersong for the time being, assuming we find a single ether in the Valley for purchase to get the King home once he's recovered."

"Fair enough. Let's call that Plan B. What's your other idea?" Eislyn noticed Róisín shift in her seat. *She doesn't like this one.*

"The fact you're here asking us about teleportation means you probably have a basic idea of how it works. We have to be able to see or have seen where we want to go to get there. Otherwise, it can have disastrous consequences."

The other Elf spoke up. "It's a memory thing. Sight allows us to visualize the destination. It's like a map. You can try to navigate without one, and you may get where you want to go, eventually. You could also end up in the middle of the Great Sea if you're not careful."

Eislyn nodded. "I'm not going to pretend I knew that before today. But yes, I know it now, after Róisín filled me in on the process earlier. That's why she asked which of you had been to the east. The closer we get to Whispersong, the better."

Serin cocked his head and smirked. "Well, there's one place we've *all* seen. One place that would give us a vantage point long enough to see Whispersong so that we could teleport there."

Eislyn's stomach twisted. This time, it wasn't the baby. "Where is that?"

He pointed upward with a solitary finger. "The sky."

Lagen placed a cloth on Lugh's forehead. The latter had a gash along his hairline that caused a trail of blood to run from his temple to his chin. The sensation of the wet cloth caused Lugh to stir.

"Where are we?" he asked through a haze.

"Confined to a room in some type of building in Lakedon's government district."

"The mayor's offices, most likely." Lugh tried to sit up. Across the room, the other six Elves looked to be in various states of pain. Frist tended to two of them, one of which had their arm in a sling. "How are the others?"

"Not good," Lagen said. "The mayor of Lakedon, Fenwick, brought us here after the mob dispersed. He said they would do what they could to track down the perpetrators, but that it might take some time. Many of those who attacked us fled the city."

"Of course they did," Frist said from across the room. "And why did Fenwick bring us here instead of to one of the medical buildings?" He stood. "I'll tell you why. It's because Graelans don't care if we live or die."

"Frist…" Lagen raised his hand to his friend, hoping to calm him down.

"You know it, Lagen. The barbarians who slaughtered us eons ago are no different than the mob that nearly killed us this morning. Fenwick can feign concern for all he wants. The truth is, he's the same as them. Callous. Sees us as cattle. Something to be used and—"

"That's enough!" Lagen stood to his feet, ready to challenge the verbal onslaught. "Do you put Lugh and Róisín in that group, too?"

"Of course not."

"So, what makes you think Fenwick bringing us here isn't for our protection as well? The mayor seemed genuinely concerned."

"Only because *he* was hurt. A Graelan. No offense, Lugh."

Lugh shrugged as he sat up. "Frist, I can't speak for the mayor. I don't even remember coming here."

"One of the errant rocks hit your head as our Barrier broke," explained Lagen.

Lugh nodded. "Well, that explains my pounding headache." He moved face to face with Frist. "My wife and I have lived here for decades. Since long before Kyrie and my son-in-law ascended to the throne. I've known Fenwick for most of that time. Believe me, he's a good person."

Frist turned around, saying nothing. Instead, he resumed tending to his injured comrade.

Lugh turned to Lagen. "How long was I out?"

"A few hours. We haven't seen a doctor yet. Fenwick expressed his concern and said he would return, but that was a while ago."

Lugh rubbed his chin. "And none of the others have returned to teleport us out of here."

Frist spoke up. "You forget, Graelan. If our people can't find an ether to recharge their magic, they wouldn't be able to come back. And besides, where would they reappear? For all they know, Dídean Inn is a flaming inferno and we're all dead."

Lugh raised his eyebrow at the outburst and then watched as Lagen paced back and forth.

The Elf stopped and turned to Lugh. "What do we do, my friend? Do we flee during the night? Blund and Bolar are pretty beat up. I'm not sure they would survive the flight."

Lugh walked over to Lagen and put his hands on his shoulders. "Stop. Listen, the best thing for us is to stay and wait for Fenwick. He may have a solution. Potions from a nearby store. Maybe even an ether or two. You don't want to leave here exhausted in the middle of the night."

"So you think we *should* leave?" asked Frist.

"And go where? Clericsfold? Alwyn?" Bolar asked.

Lugh began to answer, but closed his mouth. There didn't seem to be any good ideas.

The door to the mayor's office opened. Everyone turned around to see Fenwick, a heavy expression spread across his face.

Lugh walked over and leaned against a chair back next to Fenwick. "What's wrong?"

The mayor swallowed. He looked to each Elf in the room, then to Lugh. "I did what I could. They want you out of here." He looked back to the Elves. "All of you. I argued with the council for as long as I could. They would not budge. All Elves are to leave Lakedon immediately." He looked back at Lugh. "This includes you. They see you and Róisín as harboring enemies."

Frist threw his hands in the air. "See what I mean? I *told you*, Lagen. This is how the Graelans see us. Less than beings. Don't you ever wonder why they call themselves by that name? It's as if they think the world is theirs to inherit and we are something to be trampled on. Discarded." He turned his body to face Fenwick. "And you. With all your power as mayor, you went along with this. Agreed to make us exiles again, didn't you?"

Fenwick lowered his head. "I did what I could. But you should know," he said as he met Frist's gaze, "The council has chosen to exile *me* as well. For *defending* you. Now, if you'll excuse me, I must break the news to my wife and pack the belongings we can grab. You have two hours to get out of town, never to return."

Fenwick turned around. With his back to the room, he lowered his head and spoke one last time. "The council let Dídean Inn burn to the ground. I'm sorry. There's nothing left of it."

"You can't be serious. The sky. What does that accomplish?" Eislyn had a feeling she already knew the answer.

"I told you this was a crazy idea," said Róisín.

Serin pounded his fist on the table. "It's crazy, but it can work if you would just listen, Róisín."

Eislyn extended a hand toward him. "Continue."

"Thank you. I *know* I can pull this off. I'll hold the doctor tight."

"Perhaps we should bind the two of you together?" suggested Róisín, with an almost mocking laugh.

"That's not a bad idea. Thanks, Róisín," he said with a grin that made her scoff. "When I teleport, I'll aim high. Almost as high as the dragons from a few decades ago. I'll look east to the skies over the Valley region in the general direction of the mountains. Then, when we appear, I'll quickly absorb another ether."

Róisín sat forward. "Let's be clear here, Serin. As you fall. You'll pull an ether out of your satchel and absorb it *as you fall.*"

The Queen raised her hand. "Róisín, let him speak. Interrupting him like this is rude and you know it."

Róisín crossed her arms and motioned for Serin to continue.

"Once I absorb it, all it will take is for me to get a glimpse of Whispersong. Then, I can teleport there."

"And as for returning home?" asked the Queen.

"I've already seen Farna. Been here, inside Castle Abria. Just take me to the infirmary where you want me to deliver the King after the doctor does his job in Whispersong. After that, I'll bring him back, straight to where he needs to be."

"Why take a doctor? If you can bring Tiernan here, why should a doctor treat him in Whispersong at all?" Eislyn asked.

Serin lowered his head. "My concern is whether he would survive the return trip in his current state. If the King has internal injuries, the jostling of the teleportation process might disrupt his natural body rhythms. If a doctor can at least treat his wounds and analyze his condition before, it will improve his chances of survival."

This can't be happening. We're this close to getting him home. He's going to survive no matter what. I won't let him die. Eislyn pushed the chair back and stood, leaving the ethers on the table. She paced around the room.

Now, she understood the meaning behind Davien's games several years ago. Sure, the definition of the word wasn't lost on her. Their implication and why her deceased father-in-law named the competition as such made so much sense to her.

It's not easy being in charge. Decisions can be difficult.

Statuo.

Chapter 10

The Awakening

Kane took a sip of the soup in the bowl in front of him. His cabin, once the only structure on the Northern Plateau, now rested in the middle of many other structures that the Elves had been building. Much to his chagrin, the view from his kitchen was now blocked, occluded by a support structure just outside of his northern wall.

Next to him rested the Soul Sword. Its colors seemed more vibrant to him today than before. He took another sip. The warm liquid slid down his throat, coating his insides and soothing them. He hadn't realized how parched and sore they were. The recipe was said to contain some Elven spices, harvested from deep within the Darkwood Forest, that had medicinal properties.

With each sip, Kane thought back to his days at the orphanage. "Cleris," he said instinctively. The founder of Clericsfold hadn't crossed his mind in years.

"Our town was named after one of its founders, a knowledgeable and mysterious man named Cleris, who developed the skills to craft — fold, as he liked to call it — various potions and other elixirs from nearby foliage."

Kane swiped the wooden bowl away from him. The mere thought of Borun, even if it was nothing more than words from a school lesson many decades ago, made him physically ill. The bowl landed on the floor, spilling its contents across his kitchen.

"Is it okay if I come in?" Folas stood at the entrance to Kane's residence.

Folas is standing outside. Waiting for permission. How odd. "Come on in. How are your wounds? Has your magic returned?"

Folas shook his head. He unbuttoned his tunic to expose his scar. "The Dragonborn left her mark." He touched the wound, running his fingers along its exposed and discolored ridge. "To answer your questions, Divider, I'm sore. Weakened. And I can't seem…" He started to say it. Instead, he decided to demonstrate.

Folas extended his hand. Snapped his fingers. Opened his palm. Thrust his arm forward.

Nothing happened. If Kane didn't know better, it would have looked like Folas was performing some kind of weird Elven dance ritual.

"So, how did you teleport the boy away?"

Folas shook his head. "I think that was all I had left in me."

"And you wasted it on him."

"I only did what *he* said to do."

Kane snarled his lips at Folas' words. He didn't like the idea that Zoran was giving orders. "What's done is done," Kane said. "Have you tried the soup? One of your minions—"

"Don't call them that." Folas rose from his seat, his emotions rising to the top.

Kane raised an eyebrow. *This is not the same Elf. He's changed somehow.*

"Fine. One of the other Elves brought me some. Said it was a recipe from your homeland." He picked up the bowl and took a sip from the contents that hadn't spilled on the floor.

"Lyran Herb Soup. I know it well. My mother used to make it for me before she…" Folas' words trailed off. "Anyway, yes, it's been passed down throughout the centuries. Rumor has it the recipe predates the New Era. We've been making it in the Forest ever since we arrived, modifying it by using the herbs and plants we harvest."

"Can it bring back your magic?"

Folas regarded Kane for a moment before answering. "You're obsessing over my magic. Did the soup bring back your strength?"

Kane lifted the bowl again, this time taking a big gulp.

"Thought so. It heals the body. Abrian thyme is the secret. When mixed into a standard potion, it has various effects on the body. In soup, it gives the body a boost. Helps it fight whatever it's facing."

Kane had enough. "Out with it, Folas. Your entire countenance has changed. What is wrong with you? Enid is gone. The King has been defeated. Their parents are dead. Those two beasts almost wiped both Alwyn and Idlewind from the map. We have the Soul Sword."

"We lost the other two items. And we didn't get the magic from under Farna. The Dragonborn made sure of that."

"Forget her. She's dead. My point is Abria has never been weaker. The time of our victory is at hand and you're acting like we've lost the war."

Folas walked into Kane's kitchen, grabbed a towel, and began cleaning up the mess.

What is he doing?

Kane let the thought pass and took his last drink. By now, the soup had cooled off. It felt less comforting than before, though just as healing.

Folas finished wiping up the mess, then placed the soaked towel by the washbasin. "Do you see how easily that cleaned up? Look at your floor and cabinets."

Kane noticed their renewed, shiny appearance.

"The liquid of the soup?"

"No. It's the Abrian thyme. Its restorative properties even work on other objects too. You have to cook it right, but once you do, it releases a powerful chemical.

"And then, when applied, everything changes. Things were a mess, but now your floor is stronger." Folas stomped on the ground as he said it. He then knocked on the wood of the cabinets. "Your wood is reinforced where it splashed. And all evidence of the mess is gone."

"Sounds like magic soup."

Folas put his hand on Kane's shoulder. "What I'm saying to you is if the King recovers from the mess we've created, it will be as if it never happened in the first place. He may even emerge stronger than before."

"Absolutely not. You cannot risk yourself like that. Do you even hear yourself?" Róisín's words filled the war room, echoing and reverberating off the walls. After her outburst, everyone else in the room sat in silence. Waiting.

The Queen's response broke the awkwardness. "This is my decision, Róisín. Serin, we have four ethers. Is that enough for four trips?"

Róisín whipped her head toward the Elf as a warning to guard his words.

Serin ignored her. He opened his mouth to speak, but stopped. He closed his eyes in order to think it over. "Yeah. Yeah, I think so." He took a deep breath. "I think so. It will take two to teleport you and I there. One for the sky, and the other to Whispersong."

"Assuming you make it!" Róisín's body language was that of a person used to maintaining control, though losing it bit by bit.

"Róisín, enough." Eislyn shot her grandmother-in-law a look, reminding her of her place. Once Róisín calmed down, Eislyn continued. "What about the return trip to get the doctor?"

"That would be a third, yes, but unlike our flight from Lakedon, I will be returning to Farna without you. I'll retrieve the doctor, then bring him to Whispersong. I'll need to use the last ether to bring you and the King home."

The other Elf tapped Serin on the shoulder. "Teleportation doesn't always take a full ether. You might get lucky."

Serin gave them a faint smile. "That's true, but we're breaking the rules here. Teleporting to the sky and then teleporting again right after, not to mention the importance of the Queen herself. I don't want to take any chances."

"Then it's settled." The Queen turned to the guards. "Take Serin to the infirmary immediately. Let him survey the room, the land, the castle, whatever he needs. When he's ready, bring him to the open field in the middle of Farna." She used her hands to dismiss Serin and the guards. She turned to another group of guards still present. "I will be traveling to the Alligator to see my parents. You will accompany me there."

"Eislyn…" Róisín tried to protest one last time.

The Queen extended her hand and placed it on top of Róisín's. "Listen, you might not like this plan. I'm not sure if I do. But I will not leave my husband out there any longer."

"Even at the risk of the Kingdom's future ruler?" Róisín's words hit Eislyn hard. She pulled her hand back and felt her belly. At the same time, Róisín looked in the direction of the attending guards who, though they tried to hide it, gave subtle indications they had just learned the news for the first time.

Eislyn kept her face focused on her stomach. "You will not, under any circumstances, mention the words you just heard to anyone until I return with Abria's King. Not your friends, not the other guards. Not to your spouse or would be mates. *No one.* Do I make myself clear?"

"Yes, Your Highness," they said in unison.

"Good. Now, I must speak with Róisín privately. Wait outside the door with the others."

After a moment's hesitation, the guards walked outside and closed the door.

Róisín swallowed hard. "Me and my big mouth."

"You could say that."

"My point remains, Eislyn. You're carrying my great-grandchild. Boy or girl, the child will one day inherit the throne *of our Kingdom.* Forgetting that detail for a moment, as a mother, how can you risk their life before you've even met them?"

It was a fair question. She would be traveling alone with a single Elf. No protection. The risk that the Elf would overshoot his target — or worse, not be able to teleport to Whispersong — hung over her head.

Do I have a death wish? Eislyn rubbed her stomach slightly. *Is this fair to you, my child?*

She then shook her head. "We will not fail. If there's one thing I've learned about this family I married into, it's that their love for each other, their bond, can overcome anything. Their motto, Family is Strength, is more than a cute saying. It defines everything they do.

"Your daughter and her husband gave their lives that I might have a chance to live. They didn't do that by accident. It was their family duty to bring their Princess home."

Eislyn felt herself tear up as she recalled the way Tiernan described the love Davien had for her when they planned the rescue mission.

It was then Róisín's turn for confession. "Lugh carries a burden I cannot fix. He regrets the way he treated Davien, and even more so that they never reconciled before that day. He and Kyrie chose to rescue you and it cost them their lives." She slammed her fist on the table. "And here I am watching another member of the royal family about to make a decision that could end the same way."

Eislyn rose to her feet. "I'm coming home, Róisín. With Tiernan by my side. That is the only option."

Folas sat by himself on a rock just outside the primary walls of the fortress. A few of his blinded Elven brethren continued to work on building portions of Kane's citadel. They seemed oblivious to his presence.

Across the grasslands of the Northern Plateau, he saw another pair of Elves standing still. Silently, Folas watched their body language. One picked up a hammer, then twisted his face in confusion. His companion reached for it, then shrugged her shoulders. He saw them mouth something, but couldn't tell what they were saying from this distance.

Curious, Folas slid off of the rock and walked in their direction. Before he arrived, he felt a presence watching him. He turned around, scanning the fields. He then mentally began recounting which Elves present had the cloak of invisibility power.

That's not it. He whipped around and looked high into the sky. There, in one of the towers of the citadel, stood Zoran at the window with his hands behind his back, observing everything.

Observing me. Folas waved Zoran off, making his indifference visibly obvious. He continued to walk toward the confused Elves, knowing that his every action would be seen by the Dark Emperor.

"Soma, Rox. Are you two okay?" Folas' demeanor of a soft, concerned Elf felt odd even to him, a stark comparison to the controlling persona he had portrayed for the past few decades.

"I think so," said Soma. "But I don't know. I feel as if I'm supposed to do something with this tool, but I don't know what. Did someone give me orders but forget to tell me how to do them?"

"It's the same thing for me," Rox said. She turned to Folas. "Can you help me? I feel…off. I don't know what I'm supposed to be doing or…" Her voice drifted off as she looked around to survey the land. "Where am I? This doesn't look like the Rosewood Forest."

Folas reached out and placed his hand on both of their shoulders. "You're with others of your kind." He turned and pointed. "Do you see that wall? We've been building it for a while. Can you go help the others by the entrance? I'm sure they could tell you what to do."

Both nodded, then scurried off.

Folas shook his head and turned around. He kept his head low for a few steps until he realized he was still being watched. Felt the gaze. He finally raised his head and made eye contact with Zoran.

Folas couldn't tell, but he thought he saw a smirk cross the Dark Emperor's face. Zoran then turned and — if Folas saw correctly — limped out of sight and into another room within the tower.

Folas continued his walk toward the citadel's entrance. As he passed the two Elves, they still seemed disoriented but somewhat refocused. *I wonder how long this will last?*

Inside the courtyard, a series of small huts lined one of the inner walls. These served as the home for the Elves, save Folas who had his own dedicated room within the citadel. Reflecting on the disparity, Folas snarled. Even those who joined willingly were subjected to this minimalist existence.

Slaves to Kane's ambition. Tricked by my leadership. And now, subjects of Zoran himself. Folas sighed deep in contemplation.

He passed another structure, a tavern Kane dubbed The Drunken Dragon. *"We should name it something more powerful than a mere alligator. A dragon seems appropriate."*

Folas shook his head as he recalled Kane's words. He walked into the establishment, looking around for a space to sit.

Behind the bar and occupying most of the tables were former Clericsfold denizens. These were the remnants of the Graelan allies Kane recruited after the first Statuo. Many had been killed by the royal family during the rescue of Tiernan's now-wife. Some had been lost during Midir's attack while others perished in the underground climactic battle.

Folas saw an open table by the eastern wall and sat at it. No one seemed to notice him or even care that he had walked in. Most of the patrons seemed preoccupied with their own stories.

Folas frowned. It had never dawned on him that these men and women had homes within the citadel itself. His eyes darted back and forth until a sinking realization hit him.

He was the only Elf here with any sense of luxury. The Graelans took it upon themselves to claim various rooms as they were completed.

Completed by Elven hands. What good are these Graelans, anyway? Folas cleared his throat and raised his hand to get someone's attention.

The bartender walked over. "Can I help you?"

"I'm hungry. Soup. And something strong to drink." She nodded and walked away.

Out of the corner of his eye, Folas saw movement. He turned his head in its direction only to see an empty space. He smirked and nodded.

"Deras, you're not fooling anyone. Did Kane send you to follow me? Or Zoran?"

She disengaged her invisibility. "Does it matter? Both of them want to know what happened to the zealous Dark Elf Master from just a few weeks ago."

The bartender delivered his drink. Folas took a large gulp before responding. "Tell me something you love."

"Excuse me?" she asked.

"I said, 'Tell me something you love.' It can be anything. Food. A family member." He noticed her hair for the first time and the way she had it pulled off to one side. "That hairdo of yours."

"I don't see why that matters?"

"Humor me."

She sighed. "Fine. My spouse. We fell in love during the exile."

"Ah. Yes, that's a long time. Now, I want you to imagine him dead."

She rolled her eyes as he took another drink.

"Fine. If not dead, then taken from you. Ripped away. Your entire identity — the person you had become through years of mutual experience and growth — gone, just like that." Folas slammed the glass on the table. The cup shattered. Behind his eyes, a small flicker of light glowed, something Folas felt and Deras saw.

"And now, rather than be trusted by your brethren during your lowest point, by those who worked alongside you, you're being questioned! Doubted. *Accused*. Do you know how angry that might make someone? How much it might change who they are and how they act?" Folas stood to his feet and rushed to face down Deras. He raised his hand and watched in amazement as she levitated off the ground.

The other patrons took notice. One Graelan at the bar elbowed the person next to him, a man almost completely drunk. Even his mouth dropped at the sight of the Dark Elf's anger. An odd aura surrounded his body, a glowing, inky, halo-like effect with hints of other colors swirling through it.

Deras tried to soothe his rage. "I'm sorry, Folas. I was only doing as I was told."

"That's a poor excuse for betrayal," he said as his voice reverberated. Finding a buried strength, Folas roared as he pushed her floating body across the tavern. Deras moved with such force that she broke through the still-curing stone wall and landed outside. As it collapsed, the debris buried her in a heap of stones.

Folas panted in uncontrolled breath. He looked at his hand, a swirling ball of magic resting in his palm. He narrowed his eyes as he realized the sphere was inky and multi-colored.

He looked back at the bartender, who held his soup with a shocked expression on her face. "I'm not hungry anymore. Give it to one of the other Elves. Not a Graelan." He stormed outside.

Once in the open field, he felt his heart rate speed up. Emotions flooded his senses. He looked left and right for a place of solitude. Between two buildings, a blacksmith forge and a tailor, he saw a spot for some privacy.

Folas rushed to it and fell to his knees. He punched the ground in anger, feeling the weight of the moment. Folas thought about the last Elven life he had taken. "Voron…" he muttered. He then thought about Deras and whether she might still be alive. Wiping the tears from his face, he stood to his feet and straightened his clothing. With calm and precision, he made his way between the buildings and near the alleyway where she had fallen.

There, a group of blinded Elves were removing the stones. As Folas walked up, he saw her broken body. The trickle of blood coming out of her mouth. Her lifeless eyes.

As they removed the stones covering her torso, he realized it was hopeless. There was no movement or breathing. One of them bent down and checked her pulse. He shook his head.

In his rage, Folas snapped his fingers. To his surprise, he disappeared.

Chapter 11

Taking Flight

Queen Eislyn knocked on the frame of the open threshold of her parents' Drunken Alligator. Behind her stood a group of guards prepared to act if anything appeared suspicious.

Her mother, Freya, turned around. "Eislyn!" She rushed to her daughter's side and tried to give her a hug.

Eislyn took a step back. "Hi, Mom. Where's Dad?"

Freya paused, noticing her daughter's unease and the guards' on-edge appearance. "Sorry, I'm still getting used to this. Are hugs not allowed for royalty?" Her face appeared visibly hurt.

"Oh. Yeah, hugs are allowed. It's just an odd day. Wishing I was back here, running this place with you." Eislyn cleared her throat. "So, like I asked. Where's Dad?"

"He's out back. I can send for him." Freya noticed the growing unease in her daughter's countenance. "Honey, what's wrong? You're not acting like yourself, even with that crown on your head."

Eislyn met Freya's eyes. "Mom, do you remember the day we lost Aoife?"

Freya stopped cold in her tracks and stared back. Her lip quivered. "Why...why would you bring that up?" The older woman, remembering the moment they found out Aoife had died, braced herself on the bar. "Eislyn, what is with you today? You know I'll never forget..." Her voice broke as she began to cry.

Eislyn breathed a sigh of relief. She turned to the guards behind her. "You two, retrieve my father. Bring him here. Now."

Without hesitation, they darted off to find him.

Freya's heart sunk. "Eislyn? What is going on?"

Eislyn shook her head. The two waited in silence until her father, Eldar, appeared at the back entrance with the guards.

He looked as worried as his wife. "Freya, what's wrong?"

The Queen's mother raised her arms in confusion. Eldar then caught sight of his daughter.

"Eislyn!" He began to run to her, but the two guards crossed their swords in front of him. "Eislyn, honey, what is this?"

"Dad, do you remember the day we lost Aoife?" Eislyn watched as pain crossed her father's face.

"Yes, on the fishing trip with her family. The merchant…" He lowered his head in grief as he recalled the memory.

"What about the merchant?"

"Eislyn, what are you doing?" asked her mother.

Tears welled up in Eislyn's eyes. "Daddy, please. Just answer the question."

"The merchant was a friend of mine. Someone who grew up on the sea. Someone who promised us the rough waters near Northwick wouldn't be an issue…" Eldar choked up, unable to finish the story.

Eislyn ran to her mother and embraced her. "I'm sorry." She looked at the guards and nodded her head. "Daddy, I'm so, so sorry." Eldar rushed to his daughter and embraced both Eislyn and his wife.

With fresh tears still running down her face, Freya drew in a breath. "What was that about?"

"I had to be certain. Come with me. It's not safe for you to be here any longer. I'll tell you more on the way."

As they walked, Eislyn brought her parents up to speed on the current crisis plaguing Abria. She could see the earlier hurt and confusion turn to understanding as she explained the connection between emotion and the Shapeshifters. Eislyn saw her father's heartbreak as she explained why Tiernan was still trapped on the other side of the Kingdom.

Freya took a seat on the central well, still working through the details. "And these Shapeshifters can mimic any one of us."

Eislyn solemnly nodded.

"We can't abandon the people. The citizens of Farna who lost their homes in the…" Freya searched for the word. "Explosion, I guess. They're hurting, honey. The community needs us. Many of them don't have a place to stay."

"I have to agree with your mother. I know you're the Queen and can order us to Castle Abria. But please don't. Post guards with us. Let us continue our work."

Eislyn wiped her face, knowing her parents were right. She then saw Serin walking out of the castle surrounded by guards.

Time to go.

The Queen rose from the edge of the well. "Okay. You win. Halfway, anyway," she said with a smile. "Let's call it my way of apologizing for all the times I made you worry as a kid."

"Oh honey, you weren't that…" Freya didn't finish her thought. She saw the Elf and the guards walking their way. "Eislyn, what aren't you telling us?"

Eldar narrowed his eyes, then followed his wife's gaze toward the approaching party. "Eislyn?"

The Queen sighed. "This is where I get to be Queen, Daddy. All those years working in the Alligator, running the place? You taught me to be a manager, right?"

"Right…But…"

"And you, Mom. You encouraged Aoife and I to pursue whatever path the Moon set before us."

"Yes, but…"

"This is mine." Eislyn removed her crown and handed it to her mother. "Daddy can stay and help the people, but I need you in the castle, Mom. I'm taking a trip. I will return, but I don't know how long I'll be gone." She looked at her father. "I guess I didn't tell you the whole story when I said you won halfway."

Freya held the crown with an iron grip as her hands shook. The guards and Serin met up with the couple.

There has to be a better way to do this.

Eislyn motioned to the officer. "From this moment forward, Interim Queen Freya is in charge of Castle Abria and the commander of the Abrian Royal Guards. Lieutenant, see that Captain Nico is made aware of this transfer immediately."

Freya's eyes showed her lack of understanding. "Eislyn, what do you mean by 'Queen'?"

Eislyn took the crown back and placed it on Freya's head. "During the wedding, do you remember how Manus Midir took charge?"

"Yes," Freya answered with a wavering voice.

"Mom, I'm asking the same of you. Like I said, Daddy can keep helping the people of Farna, but Abria needs someone who can make decisions in my absence."

"This is crazy talk, honey." Her mom shook her head and tried to remove the crown.

"Mom, listen to me." Eislyn locked eyes with Freya. "I cannot stay. I must go. Now. I'm still the Queen. This isn't me stepping down. It's just…" She smiled. "What do they call it in Smithblitz when someone replaces another player?"

"A substitute."

"Right. Well, you're my substitute." Eislyn moved in and hugged her parents. "I love you both."

With that, she snapped her fingers to the guards. One half of them followed Eldar back to the Alligator and the other half escorted Freya to Castle Abria. Though walking in opposite directions, both parents craned their heads backward and watched as a guard bound one of Serin's legs to Eislyn's.

"You ready for this?" she asked.

"Are you?" he snorted.

She smiled. "The truth? No." She grabbed onto his hand as the guard bound their wrists together. Eislyn took a deep breath. "Let's do this."

Serin gazed toward the sky overlooking the Valley Mountains. He snapped his fingers.

In an instant, the Queen of Abria was gone.

Zoran paced in the throne room. Ever since he had watched Folas earlier, a new sense of urgency permeated through him.

It's time. Things are moving along and we must act now. He bellowed orders to a nearby blinded Elf. "Bring me Kane and Folas." The Elf bowed, then scurried away. *Apparently, this one lacks teleportation abilities.*

Once alone, Zoran ran his fingers along his scar. "Worthless Graelan," he said, recalling Midir's assault. He made a fist and closed his eyes. The Dark Emperor then pictured a discarded pile of stones in the throne room. Remnants of the construction, they had yet to be cleared since the Elves had finished this area.

In his mind, he saw their shape. Roughly rectangular with an unfinished surface, their appearance reminded him of the accursed Castle Abria. Anger welled up in Zoran, which he then pushed to the side to refocus his energy. He pushed past the pile and focused on one large stone.

Instinctively, Zoran relaxed his fist and extended his fingers. He began visualizing the stone's appearance not as it appeared, but in a transformed state. Smooth. Gray. He then pictured the stone flattening. At the same time, he raised his other hand in the same gesture.

"Playing games?" a voice asked.

Zoran's concentration broke and his eyes shot open. Standing at the entrance were Kane and Folas. The former carried the Soul Sword with the blade resting on his shoulder, a curious look spreading across his face.

Folas gave the Dark Emperor an empty stare.

"Games? Is that what this is to you?" Zoran shook his head and walked over to the stone pile. He sifted through it until he found the object of his focus. Zoran picked it up, feeling its rough texture and narrowing his eyes at its golden sheen. Disappointed in the results, he tossed it aside and turned back to face his conspirators.

With a look of disdain, Zoran dismissed the blinded Elf. "Leave."

Folas watched them walk out. He turned back to Zoran and crossed his arms. "What do you want? I was busy helping other Elves clean up a mess from a structural collapse."

"Structural collapse?" inquired Kane.

Zoran gave Folas a knowing smirk.

"Why are we here?" Folas asked with rising annoyance.

Zoran gave the Soul Sword a glance before walking over to a nearby chair. His limp, though still obvious, seemed to be less pronounced. He fell into the seat and motioned for the other two to have a seat as well.

Kane walked up to a chair and sat with his legs resting over an armrest. Folas walked over to a table on the opposite side and started to pull the chair out with his hands.

Zoran made a sound, a guttural growl reminiscent of when he was first reawakened. Folas turned and saw Zoran staring at him. Kane angled his head to one side at the interaction.

Folas maintained eye contact with Zoran as he extended his hand, twirled it, and the chair followed suit. Kane bolted out of his chair with a look of shock and betrayal as Folas sat down.

"Your powers. They're back? When did this happen?"

"It's not important," Zoran said with a dismissive tone.

"I think it is," said Folas. He turned to Kane. "Today. They came back today, manifesting themselves in a fit of anger. Emotion. They seem to be returning bit by bit, but they've changed."

"How?" asked Kane.

"Yes. Tell us how," echoed Zoran.

Folas narrowed his eyes. "I can't explain it. They just feel *different*. Almost as if they're powered by the energy sphere we encountered below Farna."

Kane sat back down. He rested the Soul Sword next to him. "What about you?" he asked Zoran. "Do you feel different?"

The Dark Emperor regarded the Divider for a moment, then decided to answer truthfully. "No. Which is why I've brought you here today. It's time."

"For what?" asked Folas.

"A reclamation." Zoran's words echoed off the walls of the throne room, casting a chilling presence on both Kane and Folas.

The two exchanged a look of confusion as Zoran smiled.

The Dark Emperor motioned with his hand. "Come, Folas. Since you can teleport now, you can take me where I need to go." Zoran watched Kane for a moment. "I assume you won't do anything stupid while we're gone?"

Kane rolled his eyes and waved them off. Folas, unsure if this was the right decision, reached for Zoran's hand.

The Dark Emperor grabbed it. "The caves."

Folas let out a sigh and snapped his fingers.

Queen Eislyn gasped for air. *That was unbelievable. It was as if I didn't exist for—*

She could barely finish the thought before another overtook her mind. *We're in free fall!*

"Serin! Anytime!" Tumbling in the air, their limbs tied together, Eislyn and Serin lost control of their trajectory. Here above the clouds, the wind was powerful and overwhelming. She noticed pain beginning to radiate on her wrist and ankle that was bound to Serin. His smaller size made him more susceptible to wind shear, causing their limbs to flail in awkward angles.

"Serin!" Horrified, the Queen realized the problem.

The Elf appeared to have passed out. She shook the arm bound to his, trying to wake him. As they fell through the clouds, she got a view of the land. Far to the south, she saw the Windale Mountains. She followed the landscape and spotted their destination, a small farming settlement.

"Serin!" She shook her hand even more, kicking her feet as well. As they continued in free fall, she began scanning his body, looking for the Elf's satchel.

"There it is!" She used her free hand and, as carefully as she could, reached into the pack. She felt the first of the ethers and pulled it out.

To her dismay, one of the others fell out along with it, tumbling in the wind and flying off in another direction. Whether it would survive the fall and subsequent impact was a concern for another time.

Fighting hard against the wind shear, and watching the ground grow closer by the second, she pulled her right hand toward her left one. Then she pushed the ether into Serin's palm, breathing a sigh of relief as it absorbed into his body.

The effect continued along her hand as well, moving into her arm, up to her head, then her torso, across her stomach, and finally down to her feet. The Queen's body radiated a subtle yellow glow that dissipated as quickly as it appeared.

With the ground now even closer, and Serin showing no signs of waking up, Eislyn panicked. *This can't be. This isn't how it ends. I know I'm meant for more.*

The Queen let out a cry of frustration, one that echoed from the Valley Mountains southbound until where they intersected with the Windale range. Her voice carried the angst of a wife desperate to save her husband, a mother worried for her unborn child, and a leader determined to save her people.

"I refuse to die!" she cried out and instinctively thrusted her hand toward the ground.

Tiernan's eyes shot open, awakened by the sound of a voice he knew within the deepest recesses of his soul. "Eislyn?"

Pernella rushed to his side. "What is it?"

"I heard, no I felt Eislyn. Is she here?"

Pernella shook her head.

Tiernan refused to believe it. "I'm telling you. I heard her *here*." The King patted his chest over his heart. "Help me up."

"My King, you know that's not—"

Tiernan refused to listen. Slowly, he twisted his legs toward the bed's edge. "I said help me up. That's an order." His change in demeanor lacked the grace and platitudes he had showed so far.

Pernella grasped his left hand with her right one. She pulled the injured King up, using her other hand to place his free arm around her neck as she helped Tiernan to a standing position. "You're going to be wobbly on your feet. Take it slow, ok?"

He nodded.

"Okay. Step by step." Pernella led the King from the side of the bed to the footboard. There, he let go and rested on the frame.

"Are you doing okay so far?" she asked.

Tiernan nodded again.

"Okay. We're going to move to our living room. Ahern, stop packing for your trip! I need you now!"

Ahern emerged from the other side of their home. His face morphed with shock. "King Tiernan, you're in no condition to walk. What are you doing?"

"He won't say," Pernella answered.

"That way," Tiernan finally said, pointing toward their rear door.

"The patio?" asked Ahern.

Together, the couple helped the King take each wobbling step toward his destination. Ahern watched with trepidation as Tiernan's legs almost buckled time and time again.

"Son!" yelled Ahern.

Steve came running from outside, catching a glimpse of his father through a window and recognizing the urgency on his face. The boy ran to the back door and opened it. Upon seeing the King, he took his mother's place as support.

"I'll get you a chair," she said. As she ran out the door, she gasped.

Tiernan's head bolted upward. As he took his first step outside, the King knew why he had stumbled this direction.

Laying in the grassy field just beyond Ahern's patio was a facedown, motionless Eislyn.

Zoran blinked as he appeared in the cave where he once slumbered. Folas released the Dark Emperor's hand with a hint of disgust. Zoran looked around as the pair walked through the former tomb.

As Zoran disappeared into the depths of the cavern, Folas walked around and looked at the remaining creatures inside. He first walked over to the reptile-like bipedal beasts, a set of six. Three had a distinctly green coloration while the other three appeared more orange in hue. Like Zoran before the awakening, the creatures did not move.

Next to them, the horde of spiders rested in stillness. Folas picked one up to look at it in more detail. While some were black and insignificant, this one had a vibrant red color, almost as if it was imbued with Fire Magic.

He dropped it and continued exploring. Next, he encountered another winged creature not too dissimilar to the dragon sightings from several decades ago. Much smaller and with a blue tone similar to Leviathan, Folas reached out to grab its claw. *If this is a dragon, is it a child?*

He let go and moved on, finding a group of large Graelanoids. Each of these, if on their feet, would tower a good meter over most Abrians. They had echoes of the barbarians from the exile in their clothing, though none of those attackers were this big. They were larger and their muscles seemed built for warfare.

Beside this group he saw dozens of bipedal bear-like creatures. Some had a grayish-white hue, the others with a dark brown tone throughout their fur.

Zoran emerged from the depths of the cave. Folas turned around. In his hands, Zoran carried the severed wings of a Shapeshifter.

"Let's go," he ordered.

As Zoran tried to walk away, Folas stopped the Dark Emperor with his hands. "No. You're going to tell me what is going on. What is this 'reclamation' you mentioned? Why are we here, and why do you have that in your hand?"

Zoran laughed. "You're not afraid of me anymore, are you?"

"I've had a brush with death once."

"The Dragonborn."

"And you know what she taught me? Once my wounds healed, I realized I'm okay with dying. Better to live free than to die a coward. I demand you tell me what this is about!"

Zoran laughed, its sound echoing down the corridors of the cave and filling the passageways with his voice. "Okay. This," he said, raising the wings, "belongs to me."

"Its wings?"

"Not its wings. The power contained within the wings."

Folas shook his head. "Quit talking in riddles."

"There's more than one way to reactivate magic. All you needed was an emotional push. That doesn't work on beings like me."

A being. That confirms it. Zoran is not a Graelan. So, what is he?

Zoran put the Shapeshifter's wings in Folas' hands. "Here, hold this." The Dark Emperor then stood with his arms extended.

His breathing became labored. His hands turned white. Zoran reached out and grabbed the wings while Folas held them. An inky aura of energy enveloped both before moving into Zoran's body.

The sensation caused the Dark Emperor to fall to the ground on his hands and knees.

Whatever he is, he's pathetic.

A moment later, the wings disintegrated into nothingness. Folas raised an eyebrow, unsure of what to think.

From the ground, Zoran spoke. "I need more. Make preparations to bring the rest of the Shapeshifters to the throne room."

Chapter 12

Reunion

"No. No, no, no, no, no. Eislyn! No, Eislyn!" Tiernan used his dwindling strength to force the men to move at his desired pace. Pernella rushed to the Queen's side faster than Steve and Ahern could guide the limping King.

"Oh, Aila of the Stars, help us." The words, though heartfelt, had an air of resignation to them. As she knelt next to the Queen, Pernella noticed the Elf bound to Eislyn's arm and leg. She began checking the Queen, looking for signs of life.

Tiernan made his way to the field. Once there, Ahern and Steve helped him kneel.

"Eislyn, please, my love, don't do this to me. Not now." Tiernan placed his hand on his wife's head, running his fingers through her hair. His frantic motions were a hinderance to Pernella's efforts, though she let it slide in the King's moment of duress.

Meanwhile, the men had untied Eislyn's arm and leg from the Elf. Steve looked to his father for guidance.

"Let's get her off of her back," the older man said.

"Is she…" Tiernan started to ask before a coughing fit overtook him. He wiped the blood from his face onto his sleeve before falling to all fours and bracing himself on the ground.

As Steve and Ahern reached to grab the Queen's arm, a voice interrupted them.

"That was exhilarating." Eislyn raised her head and made eye contact with her husband. "T, what are you doing out here? You should be in bed." She looked at the others. "Help me up."

Steve and Ahern each reached for a hand and helped the Queen stand to her feet.

"Are you okay?" asked Pernella.

Eislyn nodded.

Pernella motioned to the ground. "How did you…"

"End up here, randomly in your backyard? That's a *fun* story." She bent down to speak to Tiernan. Eislyn lightly brushed his face with her hand. "I'll tell all of you about it in due time. But first, get my beloved husband back to bed."

"Eislyn, I…" Tiernan started to speak, then felt his emotions overwhelm him. Tears streamed down his face.

"Oh, my love." Eislyn leaned in and hugged him tight, then gave him a loving kiss. "I'm so, so thankful to see you." She hugged him again and whispered in his ear. "We need to talk in private."

Tiernan squeezed his wife to let her know he understood. He then looked at Ahern. "Help me back to my room, please."

Ahern motioned to his son, who followed behind. Together, both men pulled the King to his feet and braced him as Tiernan limped back into the home.

Eislyn turned to Pernella, who was busy with the Elf still lying on the ground. "How is Serin?"

Pernella shook her head. "So that's his name. I wondered. Well, that and how you ended up being bound to him." She checked his pulse and breathing. "I can't tell. He's alive, but unconscious. Is he how you got here?" She stood to her feet.

"In a manner of speaking, yes. Though the details are more complex." Eislyn kneeled down and put her hand on his shoulder. The Queen gently shook him. "Serin. Please, wake up." When he didn't respond, Eislyn motioned to the other woman. "Help me."

Together, both women rolled the comatose Elf over, with Eislyn taking the side where Serin wore his satchel. Now laying face up, Eislyn noticed his normally pale blue complexion was almost as white as snow.

It's as if all the energy from his body is gone. Eislyn furrowed her brow, unwilling to accept what she already knew in her heart. "As soon as the King is secure, can your husband and his assistant move Serin to another bed in your home?"

"He's our son, but yes."

"I'm sorry, your son. I didn't want to be presumptuous."

"It's okay, my Queen."

Eislyn sighed. "Be honest. How is Tiernan?"

Pernella lowered her head. "He's not well." An awkward pause filled the air between them.

Noticing the other woman's lack of explanation, Eislyn pushed harder. "You're not being forthcoming."

Pernella looked at the sky and sighed. "Forgive me. It's not every day I must tell the Queen that the King may die. Tiernan is in terrible shape. Coughing blood, bruised and battered. We've done all we can and my husband, Ahern, was preparing for a trip to Lorelei, hoping to find help."

"Why Lorelei?"

"Tiernan needs a doctor, someone trained in nursing the injured back to health. And he needs one *fast*. We waited for Rosk to return or an entourage from Farna to arrive in his place. When neither came, we decided it was wise to retrieve one from the closest city with an infirmary."

Eislyn extended her hand toward the Valley. "Makes you wonder why Tiernan's grandfather never built one, doesn't it?" She ran both hands through her hair. "There is something I need to do right now. Take care of my husband. I'll be back soon.

"But first, I must thank you for your hospitality. Rosk arrived safely in Farna and let us know what transpired here."

At the mention of Rosk's name, Pernella breathed a sigh of relief. "So, he is alive. Thank Aila. When will he return here? My husband and son could use his assistance."

"We'll do everything in our power to get Rosk back to Whispersong as soon as possible. Though it may be some time before that can happen."

Pernella stood. "Is something wrong?"

"Much. It's not unfair to say we're at war, and our enemies may strike again soon."

"Such as the beast that attacked Idlewind? The King mentioned another in Alwyn. I'm so sorry about Prince Wayland. Do you have any news on the whereabouts of Enid?"

Eislyn reached out and grabbed Pernella's hands. "Thank you for your kind words. Losing Wayland hit the royal family hard, especially with the passing of Davien and Kyrie just a few months ago. Enid's disappearance only adds another layer to this mess, the least of which is our desperate need for her powers. I'm afraid without her, we won't be able to withstand any kind of attack."

The two women turned to see Ahern emerging from their rear door. Pernella snapped her fingers and pointed to Serin on the ground. Ahern nodded, yelled for Steve, and rushed to the Elf's side. Steve showed up a moment later and together they carried Serin inside.

Pernella extended a hand toward the home. "I can take you to the King's room."

Eislyn shook her head. "Thank you, but as I said, there is something I must do first. I need a moment alone."

Pernella couldn't hide her confusion, but acquiesced to the Queen's instructions. She bowed, turned, and walked into the home.

Eislyn looked high to the sky. Behind her, the Valley Mountains stood tall. The bright Graelian sun shone overhead, casting a powerful light on her face. Eislyn closed her eyes to feel its warmth, giving herself a brief moment of solitude. She smiled, then walked around to the home's north side, gazing in the distance toward Farna.

"Eislyn?" asked Tiernan. The King couldn't hide his eagerness to see his wife again, and the sound of a woman's footsteps echoing outside of his door raised his expectations.

Instead, Pernella stepped into his room. "She said she would be in momentarily, my King."

Tiernan acknowledged her comment with a silent lift of his head and waited for her to leave. Once he did, he grabbed his side. The King raised his tunic, the imposing bruise now having spread from his waistline and up along the side of his body. He groaned as he rubbed it, the pain feeling different from before.

Tiernan didn't know what was causing the injury to spread. Nothing seemed to be able to slow it, and so far, he had tried to hide this specific condition from his hosts.

"You have deep internal injuries," a man's voice said as he entered the King's room.

It startled him, and Tiernan scrambled to hide the bruise by lowering his tunic. He blinked his eyes. "Doctor Brack?"

The elderly man smiled. "It's been a long time. You're well overdue for your physical."

"I've been busy."

"That's no excuse, T," said Eislyn as she walked in behind the doctor.

"My love, how did Brack get here so soon?"

Eislyn stood at the King's bed and shrugged with an impish grin on her face.

The doctor answered for her. "That doesn't matter right now, my King. What does matter is that we get you fixed up."

Eislyn put her hands on Tiernan's feet. "Abria needs you back on the throne. Not me. Besides, I'm sure my mother is ready for you to come home and take over. I left her in charge, but it wouldn't surprise me if your grandmother was already driving her crazy. I know *she* hasn't been fond of some of my leadership decisions."

"Grandma Róisín? She's in Farna? Where is Grandpa Lugh?"

"One thing at a time. Let's get you fixed up first," Doctor Brack said, interrupting the conversation. He looked at Eislyn. "I could use some time with the King. Alone."

Eislyn nodded. "I'll be back soon, T. Do as the doctor says. That's an order."

"Since when do you order me around?"

Eislyn pointed to his head. "No crown. No orders."

"I don't see a crown on your head either."

Both laughed. The doctor scrunched his face as he raised Tiernan's tunic to inspect the bruise. He looked back at Eislyn and motioned toward the door with his head.

Eislyn understood the request. It pained her to leave him, especially if his condition deteriorated further. She buried her concern and emotions, giving her husband a huge smile. "I love you, T. I'll be back."

Eislyn nodded to Doctor Brack and left him to his task. As soon as she was outside of his bedroom, she leaned against the wall and took a massive, shaky inhale. It took everything in her not to fall apart, both in elation of seeing her husband and sickly worry that she might not have him by her side for much longer. Eislyn breathed in again, held it for a few ticks, and then exhaled, trying to get control of her breathing.

Pernella stood in the kitchen working on a meal. Ahern was out of sight, though Steve sat in the living room. The younger man had a notepad in his hand and appeared to be sketching something.

Pernella noticed the Queen's body language out of the corner of her eye. "Steve. A moment."

The boy stood to his feet, gave the Queen an inquisitive glance, and left for his room.

"Thank you." Eislyn moved from the wall to the table and sat down. "I was not prepared for that. I appreciate your discretion."

"I didn't think it was appropriate for a boy to see his Queen filled with such overwhelming emotions. Not if the Kingdom is in such a dire condition as you described. He needs to see strength from leadership." Pernella handed Eislyn a piece of fruit.

"No, thank you. I don't think I can eat right now. That was an astute observation. The past week has been challenging." Eislyn let out an exasperated chuckle. "A week. Tiernan and Enid left for the battle just seven days ago. It feels like a lifetime has passed." Pushing down the urge to vomit, Eislyn blinked and swallowed hard. "Rosk filled me in on how my husband appeared in one of your fields. What have you done to treat him?"

Pernella finished tending to the soup on the stove and pulled out a chair across from Eislyn. "Potions. We gave him what we had. Water, what little bit of food he would take. I'm not a doctor."

Eislyn shook her head. "You did what you thought was best. No second guessing yourselves on my watch."

Ahern walked into the kitchen area from down the hall. "Steve said you were back, and that you had a doctor with you."

"Speaking of that doctor, we didn't see him arrive with you. Where'd he come from?" asked Steve from around the corner.

The three stared in his direction. Now discovered, Steve emerged and plopped into a seat in the living area.

Pernella shot her eavesdropping son a stern look.

He shrugged. "What? We didn't see him. Tell me I'm wrong, Mom."

Eislyn smiled. *He reminds me of Tiernan when I first met him.* "The doctor arrived on his own."

Unsatisfied with her answer, Steve pushed the issue. "What is going on? Something here is off. You're not telling us something."

"Steven!" yelled Pernella. "That's enough."

"He's right." All three turned to the Queen. "I'm not telling you everything. Rosk has not returned because of a weapon of our enemy known as Shapeshifters. These are creatures that not only can mimic us, but absorb us."

Eislyn let the words sink in before continuing. "By absorbing us, I mean that they literally reduce us to nothing and take our essence into their body before transforming into the person they just devoured." She chose the last word for its dramatic emphasis, making sure that the family understood there was no coming back from the effect.

"Is that why Rosk has not returned?" asked Ahern.

"Partially, yes. Rosk is safe, last I knew anyway, in Castle Abria." Eislyn closed her eyes as she explained the situation in detail.

As she finished, she looked up. Both Ahern and Pernella stood with their mouths slightly agape. Steve, on the other hand, seemed to be more fascinated than horrified.

Chapter 13

Time to Heal

He's banged up, but he'll live." The doctor's words comforted Eislyn, though they did not reassure her. His simple explanation seemed to defy what she saw with her own eyes: a growing, unmistakable bruise that screamed impending doom.

"Is that all you're going to say?"

The doctor smiled at the Queen's inquisitiveness. He rummaged through his carry bag and pulled out a small bundle of potions with three varying colors. "These will help with the pain and with healing. They're my own special mix. Something I learned from my connections in Clericsfold. Give him the green one daily, just as he wakes up, until the bruising is gone. The blue ones are for pain. The white ones will restore his strength. In two weeks, he should be back to normal. Oh."

The doctor rummaged through his bag again and pulled out a deep orange set of potions. "Here. These are for you."

"Me?" Eislyn asked with a feigned sense of confusion, though she recognized the prenatal significance of the orange potions right away. It had been developed at the explicit request of Queen Kyrie so that no woman would ever experience the misery of morning sickness as she had with the twins.

"They will help with your condition," he explained.

Pernella and Ahern exchanged a look.

The Queen's eyes narrowed and her brow furrowed. "I'm not sure what you mean." A lie, of course.

Noting her uncomfortableness, Doctor Brack shrugged. "Ah. Well, I must have been mistaken. Hold on to them. You may need them someday, perhaps when the King is feeling more like himself."

Eislyn's face flushed. Not only did she find the conversation inappropriate, but Doctor Brack's gross indiscretion among random denizens of the Kingdom risked spoiling their news.

The doctor looked around. "From what I understand, I may be here for a while. Is there a place I can stay?"

Pernella pointed down the hall. "There are a few spare rooms where we host visitors. Pick any one you want."

Doctor Brack left the room without saying another word.

Queen Eislyn's jaw tightened as she searched for what to say next. Anger rose within her, a growing frustration that the doctor may have revealed her secret to yet another group before the King himself had a chance to announce their news. Instead of saying anything she might regret, she turned and walked into Tiernan's room.

Resting flat on his bed, the King seemed more coherent than earlier. He had enough strength to sit up, smiling at the sight of his wife. "Eislyn. I've missed you."

"I wasn't gone that long."

"You know what I mean. Come. Sit."

The Queen walked over to his bedside. She sniffed the air and scrunched her nose. "You need a bath, Tiernan. And your hair. It's matted."

"Is that the first thing you planned to say to me after all of this time?" He smiled, hoping to ease the tension with his charm.

It worked. "No. It's not. I'm sorry. A lot's happened since you and Enid left. And speaking of your sister, where is she?"

"I wish I knew. All I can tell you is what I saw. The Shapeshifter's claim was right. There was a gargantuan ball of magic energy below Farna."

"I know. It tore a chasm through the northern end of the city. There is so much damage, T. So many lives impacted."

"She did it, Eislyn." He put his hand on his wife's. "Enid kept the magic away from our enemies by releasing it back into the world."

"How?"

"All I know is that her…" He searched for the words. "Do you remember that day on the beach? When we lost…" Tiernan couldn't bring himself to say his cherished best friend and brother-in-law's name.

"Yes."

"And the wings. How they emerged when she besieged that blue beast?"

"It happened again?"

"This time it was more powerful. Her eyes. They were white with fire. She used all of her powers and each of the three ancient relics to do something. I don't know what. She attacked the sphere, it exploded, billowed upward, and disappeared.

"Then she was gone. Just like that. The three relics fell to the ground along with a red jewel."

"A red jewel?" Eislyn's eyes darted from left to right, trying to recall a memory. When it resurfaced, her eyes widened. "Didn't your mom mention something about a jewel on the day of your birth?"

Tiernan nodded. "I thought about that too. We have to find it, whatever it means."

"So what? Your sister left this jewel in her place as a, what? A beacon? A remnant of her power?" Eislyn swallowed. "Is she dead?" She hated asking the question, but knew she must.

Tiernan closed his eyes. "I don't know, Eislyn. I don't. I only know she's *gone*. The last thing I heard her say was 'Wayland, my love' and that was it. Like he was there, beckoning her to join him. The magic thing exploded, and she was gone."

"Way…" Eislyn teared up at the mention of his name. Talking in code about Tiernan's departed friend made it easy to bury the emotions.

Saying his name out loud brought up a swell of feelings Eislyn had been struggling to let go for a long time. She sobbed, grabbed Tiernan's right hand, and squeezed it tight.

Tiernan rubbed his wife's hand with his left. "I know. Did she see him welcoming her to join him in whatever happens after this life?" Tiernan's voice broke at the thought of those words.

"Tiernan. My love." She leaned in and kissed her husband, their tear-soaked faces blending with the dirt spread across the King's. "We'll get through this. You and I. Family is Strength, remember? That's us now, along with this little one," she said as she rubbed her stomach.

The reminder of their coming child comforted the King more than he expected. "How have you felt since I left?"

"Let's just say we can't keep this quiet much longer. As soon as you're well, we have to make the announcement. The doctor picked up on it just by looking at me."

"Well, it's possible I might have let it slip as he was treating me."

"Tiernan!"

The King smiled. "I cannot be held accountable for the things I said under duress," he said with a slight grin.

Eislyn frowned, giving the impression she was more annoyed than willing to take part in this particular banter. "Moving on," she said with a sigh, "There are some things you should know. I locked down the city. No one in or out of Farna, and no one travels alone for fear of this Shapeshifter threat."

"You mentioned Grandma Róisín? How did she get there?"

"She arrived with a group of Elven refugees. Teleported in. There was some kind of riot in Lakedon. Lugh stayed behind."

Tiernan slightly nodded, processing the implication of his wife's words. "What caused the riot?"

"Róisín described it as fallout from when a Graelan boy showed magical abilities, then disappeared with an older man with teleportation. Assumptions were made, the villagers blamed the Elves, and things got out of hand."

Tiernan couldn't believe his ears. "Magic? Mages besides Enid and Way?"

Eislyn nodded. "They're not the only ones, my love." Eislyn swallowed. "The world is changing and changing fast."

"So, how did you get here?"

Here it comes. Eislyn raised her eyebrows and smiled. "Well, it's somewhat of a long story. We just knew we needed to get you home as fast as possible."

"We?"

"The Elf who came up with the idea. One of the refugees from Lakedon." Her eyes widened with excitement as she recalled the experience. "It was exhilarating, if I'm being honest. I was against the idea at first, but looking back on it, I dunno. It could become a new way to travel. Look high to the sky, see your destination above the clouds, snap your fingers, and there you are: in free fall." She laughed. "You just need to make sure you don't pass out, can see where you want to teleport again, and absorb an ether before you hit the ground."

Tiernan, if he could, would have jumped out of his bed. As things stood, he shifted his body with a painful groan. "Wait. Are you telling me that's what happened?"

She put her hand on Tiernan's arm. "We had no choice. None of the Elves had been to Whispersong, but everyone has seen the sky. But that's not quite what happened. Serin, the Elf that is, passed out in the air before he could complete the second teleport."

Tiernan scrunched his face, though Eislyn couldn't tell if it was because of the pain or his lack of understanding. After a moment of internalizing the story, he asked another question. "So, how did you land if he was passed out?"

Eislyn laughed and ran her hand along the side of her husband's face. "You're not very bright, are you, *Mr. Prince?*"

Tiernan's eyes widened, and his mouth fell open as he saw the most subtle hint of yellow-toned magic twinkle in the pupils of his wife's eyes.

"Eislyn, is that what I think it is? How? You're a mage too, like Enid and Way? But…" At a loss for words, Tiernan shook his head, leaned his head back against the pillow, and closed his eyes.

"Do you want the truth?"

He opened his eyes and gave her a look that said yes.

"You're not going to believe this, but it happened *during* our flight. Fall. What should we call it?" She laughed at the perplexity of it all. "We had just enough ethers to teleport me here, for the Elf to return to Farna, for him to retrieve the doctor, for them to come back here, and then to send you and me home once you were better.

"Serin, however, passed out as soon as we appeared in the sky. Or maybe he passed out in that moment of nothingness."

"I know what that's like."

Eislyn turned her head to the side. "The messenger, Rosk, mentioned you appeared out of nowhere and fell to the ground."

Tiernan nodded. "After the battle. The Dark Elf teleported me here. It's an odd sensation, isn't it? It's as if you…"

"…don't exist for those ticks." They smiled as they said the words in unison.

"You and I, T. We've always been on the same wavelength."

"You could have made a move earlier, you know," he said with a playful grin.

"Ha! Me? Who was I, nothing more than the daughter of a tavern owner, to approach the Prince himself? The man who just happened to hug me in an impulsive moment of excitement?"

"You felt it too, then. A connection. An instant spark between us."

Her face softened as she leaned in and kissed him. Eislyn felt him grit his teeth. "Well, that's a first. Does it hurt that much?"

"Everything hurts," he said with a downtrodden look.

She put her hand on his cheek with a tender touch. "My precious husband. We'll get through this." She pulled her hand back. "And yes, I felt the spark the moment you hugged me. Maybe that's your magic power?"

"To make women fall in love with me?" He laughed at the idea. "No. You were the first. And the only. Now and forever."

Eislyn's heart skipped a few beats. She blinked her eyes a few times. "So, where was I? Ah, right. Serin passed out. I assumed he needed an ether and rummaged through his satchel to find it. We only had four, T. In all of Farna. We wanted to play it safe." She pointed to her stomach. "Clearly, it's more than just you or me now. We have this one to worry about, and Serin didn't want to take chances.

"Unfortunately, I lost one of them in the commotion, and I'm sure it landed somewhere in the fields between here and the Valley. Far too large of an area to search."

"Someone will find it someday. When they need it."

The Queen nodded. "So, when I pressed the ether into his palm, a strange aura flowed from his body into mine. He wouldn't wake up, though. It was as if all the energy in him was gone.

"I began trying to get him to wake up. I pictured being in the fields with you, embracing you, being with the man I loved. And the next thing I knew, I was face down in the yard just outside of this home. Alive."

"You *teleported*?"

Eislyn nodded.

Putting the next details together in advance, Tiernan smiled. "And that's why they didn't see the doctor when you arrived. Because you were the one who retrieved him!"

With a hint of hope and excitement, Tiernan grabbed his wife's hand. "Can you do it again to get us home?"

Chapter 14

Darkness Before Dawn

Folas teleported into the throne room with the last batch of Shapeshifters. From one end to the other, the space was filled with the creatures. He turned to a nearby blinded Elf.

"Did you get a count?"

The Elf nodded.

"How many?" Folas asked.

"With the ones you just brought, two hundred and seventeen." The Elf left Folas' side, scurrying out of the throne room and into the adjoining hallway.

Folas swallowed, wondering what the Elf's name was and if they had any idea what was going on around them.

Each Shapeshifter stood side by side. Their golden wings often overlapped with the creature next to it. As far as Folas could tell, they were identical. Each wore an amethyst robe with gold fringe. Their claw-like appendages were open, with each talon appearing almost two hundred millimeters in length. Their feet — or rather, the claws they stood on — had the same dull grey appearance.

Every Shapeshifter had a long beak protruding off of their face, curled down at a forty-five degree angle. Their eyes were a darkened gray, showing no indications of life. Their rounded heads had a distinct bird-like appearance, the only element of variation between them. Some were white; others light brown. A vast majority were solid black, darker than their claws but lighter in tone than Folas' own complexion.

Folas made his way through the hall until he reached the throne area. There, a set of Elves and Graelan accomplices stood motionless, mostly awaiting orders. One particular Elf seemed to be struggling.

Banix. I blinded him many moons ago. The effect must be wearing off. Folas walked up to the smaller creature. "Pull yourself together. Bring honor to your clan."

Banix nodded, still unsure but obedient. The Graelan next to him smirked. Folas made a note of the disrespect. *Someone to eliminate later.*

"Such ugly creatures. And so many of them. Why did you bring them here?" asked Kane as he walked in next to Zoran.

The Dark Emperor seemed indifferent to the Divider's line of questioning. Instead, he squeezed past the Shapeshifters and made his way next to the attending conspirators.

Unfazed, Kane followed. He proudly brandished the Soul Sword, resting it on his shoulder as usual.

Once both stood at the front, Zoran put his hand out for the weapon. Kane hesitated, at first unwilling to yield his trophy. Zoran's countenance shifted and intensified. Reluctantly, Kane passed the sword to the Dark Emperor.

Zoran inspected the relic with visible curiosity, then gripped the hilt with a firm hand. The weapon seemed to respond to him, softly emitting an inky glow.

"Awaken," Zoran said as he extended the Soul Sword toward the motionless Shapeshifters. A dark purple haze emerged from the tip of the weapon, covering the first row of Shapeshifters from head to toe. The effect spread from left to right and all the way to the back, increasing with speed as it grew.

Slowly, the grayed-out eyes of each Shapeshifter returned to life. A small black iris appeared in the center of each eye. Their talons began moving. Some tried flapping their wings before realizing how close they were to others of their kind.

Ticks and clicks filled the room. The sound rose in intensity as the collective group of Shapeshifters sprung to life. By the time the last one awoke, those sounds overwhelmed the gathered Elves — including Folas. While the Dark Elf stood with his hands over his ears, his brethren cowered. Two fell to their knees in tears.

Kane and the other Graelans merely winced as if the sounds were uncomfortable but bearable. It was in this moment Folas realized Graelan ears must be less sensitive than Elven. *Another thing to hold over our heads. Superior Graelan hearing.*

"Fos-da-lin!" Zoran's voice boomed over the ticks and clicks. The commotion, though subsided, continued as he used all his energy, emitting an angry growl that shocked everyone in attendance.

This sound was the final push Banix needed to snap out of his haze. "Where am I?" he asked in a panic. He looked from person to person, pulling on the shirt of the Graelan next to him. "I said, where am I?"

Zoran looked back at Banix, then returned his focus to the Shapeshifters. Beastly and menacing, Zoran spoke again. "Scra-ut-lin-fos!"

The noises subsided to a quiet murmur.

Zoran dropped the Soul Sword. It clanged to the ground loudly as the Dark Emperor raised his hands.

"What is he doing? Who is he?" Banix pressed, now deeply aware of his predicament.

"Banix. Quiet," commanded Folas. He gave the smaller Elf a look with his eyes, then mouthed the word 'Later.'

Zoran closed his eyes. This time, a pink haze emerged from the bodies of each Shapeshifter. They started shrieking, panicking as ticks and clicks of desperation and fear filled the surrounding space.

Every Shapeshifter in the room found itself immobilized. Their bodies glowed with a bright pink aura, obscuring their form. The effect increased in intensity, blinding the Graelans.

Though horrified, Folas also felt a small sense of satisfaction. *Graelans might have stronger ears, but Elven eyes can handle more.* Folas engaged his gift of Second Sight.

Almost immediately, he regretted it. No longer obscured by the pink light, Folas could see the agony of every Shapeshifter. Each of their bodies seemed engulfed with pain, explaining the panicked sounds. Folas could see energy leaving their bodies in a ghostly apparition, almost as if Zoran was taking the very life essence from them.

The Dark Elf's mouth fell agape as their bodies coalesced into smaller versions of themselves. Their wings retracted. Their arms and legs, if they could even be called such, shrunk as their talons disappeared and their beaks grew smaller. Their torsos hunched over.

As the effect diminished, so did the ticks and clicks. One by one, the Shapeshifters lost the ability to communicate. Moments later, the species fell silent.

Folas opened his eyes to dismiss his Second Sight, as it was no longer needed. Before him was a room of discarded robes. Folas bent down and moved the one closest to him, inspecting the remains of what had been this Shapeshifter.

Below the robe, a small charred husk was all that was left. Folas dared to touch it, and watched in amazement as it crumbled into a small pile of stones and granite. It continued withering away until it was mere dust.

At the same time, the last of the pink energy made its way to Zoran's body. Once he finished absorbing it, the Dark Emperor fell to the ground, unconscious.

Much to Kane's annoyance, Zoran fell on top of the Soul Sword in an unconscious and immobile state.

"Great," complained Kane.

He's only concerned with the Soul Sword. As the Elves and gathered Graelans started picking up the fallen robes, Folas walked over to Kane.

"What was that about?" asked the Divider.

"I used Second Sight to watch the transformation. If I had to guess? We know they contained a part of his essence. We saw that with the one I killed a few years ago. I think he took that back from them. And more, I think."

Kane began pacing, stroking his chin as he walked.

"What are you thinking?" asked Folas.

Kane looked annoyed. "Something doesn't feel right."

"You're just now realizing this?" Folas shook his head, then looked across the throne room. He also noticed Banix cowering in the corner of the room. The Tall Elf started to walk over to him before Kane interrupted.

"What do we do with him?" the Divider asked, pointing at the comatose Zoran.

Folas knelt down and felt the Dark Emperor's back. Zoran appeared to be breathing, though unconscious. Folas tried to move him, though Zoran's weight made it an impossible task.

Frustrated, Kane stormed out of the room. He cast a look back at Folas before he left. "I'll find a group of Graelans to help. I'll be back soon." He motioned to the Graelans in the room, leaving the Elves to deal with collecting the fallen robes of the Shapeshifters.

Folas waited for them to leave. *His obsession blinds him.* He smirked and used his magic to raise Zoran's body up by a few centimeters. The Tall Elf quickly pulled the Soul Sword out from under Zoran's unconscious body, then lowered him gently back to the ground.

Folas then turned to Banix. "I need your help."

Kane was known throughout the Kingdom for his anger and rash decisions. Many, including those in his rebellion, knew him to be impulsive and temperamental, though a powerful orator who could sway others to his side easily. While this paled in comparison to his temper, it had made him a force for change throughout the Abrian nation.

No one had ever seen his fury so intense that he couldn't react. Not, at least, until this moment. Kane froze in place at the news. He blinked after a few moments of awkward, unbearable silence. His voice began low, rising in volume with each word. "What do you mean, Folas is gone? Gone *where*? And where is the Soul Sword?"

Kane's last question drove the man delivering the news to take a step back as a precaution. "It's like I said. When the group of us went into the throne room to move Zoran's body and retrieve the weapon, it was gone. The others relocated his body to the infirmary while I came here."

He stuttered his next attempt at an explanation. "They, they may be *elsewhere* in the camp—"

Kane cut the man off with an angry yell. He picked up a nearby side table and threw it across the room.

Much to the man's surprise, the table did not move as far as he expected, landing with a thump only a few meters from where Kane was standing.

Kane leaned against the ledge of one of his windows, his mind racing. *He's taken the Soul Sword, I know it. But why?* He stood in place silently, fueling the uncertainty and discomfort between the two.

Finally, he made a decision. Kane pushed himself up from the ledge and pointed to the man. "Round up everyone. Elves and Graelans. We need to take an inventory of our weapons and gear.

Everyone must report to the fortress courtyard by sundown. Am I clear?"

"Yes." The man swallowed. "But I have to ask. What are you planning? And do you think the Elves will follow you without the Dark Elf?"

Kane didn't appreciate the question and pointed toward the door. The man shook his head and left.

Deep down, Kane had been asking himself that exact question. He left the window and walked over to his kitchen. He kneeled down to inspect the area where the soup had landed. Everywhere it had touched emitted a brilliant sheen. Even the tiny drops where the splatter had spread across his cabinetry were a stark contrast to the worn appearance of the rest of the wood grain.

"Stronger than before. We'll see about that." Kane stood and walked over to one of his knives. Treating it like a dagger, he flipped it around in his hand and then threw it at the flooring.

His lack of strength once again reared its ugly head as the knife bounced off the floor without causing any damage. "Gah!" Kane rushed over, grabbed the knife, and started scraping at the finish with the blade.

"Stronger than before. Stronger than before." His eyes grew wide as he, with a maddening intensity, began scraping at the flooring even harder. "I. Will be. Stronger than before." He threw the knife to his side. To his satisfaction, the blade penetrated the nearby wall.

He smiled, then returned his gaze to the floor. Satisfied with the scuffs and damage, he continued with his monologue. "I will be the strongest ruler Abria has ever seen. An immovable rock. A force so powerful Zoran himself will marvel at my power. Folas, you will regret this day. I guarantee it."

Just outside his open front door, an invisible form walked away.

Kane stood before the gathered group of his accomplices. Much to his relief, more Elves than he had expected stood among them. He couldn't get an exact count, but assumed one of his men would have handled the task.

There were plenty of Graelan dissidents. Most of these had come from Clericsfold, unhappy with the results of the first Statuo. He recognized the majority, knowing the names of several with most others unfamiliar to him.

Are they from other parts of Abria? This could prove useful. He chastised himself for not getting to know his Graelan army better, instead relying on Folas to handle most of the field labor.

That ends today. This is my war. He cleared his throat to address the group. A hush fell over the crowd as they waited for him to speak.

"Since we broke away from the Kingdom, we've been patient. We built this fortress with the help of our Elven brethren, many of whom are still here with us." *How many blinded Elves did Folas free?*

Kane pushed the thought aside. "This fortress has, in many ways, been a refugee camp. A haven for those exiles from Clericsfold who felt betrayed by its leadership and the failure of the first Statuo. They traded our freedom, slipping right back into the fold and pledging allegiance to the imposter who sat on the throne.

"As you know, we eliminated him earlier this year. His son took his place. We must dispose of him, too. His sister is dead. We killed her during the battle below, and her legacy now only exists as a memory, of a reminder that we will be triumphant!

"I see faces here that I do not know. Graelans from…?" Kane let his words trail off.

People in the crowd shouted out the names of various cities and regions.

"Lakedon."

"The Valley."

"Oakshadow."

"Idlewind."

"Milston."

Kane noted the absence of Farna, Alwyn, and Northwick. After the crowd stopped speaking, he continued. "I'm sure you had good reasons for joining our group. Those are stories I long to hear one day.

"But I won't entertain them until we have eliminated the threat of the imposter's son. He is all that remains between us and total victory.

"That's why we're going to go on the offensive. It'll be subtle at first. We must secure more allies, especially from Alwyn and Northwick. We must show the populace of this Kingdom that their leadership is a failure and that the peace they portray is a lie.

"As for Farna, that is the ultimate prize. I want to see Castle Abria burning and the city of Farna itself in ruins. For that, I will need Fire Magic."

As expected, the gathered Elves with Fire Magic raised their hand in a show of power. A few others put Fire Rings on their fingers to join the display.

"Excellent. We must also deal with the traitor, Folas."

"He's probably back in the Darkwood Forest," an Elf yelled.

Kane nodded, both in appreciation of its new name and a sign of their solidarity with his cause. "Whatever it takes, he must pay for his disloyalty. He stole what is rightfully mine. The Soul Sword. With it, we will awaken the rest of Zoran's forces below."

Kane raised his right fist, bringing it down hard onto his left palm. "Remember in all you do that we are at war with the

Kingdom of Abria. And it's a battle that we will win. I promise you that we will be victorious!"

Those in attendance erupted in cheers. Kane raised his fist in defiance. Elves in the crowd activated whatever magic powers they had. Graelans raised their weapons in solidarity. Some of Kane's acquaintances from Clericsfold rushed to his side, congratulating him on a rousing speech.

The crowd dispersed, with groups of Elves and Graelans breaking off together, talking about their eventual victory. One solitary Elf smiled in feigned support, scared senseless and wishing for it to all be over soon.

As more of the crowd broke up, he finally felt he was safe. He clapped hands with some of his brethren as he walked through the courtyard, pretending to be heading toward the structure where he had lived as a blinded Elf for the past several years.

Once he walked inside, he activated his Cloak of Invisibility. Banix raised a hand, snapped his fingers, and teleported away.

Chapter 15

To Go Home

Are you ready to go home?" asked Eislyn. She smiled at her husband as he walked out of the bedroom. Though still moving with a limp, the Queen was relieved that Tiernan could walk without the assistance of someone else.

"And leave the hospitality of these wonderful people?" Tiernan nodded toward Ahern and Pernella as he spoke.

"You're welcome to stay as long as you need," Ahern responded.

Tiernan bowed. "I think we've been here long enough. It's been, what? A week since we arrived? I've lost track of time, but I'm ready to get home. And I'm sure Eislyn's mom is tired of running Castle Abria."

Tiernan walked over and gave his wife a kiss. He then gave her his hand to help her stand. As she pulled on it, he winced.

"The injury still bothering you?" she asked.

Tiernan nodded.

"Maybe the doctor should check you out one more time?"

"No. It's time to go. Besides, we don't know how long your magic will last. If you even have enough left in you to get us home."

Ahern stood and walked over to the King. He extended his hand. "We'll take care of Doctor Brack and Serin until you can figure out how to get back here."

Eislyn bowed with grace and humbleness. "When he awakens, please tell him what happened. And that I had fun on our trip in the sky."

Ahern nodded. Pernella walked over and gave Eislyn a hug. Their son, Steve, just stared from across the room, keeping his distance while observing it all with an unreadable yet curious expression on his face.

After Pernella let go, the royal couple headed toward the door. Hand in hand, they opened it and walked outside.

Eislyn squeezed tight. "Are you sure you're ready to try this? Maybe a couple more days of rest would be best?"

He leaned over and kissed her cheek. "Let's go. I'm with you. Whatever happens, that's all that matters. I'll be fine."

Satisfied with his answer, Eislyn raised her free hand. *Here goes nothing.* She pictured the throne room in Castle Abria and snapped her fingers. Both husband and wife disappeared.

A few ticks later, Tiernan fell to his knees in pain. He tried to breathe and found it difficult. He thought he heard his wife's voice yelling his name, but couldn't bring his mind together to focus.

Tiernan touched his bruise and realized the pain felt more intense than it had been a few moments earlier in Whispersong. The mere act of touching it brought excruciating pain to the fallen King, who looked up and caught his wife's eyes before rolling to the side and passing out on the throne room floor.

Banix walked through the place he once called home. The Rosewood Forest, now rechristened as the Darkwood Forest, physically looked the same as the last time he remembered being here.

From what Folas had told him, that was over two years ago.

Two years of lost time. Banix told himself to let it go, though he couldn't help but feel a great deal of resentment toward Folas.

An Elf who now needed Banix's help.

Despite the physical similarities, there was an uncomfortable eeriness throughout the Forest today. There were no distant sounds of his brethren toiling away in their settlement. The bugs, birds, and larger creatures made little noise. Once in a while, Banix heard the crack of a stick or another disturbance.

If he didn't know better, he'd think the Forest itself knew the stakes of what would be coming soon.

Banix pushed past the overgrown shrubbery, walking toward his former home. One thing was for certain: the Elven rebels may have claimed this as their own with a new name, but none of them lived here.

Banix eventually saw his destination ahead: the settlement where they had lived for centuries. He walked through the entrance and into the clearing. Here, formerly blinded Elves scurried about, some cleaning up the overgrowth while others tended to their homes.

He approached one of his friends. "Min."

She turned around, surprised by his appearance.

"Banix. You're back." She hugged him. "How did it go?"

He shook his head.

"That bad?"

"Folas is a marked Elf. Kane's rhetoric is going to make this a very dangerous place. I spied on his men as they traveled throughout the land. They're building an army, finding those who are disgruntled with small things. The rough waters surrounding Abria are somehow the Kingdom's fault. It snowed too much and ruined a batch of Lorelian Mead. Dumb things like that. They're falling for the rhetoric, not reality."

He grabbed her hand. "We can't stay here long. The Elves who are aligned with them already suspect Folas is here."

"They do, do they?"

Both turned to the new voice, though neither was surprised at who it belonged to. Folas walked toward them.

Banix leaned in to hug Min again and whispered into her ear. "Get out of here. Now. Take as many as you can." He let go and turned to face the Dark Elf.

"Let's go for a walk." Folas motioned away from the settlement.

Banix gave Min a final look before following the Dark Elf. They walked for a while in silence. *Is he leading me to my death? Wouldn't surprise me. He'll get the information he needs, then finish me off.*

Folas stopped and sat down on a fallen log. He motioned for Banix to sit next to him.

"Are you going to kill me after this?"

Folas tapped the spot next to him. "What did you find out?"

Banix sat down. "Kane has declared war on Abria. And you for taking the Soul Sword. You should expect some of his Elves to show up soon."

"When?"

"I don't know. I wasn't a part of those conversations. Someone threw out the idea that you'd return here, and I think Kane has latched onto it. Could be today, maybe tomorrow." His thoughts trailed off, circling back after a brief pause. "Who knows? I did as you asked. Followed them around for a week. I'm surprised they haven't already been here."

"How is Kane handling the sudden turn of events?"

Banix grinned as he answered. "I stood outside of his home, observing him each night like you asked."

"And?"

"He's losing his sanity. He used a knife to tear up his floor. Something about being strong. Every night it was the same routine."

Folas smiled, picturing his former accomplice on his knees, trying to undo the healing powers of the soup. "Anything else?"

"He wants the Soul Sword back so that they can awaken the rest of Zoran's minions."

"Zoran is still unconscious?"

Banix nodded.

Folas stared off into the distance. "I won't lie to you. I don't know what effect this reclamation had on his body." He turned his head to the side. "Its body. I don't think we figured it out."

"Zoran rests in what was your room. The tall tower, wasn't it?"

"You remember?"

Banix erupted in anger. "I remember *nothing*, Folas! Nothing. You took two years of my life from me. I heard you mention it before you sent me on my little journey."

He calmed down, wondering if his outburst just cost him his life. "I watched in invisible silence as our Elven brethren tended to him. Kane makes them do that just in case he reawakens. Zoran sleeps day in and day out, never moving except for his breathing."

Banix harrumphed. "Elves are still second-class citizens in that rebellion. Doing Kane's bidding while the Graelans are in charge." His voice rose again, his anger bubbling to the surface. "Just like you made me and others like me do the hard work. Blindly. Why, Folas? Why did you—"

Folas waved him off. "My answer to you would never justify my actions. I made choices, Banix. Some of those you don't come back from." Folas snapped his fingers. The Soul Sword appeared in the air. Before it fell, Folas grabbed the handle.

Banix braced for his imminent death.

Instead, Folas flipped the ancient relic in the air and held it by the blade, with the handle facing the smaller Elf. "Do you remember my story of the two great beasts? Leviathan and Gamelyon? This woke them up. They seemed to attack Alwyn and Idlewind in a mindless rage. It was Kane's idea, and at the time, he held this." Folas pushed the Soul Sword toward Banix.

He grabbed the handle. The relic lit up in a bright glow.

Folas smirked. "You feel its power, don't you? We don't understand all this sword can do." Letting go of the blade, Folas opened his palms and looked at both hands. "I've wondered if it can undo my transformation." Caught up in a rare moment of vulnerability, Folas didn't see the look on Banix's face.

The other Elf considered, for a moment at least, running Folas through with the relic. *I'm not a killer.* His mouth tightened. His hands began to shake. With Folas staring at his skin, Banix made his decision.

He raised a hand and snapped his fingers.

Folas saw the flash before he could grab the Soul Sword. His eyes widened. Using his powers, he closed his eyes to search for the smaller Elf's location.

Nothing. Try as he might, Folas could not find Banix. He opened his eyes and raised his head to the sky.

"Even my own kind betray me?" His face contorted into pure, unadulterated rage.

"We'll see about that."

Eislyn held her husband's hand in the infirmary. Another doctor, one she had never met named Milek, inspected his injury. As the Queen waited for an answer, Róisín and another Elf walked into the room.

"Eislyn." The Queen looked up and locked eyes with Róisín. "How is he?"

Milek answered. "It's as we feared. We don't know enough about teleportation with the Graelan body. It's as if his internal injuries returned."

The Elf spoke up. "I have a theory, but we would need to test it." He reached his hand to Eislyn. "I have minor curative abilities. It's not enough to heal his wounds, but maybe with some extra help?"

Everyone exchanged a look.

"What do you mean, *help*?" the doctor asked.

The Elf extended his hand to Eislyn. "From you. Please, I can't do this alone."

The Queen stared at him for a moment. Without thinking, she grabbed his hand.

His mouth shifted into a wide, sinister grin. "The King is going to die. Your husband will not survive his injuries. He'll slip into the beyond, and you'll never speak to him again. You're going to rule this Kingdom alone."

"Excuse me?" Angry, Eislyn tried to pull her hand away.

The Elf refused to let go. "I said he's going to die. Until the magic takes his life, Tiernan will be a shell of the man you—"

Eislyn gasped in horror. The guards across the room rushed over, weapons drawn and prepared to defend their leader. The Elf fell to the ground, though he refused to let go.

He coughed hard. "There. That was the reaction I needed." A subtle glow moved from his hand to hers. Once it spread across her body, he released his grip. "Your magic is *rare*. Absorption Magic. I've only known one other Elf to possess it. Supposedly, the Dark Elf has a *form* of this ability, though not to this magnitude. What he can do is only a shadow of true Absorption Magic."

The Queen raised her hands to the guards. "What do you mean Absorption Magic?"

He held his chest as he struggled to catch his breath. "In moments of intense emotion, you have the ability to steal magic from another being. It's why Serin never awoke and may never again. You took his teleportation ability from him by accidental force. The shock to his system was too much."

"You mean *he's dead*?" asked Róisín.

He shook his head. "More like an eternal coma. I don't know how to bring him back. The only ones who did would have died during the Exile centuries ago."

Eislyn leaned over. "And all the things you just said?"

"I did not mean to hurt you or cause concern. All I wanted was to provoke an emotional response so that you could take my ability to heal." He nodded to Tiernan. "Touch his injury."

"Are you sure that's wise?" the doctor interjected.

"Are *you* sure you know how to treat him? His injury points to Ultimus and internal bleeding. Whatever potion the other doctor gave him cannot defend against this magic if his organs are damaged from it," the Elf retorted.

The doctor stood to his feet. "I don't know what this Ultimus is, but how do you know it's just not a damaged muscle that needs repaired?"

"The teleportation did as we feared. This is a magic injury."

"You don't know what kind of magic they used in the battle!"

"Because you're an expert on magic?"

Eislyn's head moved from Elf to Graelan and back again as each tried to convince the other of their position. Her frustration welled up. *Statuo,* she thought.

"Enough of this." The Queen stood to her feet and walked over to Tiernan's other side, where his bruise had resumed its spread. She looked at everyone in the room. "I am the Queen. This is my husband. The decision is mine and mine alone."

Under her breath, she muttered to herself. "Let's hope this works."

Eislyn placed her hand on his side. Even in his unconscious state, Tiernan shifted in response to her touch. A warm, golden glow moved from her hand across his abdomen. It enveloped his entire torso, emitting a bright light which grew in intensity with each passing moment.

As fast as it enveloped him, it dissipated.

To everyone's relief, Tiernan's bruise was gone.

The act drained Eislyn. She gasped as a new sensation washed over her. She looked up at the Elf for guidance.

"You need an ether. That's what it feels like. If you tried to heal anyone else right now, it wouldn't work."

"So that was the last little bit of magic left in me after teleporting here?"

He nodded.

"And how long will I have this power?"

"The Elf I knew who possessed Absorption kept whatever magic profile they had until they absorbed something from someone else. This included their current magic level."

Confused, she shook her head. "Meaning what?"

"Rather than absorb an ether, you can drain the power from them and recharge yourself that way. Your profile would change, but it could come in handy in a tight spot. Also, you should be able to cast Poison right now."

"Poison! Why would I want to do such a thing?"

He laughed. "It's my curse, I guess. I can heal and destroy. Well, I could until now anyway."

"Why Poison?" asked Róisín.

"All Elves have at least one type of offensive magic. Fire and Frost are the most common. A few of us have Poison, though why you would ever want such an ability is beyond me. We may have additional abilities, such as Second Sight, teleportation, Barrier, and so on. Mine are, well were, Poison and Heal. Now they're yours."

"Will they ever return to you?" Eislyn asked.

He shrugged. "No one knows. Remember, this is rare. The Elves who understood it are long gone. It's so uncommon that we don't even have any kind of studies on it. The last Elf who had Absorption died during a rogue barbarian attack. Like I mentioned, Folas has a form of it, but it's fueled by something else. Ultimus, if I had to guess."

Milek spoke up. "This has been a fascinating insight into things that, well, don't really matter to me. Right now, the King is my focus. He needs to heal, so please take the magic lesson outside."

The Queen shot him a look.

He shook his head. "I said please because I didn't want to be rude. I need to tend to my patient. *The King of Abria.*"

Eislyn huffed in frustration and motioned for everyone to leave. She looked at Róisín. "Meet me in the throne room?"

Róisín smiled and left with the Elf.

Eislyn faced the doctor. "Send for me when he wakes up."

The doctor nodded before returning to his notes.

Eislyn walked out with her contingent of guards behind her. As the Queen moved through the halls of Castle Abria, she felt both at peace and on edge. This was *home.* Yet the simple, relaxed atmosphere of Whispersong was more than alluring. Eislyn sighed.

One of the guards heard her. "Are you okay, my Queen?"

"Me? Oh, yes. I was just lost in thought." She said nothing else as they navigated the hallways and stairwells leading to the throne room.

When she walked up to the threshold, she froze. Standing in the middle of the room was an Elf surrounded by guards. He looked frightened and was shaking almost uncontrollably.

One of the guards shifted their stance. In that moment, the Queen realized the gravity of the situation.

He has the Soul Sword.

Chapter 16

War Dawn

Eislyn's voice bounced off of the walls, asserting her command of the situation as she rushed into the room. "Everyone stop. Now. That's an order!"

The guards surrounding the Elf took a step back, but remained at attention with their swords and spears drawn. Róisín and Freya both stood off to one side, unsure of what to do.

Dismayed at their hesitation, Eislyn forced the guards to take a step back. "I said stop! Give him space and lower your weapons. Now!"

With great reluctance, the assembled guards moved away and cleared a path for their commander. Banix's eyes darted from left to right as he sized up the situation.

"Who are you?" the Queen asked. "And why do you have the Soul Sword?"

Keeping the blade pointed downward, he handed its handle to her. "My, my name is Banix. I came to give you this." He kept his hand extended as Eislyn approached him. "Please. Take it," he implored.

Eislyn reached out and grabbed the relic, her hand cupping around his for a moment. Banix immediately closed his eyes. All around the Queen, everything changed. The golden-hued walls of Castle Abria dissolved into a forest scene. Greenery replaced the stone. In an instant, the air smelled crisp.

The Queen looked around. Everything had a distinctive blur to it, as if details weren't quite in focus but were distinguishable enough for her to comprehend. After a few moments, she spoke. "Where are we?"

Banix smiled. Eislyn looked deep into his eyes, searching for any sign of ill will. She saw none.

"This is unexpected, but incredible. We're in Nivala, the world of dreams." A sense of wonder filled his expression. He looked around, almost giddy. A sound from Eislyn snapped him out of it. "I'm sorry. This is the first I've shared this gift with a Graelan. I didn't know it was even possible."

"What gift? Don't we all dream?"

"Yes, but not everyone has the ability to observe the dream world. I thought I could only share it with other magic users."

Eislyn raised an eyebrow and gave him a small, half smile.

"Oh. Oh, I get it now. You're a *mage* too? Like the Dragonborn?"

Eislyn shook her head. "Not exactly like my sister-in-law. I'm not sure mage is even the correct word. So, a dream world?"

"Right, we call it Nivala. All living beings come here to dream. Some Elves, like me, have the ability to observe it when we're awake." He pointed in the distance where a father and son walked hand-in-hand.

The man said something, though Eislyn couldn't make it out. She squinted as she tried harder to hear their voices.

Banix noticed. "It takes a lot of concentration to interact with their Nivalan experience. And besides, look. They're moving away." As quickly as they appeared, they faded into the scenery. The area shifted. Eislyn and Banix were no longer in a forest, but were now near a river.

"I've been here before," she said. Eislyn ran to the river and reached down to feel the water. "It's not any river I know, but I dream about it all the time." Her hands came out dry as she turned back to Banix.

"Everyone's Nivala is different. You know how odd they can be. They're nothing more than how our minds process the world around us. We experience it here in the dream world. Next time you touch the water, your hands might be wet. Or a fish might nibble on them." The scene shifted again, this time to a beach.

Eislyn stood and looked around. Far above, the sun's warmth replaced the chilly air of the riverbank. The smells shifted too, this time to a semi-salty breeze with a hint of pastry.

Eislyn felt the grains of sand wrap around her feet, a sensation that caused her to look down in surprise. She moved her toes and buried them deeper in the sand. When she pulled them out, she had on a pair of beautiful shoes. Her clothes were different now, too. She ran her fingers through her hair. It was now done up in a regal, formal design.

Though just as blurry as the forest experience, in the distance she saw Leviathan terrorizing a small group of beach goers. She froze in place as she recognized the determined face of a brave warrior charging toward the imposing beast. From his hands, a blast of Frost Magic attacked the creature's tail. It distracted Leviathan long enough that the beach goers escaped.

Except, they didn't escape. They were just *gone*. It was as if their hero's attack allowed them to teleport away. He swung a sword, piercing the charred tail of Leviathan. He dug it in deep, enraging the beast which bellowed in fury.

No blood came out despite his aggressive twisting. This appeared to paralyze the beast. It bellowed louder, so much that Eislyn had to cover her ears.

Then, silence. Victory appeared to be at hand as Leviathan collapsed on the shoreline. The hero pulled out his sword and rushed for its head, prepared to slice it off.

Instead, the beast disappeared. It reappeared behind him.

"Wayland, get out of there!" Eislyn cried. She tried to run, but her feet felt like bricks. The harder the Queen pushed, the slower she moved.

The creature's tail, lacking any sign of an injury despite its charred appearance just a moment ago, came sweeping from the left, though seemingly unattached from its body. Wayland turned around at the last minute and glimpsed Eislyn.

Unlike everything else in the dreamscape with its blurry edges, Eislyn could see his face as plain as day.

Less than a tick later, he stood face to face with the Queen. His eyes grew large. "Tell Tiernan…" He paused, then screamed. "Eislyn! Eislyn, help me!" Wayland reached for her hands as the tail passed through the Queen and hit her brother-in-law squarely in the chest.

Eislyn flailed her arms, trying hard to save him. The tips of their fingers touched as the beach dissolved into a wet grassland. Overhead, storm clouds unleashed their pent-up fury, drenching the land in water.

"Wayland, no!" Eislyn fell to her knees and sobbed.

Banix placed his hand on her shoulder.

She turned her head back to him. "Why? Why did you bring me here, to these awful memories I want to forget?"

"I didn't. You brought us here. Is that the King?"

Eislyn looked up and, through the haze, saw her husband riding toward her on a horse.

"Tiernan, we have to help Way!" she yelled. Without warning, Tiernan appeared further away, as if his entire journey had been undone. Now, his face was nothing but a blurry silhouette. Eislyn waved, trying to get his attention, but stopped as another horseback rider rode up alongside him.

"Enid," she said as the two dissolved back into the forest from earlier. Keeping her gaze fixated forward, she began to process the absurd nature of the experience. "You said your name was Banix?"

He nodded.

"Get me out of here."

"I *can't*," he replied. "You have to be the one to wake us up."

Eislyn stood, realizing she was wearing the tattered and soiled clothing from her capture earlier in the year. "Why are you here? Not here in this dream world. I mean in Farna. And how did you come to possess the Soul Sword?"

Banix angled his head to one side. "You just passed control to me. How did you do that? What kind of mage are you?"

"Don't ask me. This is all brand new." Eislyn put her hands on her hips. "Banix, please, just answer my questions. You're the expert in all of this," she said as she motioned to the surrounding haze.

The forest dissolved into a representation of the Northern Plateau. "I haven't been here before, but yet I know where we are," she said.

He nodded. "The details aren't right. But I guess you should know the truth."

Eislyn looked down at him.

"I was blinded almost the entire time I was here. I toiled away in a dreamlike trance, unaware of what I was doing. I helped build this place, though I have no memory of it." He pointed. In the distance stood Folas, though he quickly transformed into Kane.

Banix winced. "It's all so fuzzy. Like a dream you've forgotten." He looked up at her. "Two years of my life. Gone, wasted away in a haze I'll never remember."

As he finished speaking, two Shapeshifters appeared before them. Both were short, coming up to her waist. "Is this their true appearance?" Eislyn asked.

"I don't think so. Folas had some kind of control over me. It faded about the time this happened. I only glimpsed what they looked like. This is how my mind remembers them, but they could be different."

Eislyn watched as both shrunk, collapsing into small rocks and then dissolving into rubble. "They're dead?"

"All of them, at least the ones in Abria. They're no longer a threat. The Shapeshifters, I mean. They were imbued with the power of Zoran. He took it back and more."

A bronze silhouette appeared in the place where the Shapeshifters had dissolved. "That's Zoran. Also, the two great beasts are missing."

"Leviathan…"

"And Gamelyon." He sighed. "Folas stole the Sword from Kane and I stole it from him, bringing it here."

Eislyn couldn't decide if she should believe him.

"I know what you're thinking. Is anything I've said true?" He looked up at Eislyn as the scene shifted back to the forest. "I don't need to be linked to you in Nivala to know your thoughts, though I can hear them through our connection. You're asking the same things anyone would ask in your situation. Read my mind."

Eislyn focused her thoughts on the diminutive being next to her. Almost immediately, she experienced the emptiness of two years of lost time. She saw many of the memories Banix had recently encountered, though they were just as blurry as the dreamscape.

Banix spoke again, breaking the moment. "I don't know what Folas is planning next. He'll be enraged that I stole the Soul Sword." After he said that, everything exploded in a brilliant flash of white light.

Together, they both opened their eyes. Eislyn and Banix stood with their hands overlapping on the handle of the ancient relic.

The Elf took a deep, painful breath. His eyes widened. "Something's different. Something is missing. Nivala…"

Freya walked up as Banix released the Soul Sword and dropped to his knees. Eislyn quickly grabbed it before the ancient relic fell to the ground.

"That was an experience," the Queen said.

"What was?" Freya asked.

Eislyn continued to stare at the Soul Sword.

Freya panicked. "Are you okay, honey? Do you need me to summon a doctor?"

Eislyn allowed a half-smile. "Nivala. He took me there."

Róisín moved over to the other two ladies. "What's Nivala? And when? You grabbed his hand, and he fell to the ground a few ticks later."

Banix gripped his chest as he stood. "All the things you saw happened in the blink of an eye." He took a deep breath. "Just like a dream."

It was more than a dream, a voice said to Eislyn.

The Queen looked down and realized where it came from. In her hand, the Soul Sword glowed brightly. She closed her eyes once again.

Eislyn opened them and stood in a different Nivala-like realm. This dreamscape was unlike the last one. Around her, tendrils of red energy flowed around a darkened room. Eislyn looked down and saw that she wasn't standing on anything, but rather free-floating in this plane of existence.

A ghostly silhouette appeared in the far distance. The form lacked any distinguishable features, instead appearing as nothing more than an outline of a head attached to a cylindrical body.

A voice spoke. "Unite us. Only the combined efforts of the Fourth can stop the Calamity."

Eislyn reached out, grasping at the air to touch the entity. "What is the Fourth? And what Calamity?"

A moment later, Eislyn found herself holding Freya's hand. The Queen looked left to right, then back to the ancient relic. No longer glowing, it was as if it had never happened.

"Are you okay?" Róisín asked as Freya braced Eislyn.

"Yeah, I think so. That glow was intense."

Róisín shook her head. "What glow?"

Banix stood. "No one saw it but you."

All three women turned to face him.

Tears welled up in his eyes. "You took Nivala from me. How did you do that?"

"It wasn't intentional, I assure you." Eislyn handed the Soul Sword to Freya and addressed the Elf, kneeling down to his height. "I'd ask you how you got in here, but if I had to guess, it was something like this." She snapped her fingers, disappeared, and then reappeared behind him.

He raised his eyebrows in surprise. "Yeah, I came here from the Forest. Just like that."

Eislyn frowned as she realized what that meant for him. "And now, try to teleport across the room."

He snapped his fingers, though nothing happened.

Banix shook his head. "No. No, it can't be true."

"I'm so, so sorry, Banix. I have some kind of power. Something I don't understand called—"

"Absorption." The Elf let his tears flow and trembled.

She teleported back to her kneeling position next to him. "Listen. You are welcome to stay here as long as you need. Farna is a place of refuge for your people. I'll also take you anywhere you want to go if staying here is too much."

He wiped at his eyes. "I suppose my Frost Magic is gone too, isn't it?" He sighed. "There was more we needed to talk about, Queen of Abria."

Eislyn's face shifted at the mention of her title. "Such as?"

"War is coming."

Chapter 17

The Announcement

Tiernan took a deep breath. On the opposite side of the infirmary, an attendant heard the commotion. She walked over to his side. "How are you feeling?"

The King opened his eyes. "Foggy. What happened?"

Another voice chimed in with the answer, a doctor sitting at a table on the other side of the infirmary. "Your wounds didn't respond well to the teleportation process. They were still healing and coming here undid everything my colleague did for you in Whispersong. You're lucky to be alive."

Tiernan shifted his head toward the voice. "Who are you?"

"I am your attending doctor. My name is Milek. Guards!"

A set of guards rushed into the room.

"Send for the Queen. Her husband is awake."

As they left, Tiernan tried to move. "How long was I out?"

"Three days. Lay still. You had severe internal injuries. Without healing magic, you'd be dead. Your body needs to rest."

Tiernan rolled his eyes upon hearing Milek's words, though after a moment, he nodded in compliance.

Another pair of guards walked in. "King Tiernan," they said, as their leader turned his head in their direction.

Tiernan squinted. "Gentlemen. How may I help you?"

One of them stepped forward. "The Queen has had us posted outside since the battle."

"He doesn't need to hear about that right now!" Milek snapped.

The other guard shrugged. "Queen's orders. We were to bring his majesty up to speed the moment he woke, even before she made her way here to see him."

Annoyed, Milek returned to his work.

Tiernan leaned up on his elbow, groaning as he shifted his body weight.

Milek's head shot up. "I said be still!" He rolled his eyes. "*Sire.*"

Tiernan waved him off. "When did this happened?"

The first guard answered. "Two days after the retrieval of the Soul Sword."

"Wait, the Soul Sword? We have it?"

The guard continued. "Yes. An Elf stole it and brought it to the Queen. Two days later, Farna came under siege. A dozen Graelan rebels and several Elves appeared and began the assault."

Two Elves materialized on the northern side of the Abrian Plateau. One of them raised their hand as a ball of blue Frost Magic appeared in his palm. He pulled his arm back, then threw it forward. The magic left his hand and hit the wall, freezing the blocks. His companion did the same, this time with Wind Magic. It shattered the ice. The first Elf added to the barrage, and they continued back and forth like this until a patrolling Abrian guard spotted them.

From a window in Castle Abria, Queen Eislyn pointed to the attackers. She issued commands to two of her captains, both of whom disappeared into the castle to assemble the guards. Not long thereafter, Eislyn watched as the doors protecting Farna opened to allow the Abrian forces to exit. These men, swords and shields drawn, rushed around to the northern wall. Once they arrived, two of them took up backup defensive postures while the other four approached the attackers.

The small crack in the doors was all a third invisible Elf needed to see through the gates protecting Farna. Still cloaked, he teleported just inside. He deactivated his Cloak of Invisibility and threw several volleys of Wind Magic against the still closing doors.

His magic stopped the doors from closing, which allowed time for his next attack. Using his other hand wearing a Fire Ring, he sent several blazing blasts toward the door mechanisms. These ignited in a spectacular display of flame and smoldering embers.

This same Elf continued the assault with multiple attacks of Wind Magic. These blasts sent Abrian Guards scattering, with a few knocked unconscious as they landed.

Eislyn watched in horror as a band of rebels burst through the gates, having hidden along the rocky steps leading up to the Abrian Plateau and waiting for the moment to strike. She turned to the guard with her and issued new orders.

Upon hearing the commotion outside, an Elven refugee from Lakedon walked out of a nearby tavern. He watched as more guards rushed toward the attacking Elf. One by one, their opponent bested them with his Wind Magic.

Eislyn caught sight of the refugee and gasped when he vanished. At first, she wondered if he was a collaborator. She breathed a sigh of relief as he reappeared beside the rebel Elf and tackled him.

This pause allowed the nearby Abrian Royal Guards to regroup. A handful of them dealt with the fires while the rest battled the Graelan rebels.

Meanwhile, the two Elves wrestled with each other. The rebel Elf twisted and turned, trying to break free. The refugee Elf swung his fist into the other's jaw, stunning him for a moment. Seeing no other alternative, he reluctantly cast a fatal dose of Poison Magic at the rebel Elf.

Enraged, he retaliated with Wind Magic. It threw the refugee Elf across the field who cracked his head against a rock in the alleyway. Satisfied, but knowing he had limited time as the poison now coursed through his body, the rebel Elf resumed his onslaught. With nothing to lose, he opened himself up to attack while taking as many guards down with him as he could.

A defending Abrian Guard saw the refugee Elf fly across the field and the increased intensity of the attacks. He slipped around a bend in the road behind the rebel Elf. Taking a deep breath, he raised his sword and ran at full speed toward him.

The Elf saw him three ticks too late. The guard's blade pierced the rebel's chest. Wounded, he fell to his knees. He looked down to see the metal coming through his torso. The Elf tried to snap his fingers, but it was too late. He fell over, weakened from the injury and growing poison spreading through his body.

The Graelan rebels froze as their Elven ally perished. One of them signaled for retreat. The two Elves on the northern side of Farna also fell to Abrian Guards who had snuck around the other side and eliminated them in a surprise attack.

Tiernan rubbed his head, processing the details of the story as relayed to him by the guards. *I wish I could have been there.* "How is my wife?"

"I'm fine, my love," Eislyn said as she walked in. "You filled him in?"

The guards nodded.

"Dismissed."

They left the room as Tiernan sat up. "Eislyn, I'm so sorry." He pointed to his abdomen. "This must be worse than we thought."

She sat next to him on the bed. "An Elf gifted with healing thought it might be an injury from an Ultimus attack. Did our enemies use that during the underground battle?"

Tiernan scrunched his face, thinking hard. "I can't remember, but I guess I don't know what an Ultimus attack would look like. I'm sorry. If only I had been stronger, none of this would have happened."

She kissed his cheek. "Stop it. I'm doing okay. We held our own during the battle. I guess all those years managing my parent's Alligator paid off, along with the quick response on the field by the guards and our Elven allies."

Tiernan smiled. "You're a natural born leader."

Eislyn winced. She put her hand on her stomach.

Tiernan reached out and touched her, covering her hand with his palm. "How is he or she doing?"

Behind the couple, Milek made a grunt. The attendant walked out to give them privacy.

Eislyn punched him on the arm, though it was more of a love tap than anything. "You sure can't keep a secret, can you?"

He chuckled. "Right. We haven't announced it yet."

"I've been waiting for you to be healthy. This is something we should do from the grand balcony of Castle Abria. Together." She laughed. "And soon. Word keeps creeping out like that. I'm tired of hiding it. This is our news, and we need to let the Kingdom know. We might face insurmountable odds, but this is news worth celebrating."

Two weeks later, a still limping Tiernan put the crown on his head for the first time since the morning he departed with Enid for the Cave of Tera. He swallowed as he looked in the mirror at himself.

The bruising on his torso was gone. Tiernan bent over and touched his knee, which ached whenever he was awake.

The King still did not know how he injured this part of his body. His best guess was that something happened when he rushed Kane and fell, trying to retrieve the three ancient relics and the jewel.

"I wish you were here, Sister. You too, Way. I need both of you more than ever." He turned around and looked at his bedroom. Everything looked the same as the eve before the underground battle, but felt different. The walls, despite their golden coloration, seemed colder. The room, though no less empty than before, echoed with each footstep.

He pulled back a curtain. The sun shone overhead, but if Tiernan didn't know better, he would have bet his family's fortune that it lacked the usual brilliant illumination of midmorning. The wind blew into their bedroom, though its cooling breeze now seemed different.

Birds flew overhead but did not sing. In the fields and streets below, people moved about, but with an obvious sense of trepidation. Tiernan glanced toward the large exterior doors guarding the city. Though mostly repaired, they appeared less sturdy and protective.

"The magic is gone."

Tiernan turned around at the sound of his wife's voice. Dressed in her most regal outfit, her face shone with the magnificence of a twinkling star. Her smile and eyes exuded warmth and love toward her husband. "You should finish dressing."

He nodded and walked over to his armoire. He placed his crown on a shelf and pulled out a royal tunic and robes. Tiernan breathed deep. "What do you mean?"

With an extra bounce in her step, Eislyn pulled open the rest of the curtains. "Well, I don't want any other maidens in the village getting a glimpse of my husband's muscular physique." She put emphasis on the last two words with a teasing grin. "Can't have the populace staring at their Queen with jealousy and thinking how lucky I am, Mr. Prince."

He laughed. "Thanks, I think." Tiernan walked over to a mirror and flexed, looking at his arm muscles with disapproval. "I think the weeks of inactivity have taken their toll." He puffed his chest out and tried to flex his abs, instead doubling over in pain. He shook his head in disgust before pulling the tunic over his head.

Tiernan turned toward his wife. "But that wasn't what I meant and you know it. What did you mean *about the magic?*"

Her playful smile turned sour. "I knew that, Tiernan. I was trying to lighten your mood." She ran her hands down her robes to smooth them out. "I meant what I said. The magic that made our home a perpetual paradise is gone."

She looked out toward the chasm that had disrupted northern Farna. "The legend was true, T. Haven't you noticed the leaves beginning to wither already? Today is the ninth day of the ninth month of the year and that's never happened in my lifetime. I mean, look!" She motioned toward the streets below. "The grass down there is already turning brown."

Tiernan tightened his jaw and thought about the underground battle.

Eislyn continued. "Rumors are swirling that the season of Frost will be the first time in recorded history we have snowpack here in the city." She placed her hands on her belly. "Can you believe it? Accumulating snow in Farna! I'm just sad they'll miss the bulk of it."

He put his royal robes over his outfit, then retrieved his crown. After adjusting it, he walked over and put his arms around her with his hands resting on her stomach.

"When did the doctor think our little one would show up?" He put his face on her neck.

Feeling his warm breath, Eislyn leaned her head into his. "Sometime near the end of Frostend or first week of Windbloom. Assuming the baby doesn't come early."

He grinned and kissed her on the neck. "Or later," he said into her ear in a low, whispering voice full of mischievousness.

His words made her push his hands away as she spun around. "No way, Mr. Prince." She smacked his chest, causing him to cough. "Sorry. I forgot. 'The King needs to heal' or some nonsense. I'm beginning to think you're pulling one over on us and dragging the process out."

"Ha!" Tiernan kissed her on the cheek and walked back over to a tall mirror to straighten his robes one last time.

Eislyn persisted. "But *why* would you say such a thing? 'Or later!' Don't even speak such heresy into existence, Tiernan. This baby is coming on time, whether they like it or not." She walked up behind him. "You look handsome. Stop checking yourself out in the mirrors or I'll have them removed." Eislyn tipped the crown atop his head to one side, earning Tiernan's playful ire yet again. She put her hands on his shoulders and turned him around to kiss his cheek. "I think I met him last night."

"Excuse me? Met him? Who is him?"

She grinned as Tiernan fixed his crown and then grabbed his hand to pull the King along. "Come on. We need to get moving."

"Who is him?" he asked again as they pushed open the doors of their bedroom together.

"That's right. *Him.* Edward. Your son, T. The future King of Abria."

The news hung over them in a way neither expected. In silence, the King and Queen moved into the hallway, hand-in-hand, toward their intended destination.

Tiernan's mind raced, trying to understand. He stopped in his tracks. "Did you have another Nivalan experience?"

Eislyn grinned big and nodded with an excitement she couldn't contain. "He was so adorable, T. This little ball of joy. Perfectly healthy. Ten fingers, ten toes, and a cry that'll keep us up all night." She pulled on his hand to keep him moving along.

Tiernan felt the tears in his eyes well up, but pushed them away. He had to maintain composure, not devolve into a blathering, emotional pile. He stopped again and pulled his wife to him. Embracing her while placing a kiss on her forehead, a surge of thoughts and feelings flooded his mind.

"A boy, huh? Well, I hope you're right. I can already see it. I'll take him to Dad's workshop in the city when he's old enough. Who knows, maybe he'll follow in his footsteps and become a carpenter!"

"I am right, Mr. Prince. I can't explain it other than I saw him." Her face lit up. "Come on, let's go announce this to the rest of Abria."

Neither said anything else until they reached the balcony overlooking Farna.

The same balcony where his grandfather had died during the first Statuo.

Instead of sadness, Tiernan felt his countenance lift. If he tried hard, he could almost see an apparition of his parents, Davien and Kyrie. Tiernan smiled as he imagined his mother's beaming face and his father's proud eyes.

Deep down, he knew it was a fantasy. Still, he allowed himself the moment as he next saw the man with which he wished he could make things right: Borun. And to his elation, standing beside him were...

Enid and Wayland. Impossible.

He blinked, and the balcony returned to normal. Instead of hallucinations, Tiernan saw Eislyn's father Eldar and mother Freya. Across from them stood Kyrie's parents, his Grandma Róisín and his recently rescued Grandpa Lugh.

Tiernan and Eislyn exchanged one last look before walking onto the balcony. Almost all of Farna had assembled in the streets below, unsure of the reason for the unexpected assembly.

Most were expecting additional bad news, such as another attack from one of the terrible beasts or an announcement proclaiming the loss of one of the northern cities.

When the people saw them, the atmosphere changed. Many of the women in the crowd realized what was about to happen, with their dumbfounded husbands only processing it after their wives pointed to the Queen's obvious countenance.

With one hand, she held Tiernan's. She rested the other on her stomach with maternal affection.

With five simple words, Tiernan confirmed their suspicions. "His name," he said as his voice rose, "will be Edward!"

In a moment rivaling when the ground exploded, Farna itself erupted with joy.

Chapter 18

Eight Months Later

Chaos filled the council hall-turned war room. Sitting around the table were mayors from each of the major settlements across the Kingdom, save for Lakedon. Ulrich of Milston sat next to Kettil from Northwick. The two were reviewing a report and arguing over strategy. Across from them, Tibor from Alwyn sat next to Penrod of Oakshadow, both men deep in a heated debate.

The new Manus of Idlewind, Rhys, mayor Tomek of Clericsfold, and King Tiernan stood with their backs to the rest, reviewing a map of the Kingdom. Ahern came as a representative from the Valley and Whispersong, though he seemed out of his element and mostly sat without speaking.

After a lengthy discourse, Boswell from Lorelei addressed the group. "Gentlemen, we have to take the battle to them."

The mayors settled down. Rhys, Tomek, and Tiernan turned to face those sitting around the table.

"The fight near Oakshadow was the third skirmish this month," Penrod said. "Our city guards held them off, though not without losses."

Rhys pointed to the map. "Have you been able to gain access to Mystic Mornings?"

Penrod shook his head. "No. A small group of terrified Elves emerged from it some time ago. They said it was too dangerous for Graelans."

Tiernan glanced at Enid's hanging axe as he paced. "Did they say why?"

"They were traumatized. Said there had been some kind of catastrophe, and that one of their own had turned against them."

Tiernan paused, reflecting on Penrod's words. "Folas. It has to be him."

Tomek pointed to the Soul Sword resting against the wall. "Do you think that relic has anything to do with it?" Noting an absence of opinion, he motioned to the map. "What about Lakedon?"

"The rebel forces invaded the town not long after they exiled Fenwick. He and his wife took up refuge in Lorelei," answered Boswell.

Ulrich broke in. "In other words, Kane took advantage of the internal dissension within the village to claim fresh territory for his pseudo kingdom."

Tiernan's head snapped at the suggestion of a new kingdom.

Ulrich pointed to the map. "I'm sorry, Your Majesty. But we cannot continue to pretend that isn't their goal here."

"My father ensured that would never happen!" Tiernan cast Tomek a cursory glance, hoping his words didn't offend the Clericsfold mayor.

Tomek agreed. "Then let the good King Davien did all those years ago be our rallying cry today."

Satisfied, Tiernan walked over to the corner of the room and picked up the Soul Sword.

"Folas might not even know it's here. The Mind Shield might be hiding it from him." The King sighed. Without taking his eyes off of the blade, he continued. "It's been eight months since they declared war. The first battle was here in Farna. How many more since then?"

The mayors started talking amongst themselves. Tiernan continued to stare at the Soul Sword as he waited for their response.

"Twelve, including the initial attack on Farna and the three this month," answered Rhys. "So, about one every three weeks."

The room fell silent as they waited for the King's instructions.

Dad, I could use your help right now. Tiernan put the Soul Sword back against the wall next to the Mind Shield. "The first Statuo was something my father did to protect the Kingdom, to keep it from fracturing. Afterward, he named my sister and me the 'Protectors of Abria.' She may be gone, but that doesn't mean the mission King Davien gave us is any less relevant.

"Most of you know I was content to act as the organizer of the annual games. This," he said as he pointed to the crown, "was not something I wanted. But I can't change that any more than we can change the color of our eyes. We need to end this rebellion. I'm open to suggestions."

"Take the fight to them," said Tibor as he pounded his fist on the table. "Kane's actions with that blue sea serpent caused immense damage to Alwyn, not to mention the loss of so many lives. That beast did what it did because *he* sent it there."

"We tried to stop him in the underground battle last year," retorted Tiernan.

Rhys turned to the map. "Yes, but back then, you faced three *united* enemies. Folas is off doing his own thing here," he said as he moved his finger to the Rosewood Forest. "And, according to that Elf friend of yours, wait, what was his name?"

"Banix," answered Tiernan.

"Right, Banix. Well, according to him, Zoran is unconscious here." Rhys pointed to the Northern Plateau. "The time for Abria to strike is now."

Ulrich spoke up. "And we have many more Elves on our side than before. They could teleport our troops to the top of the Northern Plateau."

"Let's not forget about the continued emergence of magic within our own forces," said Rhys. "We could take a survey. See if any of the guards can teleport. That would make the job easier on our Elven friends."

A knock at the door interrupted the debate. Everyone turned to see an Abrian Royal Guard standing in the entryway.

"Yes?" asked Tiernan.

"The doctor said it's time."

Tiernan ran through the castle halls, ignoring the pain still throbbing in his knee. *Why didn't Eislyn heal that for me too?* As he passed different attendants, he could see the look of joy on their faces. He smiled at a few, though with each ticking moment, his fear increased.

What if the baby is breech like I was? What if there are other complications? I can't lose her too. Not now. Not during this war. Or ever, for that matter.

He picked up the pace, ignoring the rest of those he encountered with a determined focus. As he approached their chambers, he could see a group of guards standing at attention.

Before Tiernan made it to the room, he heard a blood-curdling cry. *Eislyn, no!*

Tiernan pushed past the guards and burst into the room. "Are you okay?" he asked, a frantic expression on his face.

The attending doctor tilted his head toward the King with an amused smile. "Everything is fine."

"But that sound?"

Eislyn raised her head and laughed. "It's called a contraction, Mr. Prince. They're—" she tried to say as another one washed over her, "painful!"

Tiernan ran up to her and grabbed her hand.

"Now push," the doctor said.

Eislyn nodded and gave it her all. She squeezed Tiernan's hand tight, and the King did his best not to show a reaction to her impressive grip strength.

"Good. I can see the baby's head beginning to crown. The next one is going to be a big one. When I tell you, bear down and push with all that's within you. The child is almost here."

Tiernan smiled at his wife as she listened to the doctor's every word. He realized how sweat-drenched her skin had become, with the dampness glistening in the sunlight.

She looks stunning. I'm so lucky to be her husband.

Eislyn tightened her grip on his hand.

Oh Aila, she's going to break it!

"Here it comes. Tiernan, our baby is coming, ahhhhh!" The intensity of her voice echoed off of the walls of their bedroom.

Tiernan kissed her forehead. She looked up at him, a slight yellow haze of magic swirling within her irises.

"Now, push again. This time, harder!" ordered the doctor.

Eislyn bore down, squeezing her husband's hand while using every ounce of energy in her body to push the baby out.

The doctor smiled. "The head is out. Just one more push and they'll be here. Bear down, like I said. Push, Eislyn. Push!"

Eislyn screamed while following his instructions.

Tiernan looked and saw his newborn baby's head nestled carefully in the doctor's hands. His eyes grew wide as he watched the rest of the child emerge, fist clenched in a victorious act as if to say, 'Here I am, world.'

The baby cried with an incredible vocal capacity, announcing their presence to the rest of Castle Abria and those within earshot in the city.

A nearby midwife was on her knees with a towel ready. The doctor twisted the child around, laying them in the open blanket as he dealt with the rest of his delivery duties.

"My King, would you care to do the honors?" The doctor handed Tiernan a pair of snips.

Eislyn let go of her husband's hand. Tiernan kissed hers in return, then moved to the edge of the bed.

"Cut here," the doctor said.

Tiernan, still in a euphoric haze, did as instructed while gazing upon his newborn child.

The doctor cleared his throat. "Congratulations on the birth of your son."

Tiernan looked back at Eislyn as she smiled. "I *told you* our baby would be a boy."

The King returned to her side and kissed her. "I never doubted you. After all, I announced it to the entire city!"

The midwife finished attending to the baby, then transferred him to a clean towel and swaddled the child with careful precision.

Eislyn let her head fall back onto the pillow. "Listen to his voice. We're going to have our hands full."

Tiernan rested his head next to hers from the edge of the bed. "I'll have a guard send for your mother and father."

Eislyn nodded, appreciative of his thoughtfulness.

Tiernan stood and turned. He mouthed 'Freya and Eldar' to a guard at the door, who took off.

The midwife brought the baby to the Queen.

Eislyn gasped. "He's beautiful, T! Look at him!"

Tiernan looked back at his wife as she nestled the baby in her arms.

Eislyn ran her fingers along their baby's face, which seemed to calm the child's crying. "Hello there, Edward."

Edward opened his eyes to a squint, just enough to give his parents a look at them.

Tiernan touched Edward's face with gentle care. "Strong little man. We're going to have so much fun together." He leaned over and kissed his wife again.

For the first time in ages, Tiernan realized he felt at peace with the world.

A purple haze surrounded the Graelian sun. Its somber rays pierced the windows of Castle Abria, acting as a bookend to an eventful day. Tiernan walked back into the war room as the light began to disappear from the windows. At this hour, only Manus Rhys had remained.

"The others?" asked Tiernan.

"Back to their rooms. They will reconvene tomorrow. They've all been gone for quite a while."

"Why are you still here?"

"I couldn't shake the feeling we were missing something with the attacks. So, I came back here to review the reports." Rhys smiled. "How did it go?"

Tiernan pulled out a chair and sat in it while resting his feet on the table. "He's perfect, Manus. And you know, the moment I laid my eyes on him, I knew something."

"What's that?"

"I knew he was *mine*. And that I would do anything to protect him." He motioned his head at the map on the wall. "That includes winning this war."

Rhys stood and walked over to the hanging map. Tiernan crossed his arms as the Manus spoke. "Something was bothering me." He pointed to different parts of the Kingdom. "Since they took Lakedon, most of their efforts have been in other parts of the Kingdom. Here, in Oakshadow. Fabled Wonders." His finger moved down to the bottom of the map. "Alwyn." He knocked on it with his knuckle near the Abrian Plateau. "Farna a few times. They always seem to avoid Central Abria and our eastern cities. Why?"

Tiernan shrugged. "Maybe they want to keep the fight near Castle Abria?"

Rhys shook his head and pointed at Lake Conchobar. "I don't think so. I think there's something going on here, at Lakedon." He turned back to Tiernan. "Maybe we don't need Graelan mages who haven't even figured out their own powers or our Elven allies to teleport our forces to the Northern Plateau."

"You think Lakedon is their staging ground?"

Rhys nodded. "With Lakedon in their possession, no one from the east is using the Northern Path to get *here*. We're taking the long way, using the bridge near Whispersong to cross into Central Abria. And when the rebels attack, it's almost always one of the western cities."

"They don't want us near Lakedon," Tiernan leaned forward in his chair. "And that's exactly where we're going to take the battle to them." Tiernan stood up. "Wake the other mayors."

As the light broke over the Valley Mountains signaling the start of a new day, economic trade did its best to resume. In Idlewind, city residents continued to rebuild after the destruction from Gamelyon. In the Valley, businesses opened their doors, though with increasing trepidation and fear.

Northwick dock workers loaded a late shipment of Lorelian Mead to be sent to Alwyn. Miners in Milston toiled away, excavating supplies for a planned fortification of the Lorelei city walls. The consensus, after great debate, was that Abria needed a place of refuge in the east. Lorelei would reinforce their stronghold similar to Farna in the west and Clericsfold in the central region.

Within the latter community, a former member of the council named Teska prepared her duties as a teacher, having abandoned her political career after the passing of her former friend, Davien. Alongside a new couple named Minmi and Omi, as well as a mysterious man named Isoshi, the four of them continued the work of the late Borun.

As the sun rose higher, a legion of Abrian Royal Guards prepared to disembark from Farna. The group had assembled outside of the city walls on the eastern side of the Abrian Plateau.

King Tiernan walked out through the gates with his security detail not far behind. Once he made his way to the front of the group, he addressed them. "I've run our plans by your commander, the Queen. She approves. However, neither of us will accompany you. Our son is less than a day old and our responsibility to him is great. Instead, I will trust Manus Rhys, our new if temporary supreme Captain, to lead you into battle.

"We don't know what to expect. There may only be a dozen rebels or they could have moved their entire army to Lakedon. Either way, Rhys will guide you to victory."

Manus Rhys, mounted on a horse, waved toward the guards. Cheers erupted as he turned and led them down the rocky steps of the Abrian Plateau. Mayor Tibor walked up behind Tiernan.

The King felt a presence and turned around to see who had approached him. "Tibor, tell me. In all of those meetings before the first Statuo, did Dad and Manus Midir ever discuss his son's military acumen?"

"No. But King Davien and the former Manus had many private conversations. They were good friends, almost a kinship of brotherhood."

"Dad talked highly of Midir's counsel. I think the Manus' friendship with my namesake created a natural bond between the two of them. I just..." Tiernan sighed. "It saddens me to say I never got to know Midir that well before he died. Mom and Dad passed, then Way, and then Midir in the caves below."

He paused. "Not to mention my sister. It all happened so fast. I went from running the games to running the Kingdom alone. And with none of them to rely on."

Tibor put his hand on the King's shoulder. "You're doing fine. I think your family would be proud."

"Family is Strength. I know."

Tibor removed his hand. "I'll leave you be. Don't let worry consume you. The day is ours. You can be confident of that."

Tiernan stood long after Tibor left and watched as the legion of guards continued to grow smaller and smaller in the distance.

Eight days later, Manus Rhys returned to Farna. Tiernan, exhausted from the lack of sleep associated with having a newborn, sat in one of the dining halls holding Edward. The baby rested on his dad's shoulder, fast asleep in a peaceful moment of silence. Tiernan had his head against the seat back, catching a few ticks of shut eye before his son woke up.

With soft, careful steps, Rhys walked up to the King and whispered his name.

Tiernan opened his eyes and smiled. He placed his hand on Edward's head and shifted him into a new position. "How did it go?" he asked in a hushed tone.

Rhys motioned to a chair to ask if he could sit. Tiernan nodded. Rhys tried his best to pull it out without making a sound lest he wake and incur the wrath of the newborn Edward.

"We liberated Lakedon. We were *right*. Kane's forces were using it as a staging ground."

"Resistance?"

"All Abrian rebels. No Elves in sight."

"Where were they, I wonder?" Tiernan braced himself for the next question. "What were our losses?"

"Thirteen."

"That's far lower than I expected."

Rhys opened his mouth to speak, but stopped.

Tiernan raised an eyebrow. "I saw that. Say what's on your mind."

Rhys tightened his jaw. "Seven within the guards exhibited powers for the first time. All were under moments of duress."

Tiernan shifted in his seat. "Eislyn said the Elf who transferred his healing powers to her used emotion as a catalyst."

"Of those seven, most of them were about to be killed when their powers manifested. One threw his attacker back with Wind Magic. Two others froze their assailant, one subdued his opponent with Gravity Magic, and the other two burned the hands of their attacker just before the fatal blow."

Tiernan counted in his head. "You said seven. That's only six. What happened to the last one?"

Rhys smiled. "Yeah. Well. Him. That person realized they had powers when they celebrated the victory with their team." Rhys opened his hand as a small, glowing yellow ball appeared. "It was spectacular. I raised my hand and knocked a bird out of the sky. Still feel bad about it."

Tiernan cradled Edward's head closer. "Careful around my kid with that thing, Rhys!" Then the King chuckled as his voice woke Edward. The child let out a cry that made both men smile. "No point in being quiet now. I guess I should say congratulations on your new powers and successful campaign. Captain Rhys. Has a nice ring to it. Would you care to make it permanent?"

Chapter 19

Moonshadow 922NE

Enraged, Kane punched the jaw of a nearby general. "It has been twenty months since you lost Lakedon. Twenty. We declared war against Abria almost a year before that, and what do we have to show? Nothing. No new ground. The only area we captured is back in enemy hands. We had the advantage, wearing down their western defenses until they ambushed us near Lake Conchobar.

"And worse yet, the Soul Sword is still missing."

"Don't forget, it may be in Farna," said the Elf, Frist.

Kane twirled around to face him. One of his most recent commanders, Kane didn't quite trust him, even if the Elf had proven himself in battle many times.

"Yes, yes. According to your Elven scouts, Folas let it slip that one of your number stole it. But why haven't any of your spies combed the halls of Castle Abria to find it?"

Kane waved him off as he paced in his living room. "Over two-thirds of our forces have been killed or captured. Stopped at every raid. This Abrian Captain, what's his name?"

"Rhys," one of them said. "He's also the Manus of my hometown, Idlewind."

Kane grunted with dissatisfaction. "We must stop him and get the Soul Sword back, or else we cannot reawaken any of Zoran's other minions." He pointed to the door. "Tomorrow, I want to hit every Abrian settlement at once."

"All of them?" asked one of his men.

"What makes you think this will be any more successful than your concentrated raids?" Frist asked.

Kane eyed Frist with distrust. "I said all. We cannot give Abria a chance to breathe. Hitting their cities one at a time? I understand now. That strategy gives them time to prepare, to regroup." He cackled. "If we hit them all at once, it'll throw the entire Kingdom off balance. Our unified attack will be their downfall."

Kane turned his back to them and stared out the window. The Graelans and Frist exchanged a look of disbelief, then left the home.

Kane slapped his palms together in frustration. Their reduced Elven forces, since many of the blinded Elves had returned to the Forest or taken up refuge in various Abrian towns, had only partially completed the citadel.

Castle Kane. The thought made him laugh out loud, giddy with the idea of the immortalization of his name. He walked over to his kitchen and looked down at where the soup had fallen years ago.

Now, all that remained was debris. Kane left it that way to act as a reminder to himself that no matter how strong Davien's son tried to be, he would be nothing but a failure.

Kane laughed again. *Our victory is almost at hand!*

Deep below the citadel, a forgotten red jewel rested on the ground. It seemed to lack any power or significance, and was stored here next to a slumbering form that slowly breathed in and out.

Like the jewel, this form had been long unguarded and forgotten for the past year.

Together, the two occupied a darkened room in the only catacomb on the Northern Plateau, an underground storage that had been excavated not long after the Elves expanded construction efforts.

Unguarded. Forgotten. Abandoned.

No one saw when the form's finger twitched.

As the sun rose the next morning, all of Kane's remaining forces gathered in the courtyard. He left the planning to his generals. One of them informed Kane that the bulk of their forces would besiege Castle Abria with the rest dividing to attack each of the remaining towns.

Kane wasn't in the mood for a speech today, but knew he had to say something. He took a breath. "We have suffered setbacks, I admit. But now, I see the error of our ways. Abria must understand they will not, cannot win. Our unified attack will be their downfall!"

He cleared his throat, raising the volume of his voice. "As a special reward, I will offer two thousand gold din to anyone who can bring me the head of Manus Rhys. Twice that for the head of Davien's son. When this day is over, the Soul Sword must return to its rightful home. I want it here, in my castle, before the sun sets over the western mountains. Remember, we will be victorious!"

The crowd seemed less enthusiastic than Kane would have liked, though the offer of din seemed to generate some interest. He nodded, and their Elven accomplices with teleportation powers began grabbing the hands of nearby Graelans. This continued until he stood alone with a single, quiet Elf.

Kane looked around at the citadel they had built. The walls weren't as high as he wanted, but would suffice. Elves had completed most of the interior of the citadel. Some structures, such as two guard towers, still needed work.

Despite its unfinished condition, he felt proud of their efforts. A hand brushed his, and Kane looked down at his last companion, an Elf who would act as his personal escape should events proceed in an unfortunate direction.

"I want to be a part of the attack on each city. Take me to Milston first."

The Elf pushed an ether into his palm. He let the power flow through his body, grabbed Kane's hand, snapped his fingers, and teleported the Divider to their destination.

Tiernan ran through the halls of Castle Abria. Below his feet, the ground shook. *Impossible.* As he continued to run, he felt the sensation again. He changed course and moved to a nearby window. From this vantage point, he could see Elves along the Abrian Plateau casting purple blasts of energy toward the city.

Gravity Magic. They're trying to bring the walls down. Nearby, he heard a voice issuing orders. He looked toward it and saw his wife giving commands to several members of the Guard. After those men ran off, the King and Queen met up.

"Where is Edward?" Tiernan asked.

"With Mom and Dad. They wanted to watch him today," she answered as another volley shook the ground. Both looked out the window.

"There's so many of them," Tiernan lamented.

Eislyn grabbed his hand. "There's more of us, but most of our Elven companions are in other towns."

"Our relocation efforts."

She nodded. "Do we have anyone who can fend off these kinds of attacks?"

Tiernan didn't have the time to answer as another volley of Gravity Magic rocked Farna.

Kane had never been to Milston. The town's dreary appearance, a byproduct of the stone-based construction of their homes, made it seem as if the town would be an easy target.

Instead, two dozen members of the Milston city guards held their ground and kept his forces at bay. In his frustration, Kane began issuing orders, overriding his general's authority.

"Push in. Don't let them defend," Kane said as a spear from one of the Milston city guards flew by his head. It hit the man behind him, who fell dead.

"That man died for nothing unless you press forward. Take the city!"

Kane took three steps backward. His Elven companion did likewise as their forces advanced deeper toward the defenders. One by one, the rebels fell to the unified front of the Milston city guards.

This can't be. He looked at the Elf. "Clericsfold."

The Elf grabbed Kane's hand and snapped his fingers as even more of their number perished.

In the catacombs below the citadel, the slumbering form took a gasping breath. Its hand switched from an open palm to a fist.

The jewel glowed, the first activity from it since the Dark Elf had tried to steal its power.

Anger fueled the form as it awoke. Rage boiled up within its body. Determination set in to right this wrong.

Both of Zoran's eyes shot open as he bellowed a furious cry directed at one Graelan and one Graelan alone.

"Kane!"

Clericsfold had worked hard to transform the city's appearance since the last time Kane was here. It appeared as if his hometown had painted the exterior walls. They no longer possessed the imposing appearance he relished.

Instead, it was as if they happily rejoined Abria after the first Statuo and surrendered their culture to the whims of Farna's leadership.

Now, every meter of the Clericsfold walls had a bright, golden hue. It was artificial, as the city planners were using some kind of paint to mimic the appearance of Castle Abria.

Disgusted, Kane stood at a distance, observing this battle. Like Milston, the city guards of Clericsfold — no longer the co-opted orphans, but trained professionals — repelled every attempted attack and advance from Kane's forces.

Kane had wondered if sending most of the Elves to the Forest and Farna had been a mistake. It irritated him to know that many of his Elven accomplices had to be allocated to those two battlegrounds. He shook his head as more of his army fell than those from Clericsfold.

"Traitors. When this day is won, we will avenge this. Clericsfold will be my capital," he said, forgetting about his home atop the Northern Plateau in his rage. "I will subdue and execute every member of the population that stood in opposition to us."

He huffed and grabbed the Elf's hand. "Let's get out of here. Farna."

High above the skies over Kane's citadel, a gigantic winged form surveyed the land. The Northern Plateau was empty, so it rose higher and began flying over the other nearby towns. First, it surveyed Milston and Northwick and watched as the last of Kane's forces fell to defenders from both communities.

From there, it flew south to Lorelei and the Valley, where it saw the same situation play out. Further south, it observed a small, inconsequential farming settlement. It continued on its journey toward Idlewind.

The flying form watched as the Elven attackers had better success here. Then, it roared in surprise as the Graelans began casting magic in retaliation. This sound caused those on the ground to stop and look high into the sky, trying to find its source before resuming their conflict.

The winged beast turned back to Central Abria, where the rebel Graelans were failing yet again. It didn't bother to inspect the lake town, as it suspected the results would be the same there.

It turned northwest and flew over the Forest. There, it could see flashes of magic through the trees. Wind, Fire, Frost, Gravity, and even Poison seemed in play.

Ignoring Oakshadow, it flapped its wings and turned toward its intended destination further south.

Farna.

Tiernan and Eislyn ran hand-in-hand through the halls of Castle Abria and through its front doors. In Tiernan's free hand, he held the Mind Shield. His wife gripped the handle of the Soul Sword with her other hand. Behind the couple, multiple guards followed, there to ensure nothing happened to the royal couple.

"It's a disaster," Eislyn said as they ran through the streets toward the Drunken Alligator. Every volley of Gravity Magic seemed to shake the homes and structures within Farna.

"You didn't tell me. Which direction did you send your guards?" Tiernan asked.

"Both ways, actually. I told them to use their discretion with whom to send where, but to attack from each side. They're making their way around the outer walls to surprise them."

"Very clever. Why didn't one of those old kings build doors on both the north and south sides of the city? Wouldn't that make it easier to defend the capital?"

"How would I know? They're your ancestors," she said as they entered her parent's tavern. Within the Drunken Alligator, it was even more chaotic. The royal couple looked around for Eislyn's parents and their son.

Freya had Edward on her hip, carrying the toddler around while trying to tend to those who had taken refuge within its walls. Some had bloodied faces, others broken bones. All wore looks of exhaustion on their faces.

"Mom."

Freya looked up at her daughter.

Edward saw his parents. "Mama!" He twisted and turned to get away from his grandmother, who let him down with care. Edward ran to Eislyn, who scooped him up as she handed the Soul Sword to her husband.

"Hey, big boy," she said as she hugged him.

Tiernan ran his hand through his son's fire-red-colored hair.

"Daddy! Booms!" Edward giggled, unaware of the severity of what was happening around him and seeming to take the shaking in stride.

Eislyn and Tiernan exchanged looks that screamed heartbreak, both at his childhood innocence and the war zone unfolding in real time.

Another intense volley rocked the city. Some people fell to the ground while others steadied themselves on a nearby table.

"Stay here." Tiernan gave his wife and son a kiss, then motioned to a few of the guards to follow him.

Outside, Tiernan looked at the tall, nearly impenetrable walls of Farna. *That's what I thought I saw from the castle.*

Cracks.

Tiernan turned to his guards. "I want to get my wife, our son, and her parents into Castle Abria. If these walls fall…" He shook his head.

"Understood," one of them said.

"Then let's go."

Chapter 20

The Last Day

Outside of the walls of Farna, Manus Rhys commanded a group of Abrian Royal Guards. *I should be in Idlewind. How much longer can I split my duties between my home and the Kingdom as their supreme captain?*

He pushed the thought away as he swung his sword at an attacking Graelan rebel. The man used a wooden shield to defend himself, so Rhys retaliated with a blast of Wind Magic toward him. It knocked the man backward and off of the edge of the Abrian Plateau.

"Whoops," he said before a powerful force pulled him to the ground.

Behind him, an Elf was sending a continuous blast of Gravity Magic at the Manus.

At least if he's attacking me, he's leaving the city alone. The sensation was a whole-body pain that Rhys hadn't experienced before. He groaned, dropped his weapons, and fell to his knees.

And just like that, the pain ceased. Rhys flipped around to see that one of the other Abrian Royal Guards had impaled the Elf with a broadsword.

The man rushed to him. "You okay, Captain?"

Rhys waved the question off. "There are other Elves with Gravity Magic. They are the priority here, otherwise they could bring the walls protecting the city down."

As he and the guard turned back toward the battle, Rhys felt a chill as the sun disappeared overhead. He looked up, expecting to see a thick, dark cloud.

"By Aila's sword, that's impossible," he said as his eyes focused on the unfamiliar shape hovering above.

Tiernan and Eislyn ran through the chaotic streets with her parents. The Queen held Edward tight.

"Slow down," Freya said. "We're not as young as you two."

"There's no time," Tiernan replied. "We need to get you into the safety of Castle Abria."

Eldar turned his head back toward the Alligator. "It doesn't seem right."

Freya silenced him with her eyes. They had already had this discussion earlier. There was no way they could fit the entire city within the castle. This was a choice Tiernan made to protect his family.

Halfway into their trek through the streets of Farna, the sun grew cold. All four of them stopped running and looked up. Across the city, everyone paused. Outside of the city walls, both the rebels and Abrian fighters froze in place.

"Tiernan, is that what I think it is?" Eislyn asked, though she already knew the answer.

The King's mouth fell agape. He had only heard about something like this happening twice before, and both times were on The Day of Tiernan. The day of his birth. "Another dragon," he said in a hushed tone.

Tiernan's stomach twisted. This dragon seemed to inspect the battle rather than interact with anyone. The archives mentioned the previous ones engaging with Graelans and described a peaceful, serene atmosphere in their presence.

This dragon seemed to keep its distance.

"Is it seeing how we respond?" asked Eldar.

"Or maybe it's watching the battle to see how we treat each other," Freya offered as a counterpoint.

Before other opinions could be offered, the giant beast dropped low to the ground and flew through the streets of Farna. The royal couple ducked, even if the dragon itself remained above their heads. It rose higher into the air once again, surveying the city from the other side.

As the dragon hovered over Farna, Tiernan got a clarifying look now that the sun's light shone across its body. From head to tail, this dragon possessed a golden bronze hue. Even its eyes were this same color.

"Is this how they always act?" asked Freya.

Eislyn and Tiernan's worried expressions answered her question.

The dragon turned its head toward Castle Abria. It opened its mouth and breathed a series of boulders toward the ancient structure. As those rocks found their various targets, the ensuing impacts caused one of the majestic towers of the historic stronghold to collapse. It fell onto other portions of the city and structures below. The beast roared in what Tiernan thought sounded like elation.

Kane stood at a safe distance in the fields near the Abrian Plateau, enraptured by the appearance and actions of the dragon in the skies. As the tower fell, he felt an immense sense of pleasure.

"I don't know where this dragon came from, but I'm impressed."

Next to him, his Elven companion quivered in fear.

Kane noticed, dismissed the Elf's reaction, and returned his gaze to the creature's attack on Castle Abria. "What's your problem? That beast is undoubtedly on our side. He, she, whatever it is, has already done more than Zoran did the past few years."

The Elf's voice shook. "We shouldn't stay here."

Kane looked down. "Why? We're safe. Let's enjoy the show."

The dragon swooped up high into the sky and circled around. The King tried to anticipate its next target.

To his horror, the dragon soared to the north, picked up speed as it tore through the city, flipped around in the air, and flew at an impressive pace toward the city gates to the south. Tiernan watched as it raised its front claws, which appeared to be glowing with a new and unknown bronze magic that matched the color of its skin.

As the beast drove itself through the wooden gates, they splintered into a thousand pieces, raining sharp, fractured debris onto those standing nearby. As it passed through the broken entrance, the dragon raised its front claws high. The ground on either side rose with them, tearing the walls from their foundation. Dirt and soil below continued with the masonry on an upward trajectory.

It then spread its claws. The crumbling walls followed as debris from what used to protect Farna flew in all directions. The dragon swooped in an upward arc, appearing to survey the damage it had caused.

"It's going to destroy the city," Tiernan said.

"What should we do?" asked Freya.

Tiernan turned to his wife. He looked down at the Mind Shield as the beast prepared for another strafing run high above them. "I don't think it can see us because of this. I don't know if it can see *any* of us within the Mind Shield's range."

"Which is how far?" asked Eldar.

"We never figured it out," Tiernan said.

The dragon came back around, performing the same swooping maneuver on the fortifications to the north. Using its powers and speed, it rammed those walls and pulled the crumbling enclosure from its foundation as before. Those nearby panicked. Some ran through the hole, desperate to get out of Farna. Others ran back into the city and to the shelter of the Alligator.

Tiernan swallowed hard. He looked to the sky, then back to his wife. "You have to go. All four of you."

"Go where?" asked Freya.

Eislyn looked into her husband's eyes and knew what he was thinking. "T, I don't know if I'm powerful enough to—"

Before she could finish, the bronze dragon returned. It breathed another series of boulders at Castle Abria, destroying even more of their home.

"Listen. There is no time. Look." Tiernan pointed through the gap where the first tower used to stand. "That way. Get them out of here."

"You mean teleport. *The sky trick.* No. I'm staying with you." She grabbed his tunic. "Not again. Do you hear me? I will not leave your side. This can't be happening." Eislyn sobbed. "We don't even know what's beyond the western mountains. Besides, I don't have enough in me for everyone." She pounded on his chest. "I will not leave you, T."

Tiernan pulled his wife in close. Tears welled up in his eyes. "Eislyn, you have to go. At least take Edward. I'll find you when this is over. I promise." He held his wife tight, tears now streaming down her face as she buried it in his chest. "This is not the end of our story. But for now, you must protect our boy."

Eislyn pulled her head back and turned to her parents.

"There's no time, honey. Go. We'll be fine," her mom said.

Eislyn let go of her husband and ran to them, hugging both with Edward wedged between the three. She turned back to Tiernan, rushing into his arms for one last embrace. He pulled her in close, ran his hands along the side of her neck, and gave her a long kiss. He felt the wind of the dragon above him and knew it was coming back in for another destructive pass. Tiernan let go of her so she could do what she had to do.

The King leaned over and gave Edward a kiss on his forehead. "Be strong, my son. I love you."

"Lub ewe."

Eislyn looked deep into her husband's eyes. "I love you, T."

"I will find you." Tiernan took a step back. "I love you, Eislyn."

With that, the Queen grabbed her son, held him tight, and looked high to the western sky. She raised her free hand and snapped her fingers.

Circling above the city, the bronze dragon roared in vehement anger.

✛ ✛ ✛ ✛ ✛ ✛ ✛ ✛ ✛

From his vantage point, Kane laughed as the dragon destroyed Farna bit by bit. With each attack run, more of the walls fell. He yelled with excitement when another tower of Castle Abria fell and crushed other sections of the city.

The dragon came back by and began breathing boulders all throughout the Abrian Plateau. Kane stopped reveling in the destruction as he saw his own rebel forces falling victim to the crushing debris as well.

"What's it doing? It should only be attacking Abria. Those were my men."

"And my brethren," the Elf responded.

Kane regarded his words and, in a moment of uncharacteristic empathy, understood the Elf's pain. "Davien's son needs to see the glory of his home falling apart. I want him to feel as helpless as the two of us just did. Retrieve him. Deposit him into a nearby field. One far enough away that he can't do anything but watch his home crumble.

"Then come back here and return me to the Northern Plateau."

Tiernan led his in-laws through the crumbling streets of Farna. As they ran, he got a glimpse of his parent's original home, their humble abode before they became King and Queen. As if to rub defeat in his face, one of the nearby structures fell victim to the dragon's attack and crushed the smaller house with callous abandon.

Tiernan swallowed and fought back his rage. He turned his head toward the entrance to Castle Abria. To his relief, Royal Guards appeared to have begun the evacuation of the castle as soon as the dragon started its attack. Tiernan caught the attention of several of them.

They ran up to him. "Yes, sir?"

"There are more denizens back near the northern section of the city. Some of them are trying to escape through the gap the dragon made in the wall. See that they make it to safety."

A tick later, Tiernan felt something throw him back across the field. Freya gasped and started to rush toward him. Eldar grabbed her arm to hold her back. Tiernan jumped to his feet and looked around, but he saw no sign of the attacker. Another blast came flying out of thin air and hit his hand holding the Soul Sword. The ancient relic went flying across the streets and landed in a pile of debris.

"Was that an invisible Elf? Or an invisible Graelan? Either way, it doesn't matter." Tiernan made eye contact with Eldar, who was still holding onto Freya. The King shook his head slowly, the men sharing a mutual understanding. "Keep her away from me, Eldar. Go now! Get her to safety." Tiernan turned to a nearby group of guards. "Retrieve the Soul Sword. Bring it to me at the steps leading up the Plateau. I have to get these people out of here!"

Freya tried to argue, though Eldar pulled her along. Standing alone and unguarded, Tiernan motioned for the other refugees from Castle Abria to follow the couple. As the crowd filed out behind Eislyn's parents, the dragon came back. Using what appeared to be its favorite maneuver, it blew another hole in the eastern wall of Farna.

Tiernan called out to more members of the fleeing community. "Let's go! Hurry! Don't stop until you make it down the steps of the Plateau. No matter what, do not stop until—"

Before he could finish, Tiernan disappeared.

The King knew this sensation all too well. *Teleportation!* He looked around and saw an Elf behind him.

"Why?" Tiernan rushed at the Elf, one fist raised and the other holding the Mind Shield in front of him.

"Kane wanted you to watch." With that, the Elf disappeared.

"Kane!" Tiernan looked around. He was in a field near the Western Path. *Too far to make it back to Farna.*

He watched as the dragon, now more aware of the city and able to sense its residents because of the absence of the Mind Shield, increased its rampage.

It ravaged Farna with its breath of boulders, then raised its claws high in the air. The remnants of Castle Abria followed the beast's motion. It flipped its arms high and back down fast. Likewise, every stone, every room, every square meter of the historic, fabled structure that had served as a beacon of peace and prosperity for centuries came barreling back to the ground at breakneck velocity. The structure imploded, folding in on itself and crumbling into a heap of rubble as it landed.

Using its speed, the bronze dragon flew through the city, knocking down many of the remaining structures and the vast majority of the remaining segments of the outer walls. Tiernan could see the movements of those evacuating. He didn't know if his in-laws were among the group, though their proximity to the city gates before the Elf teleported him here gave the King a glimmer of hope.

Tiernan breathed deep, steadying himself as the dragon began its final assault. In a back-and-forth combination of attacks, it tore the remnants of the collapsed walls from their foundation with its claws, pulling them into the air and dropping them wherever they fell. The King knew in his heart it would be impossible for everyone to survive. The missing eastern wall gave him a direct line of sight to toppling structures that had been people's homes falling into the chasm in the northern section of the city. Tiernan couldn't tell for sure, but he got the impression much of the castle fell in alongside those buildings.

He didn't know what happened to the Soul Sword. Nor did the King know where this dragon came from and why it was intent on destroying the city he had called home his entire life.

The only thing he knew was that, as the sun set over the western mountains on 16 Moonshadow 922NE, Farna and Castle Abria were both gone.

Chapter 21

A King's Statuo

K ane gloated from Folas' old room, staring westward toward the ruins of Castle Abria and the city of Farna. An ear-to-ear grin spread across his face and his eyes shone with euphoria as he realized the view of the western mountains was no longer occluded by the offensive silhouette of the old capital.

Zoran walked into the room carrying the red jewel. His presence startled Kane, disrupting him from his elation.

"So, you finally woke up?" Kane's stare moved to the jewel. He rolled his eyes.

Zoran's face remained stoic and focused on Kane.

"Of course. Not going to say anything, are you? No matter. Did you see what that dragon did to Farna, or were you still slumbering away in the basement?"

"What about the dragon?"

"All this time we thought we needed you to bring our enemies to their knees? Instead, the giant beast did all the work for us, without your help, and without being asked." Kane returned his gaze to the window. "I don't know why the Archives even mentioned you. We didn't need you to accomplish any of our goals and all you've done since we brought you back from the brink is sleep."

Kane snorted. "As if centuries of rest weren't enough, you needed more! Going back to bed soon too, I imagine."

Zoran's face remained deadlocked on the back of Kane's head. "Where are your forces? Your Elven accomplices? The Dark Elf himself? All your Graelan rebels?"

Zoran's questions, with his reverberating tone, made Kane uncomfortable. The Divider ignored them. "And we didn't even need the Soul Sword to destroy Farna. That ancient relic was overrated." He looked back at the jewel in Zoran's arms. "And I'm not sure why you were so worried about containing that thing. It hasn't done anything since you dozed off."

"You do not understand the power of the Soul Sword if you think that. Nor do you understand the importance of this jewel. If you did, you would have safeguarded it with your very life."

Kane huffed. "Please. Once we find the dragon and sway him to my side, I'll be unstoppable." He turned back to the window, dismissing Zoran with a wave of his hand. "Go back to your dungeon. Get some more sleep if you need it. Take that worthless thing with you."

Zoran's jaw shifted. His eyes, if they could pierce skin, tore a hole through Kane's back. "You failed. You squandered all that you had, including the advantage I gave you in the battle below the surface. You left this unguarded, a grave mistake.

"Beyond that, you allowed the very thing I needed to fix your mistakes to slip through your fingers. You may think you've won, but this is far from over."

Kane shrugged, still caught up in the moment. "The thing you needed? What did you need, one of their pillows?" He laughed at the joke. "Whatever it is, go find it yourself."

Zoran turned back to a cloaked Elf, the same that had taken Kane from place to place. The Dark Emperor nodded. The Elf walked up to Kane and grabbed his hand.

"Hey, who is that? Let go of me!" he said as he tried to twist his arm away from the uninvited presence.

Zoran looked Kane square in the eyes and shoved the jewel into his arms. "You think you're an immoveable force. Something to be reckoned with. An impenetrable rock. A caudex." The Dark Emperor grunted. "So be it. You do not know what I'm capable of, and the punishment you're about to experience is only the beginning. What I'm about to do from here on won't require you, the Dark Elf, or even the Soul Sword."

Zoran turned to the empty space where the invisible Elf held Kane's arm. "Take him to the caves along with the jewel. I'll join you shortly."

Kane tried to protest, but had no time before the Elf snapped his fingers. In a flash, he disappeared along with the jewel.

Two weeks after Farna fell, Tiernan walked up to the city gates of Lorelei alone, save for his beloved steed, Chocolate. Tiernan held the reins in his hand with an iron grip, determined not to lose her as well. Never in his life had he felt more defeated.

When the city guard saw him approach, he bowed with respect and knocked on the doors. A small window opened. "It's the King."

The doors parted enough for Tiernan to slip through. The first guard took Chocolate's reins from the King. He nodded as Tiernan entered the city. A wave of sadness washed over him. The last time he visited Lorelei was with Eislyn, Wayland, and Enid during Moon Rise celebrations almost three years ago.

"This way, my King," said the second city guard. He led Tiernan through the winding streets of Lorelei.

Tiernan didn't need an escort, but allowed the decorum to proceed. Time seemed to crawl by with each step. The sound of their boots on the cobblestone streets echoed, or at least appeared to echo, off the walls of the surrounding buildings. Tiernan saw some muddy snow along the edges of the homes and businesses, remnants of a storm that had swept across the northern communities the day after the destruction.

Near the rear of the city, hidden in the northeast section, was a stone structure. It had a subtle, castle-like appearance, a building that served as the mayor's house.

Here, Boswell was hosting the other mayors to discuss the events of 16 Moonshadow.

When Tiernan walked up to the door, he stood motionless for several ticks. The guard waited for the order, understanding the depth of the King's turmoil and giving him the space he needed to prepare for what waited behind the doors.

Tiernan gave the order with a swift movement of his head. The guard tightened his face and reached for the door. Before he pushed it open, he shifted his hand toward the King.

"I'm sorry, Your Highness." His extended hand hung in front of Tiernan like a heavy weight. "I had a brother in the guards. I have not heard from him. You have my word that I will do whatever you need to avenge him and those we lost in Farna."

Tiernan's face remained hardened, a facade he had practiced on his way here. He gave the guard a curt nod, grabbed his hand, and held it for several ticks. "What was his name?"

"Phineas. He was a second lieutenant."

Tiernan let go of the guard's hand. "I did not know him, but if he's out there, we will find him. And if not, then this meeting will ensure that Abria honors his memory." He shifted his head to the right, motioning toward the door. "I'm ready."

The guard resumed his formal stance and turned to the door. He pushed it opened and, with a loud voice, silenced the room. "All hail the King of Abria."

The other mayors stopped talking. Tiernan walked in and took a seat at the table. The guard closed the door, leaving the mayors and the King to their business.

An uncomfortable silence filled the air. Boswell extended a hand to the group. "Right. Let's get started," he said. He stopped his arm in front of Tiernan. "King Tiernan, do you have anything you want to share from your trip to Farna?"

At first, he wanted to say no. What he saw there was too painful, too overwhelming to discuss. Then, he remembered, as King, it was his duty to push aside those feelings and lead his people.

The very reason for his stone-cold facade, lest he breakdown in a crying, emotional mess in front of the mayors.

"The destruction was absolute. A group of Abrian Royal Guards and I scoured the ruins. The Soul Sword is gone. I don't know if was destroyed or stolen. We saw many bodies, men, women, and…" His jaw shifted. "…children crushed by the fallen walls and buildings."

A hush fell over the room. Tibor, in his fatherly understanding and tone, shifted the topic from those they lost to the ones they saved. "Let's talk survivors. Many of us from towns near Farna have had an influx of refugees. Do we have an estimate? A general idea of how many survived?"

Rhys raised his hand. "I took it upon myself to tally those numbers. Based on the census from the western communities, we believe sixty-five percent of Farna survived and made it out of the city."

Thirty-five percent lost. Tiernan cried inside, but maintained his composure in front of the group. "Did you find my in-laws? And what about my grandparents? They were helping to relocate Elven refugees from the Forest. I lost track of them these past few months."

Tomek raised his hand from across the table. "Lugh and Róisín are in Clericsfold. They were helping a group of Elves get settled in before the attack, and I saw them myself before setting out for Lorelei."

"Before I left Alwyn to come here, Eislyn's parents had been located. They're staying with my son and his family. We'll make certain they have whatever they need," said Tibor.

Tiernan gave the men a slight smile of appreciation. "Thank you both. We need to talk about the rest of the survivors. Abria just lost its capital city. Can a place like Lorelei or Clericsfold, our two most populous cities now, take them all in? I would think those two communities would have the infrastructure to handle the influx of refugees."

Penrod of Oakshadow chimed in. "Right now, Abria is facing a crisis unlike anything in recorded history. We have Elven refugees spread out across the land, and the late Queen's parents' efforts have only scratched the surface of helping the Elves find a new home. But now? We have refugees from Farna as well. Not to mention Kane's faction running around."

Tomek coughed. All eyes turned to him.

"You have something to add?" asked Boswell.

"That was unintentional, but since you asked, yes. Two things, actually. One, like Rhys, I took it upon myself to calculate *their* casualties. I don't know how it compares to their overall numbers, but every attack on our cities appears to have led to their collective demise. Newfound Graelan magic powers seemed to help with the defense, not to mention the fortitude of city guards themselves. All things considered, our losses outside of the capital were minimal, whereas theirs seemed almost absolute."

Tiernan shifted at the mention of the deaths in Farna.

Tomek continued. "Combining that with our scouts' report of complete inactivity on the Northern Plateau, I think we can say their coup has failed."

Ulrich of Milston spoke up. "Over the years, we've built watchtowers on a few select peaks of the mountains to observe the Northern Plateau. There has been zero activity since that day. The report from Tomek's scouts would confirm our findings as well."

The group looked at each other, some showing signs of victory and others relief. "It's over," one of them whispered.

Tiernan's cold visage did not change. "You said two things, Tomek. What's the other?"

The assembled mayors quieted back down.

Tomek looked at Ulrich, his annoyance evident. "Kane's forces may have been decimated, but we've also been observing a significant number of other creatures exiting from the Cave of Tera. Something Ulrich's watchtowers would be unable to see from their high and mighty vantage point."

Tiernan groaned inside a little. *That was an unnecessary dig. We cannot defeat our enemies if we're trying to one-up each other.* "Other creatures?" he asked, hoping to deflect any potential conflict between the two.

Tomek shifted uncomfortably in his seat. "One group was of what I can only describe as bipedal lizards. About as tall as any of us. They had claws like dragons and teeth like an alligator. Some were green, others had a sandy appearance. All of them headed southeast toward the Valley."

The group fell silent once again. Creatures like these were unheard of in Abria and only rumored to exist in other lands.

After letting the image rest in the other mayor's minds, Tomek continued. "Other creatures too. Bear-like Graelanoid creatures. Giants. One-armed green creatures that seem to match the Elves' description of the orcs from the exile. The list goes on."

"If they're coming from the underground caverns, it's not unreasonable to assume these are somehow related to Zoran," Tiernan stated without emotion, trying to maintain his facade.

The other mayors, accustomed to Tiernan's typical attitude and charged responses, found his lack of reaction unsettling.

"So, what now? We've replaced Elves and Graelan rebels with *monsters*?" asked Boswell. "It's another Dark War, especially if Zoran is the one leading the charge."

The silence in the room was deafening.

Boswell contorted his face in displeasure. "Okay, moving on. What about this magic element? Every settlement in Abria has reported the spontaneous appearance of magical abilities within its populace. Is it a widespread phenomenon?"

Tiernan motioned his head to Rhys. "Your power seems limited to Wind Magic. No other powers like teleportation or a Cloak of Invisibility?"

Rhys confirmed with a slight tilt of his head.

"Even my wife, wherever she may be, has a singular ability. Absorption. It gave her the power to manifest other skills, sure. But as soon as she absorbed another being's magic, what she could do changed because her only gift is Absorption. Her profile matched whatever capabilities they had."

"What are you saying?" asked Penrod.

"It seems as if full mage-like abilities are rare. My sister had many and would fit the accepted description. She could heal, cast fire, encase enemies in a weird glass-like prison. Stuff like that. What we're seeing across Abria is more like a singular ability that only manifests itself during intense emotional distress. There's a difference between a population of mages running around and powered citizens with an extra-special skill or two. I don't think magic in Abria is something for your next King to worry about as they deal with these monsters."

Tiernan let his words linger. One by one, they realized what he was saying.

"Next? What about our *current* King?" asked Tibor.

Chapter 22

Intermissio

Tiernan put down the quill. Tibor's question had been a difficult one back then. Recalling it now was just as hard. Tiernan leaned back in his chair. Next to him, a crackling fire burned bright, its flickering glow bathing his solemn face in the light of its orange flame. He stood up and walked over to it. He rubbed his hands together over its warmth, then turned around to heat his back.

Tiernan moved over to the window in his bedroom. One change he hadn't adapted to in Lorelei was the weather. The first month of the year, Begynde, was never cold in Farna, at least until after the magic dispersed.

He had never seen such snowfall as he had here. Glistening powder blanketed the community as an icy breeze blew in through his window. Tiernan shivered, pulled the shutters together, and returned to the table. He read the last sentence he had written.

"Next? What about our current King?" asked Tibor.

Tiernan closed his eyes and picked up the quill.

It was in that moment I announced my intention to step down as the King of Abria. Despite my efforts, I had failed, miserably so. There was nothing more I could do for my people.

My wife was gone, living somewhere in a distant land. My son was with her. I hoped to Aila, anyway. Eislyn was raising the presumed heir to the throne alone because of my failures. While these circumstances had forced me to become an absent father, I could never forgive myself. Family is Strength, and mine could not rely on me to help them.

Instead, I volunteered to travel the land. To tend to the refugees throughout Abria as best as I could. To find the guard's brother, Phineas, if he had survived. My role, the title Father had given me as a Protector of Abria, would take on a new form. I couldn't save my people as their King, but I could at least assist them with whatever difficulty they faced.

My wife and I had sold Borun Mill not long after the birth of our son, and the considerable dinage I earned from the sale would help the displaced from Farna instead of gathering dust in my family's already overflowing coffers. Dad's carpentry business had made us rich, something their simple home betrayed before becoming King and Queen.

So, on the second day of Darkember of 922NE, just a few weeks before the next Moon Rise, I resigned. I recommended Rhys as my replacement to lead Abria and promptly left the room. I later learned the mayoral council agreed and, with a unanimous vote, put him on the throne. Since Rhys was unmarried and had no heir, someone else would become Manus. The city elected a man named Driscoll who had a passion for ancient Abrian history.

Lorelei, with its fortified walls and proximity to the shipping lanes at Northwick, despite the inclement weather, would serve the Kingdom's new capital. I don't know how Tibor took this news, as their relative isolation now that Farna was no more would leave Alwyn unguarded from another attack. Perhaps they would follow in the footsteps of Idlewind and become another kingdom-within-the Kingdom.

I learned there was even talk of renaming Abria. I didn't care. Like the situation in Alwyn, the election of a new Manus in Idlewind, forming a new council, and so on, those political decisions were none of my business. I kept my head out of any discussions such as those whenever possible from that moment forward. No one needed my failed leadership telling them what to do or how to do it. I only made one request of the new leadership, that they would send an expedition to find my wife and son.

And thus began my travels. I spent the first four months of 923NE in Oakshadow and another four in Alwyn. Thousands of Farna refugees moved to these two cities. I never asked Tibor about Rhys or about the potential dispute with Northwick. It wasn't any of my business.

I left Alwyn and finished the year in Milston, helping skilled laborers from Farna find new occupations in the mines. From there, I drifted for almost all of 924NE. I don't remember much of the year, instead spending my time sleeping in tents or the occasional stay at Fabled Wonders.

Almost two years to the date after Farna fell, I decided to go back to where it all began. I walked into the Drunken Alligator in Lily of the Valley, lamenting my journey and failure as this land's ruler. There, a chance encounter with an old man inspired me to write the first half of my story: The Tale of Tiernan.

This is the second half, The Legacy of Enid.

Tiernan paused. "Is this the end?" He flipped through the pages. The story bearing his sister's name was so much shorter than the one carrying his.

"Her legacy is ongoing, my King."

Tiernan turned around and rolled his eyes. "Of course you'd show up now, Old Man. I was wondering when you'd make another appearance, if ever." He smirked. "I was hoping it might be never."

Zachary laughed. A loud, boisterous laugh. One that wasn't too dissimilar to…

Tiernan shook his head. "So, where have you been these past few months?"

Zachary picked up a book from Tiernan's table.

One that hadn't been there a moment ago. Tiernan rolled his eyes again. He recognized the binding as one of the transcribed versions of *The Tale of Tiernan.*

Zachary made what sounded to Tiernan like a mocking grunt. The Old Man flipped through various pages, circling the room with his head buried in the book. "Interesting. Curious insight. Hey, how did you know some of this?

"Some of it came from other people. Things I heard over the years."

"Ah. I see." Zachary closed the book. "Well. I can already see from this side of the room that you have far fewer pages than this story. What would Enid say? What does the shortened manuscript tell you about her legacy?"

Tiernan shrugged. "I'm running out of things to talk about?" He chuckled. "No. No, she'd say I'm stupid and never should have started writing in the first place."

Zachary laughed again.

I wish he would stop that. Tiernan raised his eyebrows, realizing he was okay with self-deprecating humor but not laughter from others, especially the Old Man.

Zachary appeared next to Tiernan in the blink of an eye, somehow traversing the length of the room in less time than it took for a tick on a tokei. "That's not what Enid would say. Remember this. Wherever you go next, keep notes. This story, her *legacy*, has a lot left in it." Zachary put his hand on the former King's shoulder.

"You heading out again?" Tiernan asked.

Zachary changed subjects by pulling Tiernan around with his hand. He got close enough to his face that the latter could feel the Old Man's breath on his cheek. "Listen to me. I know you're still working through things. You wanted closure back in the Valley with your first book. You might not realize it now, but you started the process. This will finish it. When King Rhys summons you today, answer him. Things are about to get interesting."

Tiernan turned his head back to the piles of papers on the table. "But how—" Before he could ask, Zachary's hand left his shoulder. He shook his head at the Old Man's behavior. Tiernan didn't even bother to turn around to see if his visitor was gone.

He knew Zachary had already disappeared.

Instead of trying to find him, Tiernan picked up the quill.

After I finished writing The Tale of Tiernan, *I moved to Lorelei, taking King Rhys up on his original offer of residency from almost two years earlier, one that came just before I began my travels. Back then, he said I could live here, out of sight for as long as I needed.*

When I arrived in Lorelei after my time in the Valley, his offer stood.

One day after settling in, I found the courage to request an audience with him. There, I learned that, in my absence, Zoran's presumed monsters had wreaked havoc. Almost every community in the land had felt the heartache of his minions. This explained why Tammith said too many had forgotten a time before Zoran.

The Second Dark War had terrorized the populace. Zoran himself had not been encountered. Kane was gone as well, with no one knowing what happened to him. Some wondered if he perished in one of the attacks, though Rhys' guards never found a body.

No Graelan dared venture into the Rosewood Forest to search for the Dark Elf. His absence led to rumors of his demise during the battle as well, or possibly during a monster attack, though exploring the Forest for his body was not worth it. If Folas was still alive, he left the people alone, and that was enough.

I found it strange that I had never encountered any monsters myself, even while sleeping in tents throughout the plains or the occasional overnight in the eastern half of the Valley Woods. The ferociousness of the creatures and my continued safety made no sense until I remembered the Mind Shield. Its power continued to surprise me. Did it keep the monsters from attacking? Or did it merely keep them from seeing me? Did the dragon that destroyed my home know I was there? Or was it unable to see the city until the Elf teleported me away because of the shield's power?

These things didn't make sense, but I accepted them as the new normal and moved on.

On my first day in Lorelei, I gave Rhys my manuscript. He immediately turned it over to his scribes for duplication and binding.

Within a month, he disseminated copies of the story throughout all the Kingdom. Told me that too many people had forgotten what it was like before Zoran. Before Kane.

Just like Tammith had said.

To be honest, I don't know what good sharing my story was for the Kingdom. Rhys seemed to think it would give the people hope.

If I'm being honest, I'd like some of that hope too.

Chapter 23

Three Defenders

Tiernan walked through the halls of the much smaller Castle Midir. The naming was obvious. Rhys chose to honor his late father and renamed the stone construction after the fallen Manus. Compared to Castle Abria, it only had two much smaller towers, one of which acted as Rhys's private study and bedroom.

Tiernan occupied the other. Both structures had been built since Rhys ascended to the throne. *Stone cold gray. A far cry from the vibrant golden hue from back home.*

"Hello," said a passing castle attendant.

Tiernan nodded. He had been lost in thought again. *I wonder how many people here know who I am.* Tiernan ran his fingers through his hair. Now short and almost a boring standard haircut more common for a member of the Abrian Royal Guard, he also had recently began growing a goatee. He hoped these two changes might act as enough of a disguise if anyone thought they recognized their former leader.

A gust of icy wind blew in through a nearby window. It felt like needles on Tiernan's skin. Though he didn't react, he mentally huffed in annoyance. *Why would* anyone *choose to live in this part of the Kingdom? It's nothing like Farna.*

The mere thought of his hometown brought sadness to his heart. He stopped and closed his eyes. He could still see the joy, the love, and the sense of excitement that predated Kane's rebellion. The sun shining overhead, children playing Smithblitz in the streets, dogs and cats running free. Even as a child, he knew his home was special.

No more. I need to stop this. He opened his eyes and continued walking, ignoring the wind blowing through the lower level of Castle Midir.

Just outside King Rhys' private study stood two guards. One of them raised his sword as a matter of instinctive caution. The other nudged him and mouthed 'It's him.'

The guard with the raised sword mouthed the word 'Who' in response.

Tiernan let out a quiet sigh, relieved that his changed appearance seemed to be working.

"Come on through, sir. King Rhys has been expecting you," the other guard stated. Tiernan nodded and smiled with a feigned sense of politeness. As he passed through the entryway, he thought he heard the man say, "King Tiernan."

But that's not right. Maybe he said former King. That would make more sense. Also, only one of them recognizes me. Maybe the longer my goatee grows, the fewer who will remember my face.

"Tiernan!"

Rhys was out of sight. It took Tiernan a moment to realize the King's voice came from the adjoining wash room. He walked over to Rhys' desk. On the top were battle plans, casualty reports, and updates from the various cities across the land. He picked up one.

Oakshadow. Four bandit raids. Two subsequent attacks from tall Graelanoid-like giants. Ninety killed since Moonshadow. He swallowed. He had left Oakshadow before he visited Alwyn. Things had been peaceful the entire time.

Sickened, he picked up another. *Lily of the Valley. The bipedal lizards raided a gathering in the Tolith Market. Valley residents fended them off, but not before…*

Tiernan dropped the report, unable to continue reading. He had never seen the bipedal creatures in person, but had heard stories of their ferocious nature. Another one caught his eye.

Milston. Continual attacks from tall, bipedal bear-like creatures. Fourteen residents killed in the past month.

"They only get worse. An entirely new species we haven't seen before has been sighted flying over the Rosewood Forest. Or is it the Darkwood Forest? Do you know what we're calling it these days?"

Tiernan turned around to see Rhys walking in and pulling a tunic over his head. "Did I come at a bad time? I didn't mean to intrude," he asked the still-dressing King.

A look of confusion crossed Rhys' face. "Hmm? Oh. Sorry. No, I just got back from a military exercise with the Royal Guards. I needed to get cleaned up before our guests arrived. Besides, I sent for you."

"I think the answer depends on who you're talking to," Tiernan replied.

"Answer? What answer?"

"The question you asked about the name for the Forest. In my travels, I found the formerly blinded Elves call it the Darkwood Forest, almost as if their time under Folas' control imprinted the new name on their psyche. But if an Elf was always aligned with Abria, they still call it by its original name."

Rhys continued dressing. "I wonder if the blinded Elves will ever go back to the original name? Then again, changing the names of places seems to be the norm. How are your accommodations here in Castle Midir? I thought it was a fitting tribute for my father."

"It is. Did this place have a name before?"

Rhys laughed. "Just the mayor's house. I'm sorry we haven't had much time to talk since you moved here a few months ago." He pulled his robes over his shoulders but left them open, smiling at Tiernan. "I'm glad you did. It wasn't safe for you to be wandering the countryside unprotected, especially with all those monsters out there." He buttoned the robe and tied it with an ornamental belt.

Tiernan raised his eyebrows and leaned on Rhys' desk. "I dunno, it wasn't that bad. I don't know that I encountered anything more than a few bandits here and there. Speaking of which, I thought we dealt with all the rebels years ago."

Rhys made a sound that sounded like a half laugh and a half grunt. "You'd think so, right? Here's the odd thing. They keep appearing! We can't figure it out. I talked with the mayors and none of them were aware of any missing persons or dissenters. So, these aren't new rebels, but they're also not the ones from before. It's very strange.

"In any case, that's not why I called for you. I just felt it was important for you to know."

A strong sense of unease hit Tiernan. "For me to know what?"

Rhys put on his crown, though it was less of a piece of metal and more of an ornate hat. He saw the former King's expression. "It's something they used to wear in Idlewind. A tonglin. My father stopped the tradition, but I thought it would be a small way to honor where I came from."

"Know what?" Tiernan didn't want idle pleasantries to detract from the issue at hand.

Rhys turned and looked in a mirror to straighten his tonglin. "Two months ago, right before you arrived, I sent letters to all the Kingdoms we've traded with over the centuries. The Isles, Lonlin, Watodo, and Lyra, as well as others we haven't encountered, such as Kinswatch and Infernus. We used an old map we found buried in the back of a book in the Alwyn Böchord to send ships to those we thought we could reach. Here." Rhys handed the map to Tiernan as he continued to mess with the tonglin.

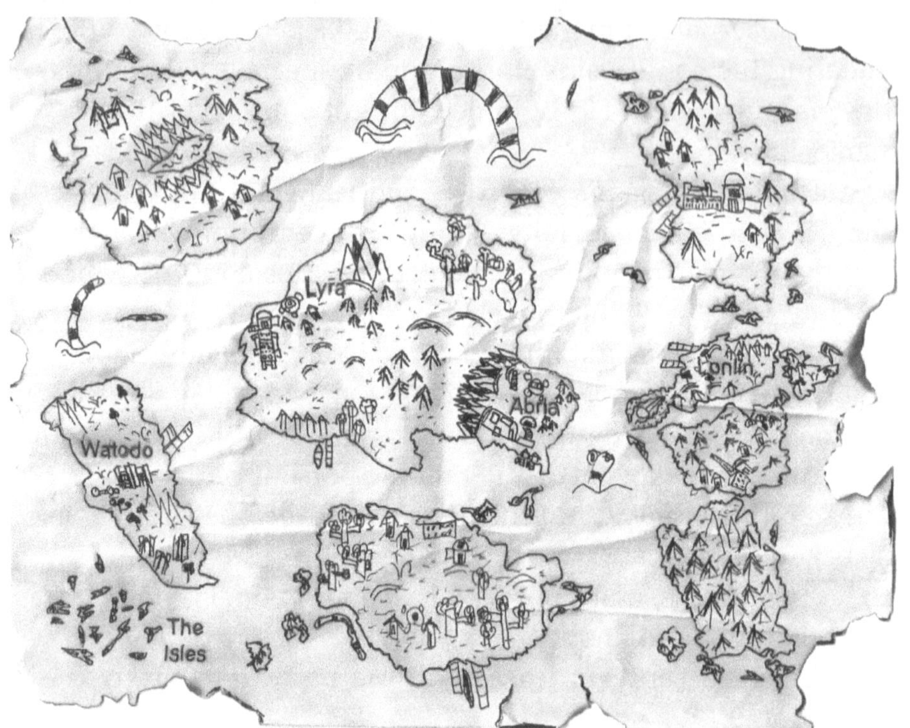

Rhys continued, growing impatient with the tonglin. "This must be why my father stopped the tradition. This thing is impossible to straighten. No matter."

Tiernan inspected the map, pulling it close to his face and trying to make out the details.

"We don't know how up-to-date things were with it. It appeared to be based on a loose understanding of the world from centuries ago, and we know it's incomplete with some liberties. Our land's coastline isn't exact, as you can see here." Rhys pointed at the Windale Desert.

"But it was a starting point. So, I commissioned expeditions, brave souls willing to risk their lives to try to reach the other regions. We all know how rough the waters are out there."

Tiernan handed the map back. "It's why trade outside the Kingdom is so difficult. It's why my wife lost her sister on a simple fishing excursion." Tiernan's voice shifted. "Speaking of my beloved wife, have your search parties had any luck finding her?"

"Not yet, but we will."

Tiernan shifted his gaze toward a window to the west.

"We've been following the routes your father mapped for us when they began trading with Lonlin through the Port of Alwyn. While we never heard from several of our ships, three new individuals will arrive today. In fact, they made landfall in Alwyn two days ago and, after resting up, booked passage on a ship traveling around the Abrian coastline toward Northwick. If all is on schedule, they should have docked there this morning and be on their way here right now."

"Wait. Back up. Letters? New arrivals? Who are we talking about? And why?"

Rhys put his hand on Tiernan's shoulder. "They're the defenders who will help us secure the future of the land we once called Abria."

A quiet woman walked down the streets away from the Northwick ports. Her long, brown hair extended from a top knot as the rest flew in the breeze, which was especially chilling compared to the temperate climate she preferred. She shivered, annoyed by the temperature of the surrounding air. It was much, much colder here even if they were at the same general latitude as her homeland. The currents of the Great Sea brought warm air from the south, creating a perfect environment for year-round planting, harvesting, replanting, and so on. Those winds were what made Lonlin a proud community of farmers, providing food to other kingdoms and lands throughout Grael.

The woman was thankful her cloak and connected wool skirt provided some protection from this season of Frost. She smirked to herself, thinking its cerulean to indigo gradient would make it impossible to know if it was a natural coloration or if was freezing like her skin.

Her large arrowhead shield, secured to her back atop her preferred long bow, reflected the rays of Graelian sun. It twinkled in the light with a unique design embossed on it: a series of small, glimmering pink flowers circling a single golden figure. This caught the attention of several nearby dock workers. She shivered again, and this time heard a slight rattle as her bodily reaction caused her golden armor to clank against her weaponry.

As she moved through the streets, her stomach growled. She decided it was time to look for a place to eat. With her emerald green eyes, she spotted a name of an establishment she had seen in Alwyn when she first arrived in that community.

"The Drunken Alligator. Does every town in this frozen Kingdom have one of those things?" she said.

"I ate there twice yesterday back at the beach town. They have this drink here, Dori's Ale or something. Disgusting stuff. Pales in comparison to what the Emperor serves in the Royal Palace."

The voice interrupted the woman's thoughts. She turned to see the first of her two companions standing next to her.

His green outfit contained all the markings of a seasoned soldier. It consisted of a repeating pattern of circles along the bottom of his surcoat. His coal black hair had what she assumed to be an artificial red streak from the front to his crown. He carried a long stringed instrument on his back that never seemed to be in the way despite its impressive size.

He smiled as he spoke again, the warmth behind his hazel eyes exuding joy. "I heard one of the other patrons say something about a beast of the ocean back there. What do you think, Firefly?"

The woman, broken from her observations by the mention of her name, found herself unsure of what to make of him or their other ally. Firefly turned away. "There are always rumors of beasts, Shig. We hear about them in Lonlin too. I've seen plenty of creatures and monsters these past few years, though nothing the likes of which they described."

"Just because you cannot see something does not confirm its absence," a soft voice said.

Firefly stopped and turned around to acknowledge her.

It came from a woman standing next to Shig. A woman who had caught the attention of every passing man in Northwick. Her flowing navy cloak surrounded her equally grand green skirt. It touched the ground, yet didn't seem to absorb any of the snow along the path.

Firefly noticed her outfit wasn't a two-piece tunic and skirt, but rather a full dress. The top featured a vibrant floral pattern. Her belt and satchel, with its long extension down her left side, looked to be more practical than functional.

Her skin glowed with a pink, rosy-like quality to it. Firefly wondered if it was a reflection of the woman's striking red hair that extended down her back.

"So, Airvede, isn't it? You're telling me there really are great beasts that roam the ocean?" Firefly asked with a hint of sarcasm.

Airvede just smiled. "What I'm saying is that until about four and a half years ago…" She paused as she put her hand over a still-healing wound on Shig's hand.

"Hey, what are you doing?"

Airvede's hand glowed bright white, an almost eye-searing light that faded as fast as it appeared. "As I was saying, I couldn't have done that," she finished. "And do I look any different from how I did back then? No. Just because you can't see it, Firefly, doesn't mean it isn't there."

Airvede looked up at the Drunken Alligator. "I know we're all hungry, but isn't the King of this land expecting us? To delay may offend his leadership, and then what? Will he send us home without accomplishing our task? His letter to my country's Paxtin made it sound urgent."

Shig rubbed his stomach. "I mean, I would like to eat soon too. But, maybe she's right. What do you think, Firefly?"

Firefly looked at both of her companions. She sighed deep. "Fine. Let's find the person we're waiting for. They said he'd be by the central well, didn't they?"

Firefly motioned with her right hand for the other two to lead the way. Airvede stayed motionless. Shig looked at the two women, shrugged, and bolted off.

"After you," Airvede said.

Firefly wasn't sure what to make of it, but didn't push the issue. She turned to follow Shig. By now, he was weaving through the streets toward the well. In the town's busyness, she would have lost sight of the peculiar man if it hadn't been for the odd instrument he called a sanshin strapped to his back bobbing above people's heads.

Chapter 24

A Meal with the King

Tiernan stood along the wall of the main dining hall within Castle Midir next to a group of gathered attendants. He asked Rhys if he could be here, a request that seemed to excite the former Manus. Tiernan didn't know why it mattered to either of them, other than perhaps a curiosity if there was any connection to Zachary's mysterious reappearance.

He looked at each attendant. Each held something for the King and his new arrivals. Some had food, others a platter of drinks, and so on.

Tiernan looked down at his pad. *"Continue doing what you've been doing. Just make notes. Your role can be the official castle scribe."* Tiernan mulled over Rhys' words as the door opened. Through it walked a brown-haired woman wearing a blue cloak with a unique color gradient.

An attendant rushed to her and escorted the woman to one end of the table. *A head seat? Who is she if they placed her in such a position of honor?*

Another woman walked in. Tiernan raised his eyebrows, unable to ignore her grace and beauty. She seemed to glide across the room with ease, minimal foot movement visible below her dress. *Oh, Eislyn, how I wish you were here with me.* A second attendant rushed to her side and seated her to the first woman's left. They smiled at each other as if they had already met.

"I'm sorry. I got sidetracked. A vendor was selling the most amazing smelling concoction." The first woman flipped her head around to the voice of the third visitor and gave him a look that said to be quiet. He waved her off and continued walking in as a third attendant seated him on the right.

Rhys is assigning their positions. But why? Tiernan noted this in his journal as the King entered.

"Welcome to Castle Midir!" Rhys walked in from one of the side doors with his arms outstretched, his voice loud and full of energy. Tiernan noted this, too, an uncharacteristic mannerism he hadn't seen before from the former Manus.

Rhys took his seat, waving off the attendant who tried to pull it out for him. "As you might have guessed, my name is Rhys. I'm the King here and I'm sure you're wondering why I summoned you from your homes to this strange land."

"I wouldn't say strange. Nothing has seemed out of the ordinary so far, but the question of why has crossed my mind several times," the first woman said.

"Straight to the point. I like that. The letter I received back from your Prime Minister spoke to your leadership capabilities, Firefly. The Heroine of Lonlin. Thank you for coming. The work you did saving your school was incredible. The Prime Minister said you're inquisitive and not afraid to take charge too, which means I know exactly what role you're going to play here."

Tiernan froze as Rhys said her name. *Firefly.* As he repeated the name in his mind several times, the mental images Zachary had showed him back in Borun's living room rushed to the surface. He looked at the other two. *Right. That means the other woman is named Airvede. And the man. His name is…*

"You can tell all of that from what she just said? What are you, a mind reader?" The young man chuckled at his accusation.

"No, Shigeharu, I am not—" Rhys began to say.

"Shig," the man corrected. "Call me Shig."

Right. His name is Shig. Zachary, who are these people? Why did you show them to me last year? Tiernan made some more notes in his journal. *If these three can make it here, it means I can make it out, too. Eislyn, I'm coming! No matter what it takes, I will find you.*

Rhys smiled. "Okay. Shig. I am not a mind reader. Instead, look at Firefly. The way she sits in her seat. The way she's taking this all in. Her face says more than her words."

Tiernan and Shig looked at Firefly, the latter silencing the room with an icy gaze. Tiernan noted this interaction and resumed scribbling notes in his journal.

"See. Right there, she's telling you who's in charge," Rhys explained. "But did you not pay attention to my words? I said her Prime Minister sent a letter. Just as your Emperor sent one along with you. Interesting title, by the way. Ashigaru Paladin. Here, a paladin is just an outdated description from centuries ago, but your people have adopted it as an official title of honor."

"You still haven't answered the question." Tiernan looked up as Airvede continued. "The letter you sent said it was urgent. That this land was under a grave threat. An ancient evil, if I remember correctly. I didn't get to read it, but its contents were explained to me, nonetheless."

Airvede gestured around the room. "Forgive me, King Rhys, but things seemed peaceful in Northwick. Here, they're somber but not desperate by any means. People are busy buying and selling. The beach town to the south mentioned a great beast, but that was several years ago from what I gathered."

She's perceptive, Tiernan thought.

Rhys put his hand on the table, pounding it slightly. Then he snapped his fingers, pointing one at her though in a respectful manner. "You, Airvede, are the one I'm most curious to meet. A White Mage. Your country's Paxtin — curious name for a leader, by the way — said you had grown fond of levitating. Something an old healer friend of yours taught you, if I'm not mistaken."

Tiernan stopped writing once again. The other two arrivals looked to Airvede as if this was new information to them, as well.

Rhys continued. "You're full of mystery, Airvede, that's for sure! You're the first mage we've had here in several years. Don't get me wrong," he said as he tore off a piece of bread from the table and passed it around. "We have magic in this land now. It's just that, except for a brave warrior who gave her life to protect us, most Abrians can only wield one magic power. Like this."

Rhys opened his hand and generated a ball of Wind Magic. He released it, hitting a decorative shield on the wall. It fell to the ground and made a loud clanging sound that bounced throughout the room.

"That's mine. Wind Magic. Comes in handy during battle, I admit. But you, one that can levitate and heal? That's two powers. The last person who had more than one magical ability was named Enid." He smirked. "Wonder what else you can do?"

Tiernan raised his head, pausing his note taking as Rhys said his sister's name. Images of the battle flashed through his mind, along with memories of the unusual jewel that had not been found or seen since that day.

Rhys motioned around him. "In fact, it's because of her sacrifice that we now call this Kingdom by its new name: the Land of Enid."

Tiernan froze. He had heard the rumors, but never anything formal. Those he had spent the past two years with would have been indifferent to the name of the Kingdom when they were more focused on rebuilding their broken lives.

Rhys gave Tiernan a sideways glance. "Here, we called her the Dragonborn, a title worthy of her reborn nature and enduring legacy. Indeed, it's her legacy that gives us hope." He turned his attention to Airvede. "Let me see, about four and a half years ago, you woke up and had magical powers. The night before, you went to bed yourself. The next, you could do miraculous things. No explanation why, it just happened. You went to bed as you and woke up the White Mage."

Airvede didn't deny the accusation, but instead pressed the King. "You still haven't answered the original question. Why are things so desperate here that you had to summon the three of us?"

Firefly sat forward. "She's right, Rhys."

Tiernan raised his eyebrows at Firefly's decision to not use his title. *That's something only a select few of us would dare to do. She's confident in herself, that's for sure.*

Rhys snapped his fingers and a previously unseen castle attendant entered from around the corner. He carried three books, bound in a navy material. Etched in gold along the spine, Tiernan's mouth fell open as he saw the writing.

The Tale of Tiernan.

"I mentioned the Dragonborn. A man who suffered a great deal wrote this book," Rhys said as the attendant handed copies to the other three. "More appropriately, the Dragonborn's brother penned this last year before disappearing. No one knows when Tiernan might reappear, but until he does, this is what we have. Freshly bound copies of his words of wisdom. His memoirs, if you will. Come, let us eat. You can skim through these pages and we'll talk more after."

Shig closed his book.

Firefly looked up as she took a bite of the fruit on her plate. "You're done already? This thing is huge!"

Shig picked up a piece of dragon fruit from his bowl. "I didn't read the *whole* thing. I skimmed it. Got the highlights. I have a feeling I'll have plenty of time in the upcoming weeks to read the story. Shame about the guy's sister. Sounds like this Dragonborn was special. But it also sounds like she's the reason Airvede over here can do the things she can do."

Tiernan winced at the mention of Enid's sacrifice. He then noticed how Airvede sat motionless as she flipped through the pages, staying focused on her own reading of the passages.

A moment later, Tiernan saw a hint of understanding wash across her face. While the other two conversed about the page length, Airvede's eyes darted from left to right. She flipped to the beginning of the story, then back to the end again, speed reading the pages. Tiernan couldn't tell for certain, but had a feeling he knew which section she was reading.

When my sister released the magic back into the world. The red jewel that started and ended it all. Wonder if she can explain it to us?

Rhys interrupted the argument between Firefly and Shig to move on to more pressing matters. "I know you have many questions."

Shig spoke up. "Yeah. I think a big one is what happened *after*. The twins fought the bad guys. One of them died or something. You're the King, not this Tiernan guy. And I'm pretty sure your city guards welcomed us to Lorelei, not Farna. There's a lot of the story we don't have."

Rhys smiled. "Much of that you'll need to discover for yourself."

Shig sat back in his seat, frustrated.

He acts like I used to, Tiernan thought.

Rhys continued. "For centuries, the Kingdom of Abria was peaceful. Until recent years, our only conflict was the first Dark War a long time ago. This current conflict is the second. As you read the book, you'll find references to Zoran. Our people fought him in that conflict long ago, and he's the same enemy we face today. The records from that earlier war are lost to us now. All we know about Zoran is what King Tiernan recorded in his memoirs."

Firefly folded her hands together. "We've heard of Abria in Lonlin. Traded with you some, though not without grave risk because of the almost impassable waters. It's a shame too. Our two lands are so close geographically. On a clear day, you can see just the smallest hint of your eastern mountains from the highest edge of Robinson Cliffs."

Airvede shifted in her seat. "Your people were known to us as well, but your story was incomplete. My mentor mentioned his brother lived here and had mastered the art of folding plants and other items into potions."

Rhys smiled. "Well, for once that's new information. What is your mentor's name?"

Airvede cocked her head sideways. "Tolby."

Rhys shook his head ever so slightly. "Don't recognize the name. Who was his brother?"

"Cleris," she answered.

Tiernan nearly dropped his pad. He regrouped himself and, much to his relief, saw that Rhys had a similar reaction at the table with his spoon.

"Cleris founded one of our major cities. During your travels, be sure to stop by Clericsfold. You may be able to teach them a thing or two about their own history."

Airvede crossed her arms. "The biggest thing we knew of Abria, excuse me, the Land of Enid, was that it was rumored to be an extraordinary place full of joy and happiness that we're all connected to somehow."

Rhys gave Airvede a sympathetic look. "And let me guess. Your Archives *start* with the New Era just a little under one thousand years ago."

Her silence confirmed his suspicion.

Rhys pointed at the other two. "That goes for the rest of you. You probably know very little of what happened leading up to the New Era in your own lands. I'm sorry to say, you won't find those answers here either. We know virtually nothing of what came before the New Era. Just legends, such as the *Song of Aila*, that paint an incomplete picture."

Shig and Firefly exchanged another look as she shrugged. "What is the *Song of Aila*?"

"It's a play. A grand performance. One that, if this so-called Second Dark War wasn't plaguing our land, I would recommend you see over at Mystic Mornings in the Rosewood Forest. It's one of the best productions I've ever seen, and it's all based on loose records collected by a great man named Borun."

Tiernan took a deep breath. *How is it I never knew Grandpa himself helped write that?* Sadness hit his heart, reminding the former King of the decisions he had made years ago that kept a wall between his younger self and his now-deceased grandfather.

Shig lowered his head. "Those of us in the Emperor's court had always hoped what happened before the New Era could be learned in Abria. If the waters of the Great Sea would ever calm themselves and make regular passage here easier, of course. It's been one of the Emperor's passions since he ascended many moons ago. He even charged me, if possible, with discovering what came before."

"Same. Abria is spoken of so fondly in our Archives, but we know little about this land other than its rumored majestic presence." Firefly sighed. "And yes, our records begin 925 years ago."

Rhys gave Tiernan a quick glance back.

What's he doing?

The King snapped his fingers to an attendant. This man revealed an apple pie from under a cloche resting on a separate table. Rhys nodded for him to cut it.

"The three of you really should try this dessert. It's the same recipe from a royal wedding a few years ago, and the apples themselves were harvested from Northwick just up the road. I'm sure you saw the grove on your way here?"

Rhys caught the attention of a second attendant. "The deep cellar. Hurry."

They rushed away as the first served the three defenders.

"Don't eat just yet." Rhys smiled at the server. "Do your thing when your friend returns with the cream."

"Yes, Your Majesty," they said as they stood by the table.

Rhys cleared his throat. "The history of the New Era is not the issue at hand. It's Zoran. We don't know how, but it's because of him Farna is no more and Lorelei is the capital."

A coldness fell over the room with that last statement. Rhys continued. "It's because of their uprising we now call this the Land of Enid — not the Kingdom of Abria. This is our way of honoring the royal family who suffered so much in service to our people."

Rhys removed his tonglin and ran his fingers through his short hair. "A man from Clericsfold named Kane betrayed our Kingdom, and you'll find his story in that book, too. During the last push of their rebellion, a bronze dragon appeared. Somehow, it ties back to Zoran, but we don't know how.

"Just remember this: servants of Zoran do his bidding. Unfathomable monsters. Our cities have been attacked and plundered. Our people killed. Their spirits broken. Tiernan wrote his book so that we would remember what life was like *before* everything fell apart. And I believe, with your help, we can restore what we lost."

The second attendant returned, carrying what looked like a small bucket. Rhys raised his eyebrows to the man who had served the pie.

He hovered his hand over the piece on each plate in front of the three defenders. A tiny ball of fire formed in his palm, warming the slices.

"Now quickly!" Rhys said to the second attendant.

Using a small scoop, she pulled out what appeared to be solidified cream from the bucket and put a ball of it on the plate next to each. The attendant touched each with the tip of their fingers, sending a hint of Frost Magic into the cream.

"We call it iced cream. Goes well with warmed apple pie. Regardless of the answer to my next question, this is my gift to you. It's a hint of what Abria used to be like. Joyful. Happy. Peaceful. The blending of different worlds into a unified Kingdom of grand beauty."

The three visitors exchanged a look as Rhys continued. "So, my question is simple. Will you help us defeat Zoran?" He smiled. "Enjoy your pie."

Before the three answered, Tiernan discreetly slipped out of the dining hall. Though he still had his limp, he bolted back to his chambers, his speed belying the constant throbbing in his leg. He pushed the door open with a shove and ran into the room.

Laying on his bed were the Mind Shield and the robe from Zachary.

Chapter 25

On the Way to a Memory

Firefly led the group through the open doors of Castle Midir. Shig was deep in conversation with Airvede. They entered the streets in front of the building as the denizens of Lorelei went about their business.

Firefly stopped and turned back to the group. "King Rhys encouraged us to head south toward a village he called Lily of the Valley. Said something about his forces heading north to secure the town of Milston."

Shig opened the small traveler's journal Rhys gave him during the meal. "He thought we might help the owners of the Drunken Alligator in the Valley with something. Didn't say with what, though." He shrugged. "I guess you were right, Firefly. Every town in this land must have one of those taverns."

Shig's face turned into one of a man in heavy thought. "But maybe we should head north with the guards? See if we can lend some assistance?"

Airvede turned and gave Shig her opinion, arguing that they should follow Rhys' instructions. As the two of them conversed, Firefly noticed a robed man walking a few dozen meters away. Looking destitute, he limped with each step he took. Not long after she began observing him, the man sat down in one of the grassy areas near a fork in the road leading deeper into Lorelei.

Firefly glanced back at her two companions, both of whom were still deep in a heated debate. She smirked, thinking back to her time at the Maxina Dormitory when her roommates, Kai and

Minerva, would argue over the silliest of things. She walked on ahead of them and in the direction of the man.

I can see her coming. This is it. I'll know if I can trust them after this, the man thought.

Airvede and Shig finally noticed Firefly's absence. "Do you see that?" the White Mage asked.

"Yup. Wonder what she's doing?" Shig said.

Firefly kneeled next to the robed man. "Are you okay?"

The man kept his head down and didn't answer. His right leg, extended out straight, seemed to be a point of pain for him.

Firefly noticed. "Hey, is your leg okay? Did you injure it somehow?"

The man groaned. *Not much of a lie,* he thought. *This leg has never been the same since the underground battle.* He leaned down on it harder, putting his hand on his kneecap.

"Is he okay?" Airvede asked from behind.

Firefly shook her head, unsure and confused. "He hasn't said anything, but appears to have pain in his right knee." She smiled to herself while turning back to the man. "Also, apologies to you two for wandering off. It's not something I want to get into a habit of doing here in the Land of Enid. None of us know the layout, so let's stick together as much as we can. Agreed?"

Airvede gave the two of them a slight nod.

Shig smiled. "I mean, I could go check out the Drunken Alligator here in Lorelei. For reconnaissance, of course."

"Shig," Airvede said with a curt shake of her head.

He chuckled to himself. "Okay. Fine. I'll wait. It's just that Tiernan's book mentioned Lorelian Mead and…"

"Shig, let me think," Firefly said. She turned back to the Paladin with a serious expression. "Remember, Rhys said I'm in charge. And right now, this man is our priority. Then you can go find your mead. Deal?"

"Deal. So, what's wrong with him?" Shig took a bite of an apple, something he had taken from their feast as they walked out of the King's domain.

Firefly thought for a moment, pointed at the man's knee, and looked back at Shig. "Do you have one of those healing potions the king gave us?"

Shig furrowed his brow and motioned his head to Airvede. "I thought she was a White Mage. Gifted with healing and other types of defensive magic. Isn't that what he said back there? We only have four potions for now and you want to part with one of them already?"

He's practical. Full of doubt and suspicion. Reminds me of myself at his age, the robed man thought.

Airvede twisted her mouth. "You're not wrong, Shig, but it doesn't work that way. I may be able to treat his *injury*, but he'll also need something to restore his *strength*."

"I saw him limping as he walked by. A potion, Shig. We can buy more later. Rhys also gave us a small bag of their currency. Dinage or something. I'm sure a shop owner nearby carries more that we can buy." Firefly nodded to Airvede as she stood, having made her decision. "A potion, please. Give it to Airvede. She can heal his knee, let him drink the vial, and he can be on his way."

Shig opened his satchel and pulled out one of the yellow vials. He handed it to Airvede, who then kneeled down to the robed man. She placed her hands on his right kneecap.

Much to the man's surprise, he could feel the transformation within the tendons and joints. It reminded him of another healing experience from his younger years when he, in a fit of rage, punched a stone wall and had to rely on another mage to heal his broken fist.

Airvede smiled and then handed the potion to him. "Here. Drink up. You'll need to eat something soon, too."

The man stood and pulled back the hood of his robe. His vibrant red hair shone in the sun. His chiseled face, marked by the beginnings of a goatee and eyes that appeared drained, relaxed. He held the potion tight, then handed it back to Airvede as he reached for Firefly's hand to shake it.

"My name is Zachary," he lied once he was on his feet. "I wanted to see if there was goodness in you, if you would sacrifice a part of your limited inventory to help someone in need." He smiled. "You passed. Though…" He bent his knee. The pain was gone. "I'll admit, I wasn't expecting you to heal my leg. I've been dealing with that injury for several years."

"How did you hurt it?" the White Mage asked.

"In battle against the same forces you're here to defeat. I would be honored if I could accompany your entourage. Please, let me take you to your next destination. It will be my way of saying thank you. Do you have a map of the land? Where are you headed?"

"Lily of the Valley," Firefly answered. "And come to think of it, no. We don't have a map. Old Rhys back there didn't give us one."

At the mention of the Valley, a twinge of pain threatened to take his breath away. *It's okay. The Valley. Breathe. Remember, you can help them. You were just there a few months ago, and you were fine.*

"That's the village south of here. A wonderful place. Come, I'll tell you more about it. I may also be able to answer questions you have about this land."

"What do you think, Firefly? After all, Rhys said you're in charge," Shig said, a slight mocking implication within his voice.

Firefly rolled her eyes. Her jaw shifted, thinking it over. She then put out her hand. "Welcome to the team. I'm Firefly, leader of this small band of defenders." She said the last part with a commanding sense of irony, willing to accept Shig's playful joking while asserting command of the group. "This is Shig and the woman who healed you is Airvede. You said your name is Zachary?"

He paused. *It's too soon to tell the truth. Though I'm sure my sister would chastise me for lying to them.* He grabbed her hand. "I think there's a weapon vendor up the road. They should sell potions there if you need more. And I heard one of you is interested in Lorelian Mead?" He pointed at Shig. "Kinda early in the day to be drinking, don't you think? But," he said with a smile, "If you want the best, it's right here. Lorelian Mead is brewed in the city, and takes its name from Lorelei itself."

"More than any kind of drink, ethers would be helpful," said Airvede. "Do you sell them in this land?"

He nodded. "They're harder to come by in the outlying cities. You'll have a much easier time finding them in Clericsfold where they're crafted and most of our Elves now live."

Firefly put her hands on her hips. "Let's go. All this standing around and talking is making us lose daylight."

My sister would have liked her. "I'd be happy to lead the way, since you don't have a map." The group followed his lead as they navigated the busy streets of Lorelei.

While shopping at the vendors, a thought crossed the man's mind. *Sorry to steal your name for this, Old Man.* To his surprise, Tiernan chuckled as he heard the real Zachary respond to him in his head.

Why do you think I gave you the robe, my King?

The city guard motioned to the stable hand as she brought four horses to the open fields in front of the entrance to Lorelei. Tiernan hopped on one of the horses and grumbled.

Shig saw his displeasure. "Problem, Zachary?"

Tiernan adjusted himself in the saddle. "This isn't my horse."

Shig pursed his lips. "So…?"

"There's a certain bond between Graelan and steed," Tiernan explained.

"I wouldn't know," the younger man said.

Firefly rode up next to the pair. "Don't you have horses in Watodo?"

"We do, but members of my order, the Ashigaru, don't ride them. They're how we tend to our fields or how others outside of the Emperor's Court travel the land."

"So which way is Lily of the Valley, Zachary?" asked Airvede.

Tiernan pointed. "This way. Everyone ready?"

The group checked their inventory and gave him a nod.

This should be fun, Tiernan thought. "Alright then. Hee-ya!" He gave a slight squeeze to the horse's sides. The steed took a few steps forward walking before moving into a trot.

The other three did likewise, with Shig struggling the most to figure out the right amount of pressure.

They rode for a long time without talking. Tiernan looked eastward toward the Valley Mountains. They lined the coastline, starting north of Lorelei, extending southbound to the Windale Mountain range.

I wonder where Tolith lived. He had heard stories of his grandfather's Elven friend, though never had the time or the interest to learn more about him.

Until now, that is. Tiernan realized his return trip to the Valley might give him a chance to explore the market, not as the planner of the games or a former king in hiding, but as one with a genuine interest in history.

As a person wanting to know more about his past.

They approached the outer edge of the small section of the Valley Woods that bled over to the east side of the Lorelei River. Tiernan brought his horse to a stop. The women followed his example as if they knew exactly what they needed to do to stop a horse.

Shig struggled and pulled back on the reins. Instead of stopping, the horse bucked its rider off of its back. He landed on his backside, but jumped up to protect his pride and honor. Below his feet, the crunching sound of snow was the only sound any of the group made. Shig dusted the powder from his clothing and grinned at the group.

Firefly rolled her eyes and muttered under her breath. "I can't believe we're here to save this land, and he can't even ride a horse." She leaned to the side toward him. "Listen. Next time, sit up straight on your seat bones. Toes up, heels down, and say 'Whoa' with a commanding voice. Deep but soft. Got it?"

Shig nodded.

Tiernan pretended to ignore the exchange, though inside was laughing at the younger man's inexperience. *He can't be more than eighteen, nineteen at most.* "You'll do better next time, kid. So, after we cross into the woods, the Valley will live up to its name. We'll be descending, though the community gets less snow than what you see around you right now because of its geography. Don't get me wrong. It snows in the Valley. Just less than this," he said as he waved his hand around. "Also, it'll feel warmer, but don't let that deceive you. The Valley can still be quite chilly during this time of the year.

"When we arrive in the town itself, we'll have to ride through the streets to the inn on the south side of the village. That's where the stables are located."

As Tiernan finished speaking, two bandits came running out of the woods brandishing weapons. One held a long-handled axe. The other had some kind of broadsword. Both carried shields with a symbol Tiernan did not recognize.

"Kinswatch," Firefly said in a hushed tone only Tiernan heard.

The second charged toward Shig, sword high in the sky. Because he had rolled ahead of the others when his horse bucked him, he was the easiest target.

"Shig, watch out!" yelled Firefly.

The bandit slashed his sword at Shig. He avoided the blow like a well-trained fighter. As the bandit's weapon missed its target, Shig slid to the side and swiped his right foot under his attacker's leg.

The man fell into the snow as the first bandit ran at the group. Firefly pulled out the bow attached to her armor and grabbed an arrow from her quiver. With incredible accuracy, she released an arrow toward him.

As it flew across the field, Tiernan noticed the tip had a perfectly cut stone in a sharp triangle point. The arrow dug itself deep into the man's left shoulder.

The bandit dropped the shield in pain, then used his other hand to pull the arrow out. He tossed it to the side.

"Don't move, or the next shot won't be into your shoulder," Firefly warned.

Shig stood over the first bandit. The rebel rolled to his side and jumped up. He swung his shield offensively at Shig, who did a somersault jump backward to avoid it, sending snow into the man's face. As the Paladin came back around, he kicked the bandit in the chest and pushed him backward.

Airvede extended her hand. The man attacking Shig froze in place.

"Hey, I was having fun!" Shig protested.

"We don't have time for fun." Airvede made a fist with her hand, which seemed to place the man in some kind of lock.

"What did you do to him?" the other bandit asked with an underlying, angry growl in his voice.

"It's called a Barrier spell, though it's not permanent. It'll wear off in a day. I suggest you carry him from here until then. I can heal your wound if it'll make it easier."

The bandit looked to the other rebel, whose face begged for help. Instead, the axe-carrying bandit ran away, leaving his accomplice helpless.

Shig kneeled down. In the attack, the frozen bandit had dropped a small satchel. He picked it up and wiped the snow from it. "Hey guys, he dropped this. Looks like some, what do they call it?" Shig sorted through it. "Ah, right. Dinage." He raised it to the bandit. "Thanks. I'll be taking this for our troubles."

The man tried to protest, but surrendered. Shig smiled and turned to face his horse. Tiernan caught a look of mischief on his face as the Paladin flipped back to the man and pushed him backward.

The bandit fell to the ground, groaning as Shig hopped back onto his nearby horse. "What did you say? Sit up, feet down or something?"

Firefly groaned, her annoyance evident. "That's if you want to stop the horse. To move, apply pressure to her side like this." She pressed into the side of her steed with her calf muscles. "Careful, Shig. Not too much. Come on, I'll see if I can guide you."

Tiernan and Airvede exchanged a look of amusement as the group trekked off toward the Valley Woods.

As they entered the outer edge of the region and began their downward descent, Tiernan shivered. The air here, while warmer than the thick snow-covered plains they had just left near Lorelei, had a distinctive vibe he knew all too well.

Welcome home, he thought to himself. The light from the sun, now obscured by the trees, made Tiernan feel as if he was saying goodbye to one chapter of this journey and hello to another, unknown adventure.

After they were inside the Valley Woods for a while, Airvede trotted up next to Tiernan. "Your king mentioned bandits. Is this something we should expect throughout the Land of Enid?"

Tiernan winced at the name, then chastised himself for doing so. Airvede noticed, but said nothing.

"Do you want my honest answer? I can't tell you. Those shields were a symbol I did not recognize. It wasn't from Abria, it wasn't Kane's rebel forces from several years ago, and it's not something I've seen in any of the books in our Archives. If it helps, that's the first I've encountered them, but that doesn't mean it'll be the last."

"They're from Kinswatch," Firefly said with an uncomfortable air to her voice.

Airvede began to ask about Kinswatch. Before she could, the group heard a blood-curdling scream.

Chapter 26

A Healer's Journey

Tiernan looked at Airvede. His mind filled with possibilities. Did the bandit break free and attack someone else? Was another traveler in trouble? He gave his allies a look that said follow me and, without thinking, turned the horse around. He applied pressure with his thighs to push it into a gallop.

The others followed close behind. Airvede caught up to him first. ""That came from back there," she said. "It sounded fatal."

When they emerged from the edge of the Valley and approached the outer edge of the woods, all four brought their horses to a dramatic stop, including Shig, who had remembered and listened to Firefly's instruction from earlier.

"Catrin help us. A diocene," was all Firefly could say.

Standing over the man's body was a bipedal, green, lizard-like creature. It seemed oblivious to the group.

Tiernan squinted. Its eyes were glazed over, a milky-gray color he hadn't seen any creature, animal, or Graelan have before. Its claws were well over ten centimeters long, now stained in the color of the man's blood.

Airvede screamed, an unexpected combination of rage and sadness from the so far soft-spoken persona of the White Mage.

Firefly, acting on instinct, pulled out another arrow, loaded it onto her bow, and released it toward the creature. It dug deep into the beast's side, causing it to roar. It looked around, almost as if searching for who attacked it and where the defiant scream had come from. A few ticks later, it appeared to shake off the defensive instinct as it looked back to its victim and lunged its face toward the bandit's chest.

Before it tore into him with its teeth, Firefly released another arrow. Her weapon pierced its hind leg and the beast roared in anger. It ran away, disappearing in the snow-covered grasslands toward the Lorelei River.

Airvede dismounted and rushed to the man's body. "Please, by the Moon, please. Don't do this, please." She fell to her knees next to his fallen body. The creature had torn into his chest, and he didn't appear to be breathing.

"Help me!" she cried to her companions.

Shig dismounted and ran to her.

"His tunic. Remove it. Fast." Airvede's hands were already glowing.

Shig did as he was told, using his bare hands to tear it from top to bottom. The gashes across the man's torso were easier to see now, appearing as if the creature's claws dug deep enough to reach his heart. He was bleeding profusely, fast enough that Tiernan suspected he would not last long if he wasn't dead already.

Airvede placed her hands, white light and magic circling around them in a dazzling display, on his torso and closed her eyes. His body lit up from head to toe, enveloped in her healing powers.

By now, both Firefly and Tiernan had walked up.

Sister, if you could only see this.

The man's body stopped glowing with his wounds appearing to be gone. Airvede looked up to Shig. "A potion. Pour it down his throat."

Shig fumbled through his satchel and pulled one out. He popped its lid off and bent down. Bracing the man's head, Shig then poured its contents into the man's mouth.

"Good." Airvede began pushing on his chest in a rhythmic pattern. "Come on. Wake up. I know you're in there."

After a few more compressions, the man coughed. He opened his eyes and tried to move his arms. Airvede released him from the Barrier. She made a fist over his body, and his arms moved without restraint once again.

"Thank you," he said in a hoarse voice. "I thought I was—"

"Dead?" She shook her head. "You were *close*. Far closer than you want to know. Another few ticks of the filo and you'd be gone."

Tiernan walked up. "A filo?"

Airvede looked back and pulled out a small device from her satchel. Shig and Tiernan both recognized it.

"A tokei!" they said in unison.

"What's a tokei?" asked Firefly.

Tiernan gave a partial explanation. "It's a long story. They help us keep time. But I guess you call them a filo in The Isles?"

Firefly raised an eyebrow. "Do you mean a watch?"

Airvede slid the filo back into her satchel and returned her attention to the man. "You've been given a second chance. The Moon looked upon you with favor. Remember this the next time you try to hurt another person."

The man nodded. Tiernan walked around him next to Shig. "Where are you from? Your shield. I don't recognize its symbol." He gave Firefly a quick glance and remembered what she said a little bit ago. "Are you from Kinswatch?"

Before the man could answer, his body began to vibrate. He screamed again, not too dissimilar to the cry from earlier. His agony seemed even greater than before. As a pink mist enveloped him from head to toe, it resonated with an ever-increasing speed and intensity.

"Help me!" he begged of the group.

Airvede's helplessness was on full display as she tried to cast a Barrier to hold him. It had no effect. As the pink mist grew more obvious, his skin turned the color of stone. His face locked in a final, horrified expression with his slack-jawed cry for help, the last sound he would ever make. His eyes fixed on the overhead sky as they glazed over in the same stone color. A powerful vibration took hold of his new form, gigantic cracks forming all over.

The vibration increased in magnitude as his body broke, crumbling into a dozen pieces. These continued to pulsate and crumble into even smaller chunks, continuing the process until there was nothing left but a pile of small pebbles. A few ticks later, those withered away to dust, leaving no remains of the bandit.

Midir. That's the same thing that happened to him. Tiernan's rage erupted as he turned toward the northwest. He made a fist with one hand and screamed, extending it as he yelled. "Zoran!"

Despite Tiernan's visceral reaction, Airvede seemed to take it worse. She pounded her fist into the ground, her breath increasing with each passing moment.

A somber atmosphere surrounded the group on the final leg of the day's journey. They arrived in Lily of the Valley just as the sun set on the distant horizon. Tiernan looked at the sky. A pink, purple, and orange haze spread across the Abrian stratosphere. He shifted his gaze to the south, catching the first few stars of the Ailan Huntress constellation beginning to break through the sky.

"There's the Snakehead," said Shig.

Tiernan flipped his head toward the younger man. "Snakehead?"

"Yeah. That series of stars. It extends from the horizon to the sky. We call it the Snakehead after the gargantuan reptile the first Emperor of Watodo defeated just before he founded our nation."

Tiernan laughed. "That's not a snake. It's a sword. Aila holds it."

"Aila?" asked Airvede.

"Yes. You know, the famed Huntress?" Tiernan couldn't believe they hadn't heard of the most revered warrior in all Abrian history.

"If you mean the woman in the sky, her name is Catrin," Firefly said, her attitude matter-of-fact.

The four of them laughed as their cultural differences and similarities sunk in. Four nations seeing the same thing and interpreting it in their own way.

Feels good to laugh, thought Tiernan. Their horses' hooves echoed off the buildings at the northern end of the village.

The northern end. Tiernan closed his eyes, not wanting to get an unintentional glimpse of his grandfather's grave and statue. As they passed the Drunken Alligator, Tiernan pointed it out.

"Tammith and Dagnall. They're the owners of this Alligator. They're the people King Rhys said you could help." He pointed to the left. "The Tolith Market is that way. It's set in a crescent design. You'll find a statue of its namesake in the middle. I recommend Kellag's Kitchen. Its name might sound kitschy, but you won't find a better meal in the Valley.

"The stables are this way." Tiernan cast a glance at the central well, remembering the last time he saw his father leaning against its masonry. *The last time I ever lied to him. Good ole teenage angst. How I wish I could take it back.*

They arrived at the southern inn and dismounted. Shig volunteered to take the horses to the stables, while Tiernan — still under the guise of Zachary — checked them into their rooms. He paid the usual fare, and the attendant gave Tiernan four keys.

Tiernan climbed the stairs, thinking to himself how he had never been inside of this particular inn. Standing in the hallway waiting, he saw two of his companions. The women smiled as he handed a key each to Airvede and Firefly.

"Tammith is known to work late. She also has a Kingdom-famous bread you'll love." He cleared his throat. "I'm going to go give Shig his key. Before your group leaves town, meet me for breakfast at Kellag's Kitchen?"

The two women agreed, so Tiernan turned to leave.

Firefly grabbed his arm. "The bandit was from Kinswatch. I'd recognize that symbol anywhere. They invaded Lonlin a few years ago. All of their ships wave a flag with that design."

She let go and turned to her room. Tiernan wondered what story there was to tell with the invasion. All he knew of Firefly was that she was known as the Heroine of Lonlin. *Was it during this invasion she made a name for herself?*

Tiernan passed Shig as he walked down the stairs. "Here's your key. Everyone gets their own room here."

"Thanks, Zachary. Hey, can I call you Zach?"

Tiernan smirked and blinked his eyes in amusement. "Sure." He turned and finished walking down the stairs, through the inn's lobby, and out the doors. He cast a brief glance toward Borun's residence, itself obscured by the other homes from this vantage point.

Tiernan returned his gaze to the sky. Most of the stars were peeking through as the sun had set some time ago. The former King walked through the village alone, a layer of snow crunching below his boots with each step. He approached the well. He stopped to reflect. *I'm sorry, Dad. I wish you and Mom were here with me right now. I'd give you a big hug and tell you everything I ever did wrong. Please. Just let me be a kid again.*

A mouth-watering smell billowing in the air caught his attention. *Tammith's bread. Some of it might help ease my nerves.* Tiernan patted the stonework of the well and continued northbound. In the distance, he saw the famed establishment where he had spent several days last year penning his memoirs. With an unexpected pep in his step, Tiernan finished his journey to its front step. He glanced down at the door and eyed the Borun-designed knob. This time, it did not pain him to admire its intricate beauty. *Grandpa took his trade to heart.* He allowed himself a half-smile, grabbed the handle, and pushed the door open.

The Drunken Alligator had the same lonely vibe as it had when he came here late last year. This time, rather than sit at his teenage-vandalized table again, he went straight to the bar.

Tammith greeted him. "Hello, my King. Back so soon?"

"Tammith. It's good to see you again. Could I ask you a favor?"

"It depends. What do you need and will you be ordering Lorelian Mead?"

Tiernan laughed because, for the first time that he could recall, he saw a playful banter behind Tammith's eyes. She already knew the answer.

"If I was going to order mead, it would be from anywhere but here," he said with a grin.

"Get out." Tammith resumed her work, trying to appear angry. "In all seriousness, what do you need? I'll see if I can accommodate it."

"It's two favors, actually. I'm traveling with a..." He searched for the word. "...team. Rhys sent them here to help you with something. I'd appreciate if you didn't refer to me as anything but Zachary."

Tammith harrumphed. "Anything else?"

"Your bread. And water?"

"You *know* I don't appreciate it when you only order water," she retorted with a smile.

"I'm not eating it here. Here." He dropped some extra dinage on the counter. "This is for one of your staff to bring it to me."

"Where?"

"Family is Strength."

Tammith gave Tiernan a knowing nod. He turned and raised his hood as he cast one last look around the Alligator.

Tiernan sniffed the air, catching a hint of the bread already baking, along with the distinctive combined smell of mead and paint which he was growing fonder of with each passing day.

No wonder Grandpa loved it here so much, he thought as he pushed the door open.

Tiernan rounded the corner of the building and continued north. After what felt like an untold amount of time walking, he arrived at the garden he had ignored when he first arrived.

The state of the ground saddened him. He breathed a deep sigh, realizing it made sense. With the problems facing the land, keeping a garden looking beautiful was secondary to basic needs.

Basic needs such as survival.

Tiernan walked by the rows of flowers and decorations. The intoxicating smell of the Valley Rose filled the air. Unlike last year, he felt strong enough to face the memory this time.

Standing tall, its face turned toward a beloved lumber mill, hands on its hips, and possessing a long, flowing beard, the statue of Borun looked across the village with love and pride.

"Hello." Tiernan's voice was barely a whisper. He cleared his throat and said it again.

"Hello, Grandpa." Borun's statue continued to smile in the direction of the mill that once acted as a driving force of this community's economical basis. Tiernan closed his eyes.

"I'm back. Again. I, uh, I went to your home." Tiernan closed his eyes. "I read your journal. You said I'd make a great King someday. Wonderful, I think, is the word you used."

Tiernan opened his eyes. "Farna is gone. Another dragon, one that could control the ground itself, attacked. It wasn't docile or welcoming, like the two you encountered from the day of my birth. This one tore the place apart. It killed so many. Men, women, children, buried under a sea of rubble."

Tears welled up in Tiernan's eyes. "We were already under attack. Kane's forces had Farna surrounded. From what I later learned, it was a Kingdom-wide coordinated attack. We would have won if not for that accursed dragon."

Tiernan sobbed. "I failed. Eislyn escaped, but I don't know where. I haven't seen my wife in over two years. My son has probably forgotten me by now."

He wiped his eyes. "I came here last year looking for closure. I found some, but I…" He took a deep breath. "How can I say Family is Strength when my family is all gone?

"All of them. They're either dead or in hiding." He leaned against the base of Borun's statue. "Why did you give me this burden? Why did you pass the throne to *us*? I can't do this alone. I need my family."

Tiernan didn't hear the person approach him from behind. "Family gets us through the hard times."

Tiernan wiped his eyes and turned around to see Airvede standing at the edge of the garden.

"May I come in?"

Tiernan motioned toward an open bench and sat on it.

She walked in and took a deep breath.

"You smell it, don't you? That's the Valley Rose."

Airvede sat down next to Tiernan. "It's a powerful aroma." She raised her head up to see Borun's face. "This man is an important figure here."

Tiernan straightened his robes. "Are you asking or making a statement?"

Airvede continued. "I didn't hear much of what you said. I'm sure that's a story you'll share when the time is ready. What I did hear was your comment about family, which struck a chord with me."

"Struck a chord. That's a phrase only musicians say. Does that mean you play an instrument?"

As Tiernan asked, another person entered the garden. It was a member of Tammith's staff carrying bread. He also had a pitcher of water and a single glass.

Tiernan reached out to take them from the man. "Ah, thank you. Give my regards to Tammith." He looked toward Airvede. "Could I trouble you to bring us another glass? For my friend here."

The man nodded and headed back to the tavern.

Tiernan tore off a piece of bread and took a bite. The soft texture was exactly as he remembered. While still chewing, he tore off a piece and handed it to Airvede.

"When I finally had the courage to talk to the woman who eventually became my wife, I used this tactic to break the ice."

"You're married?"

Tiernan nodded. "If you can believe it, yes. I convinced the daughter of another Drunken Alligator owner to marry me." Tiernan swallowed his bite. "One from a different town. Are you married?" Tiernan wondered how Airvede would respond, as she had so far showed a curious tendency to answer some questions, but not others.

Airvede took a bite of the bread. "Yes. My husband's name is Eamon. We've been together for quite some time, long before I became the White Mage."

"Kids?"

Airvede finished chewing. "Yes, two."

She's beginning to open up to me, and she understands family, too. She left them to come help us, so she knows the pain of separation. No ordinary mother would do that. Tiernan gazed up at Borun's statue once again. "You took the man's death back there pretty hard. I get the impression you're not just a mage. Am I right?"

This question she didn't answer, which Tiernan let rest. He stared into the dusky sky. He thought he caught a glimpse of a shooting star flying overhead, though the flash was fast enough it could have been a figment of his imagination. The server from the Alligator returned with a second glass for Airvede. Tiernan gave the man two gold din for his troubles and a third for Tammith as a way of saying thanks.

"Three gold din. That's a lot, isn't it?" she asked.

Tiernan took another bite of bread. "My family has resources. Tell me about yours."

She tore off her first bite. After chewing and swallowing, she paused in a moment of hesitation. Her face softened as she opened up. "I was adopted, fell in love with the boy next door, and we've been happily married ever since. I developed an interest in becoming a healer." Airvede laughed. "I had been studying under Tolby for some time when our land was rocked with a horrible sickness. We called it the Galvan Scourge. Anyway, we had been working hard to find a cure." She smirked. "Turns out, the cure was me. Once I became the White Mage, it was nothing to heal the land. I'm just thankful my children could stay safe from it."

Airvede's story revealed something he hadn't expected. *Enid's legacy is much larger than I realized.* "One of the past rulers of this land was adopted, too. You're in good company." He pondered her story for a bit. "Here in Abria, well. The Land of Enid, as they call it now, we've had similar stories. Graelans manifesting powers without warning. It all stems from what happened during the final battle against Zoran. The Dragonborn released the magic into Grael."

Airvede pulled out the book bearing his name from her carry bag. "I haven't worked my way through this quite yet, though I did read the last chapter. When we were dealing with the Galvan Scourge, Tiernan and his sister were busy fulfilling her legacy. And by extension, she saved my home."

The White Mage stood. "I'm sure you came here looking for solitude. I'll leave you be. Thanks for the company, Zachary. And the bread."

Tiernan watched as she left the garden. He wasn't sure how much longer he could carry on this charade under a false name. He looked back at Borun's statue.

"She knows more is going on than you're willing to say."

Tiernan leaned over to rest his hands on his knees at the sound of the voice. "Welcome back, Old Man. Sorry about stealing your name."

Zachary placed his hand on Tiernan's shoulder. "There's one thing I don't understand, my King."

Tiernan sat back. "Why didn't I come here before?" He sighed. "When I left the Valley for Lorelei, I felt at peace."

"And now?"

Tiernan stood and turned to face the old man. "I don't know how you do…this," he said, motioning to Zachary's sudden reappearance. "But I assume you're at least vaguely aware of the way Zoran's minions are wreaking havoc on the land?

"When I left here after writing that book last year, I felt at peace with my *past*. Now, I'm uncertain about the *future*. I knew about the emerging monsters when I stepped down. I didn't know they were this bad."

Tiernan sighed. "Will we win this war?"

Zachary walked around the bench and made direct eye contact with Tiernan, placing both hands on his shoulders. "I'm not a fortune teller. I only know one thing. Family is Strength. I've seen it time and time again. Those three," he said as he used his head to motion back toward the inn where Airvede and the others were staying, "know that too. That's why they're here."

Tiernan lowered his head. "But how will…" He stopped talking as he realized Zachary disappeared. Again.

"Of course. Why am I not surprised?" Tiernan picked up his notebook from the bench and returned to the inn. *Guess I'll have some writing to do tonight.*

Chapter 27

Split Paths

Good morning, everyone!" Shig sat down at the table where Firefly, Tiernan, and Airvede already were sitting. "How did you sleep? Did my sanshin playing keep any of you up? I hope not."

Firefly rolled her eyes. "Are you always this way in the morning? Give me a chance to get woken up before you burst in with your overeager antics, Shig."

Shig grabbed a handful of dates from the bowl in front of them. He tossed one in his mouth and spit out the pit. "No can do. Life is too precious. I choose to embrace it from the moment I wake up until my head hits the bed. I've already been out for a morning run and did some calisthenics in my room. It's going to be a great day. I can feel it."

He spit out another pit. "So, what were you talking about?"

"Zachary was just saying that we should stop in Whispersong. He thought..." Airvede extended her hand to Tiernan as if to say, 'Help me.'

"Ahern," he answered.

"Yes. Ahern. That his team could help you refine your horse-riding skills, Shig. We're going to need them to cross this land, and we can't have you getting hurt from your horse bucking you off at every stop."

Kellag approached the table carrying several trays of food. He placed them on the table. Behind them, one of his staffers handed him another tray.

"These are on the house. Compliments of the King!" He smiled at Tiernan, who gave a return gesture that feigned understanding.

Don't let my secret out! "If you could send *King Rhys* our thanks through a messenger, that would be wonderful."

Kellag raised his eyebrows as he realized he made an error, though he wasn't sure how.

"What is all of this?" asked Firefly.

"Twelve dishes, each inspired by or directly from a community across the Kingdom of Abria. Land of Enid." He laughed. "Whatever we're calling it these days. I'm sure it'll be something else by the millennium." Kellag pointed to each. "This is Lorelian Pinsa from Lorelei. My favorite, Mystic Cake from Oakshadow. My staff loves these, Mountain Oat Bars from Milston. And this one," he said with a gleeful smile, "is Farna's Favorite Pretzel. Every time we went to Farna for an event, we fell in love with these. I haven't mastered the recipe just yet, but I'm trying."

Kellag explained the rest of the dishes, finishing with Idlewind. "A man from Idlewind, their ruler named Midir, discovered my skills well over a decade ago. He passed that info on to the leader of this town, Borun."

Tiernan lowered his head at the mention of his grandfather's name. All three companions saw it, though they were thus far oblivious to the connection.

Kellag continued. "I visited Idlewind not long after Midir passed away. I talked to his wife and son who told me many stories about the Manus. And so, I present Midir's Warming Grains in honor of the man who made me who I am today."

All four thanked him and began eating.

"Oh, that's good!" Shig said with his first bite.

Tiernan made mental notes as to which dish each person went to first. He wasn't sure if it would matter for his story, but decided he didn't want to forget this moment.

You never know when it will be the last time you eat with someone.

Tiernan pointed to Whispersong in the distance. "There. Whispersong. This region acts as the primary stables of Abria." He sat on his saddle, bringing his horse to a complete stop.

Firefly rode up next to him. "You've been so kind to bring us this far. Are you sure you want to follow us the rest of the way there? I'm sure we can find a map somehow."

Tiernan didn't want to keep going, but knew he needed to see this through to the end — wherever that may be. He also knew, after the incident with Kellag that almost revealed his true identity, visiting Whispersong might reveal his secret.

Airvede brought her horse up to Tiernan's other side. "We mean it, Zachary. King Rhys charged *us* with this quest. You don't have to go any further."

Tiernan guided his horse to walk ahead, then turned around to face his companions. His mind flew through the possibilities. "Firefly, what was that request Tammith needed again?"

Firefly pulled out her small traveler's journal and flipped through the pages.

"She asked us to find a crystal hidden in a cave on the opposite side of the Lorelei River." Firefly closed the notebook. "I figured we'd tackle the task later. Why?"

Tiernan smiled. "It's not wise to travel alone. Why don't you and I go looking for her fancy rock while Shig and Airvede head south to Whispersong? Ahern and his wife Pernella, from what I've heard, are a hospitable family. They can host Airvede for a few days while Ahern helps Shig get acquainted with the nuances of riding a horse.

"Then, the four of us can meet back up at the edge of the Windale Mountains."

Airvede nodded. "I'd like some time to read the book Rhys gave us."

"It's up to you, Firefly," Shig said in an indifferent tone. "After all, Rhys made you the leader. Whatever you think is best."

Firefly pulled her quiver of arrows around. "I have thirty arrows. I could harvest some more from the Valley Woods."

"Then it's settled!" Tiernan said, forgetting for a moment that he wasn't the King issuing orders to his subordinates.

To his relief, Firefly agreed. "We'll see you both in two days. Think that's enough time for you to get your bearings, Shig?"

The Ashigaru Paladin nodded with enthusiasm and then squeezed his horse on both sides. The steed took off faster than expected. Airvede laughed as she followed him.

"After you," offered Firefly. "You seem to know your way around these parts."

Tiernan considered lying, but answered honestly. "I had some family who used to live nearby. I didn't spend as much time here as I should have, but I know enough about the layout of the land. Come on, let's go. I'll show you a shortcut."

Tiernan and Firefly tied their horses up against a nearby tree. A small, almost indiscriminate, cave stood on the outskirts of the northwestern edge of the Valley Woods.

Tiernan swallowed, remembering the last time he approached a cave entrance. It was in this moment it dawned on him that he didn't have a torch. He looked around for a stick and dried grass to try to form a makeshift one.

Instead, his companion lit up the cave entrance with an open palm. He stopped in shock, realizing that Firefly had kept her magical abilities hidden. He then noticed the Fire Ring on her finger.

"So, you can use those things?"

Firefly responded as she crept into the entrance. "I have no innate magic, if that's what you're asking. But somehow, I can use this ring. Someone in that beach town where we first arrived was selling it, and I thought it looked pretty."

She shrugged. "When I put it on, my hand lit up. The merchant almost didn't sell it to me, but I promised I'd use it for good. He relented." She cackled with glee, remembering the incident. "After I threatened him, that is. Come on."

The two of them slowly made their way into the cave. Tiernan touched the walls with his bare hand, feeling its slick and slimy texture. He looked down and noticed the dampness on the floor. He then sniffed and wrinkled his nose. The air smelled musty at first with a putrid smell just lingering in the background.

"I heard that sniff. You're smelling the stench of an orc."

"An orc? In Abria?" Tiernan didn't care if he used the wrong name for the land. There was no recorded encounter with an orc in all of Abrian history. The only awareness his people had of the creature was from stories passed down from the Elves.

Firefly stopped and turned around. Her surprise caused the light in her hand from the Fire Ring to brighten. "You've lived in this land all this time and have never seen an orc before?"

Tiernan shook his head. "In fairness, there are a lot of new creatures and monsters roaming about. Ever since Farna fell, there have been weird sightings all across Abria. That lizard thing we saw attacking the bandit? That's new. What did you call it again?"

"We call them diocenes." Firefly turned around as Tiernan quickly grabbed his notebook to jot that down.

He put it away and continued the hunt for the crystal behind Firefly. "Do you have a lot of strange creatures like this in your country? Lonlin, isn't it?"

A bat flew toward them. Both ducked to miss it. The creature turned back for another pass.

Bats don't do this.

It growled, baring its teeth.

Firefly pulled out an arrow and fired it at the creature. The arrow pierced its chest, knocking the winged form to the ground. As it struggled, a strange pink mist emerged from its mouth as the life left its body.

"That's right, Lonlin. Remind me to tell you about it sometime. And no, we don't, at least not naturally. Just the marrens. Vicious hunting avians. The diocenes and orcs were a part of the invading force from Kinswatch I mentioned. They brought more marrens with them, along with some other creatures too vile to mention right now."

Another bat flew at them. Tiernan pulled out his sword and defended the duo, swiping at the bat and knocking it across the tunnel. The sharpness of the blade was fatal, and as the creature died, more pink mist emerged.

Tiernan pulled the Mind Shield off his back and attached it to his left arm. "Why did Tammith need this crystal?"

"She didn't say. Only told Shig and me that it would come in handy soon. Offered us a large sum of your dinage for retrieving it."

Ahead of them, they heard grunting and snarling. Firefly raised her finger to her lips, telling Tiernan to keep quiet. She motioned for him to follow her lead as she put her back as tight against the wall as she could. Tiernan followed her orders just in time as a diocene came barging down the passageway.

It blew past them, searching for its prey. Firefly mouthed 'Now' to Tiernan and pulled out a trio of arrows. One of them had a red stone on the end. Tiernan gripped his sword as the arrows found their mark on the creature's neck.

The one with the red tip exploded in a fiery flame. The diocene let out a cry.

"Now, Zachary!"

Tiernan ran toward the beast as it squirmed and twirled in the cave. He plunged the blade into its back.

It let out a cry, then fell to its knees. Tiernan pulled the blade out as the creature tried to breathe, still on fire and now bleeding from its wound. A moment later, it stopped moving. The same pink mist emerged from its body and dissipated into the air. Tiernan turned around to Firefly for an explanation.

"They cannot see. They use sound to find their prey. The pink mist is new to me, though.

"And the red-tipped arrow?"

She laughed. "A gift from the Robinson Cliffs. Come on."

Firefly and Tiernan walked up to a large opening leading into a massive antechamber. Here, the putrid smell was almost unbearable. Tiernan hoped he could take a bath after this adventure.

Firefly elbowed him and pointed. She mouthed 'orc' and removed the Fire Ring.

Curiously, the glow of a Magic Ring never stopped once removed from the user's finger. It dimmed some, but the object continued to light up Firefly's satchel as she put it away. *The effect must be amplified when worn by a magic-enabled person.*

Firefly then pulled out a blue Frost Ring.

With the faintest whisper, he asked, "Are you going to explain this one?"

"Later," she said in the same low voice back to him as she used her hand to freeze four arrows.

The ring's ambient light was a subtle blue haze. It helped to illuminate the darkened corridor, giving off an ominous vibe that Tiernan wasn't sure if he liked or disliked. He wondered if his friend, Wayland, had ever sat in darkness admiring the beauty of a Frost Ring.

Firefly finished coating the arrows in her hand from end to end in ice, then handed them each to Tiernan.

"Hold," she said in the same whisper. "And follow."

He gritted his teeth as the coldness of the arrows chilled his palm. Together, they crept up to the entrance.

Tiernan could only see the shape of the orc with the faintest silhouette against the far wall. It looked larger than a typical Graelan, close to three meters tall. It cast a shadow much wider than even the strongest man in the old Abrian Royal Guard.

It appeared to be sleeping. *Will it be this easy?*

Firefly raised her bow and pulled the bowstring taut. She closed one eye, focusing on the creature's chest. Tiernan assumed Firefly was aiming for its heart, though he wondered how thick the creature's skin might be and if the arrow would even penetrate it.

He didn't have to wonder for much longer. Firefly breathed deep, as if time stood still for her. Then she released the arrow. It flew across the antechamber and found its mark.

Firefly grabbed another frozen arrow from him and released it toward the beast's torso. She fired the third toward its head and the fourth toward the creature's left hand.

"Come on!" Firefly pulled off the Frost Ring as she ran into the cave. She dropped it into her satchel and pulled out the Fire Ring from before, using its power to light up the room.

Tiernan followed her lead. The arrows had found their mark, freezing the creature but not killing it.

"Find the crystal. Throw me your sword!"

Tiernan tossed it toward her as he rummaged through the creature's belongings, using the edge of the Mind Shield as a scoop. He almost lost his breakfast as he realized what the orc kept as trophies.

The putrid smell was that of fish and other Abrian animals it had killed, some partially eaten, all left to rot. It was the first time he knew of a living creature eating the flesh of another.

He swallowed, pushing the sickening feeling aside as he continued to dig through the rubble.

Out of the corner of his eye, he watched Firefly. She used the sword almost as a blunt force instrument and repeatedly tried to jam it into the creature's chest. It was here he realized why she shot its left hand: it did not have a right arm, missing from the shoulder down.

"Come on, you worthless, green, ugly piece of slog!" She raised her hands high, gripping the sword's hilt with fierce determination, and brought it down as hard as she could. "This is for Cykela Academy!" She jabbed the sword into it again. "This is for everyone you hurt at my school."

Her eyes flared up. The Fire Ring burned bright, and a flame moved down the sword.

"And this is for my friends. May you burn until you can't breathe anymore."

Each thrust from her sword drove the blade deeper through the orc's tough skin. With the added effect of the Fire Ring, Firefly realized the error of her attack. She made eye contact with the creature and saw awareness of her. Its eyes fluttered as the effect of the Fire Ring passed through the sword and melted the ice on its body around the arrows.

"Uh oh. Zachary, we have to hurry. It's beginning to thaw." She continued to jab at it with the sword, this time in a different spot, lower on its abdomen and away from the frozen portions of its body.

While Firefly attacked the orc, Tiernan tossed rocks and other debris around the room. "Where is it?"

The shimmer from her flaming sword sparkled on a glossy surface. He smiled. Laying at the bottom of a pile was a purple crystal. Tiernan cleared the debris away to reveal it. Once uncovered, the crystal emitted a light almost as bright as the Fire Ring except in a beautiful violet hue.

"I found it!" He picked it up. No larger than his travel notebook, he dropped it into a pocket in his satchel. "Come on! Let's get out of here!"

Firefly turned and ran, tossing the sword to Tiernan on her way by. To his disappointment, the fire effect extinguished as the weapon left her hand. Tiernan glanced behind as they made it to the edge of the antechamber. The orc's head and hand were unfrozen, and it used its freed appendage to pull out the arrows just barely lodged in its chest.

"We have to hurry," she instructed.

Tiernan nodded as they passed the various bats and another diocene they killed on their journey into the cave. They heard the sound of thumping behind them moving at an increasingly faster pace.

"If it catches us, we're dead," Firefly said without any emotion in her voice.

It carried a weight Tiernan recognized. *She'd seen this before.*

The two picked up their speed, jumping over the body of the first diocene. As they approached the cave entrance, Tiernan thought of an idea.

"Firefly! Use one of those red-tipped arrows on the cave entrance."

"Now?"

"No, not now. As soon as we clear it."

She turned around and could see the orc charging. In her mind, she made the calculations she needed for her bow, figuring out the distance on the fly.

"Good thinking, Zachary. Okay, listen! When we get outside, grab the horses. Get them away from the entrance as fast as you can."

They saw the light ahead. The orc let out a guttural, hateful growl. It stopped. Tiernan was tempted to turn around to see why.

Instead, they ran harder and cleared the cave entrance. As he headed to the left to grab the horses, the body of the diocene flew past him and tumbled down the small hill leading up to the cave entrance.

Firefly smiled. "That pause was what I needed. Go, Zachary!"

Tiernan hopped on his horse and pulled the other by the reins. Firefly ran ahead in the opposite direction, pulled out the red-tipped arrow, and turned to face the cave's entrance.

"May Catrin give me strength." She pulled the arrow taut, breathed deep again, and released it toward the grasses right at the edge of the cave. "Long live Cykela!"

The ground lit up in a spectacular display of fire, blocking the orc from exiting the cave. Tiernan brought the other horse around to Firefly. She put her foot in the stirrup and hopped on as the orc howled from behind the wall of flames.

Firefly looked at Tiernan. "That was fun."

He laughed. "You call this fun?" Deep down, he admitted to himself that he had enjoyed it too.

Reminded me of sparring with Sis.

Chapter 28

Thoughts of Family

Firefly and Tiernan rode up to the same inn in the Valley they had stayed at just a night earlier. Both dismounted from their steeds and passed them off to the stable hand.

"I'll secure us two rooms again. Maybe we'll get a discounted rate for a second night's stay," he said with a smile. They walked into the lobby. Firefly took a seat as Tiernan visited the innkeeper at the desk.

A moment later, Tiernan returned and handed her a key. "No luck. They were almost sold out. Premium pricing even."

"Doesn't matter. With that crystal, we'll more than make up for it." She stood. "I'm hungry, but it's late. Are any of the restaurants in the Tolith Market going to be open?"

He shook his head. "I'm afraid not, but Tammith is sure to have something."

She laughed. "Shig is going to be furious if we go to a tavern without him."

He gestured toward the door and together they walked through the streets of Lily of the Valley. Tiernan didn't look at the central well this time, instead keeping his eyes focused on the Alligator.

He pushed the door open. *Beginning to get used to this*, he thought. Behind the bar stood Tammith. *Time for that charm Eislyn loved so much.*

He walked in and sat on a chair with a sense of confidence he hadn't had since his teenage years. Tammith saw him and, noting his changed countenance, came right over to them. Firefly sat down, casually observing the interaction.

"You again, Zachary?" Tammith said to Tiernan with a slight twist of her head. "And Firefly, isn't it? Good to see you. Where are the other two?"

"Whispersong. Shig needed horse lessons," answered Firefly.

"We got you something," Tiernan said with a smile.

Tammith couldn't help but return the expression. "I haven't seen you smile like that in a *long time*," she said.

Tiernan pulled out the crystal.

"You found it." Tammith picked it up. "I have to admit, I didn't expect you to."

"You want to tell me why it's so valuable? It reminds me of the crystals they used when building a tokei. But it somehow seems different. Care to explain?"

Tammith shook her head. "Nope. Let's just say I have plans. Meanwhile, I'll get your din. Grab a table. Whatever you want, it's on me." She laughed. "Even water."

Tiernan knocked on the bar with an amused grin. It felt good to feel good again. He looked around and got excited when he saw that his favorite table was open. He motioned to Firefly, who waited for Tiernan to sit before heading over.

"You act like you own the place," she said. "Do you?"

Tiernan laughed. "No. Like I said, I've been here before. My family has roots in the Valley."

Tiernan noticed her face changed when he said family. He gestured to the chair on the opposite side. Firefly pulled it out and sat.

Tiernan smelled an aroma, one that made his stomach growl. Though he had already had some just last night, he felt giddy knowing what was coming.

Tammith's bread.

A member of her staff brought over a glass of water. He asked Firefly what she wanted, and she pointed to the water.

"Sometime, you'll have to try Dorian Ale. It was my father's favorite drink."

Firefly nodded. "Dorian Ale, huh? Shig thinks it's called Dori's Ale."

Tiernan couldn't hold back the grin. "You want to know the crazy part? It's not even the real stuff! They call it 'ale' only so people buy it when they're attending theatrical shows up at Mystic Mornings."

The server brought the pair a glass of water each. Firefly grabbed her glass and downed it almost immediately. "Another, please." She wiped her mouth. "Mystic Mornings. Is that the place to watch that play about the woman in the sky? *Song of Aila* I think?"

"That's the one. My father was fond of Dorian Ale. Preferred it wherever he could get it, even over Lorelian Mead."

Firefly sat back in her seat and put her feet on another nearby chair. "You've mentioned your family several times now. Would you care to elaborate?"

Tiernan raised his glass of water to Firefly. Confused, she waited for the server to bring her another pint. Once she had it in her hand, she raised it along with him.

Tiernan clinked their glasses together. "To family and what they mean to us."

Firefly smiled at Tiernan's words. "To family."

Both took a drink.

"You know, toasts like that are usually better served with Lorelian Mead. But not yet," he said.

"Shig had a pint of that drink in Northwick right after we arrived. Acted like he enjoyed it, probably why he made us stop off in Lorelei for another round."

The server brought the bread to the table. Each of them tore off a piece.

Tiernan's eyes almost rolled back in his head. "I can't get enough of this."

Firefly's eyes widened. "This may be the best bread I've tasted in my life."

He nodded. "Hey, something to keep in mind for Shig. Lorelian Mead gets its name from Lorelei, where it's brewed, right? You've been here long enough to figure that out. Here's a hint. It gets worse the further you get from Lorelei. Something about the fermentation process breaks down when they ship or haul it. By the time it gets to Alwyn, it has a distinctive sour flavor. Not the best." Remembering his drunken escapades with Wayland on the eve of the wedding, he softened his face. "Still gets the job done, if you know what I mean."

Firefly smiled. "I think I'll let him figure that out for himself when we get there." She turned her head to the left. "Forgive me for asking, but it just dawned on me you're not drinking it yourself."

Here we go. "I made a promise to someone that I wouldn't touch it again until this war ended." Tiernan cleared his throat. "It's in honor of my best friend. He gave his life to save us in one of the early attacks of the war."

Was that too much? Will she make the connection between that and Wayland? I have to be careful. Tiernan chastised himself for saying more than he should have. *If I leave it there, she might not push the issue.*

Firefly took another bite of bread and washed it down with a last drink of water. She stood to her feet. "You've done a great job deflecting my question about family, Zachary. And that's okay. Remind me to tell you about my brother sometime. I see a lot of him in Shig, somehow."

Tiernan gave Firefly a sympathetic look. "I saw your face a little bit ago. You mentioned the invasion back in the cave. Did you lose someone during it?"

Firefly sat back down. "Not personally." She pulled off her bow and placed it on the table. "This is Rivka, named in honor of one of my friends from that day."

"Who is Rivka? Family?" He asked.

"No, but she might as well be. She's someone who helped me during my proving trials, someone who gave me an idea during a critical moment. That's why I'm an Archer Master Class and not just First Class. The only one in the entire land. Rivka threw out an idea during my test and it worked."

Tiernan gestured to the bow, and Firefly passed it to him. He held the weapon in his hands, admiring its sturdy construction and smooth texture. He used his other hand to flick the string slightly. "Archery isn't common here. Most of our city guards prefer swords. We know of it, some of them practice it, though they're not any good with this kind of weapon. It was a part of our first Statuo, but I guess it hasn't caught on as a method of *fighting*." Tiernan smiled. "Maybe you can inspire us to adopt it."

Firefly tore off another piece of the loaf. "It wasn't common in my part of Lonlin, either. Not until I moved to the city of Cykela."

Tiernan handed the bow back.

Firefly put it on her back and stood again. "It's late. Someday I want to hear more about this family of yours. And the friend you mentioned. Sounds like we've both experienced great hardships." She gave him a courtesy nod and slid the chair back under the table. Firefly grabbed the rest of the bread. "I'm taking this with me. Goodnight, Zachary."

He raised his glass to her as she headed out. Tiernan sat in silence for a bit, reflecting on her story and the snippet he had shared. He heard someone at the table behind him cough.

"I had a chance to read your book. You do realize you mentioned my name in it. The one you're borrowing right now. Your companions are eventually going to put things together."

Tiernan harrumphed at Zachary's words. "Maybe I'll tell them I'm you and that I can change my appearance."

Zachary laughed and then spun around in his chair to face the rear of Tiernan's head. "And when you can't disappear? What will they say then?"

Tiernan himself then turned around to face the older man. "Tell me something. Who are you? The genuine answer, not some cryptic, half-baked remark that doesn't tell the story. I want the truth this time."

Zachary met the former King's gaze for a bit. He kept his mouth shut while meeting Tiernan's challenge with a hard-nosed glare of his own.

What's he doing? Trying to stare me down? Tiernan wondered.

"You're going to be needed soon in Idlewind. I'm telling you that now as a warning. Get some rest. Answers are coming, my King." The older man then slid his chair away from the table and stood to his feet. "I think it's time you head to the inn. I think it's this way," he said, gesturing to the south.

Tiernan turned around to take one more drink from his glass of water. As soon as he did, he realized his error and let his head fall to the table. He flipped back up and around. As expected, the older man was gone.

"Next time, Old Man. I'm going to figure out how you do that."

Two mornings later, Firefly and Tiernan rode up to the edge of the Windale Mountain range. Near the base, a herd of deer drank from a small outcropping where a stream of water from the mountains pooled. Tiernan dismounted from his horse to take in the sight.

Around the water pool, the grass was thick and a vibrant hue of green. As a gentle breeze blew in, the long blades bent ever so slightly in response.

Firefly dismounted next to him and grabbed the reins of her horse. Tiernan watched her, wondering what she was thinking in this moment. Overhead, a family of birds sung a song as they passed by the pair. Here, the ambient air temperature was already much warmer than the Valley, let alone Lorelei.

"Seems idyllic. You're telling me on the other side of this mountain range is a harsh desert?"

Tiernan pointed. "Horrific conditions, at least to those used to the more temperate regions of the Kingdom. See how high the mountains extend into the sky? Then over there," he said as he pointed eastward. "The Valley Mountains connect with the Windale range. We think this acts as a natural barrier and that the erosive nature of the Great Sea contributes to the harshness of the desert. It will take us a while to cross it before we reach Idlewind. But here? It's like a slice of the paradise the old Abrian capital city was rumored to be."

"You mean Farna? It was as nice as this?"

Tiernan pushed aside thoughts of sorrow and focused on memories that brought him joy. "From what I've heard, anyway. Those who lived in Farna never wanted to leave. Things were just too pleasant there, at least until the downfall."

Behind them, a horse neighed. Firefly and Tiernan turned around to see Airvede and Shig approaching on horseback. Shig waved. Tiernan noticed how the youth had a habit of extending his index and middle fingers, along with his thumb, whenever he said hello to someone.

As if that's his signature greeting, Tiernan thought. He decided to keep track of Shig's wave during this adventure.

"He looks more in control," Firefly commented.

As the others approached, Tiernan could see an odd expression on Airvede's face.

"Everything okay?" he asked.

Airvede brought her horse to a complete stop. Shig did as well, though not with the grace of everyone else.

"The family who owns Whispersong shared a story with us when we first arrived." Airvede dismounted and brought her horse along with her. "Their son, Steve, saw a giant winged creature flying toward Idlewind."

Shig slid off of his horse. "I did the math. It happened the day your king sent messengers to the other lands, so about two months ago."

"A dragon?" asked Firefly.

Airvede shook her head. "That's not how they described it. I flipped through the book Rhys gave us. Although the author didn't go into a ton of detail," she said with a cursory glance at Tiernan, "it sounded closer to the Gamelyon of Tiernan's story."

Tiernan's eyes grew large. He tried not to react beyond that, but his heart began pounding. A cold sweat washed over his skin, drowning out the sun's warmth and the peaceful feelings of the meadow.

If Gamelyon has returned, that must mean Leviathan… Tiernan shifted his body westward toward Alwyn. *Wayland.* Rage built up within Tiernan, thinking about the loss of his best friend turned brother-in-law. He gazed back toward Idlewind. To keep the charade going, he feigned ignorance of its contents. "In that book of yours, does it say how they defeated the beast?"

Airvede stepped forward with an analytical expression on her face. "It did not. It was a hard chapter to read."

Shig moved forward a bit. "Why's that? Sorry, I only skimmed the book so far. I've mostly read the last bit with the final battle."

Tiernan admired Shig's bluntness. *Will he ever read the full story?*

Airvede closed her eyes. "There was a wedding. The twins each married their betrothed on the same day. During the reception, two enormous beasts appeared. A sea serpent they referred to as Leviathan attacked the coastal town where they held the ceremony, the one where we first arrived in the land.

"That way," she said, opening her eyes and motioning toward Idlewind, "the beast they called Gamelyon leveled portions of the city. The Dragonborn sister used her powers to injure the sea serpent. At that time, the Gamelyon was presumed to have retreated from Idlewind, somehow sensing the injury on the other creature."

"And it reappeared the day Rhys sent for help. That's no coincidence," Firefly said with an increasing awareness. Her eyes grew wide. "He knows we're here. This Zoran, the Dark Emperor. I'm sure the other beast will be terrorizing the beach town soon too, if it isn't already."

Tiernan swallowed, realizing she was right. His instinct told him to abandon the group and to make his way straight to Alwyn. *I just want to run this sword through that monster. I want it to feel the loss and pain I felt when it took my best friend's life.*

Out of instinct, he ran his hands through his hair, expecting to pull his long locks into a knot. His shortened haircut brought him back to reality. Feeling a need to do something in preparation, he felt his growing goatee. He moved forward and pulled out his sword along with the Mind Shield from his back. He attached it to his left arm while he gripped the handle of his sword with his right.

Leviathan can wait. We're coming for you, Gamelyon.

The other three walked up next to him. Firefly stood to his right with Airvede and Shig to his left. Together, the four of them mentally prepared for the coming unknown battle against the beast.

Chapter 29

Grains of Sand

Shig threw his fist toward the abdomen of the attacking giant, a Graelan-looking being towering over him. The blow landed hard on his opponent's exposed stomach, causing the giant to recoil from the pain. The giant stood back up and shook it off, grabbing his fallen maul and gray arrowhead shield.

"Big scary man, aren't you? Come and get me," Shig taunted as he backed up.

The giant roared and rushed toward the Paladin. His red cape fluttered in the howling winds of the desert as he took a running leap toward Shig. The giant then used his shield as a weapon, intending to plow through his victim before finishing him.

Instead, Shig slid between the giant's legs. As he passed, Shig grabbed the giant's left foot and pulled on it. The larger man fell with one piece of his shoulder armor falling off and disappearing in the blowing sand. Shig jumped to his feet and body slammed the giant's back, jamming his elbow into the latter's spine.

To his surprise, Shig heard a loud, painful-sounding crack. The giant released his grip on the maul and laid still. Shig grabbed the weapon, content he had subdued his opponent. He wiped away sweat from his forehead. His skin felt gritty, a side effect of the blowing sand around him sticking to his skin.

Across the way, Tiernan was engaged with another of these giants. The only distinguishable feature between the two was the color of their kilt and tattoo on their bald scalp.

Before Shig could help his companion, another nearby creature lunged at him. This ghoulish fiend had long streaks of red, yellow, and orange hair. If Shig didn't know better, he would have said the creature's hair itself was made of fire with the way its long locks fluttered in the wind.

From its chest, a powerful flame protruded in all directions. Beyond that, the creature's skin was a dull gray, lacking any sense of give or texture. Its face screamed rage, an angry expression highlighted by its red eyes. It held a sword in one hand and a morning star in the other. The tips of both, including each spike on the latter weapon, flickered with a flame similar to that of what emitted from its chest.

It tackled Shig, knocking him to the sand and singeing his surcoat. It raised its sword, prepared to plunge the flaming blade into its victim. Shig twisted, refusing to give up though the creature had him pinned down.

A blue frost arrow came streaking across the field and hit the creature square in its chest. All signs of fire left its weapons and body. The creature fell over as a pink mist emerged from the hole in its chest where the flame had been.

Shig jumped up and gave Firefly his signature wave as a way of saying thank you. Tiernan promised to remind himself to update his tally of the number of times the kid used the hand gesture.

Firefly nodded and resumed her attack against a vibrant orange and tan diocene.

Shig turned back to make certain the giant he fought off hadn't moved. To his relief, it was still lying motionless. Shig ran his fingers through his hair to get the sand out. He then caught sight of Airvede, herself occupied with a horde of a dozen spiders. The skin of each appeared dark burgundy with a yellow and orange oval on its thorax.

Airvede appeared to be binding each of them in place using her magic abilities, though the more she froze, the more that seemed to appear from below the sands. One of them emerged and backed up rather than confront her.

Shig watched this happen and tried to get her attention. The spider extended its smaller front legs, and a small flame formed on each. Shig rushed toward it, unsure if he would make it on time.

Airvede took a breath. "After this, I'm going to need another ether. I just absorbed my last!"

Tiernan yelled back as he got an open vantage point and ran his sword through the body of the giant he had been fighting. "They should sell them in Idlewind!"

Meanwhile, the fire-enabled spider's body lit up. Shig shook his head and picked up the pace. Just before it released its magic, he swung at it with the giant's maul. The spider went flying, releasing its fire elsewhere into the Windale Desert just as a pink mist emerged from its mouth.

"Thanks!" Airvede bound another group of spiders with her magic. "Go help Firefly!"

Shig nodded and ran off. Firefly had one diocene occupied, circling it with a set of three arrows primed for release. The creature locked eyes with her, with its victim unaware another diocene watched her through the haze of the desert wind.

Shig saw what was about to happen and tried to warn her. Instead, he felt the impact of a cudgel knock him off his feet. With the wind forcefully pushed from his lungs, he could only watch as a bipedal bear-like creature he only recently learned was called a haracher hovered over him. Shig chastised himself for being unaware of the creature's approach.

The haracher raised the cudgel. Shig found the strength to breathe and braced himself for the attack, hoping he might be able to grab the weapon before it crushed his body.

Instead, a sword pierced the creature's torso, emerging from its abdomen. The haracher roared and tried to grab the blade with its free hand. It dropped the cudgel, a moment which Shig used to his advantage. He grabbed it and his stolen maul, swinging both of them in unison against the creature's body.

The combined force of Shig's momentum and Tiernan's sword in its body were more than the haracher could take. It let out a horrific howl as the creature went flying. The beast landed hard in the sand and fell dead. Shig thought he saw the same pink mist emerge from its mouth, though he couldn't be certain since it landed face down.

"Firefly!" Shig said to Tiernan as he pointed in her direction.

The latter turned around and saw the stalking diocene about to pounce on their companion.

"Let's go!" Tiernan commanded, asserting himself as he once would have as King. Tiernan put the Mind Shield in front of him as a battering ram and extended his sword. He plowed into the stalking diocene with the Mind Shield near its rib and plunged the sword into the muscle in its hip.

Shig performed the same attack on its head, using both weapons to subdue the creature. To his surprise, he heard a crack more intense than when he took down the giant.

The creature didn't have time to cry out before it fell over dead, its neck broken from Shig's attack, a pink mist emerging right away. Satisfied, the two men exchanged a look and turned to help Firefly take down the other diocene.

They didn't have to. Airvede stood next to Firefly, the diocene secured on the ground from Airvede's magic. Firefly aimed a red-tipped arrow at its throat, pulled it back, and released it. Unable to move, the fire moved throughout the body of the fallen beast, consuming it from head to tail.

Around the four, the howling winds of the Windale Desert picked up as if something or someone was aware of their victory.

Shig tossed the weapons aside and raised his hands to cover his eyes as he and Tiernan approached the other two.

"That was unexpected," the younger man said.

Tiernan nodded. "The creatures seemed unaware of us until we were upon them."

Firefly turned back to the smoldering body of the diocene. "These things could *see*. That's not normal. And I've never seen one with an orange color like that."

Airvede spoke up. "In healer circles, we call this an adaptation. It must have grown used to these conditions through multiple generations."

Tiernan shook his head. "That's the thing, Airvede. These conditions are not normal. None of this is. These things," he said, motioning around, "are not native to the Windale region. Or anywhere else in our land, for that matter."

Firefly sighed. "Some of them are from Kinswatch, but others are new. Forgetting *how* they got here, is it possible this Zoran is somehow changing them?" She shook her head. "It doesn't matter, I guess. We need to get out of this storm." She pointed toward their horses, tied up to a rock. "And this can't be good for them."

Tiernan motioned toward the city, glimpsing the outer walls to the southwest. "It's not much further to Idlewind. Even in this storm, we should be able to be there within the next hour."

Tiernan pounded on the city gates protecting Idlewind. After a moment of waiting, he and Shig both beat on the doors frantically while yelling at the same time.

Airvede and Firefly stood behind them, their clothes now a distorted shade of tan with a large amount of sand sticking to the fabric and their wares.

"Are they in there?" Firefly asked through the howling winds.

Tiernan exhaled, his mounting frustration evident. The gates appeared impenetrable. With one final act, he used his shoulder, hoping to the Ailan Huntress that the gates might push open.

No luck.

"This is the only entrance," he yelled back. "There's no way to get inside besides these doors. Airvede, do you have any magic that could work? Otherwise, I don't know how we're going to get into the city."

Airvede shook the sand from her sleeves. "Most of what I can do is defensive and restorative. It's why they call me a White Mage, Zachary." She inhaled, then exhaled slowly. "But let me try something. An idea I had from when I fought the spiders."

The two men moved aside for her to come forward. She extended her arms wide, then brought them together and cupped her hands with her right hand on top of her left. She closed her eyes, searching.

Tiernan raised an eyebrow at the motion, unsure of its purpose or intended result. Even through the sandstorm, Airvede's silhouette seemed to brighten. The effect faded fast, which caused Tiernan to remember her need for an ether.

All of the sudden, he heard a creak. Tiernan whipped his head toward the sound which emanated from the doors protecting Idlewind.

Sure enough, they had parted just enough that he and Shig could slide their hands in.

"Move quickly," she said.

Tiernan gestured toward the doors. "Shig."

Both men rushed up to them, with Tiernan placing his hands above the Paladin's. They slid their hands just inside the seam between the doors. Firefly dropped the reins of their horses and kneeled down under Shig to pull as well.

Centimeter by centimeter, the doors strained against the combined strength of the trio. Airvede parted her hands and moved her arms wide. As she fell to her knees, the doors opened just enough that a Graelan could slip through.

"That's it. I'm done. I'll need an ether if you need anything else," she said through labored breath.

Firefly helped the White Mage to her feet as the other two grabbed their gear. Tiernan slipped through the gates first and looked around. To his left, he saw the pulley system that controlled the doors. He used it to open the doors wide enough to bring a horse through.

Shig came through first, pulling Tiernan's and his steeds by the reins. The Paladin ran back through to the outside. Next, Firefly came through holding Airvede's arm, steadying the White Mage step by step. Shig came through again, guiding the women's horses behind him.

Tiernan waited for the last horse to pass through the gate before closing the doors. They creaked shut almost all the way, but enough of a gap remained, one about the width of a hand, that allowed sand to blow through and pile up on the ground.

Airvede explained. "I created a Barrier around a few grains of sand I could sense were lodged between the doors. That's what forced the doors open." She turned around with Firefly's help. "It'll take until the sun rises tomorrow to disperse. There's no point in trying to shut the doors all the way. The Barrier is too strong, and I can't dissolve it in my weakened state. I would need an ether for that, or any other magic for that matter."

Tiernan looked down at the growing mound of sand creeping through the doors. He then thought about the monsters they encountered and if any of them might try to break into

Idlewind. Frustrated, he let go of the handle and walked into the open streets of Idlewind.

Tiernan shook some of the sand off of his body as he looked around. The streets of Idlewind, usually known for their laborious and productive activity, were deserted. No one moved. Not a single sound could be heard, save for the winds of the Windale Desert outside the city walls.

Midir never described his hometown like this. Nor did he describe Windale as a torrential sandstorm like that. Tiernan pointed to the central well down what he presumed to be the main street.

"Let's head that way." Tiernan grabbed the reins of two of the horses while Shig grabbed the other two. He led the group through the streets.

"Can you walk?" Firefly asked.

Airvede nodded, and with her companion's help, took the first step to follow Shig and Tiernan. "I just need an ether, and I'll be fine. Help me catch up with those two."

Tiernan shivered. Though the Graelian sun felt hotter here, the echoing sound of the horses' hooves on the cobblestone streets gave the town a cold, eerie presence. The windows to every building were boarded up, giving the city a ghost town-like feeling.

As they approached the well, Tiernan saw a post around the bend in the road. "Shig, tie the horses up there."

"You got it, Zach. Come on, girls!" he said to the horses.

Tiernan craned his head back to see the women walking toward him. He paused and turned around. "Airvede, why don't you rest here? Shig and I can go look for a shop selling ethers and bring you one."

Firefly gave him a look that reminded the former King of his sister. A look that said to quit giving orders, as that was her job. "I agree. That's a brilliant plan. Zachary, you go on ahead. We'll wait here."

Tiernan looked around, hoping to see a map, or at least some kind of signage, to point him in the direction of the right vendor. What he saw confused him.

None of the shop names in Idlewind were written in Abrian. It appeared to be an ancient script he had never seen before.

Firefly glanced in the direction of Tiernan's gaze. "What do you see?"

Tiernan pointed. "That's not the script of Abria. That's different." He pointed around, realizing it was the case for every vendor and sign in the streets. "All of those symbols. They're different and I don't recognize them."

From across the city, a gargantuan growl and sound of anger emanated from the depths. Firefly and Tiernan exchanged looks, and Shig came running back from securing the horses.

"Did you guys hear that?" Shig asked.

Airvede, on the ground with her back against the well, tried to sit forward. "It sounded beastly. Angry."

"That must be Gamelyon," Firefly said in a determined tone.

Airvede grumbled. "Listen, I'm not going to be much good to the three of you without an ether."

Tiernan stroked his goatee again. *I miss my hair.* "This is ridiculous. How are we supposed to know where to go? And where are the denizens of the town?"

The sound echoed through the streets again, this time louder and more forcefully.

Airvede coughed, the weakness in her body taking its toll.

Firefly threw her hands in the air and walked up to a nearby door. She began pounding on it, yelling at the top of her lungs.

A moment later, a nervous vendor came to the door. With wide eyes and a worried expression, he said two words that made the town's situation abundantly clear.

"Help us."

Chapter 30

Gamelyon Revealed

Tiernan helped Airvede through the door of the Drunken Alligator. He pointed to a table. Airvede walked over to it and sat. She rested her head against the wall as Tiernan rushed to the bar to get a pitcher of water and a set of glasses.

He returned to the table. "Here. Drink up."

The White Mage poured herself a glass full and chugged it as if it was the last drink she'd ever have. She refilled it again, drinking this one slower.

Tiernan then poured himself a glass. "Did it take that much out of you?"

She swallowed another gulp. "We only bought two ethers in Lorelei. I used the first after I healed the man near the Valley Woods. Bringing someone back from near death is exhausting.

"I took the other the morning when Shig and I left Whispersong." She drank again. "It was the spiders. Fire spiders I guess, though I had no idea such a thing even existed. I've never used that much Bind Magic in such rapid succession. Casting the Barrier and then making it grow did me in."

Tiernan sat at the table's other chair and took a drink. As he did, the nervous vendor from earlier returned with Shig and Firefly. Tiernan noted how the man seemed more at ease, though still moved with a sense of fear.

"Hey guys," Shig said with his signature wave.

Tiernan smiled at the Paladin's youthful expression. *That's two. No, three times he's used that today. Even in the midst of all of this, the kid is happy. Unbelievable.*

Firefly handed an ether to Airvede. "I have five more where they came from. This gentleman took us to a supply shop down the road. That vendor donated the ethers to us. Gave us all they had, said there wasn't any need for ethers in Idlewind now." She shrugged, unaware of the significance of the words.

Next to her, the vendor lowered his head. "Mama…"

Airvede pressed the object into her palm. As her skin absorbed the concoction and its power moved across her body, she felt her heart rate slow. A serene sense of peace overtook her. Tiernan watched, fascinated by the way the item seemed to work within the White Mage. *Huh. Enid never needed an ether, though Eislyn did a time or two. I wonder why there is a difference?*

Airvede breathed a sigh of relief. "That was kind of them. I think I'm going to need all six to get through this."

Firefly pulled out one and looked it over. "Truth be told, I might need one too."

Shig's voice raised in excitement. "I saw that! You saved me back in the desert with a frozen arrow. How?"

Tiernan raised his eyebrows in curiosity. He wondered when Firefly's secret would come out.

Sure enough, she pulled out the two rings from her satchel. "I obtained these in Northwick. That's also when I found out I could use them. I thought the Fire Ring was just a pretty accessory. I had no idea it was imbued with magic."

"And the Frost Ring?" Tiernan asked, finally pushing her to reveal the story.

"I might have threatened the vendor to show me any others he had like this."

Shig reached for the rings. "Might have?"

Firefly tossed them his way. "I told him if he told anyone my secret, it'd be the last thing he did." She laughed. "And then I grabbed him by the collar and asked if he had anything else like it. He handed me the Frost Ring and told me it was on the house."

Shig handed the rings back to her.

The vendor tapped the younger man on the shoulder. "Would you walk me back to my store? I'd rather not travel alone."

Tiernan sat up. "Wait. Before you go, what's going on here? I've met people from Idlewind. They've never described the town like this."

The man looked eager to leave, but relented. Tiernan pointed to a chair at the table next to them. Shig raised his finger as if to say he'd be right back and went to the bar. Firefly sat at a third table nearby.

"Gamelyon. The same creature that attacked us during Midfest back in 920NE."

Firefly spoke up. "That was almost five years ago, if your calendar is the same as ours."

Shig returned carrying two pints of Lorelian Mead, handing one to the vendor while keeping one for himself.

The man took it graciously. "Thank you. The beast arrived during the first week of Fawnmist that year. No one knew what to make of it. As it descended, an old lady recognized it from the stories her grandmother told her many years ago. She yelled out its name as the memory resurfaced. Gamelyon."

He took a long drink of the Lorelian Mead. "It moved south, leveling many of the homes in the residential district. We call that the old city. It was only an act of pure luck that saved the northern section of town."

Shig took a drink himself and shook his head. "I don't believe in luck."

The man put the pint on the table. "Call it whatever you will then. The gates. Manus Midir, our leader for many decades, expanded our community. As Idlewind grew, we transformed the old city into our residential district. The new section became our hub of commerce, with the original gates separating the two halves. We closed those off to protect ourselves from the creature's rampage back then."

"And now?" asked Firefly.

He picked up the glass and took another drink. "Same thing. When Gamelyon arrived two months ago, it returned to the old city. But this time, it was different. Angrier. More determined. It seemed *indifferent* to the gates."

He closed his eyes. "So, some of our people made a choice. From your clothing, and especially his accent, I assume you're not from here."

"What about my accent?" Shig asked.

The others waved him off as the man continued. "Many in this land now have magic. Idlewind was no different. Though the spontaneous appearances of gifted abilities seem to have slowed down in recent months, we had numerous empowered people living here who had discovered their abilities over the past few years.

"But now they're all gone, including my mom. Every one of them sacrificed their lives to encase the old city in a near impenetrable Barrier." He opened his eyes and emphasized his next sentence with measured cadence. "Each and every one of them. They joined together with the Elves living here and put all of their collective efforts into casting the Barrier.

"When they were done, they were all dead, as if their life energies created the gargantuan enclosure." He tightened his mouth. "The windstorm picked up three days ago."

Shig whispered to Firefly as he put his pint of mead on the table in front of him. "That's the day we arrived in Alwyn."

She gave her companion a knowing look. "Gamelyon knows we're here."

The man grabbed Shig's glass. "Gamelyon is angry, and the Barrier is weakening. That's why we barricaded ourselves. A shelter-in-place decision until we figured out what to do."

The vendor took a big gulp of Shig's mead. "Before they died, one of them told our new Manus that they left seven tiles. Those tiles, when arranged in the proper order, would allow access to the old city for the right person." He threw back the last drink of Shig's mead and put the glass on the table.

"Thank you for the drinks. Now, would you mind taking me back to my shop?"

Shig jumped to his feet. "I'll do it if that's okay, Firefly?"

She smiled, nodding toward the door, and mouthed the word 'Go' to him. The vendor stood to his feet and followed Shig to the Alligator's main entrance.

Tiernan's eyes darted from left to right as another thought crossed his mind. "Hold on!"

The man and Shig turned back to him.

Tiernan motioned to a window. "The writing outside. Nothing here is in Abrian. Why?"

"Ah. That." He laughed. "Manus Driscoll thought it would be a way to honor our past. We didn't know if the Kingdom would withstand the war and made preparations in case we had to stand on our own against whatever evil emerged from its ashes. He didn't want us to forget our heritage as Abrians, so he signed a decree that we would begin using ancient Abrian in all public signage."

Ancient Abrian. Tiernan's eyes grew wide, then he narrowed them in deep thought, remembering the inscription on the back of the Mind Shield. "Ancient Abrian uses the same script as we do today. These symbols are different."

"It's something Manus Driscoll said he found in the Alwyn Böchord. Buried in one of the books. He called it the Abrian Codex. Something about the way they wrote before the New Era."

With that, the man turned around to leave. Firefly and Airvede leaned in to Tiernan.

"So, we have to decipher an ancient Abrian code to gain access to Gamelyon?" asked Firefly.

Tiernan leaned on his knees, thinking. *It can't be this difficult. Think. Seven tiles. Ancient Abrian.* He turned to Airvede. "Are you feeling better?"

"I am."

Tiernan looked up at the bar. It felt disconcerting to be in an Alligator and not see Tammith. *I think I've grown fond of seeing her face behind the counter. She understands my family more than most.*

"Family. Could it be that simple?" Tiernan pulled the Mind Shield off his back. Much to his delight, the women still did not know the importance of the shield he carried with him. He laid the relic on his lap to read the inscription.

Except this time, the script was different. *Ancient Abrian. The Mind Shield knows we're here. It knows what we need. It's acting as a codex!*

"I want to see the tiles," he said.

Firefly poured herself a glass of water, took a big drink, then stood to her feet. "Let's go then. We're wasting daylight."

Shig met them in the alleyway not long after the three of them left the Alligator. Tiernan wasn't paying attention to what the younger man was talking about with Airvede. Instead, he was focused on his destination.

He also wasn't sure they were following the correct path, instead using the approaching towers of the original city walls as his only guide. Firefly walked alongside on the right, since Tiernan wore the Mind Shield on his left arm.

The group could now hear Gamelyon with increased clarity and intensity. Trapped within the Barrier, the beast's roars and bellowing seemed to be even angrier than when they first arrived in Idlewind.

"Look up there. Are those the doors to the old city?" Firefly asked as she pointed.

To Tiernan, the gates ahead of them appeared almost identical to the current doors. "They're large and sealed shut. I think so."

Firefly waved back to the others. "Then let's go."

The group jogged forward, approaching the closed doors. A giant cry from Gamelyon on the other side confirmed that they were in the right spot.

Firefly ran her hand along the door. "The vendor said something about tiles. Look at this, Zachary." She used her finger to outline seven square indentions. Split between the two sides of the gates, three were on one side with another three on the other and the middle between each half. "So, all we do is insert the tiles here?"

"Where are the tiles?" asked Shig.

"That's a good question," Tiernan said, as he turned from the door with his left hand on his hip. He kept the Mind Shield close to his body, an instinctive protective barrier between his growing suspicion and hoping not to let the others know what he was thinking.

"Look near the walls. See the sand piled up? Perhaps they're buried," suggested Airvede.

"Dig. Find them," ordered Firefly.

The four spread out. Tiernan used the Mind Shield as a scoop and uncovered two in his first pass. Shig used his hands, moving sand by clawing it away. He uncovered two more and handed them to Tiernan.

"We have four so far."

Airvede chimed in. "Five." She handed another to him.

"Make that six," said Shig, as he found another.

"I'll keep looking for the final tile. See if you can make sense of them," said Firefly.

Tiernan spread them out on the pathway, grouping two of them together. "Look. These two are the same. The rest of these are different," he said.

"So, the word has a repeating letter?" suggested Airvede.

Of course it does. Then again, maybe my suspicion of the message is wrong. Tiernan looked at the inscription on the back of the Mind Shield.

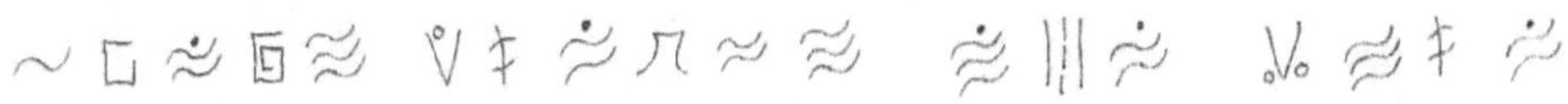

He tightened his lips. He couldn't remember the exact phrasing from the back of the relic, but noticed the script of the two identical tiles was the next to the last letter of the message on the back of the shield.

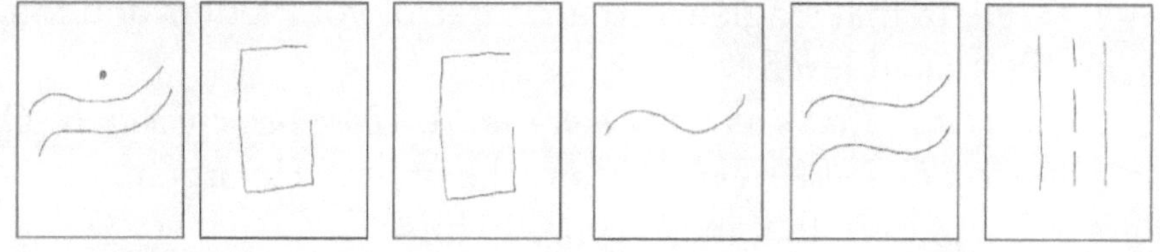

"There. Look. Those two tiles are the same as this letter here," he said.

Airvede pointed to another tile. "That's the last letter on the back of that shield. Where did you get that thing, anyway? It's like it's *magic* or something."

Tiernan picked up on her implied accusation, wondering if she was connecting the dots. *It's too soon.*

Shig then pointed. "The first letter on your shield is the same as that tile."

I remember now. It started with an A. That symbol is an A. Tiernan thought hard, trying to remember what he read all those years ago.

T. I remember the saying ended in a T. He swallowed. *I was right. But how did they know? Did one of them have a premonition about this moment?*

Firefly walked up. "Here's the last tile." Tiernan looked at it, then compared it to the Mind Shield.

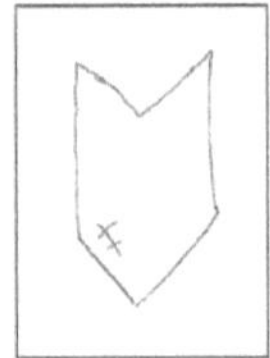

The symbol didn't appear anywhere on the shield. He put it off to the side as he remembered something. "Animo!"

"Excuse me?" asked Shig.

"It's ancient Abrian. The first word on the back of the shield. I know this word. It's Animo," he explained.

"Well, in that single word are three of your letters and four of your tiles," said Firefly.

This is a T. That's an I and that's an A. Those two are both N. Of course they would. I was right. "I know the order." He organized the letters into a pattern that made sense to him.

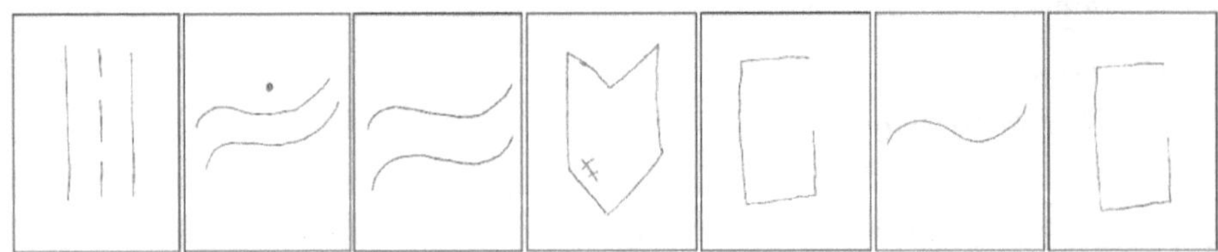

"You've got to be kidding me," he said.

"What?" asked Firefly.

Tiernan shook his head. "It's a message, but not one that matters right now. Put them in this order."

Each person grabbed two tiles except for Airvede, who grabbed just the last one. They put them in the open slots on the door.

Once the last tile was secured, the door exploded in a brilliant light show. It blinded the group, save for Tiernan, who knew what the message meant and who it was for. The group stepped back, covering their eyes from the shine and turning their heads away as they could still feel the light on their faces, even with their hands acting as a protective covering.

To Tiernan, all he saw was a door dissolve from cast iron to a semi-transparent surface to, finally, an open doorway. Once gone and the others uncovered their faces, a growl echoed throughout the old city and into the new one.

Tiernan kept his gaze fixated straight ahead and into eyes full of anger and rage.

Eyes that, though they belonged to another, had the underlying presence of Zoran within them.

No longer hidden by the Mind Shield, the group was now physically visible to the terrible beast of the desert and its controlling Dark Emperor.

"Gamelyon," Firefly whispered.

And so much more. That's Zoran too. I can feel it.

"Its face looks like a lion," said Shig. "We have them in Watodo."

"Its feet look similar to that of a dog," continued Firefly. "But look at its chest. It's like…"

"A dragon. Along with its wings," finished Tiernan.

Tiernan heard a voice speak within his mind in an ancient language. *Animo clipeo uti soli qui in pace sunt.*

"Only those who are at peace with their past can use the Mind Shield," Tiernan repeated in modern Abrian.

Shig rubbed his eyes. "What did you say?"

I've been keeping you hidden from evil. Now, it can see you with its physical eyes. Tiernan had only heard the Mind Shield speak a few times. With this most recent revelation, he now understood its power.

It kept evil from knowing his position. *All those travels. I never encountered a monster because they couldn't* sense *my location, just like the bronze dragon that day in Farna. The Mind Shield protects whoever is near it from evil's sight, at least until your enemy can lay their physical eyes on you.*

"The bronze dragon is blind," he said in a moment of revelation.

Airvede walked up and put her hand on Tiernan's shoulder. "Zachary, are you okay?"

Gamelyon took a step forward, crushing a building below its paw. The beast opened its mouth and breathed fire that incinerated another home. It then raised its head to the sky, though the fire effect dispersed along the bubble of the Barrier above.

The now missing gates were the only way to enter its domain, and the best way for the creature to leave and wreak havoc on the rest of Idlewind and, if they couldn't defeat it, all of Abria.

"Everyone ready?" asked Firefly.

Chapter 31

Battle in the Old City

Tiernan used the Mind Shield to protect himself from Gamelyon's fire breath. Thankfully, the ancient relic seemed to deflect the heat of the attack as well as the blaze itself.

Airvede, standing atop a destroyed home, raised her hands to chest height, pushed them forward, and then clapped them together in a quick motion that made a resounding snap. Two piles of rubble she had just encased in Bind Magic followed the path of her hands, extending forward toward Gamelyon and then crashing against the creature's abdomen.

The attack refocused its attention away from Tiernan and onto Airvede. She raised her hands in front of her, palms open as she cast a Barrier that protected her from Gamelyon's retaliatory fire breath attack.

"What am I supposed to do, punch this thing until it falls over?" Shig asked in frustration as he whaled on one of its legs with his fists.

Tiernan stood up from behind the Mind Shield and looked at his younger friend. "Why didn't you bring a sword or something? Or at least keep those weapons from the desert fight?"

Shig turned around and threw up both hands, one of them just barely forming his distinctive hand gesture for hello. "I never needed anything but my fists before!"

Tiernan chuckled amidst the chaos as he made a mental note to record yet another incident to his Shig tally.

Across the street, Firefly released a series of arrows in rapid succession at Gamelyon, each frozen by the power of the Frost Ring. "Shig," she said between two volleys. "Go dig through the rubble. One of those homes had to have a sword or something sharp in it!"

Shig threw up his hand in the same pose for a second time in as many minutes and ran toward a grouping of destroyed homes just as Gamelyon took a step backward to refocus its attack against Firefly. The Paladin's movement spared him from being crushed as Gamelyon's rear right leg moved to the exact spot where the Ashigaru Paladin had just stood.

The former King used his sword and charged at the same leg, yelling with a ferocious anger as he attacked and tried to wound his much larger adversary. Gamelyon's fur felt like that of a timid deer, something that unsettled him. Pushing the thought aside, Tiernan pulled out the sword and thrust it back in again. The beast roared and raised its paw.

Before it could crush Tiernan, Airvede used her Bind Magic and froze it in place. The creature couldn't shake off the effect, and instead took to the skies.

Tiernan rolled his eyes. "That's swell. Firefly, it's up to you. You're the only ranged attacker we have here." *Maybe the Kingdom should adopt archery in the guards after all,* he thought to himself.

Airvede used her hands to capture more debris and threw it at the beast again. "I can do this too! All is not hopeless!"

Just then, Gamelyon used its wings to pick up a gust of air, directing it at Airvede. The wind hit her hard and tossed the White Mage off the building and onto the streets below. It then used its tail, a long, thin, dragon-like appendage with a spike on the end, to whip around Firefly. It grabbed her, tossing her across the destroyed city streets and into a pile of rubble next to a collapsed structure.

Gamelyon turned to face Tiernan as its last standing enemy, opened its mouth, and breathed an intense stream of fire again. As the beast released the volley of flame toward him, Tiernan hid behind the safety of the Mind Shield once more.

This is hopeless. We need Enid. How are the four of us supposed to defeat this thing?

Tiernan's answer came a moment later as Shig emerged from one of the buildings, brandishing a series of swords and daggers. With precision aim, he threw what looked like a rusty and broken claymore toward Gamelyon's open mouth. From his belt, he pulled out a scimitar and prepared to throw it as well.

It wasn't obvious at first glance what effect the claymore had on Gamelyon other than to stop its volley of fire breath. This gave Shig time to make it up to Tiernan, who waved him off.

"I'm fine," the former King said.

As Gamelyon made a coughing sound that sounded as if it was trying to regurgitate something, it rose higher in the air. It made the noise with increased and more laborious effort, obvious to those below that it was trying to dislodge the claymore to no avail. It roared and flew southbound toward an abandoned section of the old city. Flailing its limbs, including its still bound leg, it knocked down some of the remaining structures as it hopped and spun, fruitlessly trying to remove the weapon from its throat.

Shig rushed to Firefly and offered a hand. He pulled her up to her feet and, as she stood, she switched from her Frost Ring to her Fire Ring.

Tiernan ducked through the destroyed alleyways to the spot where he assumed Airvede had landed. Sure enough, the White Mage was there, dusting herself off and absorbing another ether.

"You might want a potion, too. You landed hard."

She nodded and pulled one out of her satchel. "Good thinking, Zachary." Airvede flicked its lid to the ground and chugged the vial.

"Come on," he said. "The others are up the street."

Together, they ran to the spot where Shig and Firefly appeared to be pointing and strategizing their next move.

"Hey. You okay?" Firefly asked of Airvede.

The White Mage gave her a thumbs up and a slight smirk. "This is child's play," she said with a sense of irony.

"What's next? The creature is far stronger than all four of us combined." Shig flipped around to Tiernan. "I know you were just a guide, Zach, but I'm sure glad you're here right now."

Firefly rested against a fallen building. "Shig is right. We haven't stopped the beast, but without your help, I'm not sure we'd be this far even." She put her hand on her chest as she took a deep breath. "What made it fly away like that?"

Shig raised the scimitar and pointed to the daggers in his belt. "I found these, plus a rusty old sword. I threw it at the beast's throat as it attacked Zach here. Must have caught it in just the right spot."

They all gazed toward Gamelyon. The creature had stopped its rampage and appeared to be waiting for their next move.

Tiernan tilted his head in its direction. "We need an offensive strategy. If we had someone with attack magic, we might stand a better shot at taking it down. No offense to either of you, but we need a *red mage* or something." *Is that what Enid was? A mage that can attack and heal? Is that even the right term?*

"None taken. I'm here to heal and defend," responded Airvede.

"I've only known I had magic abilities for a few days, Zachary. When I froze the arrows in the cave with the Frost Ring, it was a hunch. I didn't know if it was going to work," Firefly admitted with a sigh.

"The rings." Tiernan reached toward Firefly with a thought running through his mind. "Let me see the Frost Ring."

She pulled it out and handed it to him. He inspected the jewel encased in its golden construction.

Shig walked over. "What are you thinking?"

Tiernan raised the Mind Shield and looked at the inscription. *Only those who are at peace with their past can use the Mind Shield.* He gazed deep into the jewel and thought of his friend.

Wayland, my brother. What are you trying to tell me from the beyond? Talk to me.

Tiernan looked up at Gamelyon. The creature moved one of its free paws back and forth, almost in eager anticipation of what the four defenders planned.

"Shig, hand me a dagger." Tiernan turned around as the younger man passed one his way, not wanting Gamelyon to see. Using the blade, he scraped at the jewel.

Tiernan smiled as he saw a reaction within the stone. Though barely visible, the swirling magic sped up its motion in response to the dagger's prod, as if the power within the ring was straining against the walls holding it captive. Tiernan turned back around.

"I have an idea."

Gamelyon's head darted left to right, watching as the group spread out through the streets of the old city. Tiernan watched Shig and Firefly move to the east as he and Airvede walked west.

Tiernan spoke first. "Do you think it'll work?"

Airvede smirked. "This is your idea. I need to focus. I'll take up a hidden position just around that collapsed tower."

"Got it. Look, there goes Shig." Gamelyon's head tracked the Paladin as Tiernan spoke. "It's taking the bait. It thinks Shig is going to hurt it again." Tiernan scanned the streets until he found Firefly, who was busy climbing the fallen structures. He gasped as Firefly lost her footing, and breathed a sigh of relief as she recovered.

Gamelyon roared and gave chase to Shig.

"You want me, don't you? For the glory of the Emperor!" Shig threw the scimitar at Gamelyon's neck.

The creature ducked, and the blade bounced off the beast's back and landed on the ground below.

"Nice move," Shig said through gritted teeth.

Gamelyon opened its mouth to roar and planned to release a volley of its fire breath, forgetting that it no longer had that ability because of its earlier encounter with Shig. This enraged the beast as it whipped its tail around the streets, trying to capture the Paladin but missing as he dodged each time.

Airvede closed her eyes and concentrated. "I've got this. Go, Zachary."

Tiernan nodded, then charged. "For Abria!"

Gamelyon heard his cry and flapped its gargantuan wings to take to the skies.

Airvede extended her fists and encased one of its wings in Bind Magic. Now unable to fly, Gamelyon fell to the ground and roared again as Shig threw several daggers toward its mouth. The creature's flailing made it hard for him to hit his target, though a few made impacts on its face and throat.

"Zach, I'm down to my last three!"

Tiernan jumped off the top of a fallen building, sword extended. As he landed on Gamelyon's back, he thrust the sword into its body forcefully, driving it deep near the top of the creature's spine. The beast threw its head back in pain as Tiernan slid down its back, leaving his weapon in place. Gamelyon turned away from Shig and toward Tiernan, mouth agape and sharpened teeth showing, ready to scoop up and crush the former King.

"Now!" Tiernan yelled as he ran. He passed Firefly, who stood atop the remains of the tallest building she could find. Tiernan smiled as he looked up at the archer.

Her arrow loaded, her body poised, and the string of her bow tight, Firefly took a deep breath. She held it as she focused her mind on her target. She relaxed and let the air leave her lungs as she released her battle cry with pride.

"Long live Cykela!" She let go of the string as the arrow flew across the street and into Gamelyon's mouth, a small ring affixed to its tip. A ring that, in this case, glowed with a subtle blue hue with swirling magic pleading to be released from its prison.

The arrow found its target, lodging itself in the back of the beast's throat. Gamelyon paused, almost as if it was aware of the magic now pinned within its body. It gave Firefly a look tinged with fear and understanding.

Below those eyes, another being cried out in anger as this portion of its plan fell apart.

Breaking the gaze with Gamelyon, Firefly issued an order. "Now, Airvede!"

Airvede's cupped hands let go of each other as she extended them wide with majestic speed.

Gamelyon barely had time to react as the magic ring exploded in its mouth. Frost Magic spread throughout the creature's body as fast as the flash of the explosion, freezing it from head to toe.

It stood motionless, aware of its predicament but unable to react as the reaction froze its bodily functions. Tiernan observed from what he assumed was a safe distance away from the beast.

He was wrong. Tiernan's eyes widened as he saw the magic spread into the ground below Gamelyon's paws. "We have to move. Get out of here! Everyone! Now!"

Shig, the furthest from the others, darted through the streets at lightning speed. Airvede, not far from the creature, used her levitation powers to get just above the ground as the ice effect overtook the streets below her. She floated away, narrowly escaping the spreading cold.

Tiernan ran to Firefly and helped her down the pile of rubble.

"Zachary, run!" she said as she pointed toward the encroaching ice. Tiernan looked back and then followed her through the streets, winding around the fallen remains of homes and other structures toward the exit.

As the ice continued to expand, Shig caught up with Airvede. "You'll have to tell me how you do that sometime!"

She laughed. "I'm not sure I even know how I do it."

The two of them met up with Firefly and Tiernan not far from the where the old city gates once stood.

Shig's eyes filled with horror as the ice showed no intention of slowing down. "Look, Zach. It's still spreading."

Tiernan turned back. The effect continued to expand, almost out of control at this point. By now, the ice had spread up the back of the city and along the top of the encasing Barrier.

"Barrier. Airvede, a Barrier!" Tiernan said.

Her eyes lit up in agreement. "Zachary is right. Let's get out of the old city. I'll enclose the entrance in a Barrier."

"Right," said Firefly. "And then by the time your new Barrier and the old one fade, the ice will be gone."

Tiernan cast one final glance at Gamelyon. Next to the creature, the few buildings that had not fallen over cracked. One vibrated and shattered into a thousand smaller shards.

The group ran through the entrance of the old city. Airvede turned around and extended her hands, her palms facing the open entrance. An almost impossible to perceive, yet shimmering Barrier covered the place where the gates used to stand.

The four stood side by side, watching as the ice overtook what remained of the old city. Before a thick layer of frost covered

Airvede's new Barrier, Tiernan made eye contact with the beast they had just fought.

Though an enemy, Tiernan couldn't help but feel sadness for the creature as Gamelyon's body trembled. First, its wings shattered, falling to the ground and disappearing into the layers of ice covering the streets. Then, Gamelyon's rear legs fractured with its body breaking away from its front paws as the creature's backside hit the ground. The foot within Airvede's earlier Barrier exploded, filling it with icy shards.

Tiernan couldn't be sure, but thought he heard one last cry of anguish as the rest of its body fell forward. Gamelyon's torso erupted into a million ice splinters as its head fell, releasing a mist of pink before it, too, crumbled among the deteriorating icy grave of the old city.

Chapter 32

Aftermath

Tiernan put his feet up, resting them on another chair within the Drunken Alligator. His companions were spread throughout the tavern, with Shig busy chatting with the vendor from before and sharing a drink with his newfound friend. Tiernan wasn't sure if he was correct or not, but next to the Ashigaru Paladin, a maiden appeared to sit mesmerized, captivated by Shig's every word.

Firefly conversed with a group near the fireplace, acting out the details of the battle with her hands. Despite the angle here, Tiernan could tell with absolute certainty that several of the younger men were enraptured by her storytelling.

Airvede approached him from the bar, carrying a glass for Tiernan and a different drink for herself. "Water, right?"

Tiernan laughed. "For now. Yes. Water. What did you get?"

"Something called Dorian Ale."

Tiernan smiled. "If I'm not mistaken, rumor has it a beloved former King of Abria preferred that over Lorelian Mead."

Airvede pointed to Shig. "I think he's fond of the Mead." Tiernan turned his head toward the Paladin who was engrossed in deep conversation with the vendor and other patrons of the Alligator. His rapid hand gestures drew more and more to his story, with Shig greeting each new arrival with his signature greeting.

"He's a good kid. Seems a bit oblivious of that girl next to him. Reminds me of someone I once knew at that age."

Airvede took a sip of the ale. "Yes. Almost as if he was somehow related to the Prince himself."

Tiernan took another drink. "What do you know of the Prince?"

"Just what I've read from the book so far. That he had a magic shield. That his best friend could wield Frost Magic and his sister was the most powerful mage Grael has ever known."

She took another drink. "It doesn't say so in plain terms, but I get the impression he was a master strategist planning those games each year. Something called a Statuo. Must have been a quick thinker, someone who could come up with fresh ideas on the spot."

They sat in silence watching Shig. Tiernan laughed as Shig greeted two more listeners coming to hear his story.

Airvede chimed in again, this time leaning closer. "Oh, and that he had a chance encounter with an old man also named Zachary. In a tavern, just like this one. A Drunken Alligator, if I recall. What a funny coincidence, don't you agree?"

Tiernan took another drink. "It's just a name."

"Right." Airvede sipped her ale. "I can see why your father liked this so much. Notes of apple and lemon. It reminds me of a drink we have back home called Gideon's Cider. I think your dad would have liked that one, too."

Tiernan made eye contact with Airvede. "My father?"

She smirked. "Okay then. You're not ready yet. I get it. Nice move with the Frost Ring."

Tiernan shrugged. "I just remembered how you opened the gates using those few grains of sand. And, if like that, you could sense even a single *blip* of the magic inside of the jewel, you could pull the same trick. With any luck, the jewel would explode." He closed his eyes. "We were fortunate today. I don't know if we can repeat that trick with Leviathan."

Airvede took her last drink and then patted her hands on the table. "One more thing?"

Tiernan opened his eyes and turned his head toward the White Mage.

"The other two relics. The Power Ring and the Soul Sword. What happened to them?"

Tiernan sighed, knowing his next words would confirm Airvede's suspicion of his true identity. "The Soul Sword was lost when Farna fell." He met her gaze. "I haven't seen the Power Ring since *that day*."

She motioned behind Tiernan. "Looks like you have a visitor."

"Hmm?" He didn't follow the meaning of her words.

Airvede motioned again with her hand for Tiernan to turn around. He did so and saw the grinning face of the old man.

""That's the real Zachary, isn't it?" Airvede stood. "I'll leave you two be."

Zachary extended his hand toward the back of the bar. Tiernan took one last drink and hopped to his feet to follow him.

"She's a smart one, isn't she?" Zachary asked.

Tiernan wasn't sure whether to be annoyed or grateful to see Zachary's face. "Of the three, she's the one I assumed would figure things out first. I was afraid the Mind Shield acting as a stand in for Driscoll's Abrian Codex would have given things away to all of them."

"Yes. Curious thing, isn't it? Using your real name on the tiles, but in ancient Abrian. Why do you think they did that?" Zachary asked as the two sat at a table hidden by a small wall.

"It seems like a big gamble to me. How did they know I'd be here? Why bury the tiles? None of it makes sense."

"Does everything have to make sense to you?"

"Yes!" Tiernan exclaimed. Aware that he drew attention to himself, he lowered his voice. "I don't like surprises. Something you seem fond of ignoring."

Zachary laughed. "Well, here's one you might enjoy." He reached into his pocket and pulled out a glistening ring, one with highlights of blue and fuchsia enhancing a design Tiernan knew all too well.

"The Power Ring!" Tiernan tried to grab it, but Zachary pulled it back.

"Not yet. Your companions aren't ready for it yet." Zachary pointed to Tiernan's back. "That one needs explained first."

"The Mind Shield?"

Zachary nodded. "Airvede is smart. So are the others, but their youthful inexperience blinds them to what's in front of them. Something I know about all too well." He raised his eyebrows. "But stories like that are for another time."

Tiernan wondered what Zachary looked like when the older man had been the same age as Shig. It filled the King's mind with wonder to envision a young Zachary pulling magic tricks without explaining them. "At least tell me how you found it," Tiernan said.

Zachary smiled. "In the plains near my father's field." He slid it on his finger. "I've had it for a *long time*. More years than you've even been alive." Zachary made a fist. "It's taught me a lot and soon it will be handed over to its rightful owner."

"Airvede," Tiernan said. "We'll need her abilities at full capacity."

Zachary smiled. "Maybe. Maybe not. You'll have to wait and see. Either way, it's time for me to go. I'll see you again soon. And for once, no tricks." He raised his fingers as if to snap them in the usual way a magic-empowered individual would teleport away.

Instead, the old man cupped the Power Ring with his hand and disappeared. Tiernan couldn't help but smile, having seen Zachary's trick with his own eyes.

As he started to leave the table, he sat back down. "Father's field?" His eyes darted from left to right, thinking. *Father's field. Father's…it can't be!*

"Steve?" Tiernan asked the empty space.

Tiernan shook the hand of Manus Driscoll. He handed a small bag to the former King who passed it off to Airvede. The White Mage counted their dinage, an act of gratitude from the people of Idlewind for defeating Gamelyon and stopping the sandstorm.

Tiernan hopped on his horse and pulled out his notebook, skimming through the details he had written while resting in one of Idlewind's inns, including the number of times Shig greeted someone with his peculiar hand motion.

"Is another book coming?" Airvede asked with a playful smile.

Tiernan put it away and patted the horse. He glanced toward Firefly, who kneeled in the street counting her arrows. "Where's Shig?"

"By the well. Look." Airvede pointed down the street where Shig seemed engrossed in a conversation with a young woman.

Tiernan grinned. "Is that the same maiden from the Alligator last night?"

"I think so."

"Maybe he's not as oblivious as we think," Tiernan said, as Shig bowed to her. The Ashigaru Paladin looked around and saw his companions near the city gates. He waved at them, then turned back to the maiden and gave her his signature wave as well.

Tiernan surreptitiously pulled out his notebook and added two more hashes to the tally before stuffing it back into his satchel.

Firefly stood to her feet and slung her quiver around her back. "I'm down to thirteen, so I'll need to harvest or buy more someplace. I guess archery isn't a thing here in Idlewind at all? Even for fun? Hard to believe." She grabbed the saddle and put a foot in one of her horse's stirrups. Firefly used her momentum to swing her body around and rested on the steed's back.

On the ground next to the animal, one of the lingering townsmen bowed. "Will we ever see you again?"

Firefly gave him a playful smile. With a twinkle in her eye, she pointed upward. "What do you call that woman in the sky? The Huntress? When you see her, know I'll be watching over you, too." She pressed her thighs into her horse's sides and guided the animal over to Airvede and Tiernan.

"You probably just made his day," Tiernan joked.

"Oh please. I had to say something. Bunch of loons."

"Not your type?" asked Airvede.

"Too clingy," Firefly responded with a shiver. "I prefer a man who can spar with me like Alex." She twisted her mouth sideways. "Just not Alex. He belongs to Kai." She cleared her throat to push aside the thoughts of her home. "Is everyone ready to go?"

Shig rode up on his horse, spinning one of his daggers in his hand, though it looked shinier than the ones from the battle in the old city.

Tiernan raised his eyebrows. "You seem to be getting a better grasp of riding. Is that a new toy?"

"Hey, Zach. A gift from that vendor we met yesterday. Gave me a full set of them. I've nicknamed this one Haia. So, where we off to?"

Firefly pointed northwest. "The owner of the inn said we can find more ethers and other supplies in Clericsfold. Said it was that way."

Tiernan nodded. "They're right, but a direct path would have us crossing the Lorelei River. There's a bridge back by Whispersong, but we'd lose the better part of a day taking it. We could try to cross the river. The melt from the Milston Mountains hasn't kicked in yet, so the current may be less intense."

"I'm up for a challenge!" The other three exchanged a look at Shig's words as Tiernan and Airvede shrugged their shoulders and deferred to Firefly.

"Your call," the White Mage said to her.

"Zachary?" Firefly asked.

Tiernan looked high to the sky. The sun had only just risen over the Valley Mountains. "It's going to be a beautiful day. I think Shig is right." He smiled. "It's the kind of day you want to do something challenging."

Firefly waved her hand at Tiernan. "Then, by all means, lead the way!"

Chapter 33

Crossing the River

High above, the sun reached its peak, its warmth acting as a source of invigoration. Tiernan closed his eyes for a moment, feeling its heat which reminded him of the perpetual paradise Farna used to be.

With his eyes closed, he could hear the rushing waters of the Lorelei. It reminded him of when he landed in the plains near Whispersong right after the underground battle. Tiernan opened them and squinted.

"There. See how the horizon bends? That's the banks of the Lorelei River." He turned his gaze a few degrees west. "Look!"

Tiernan pointed at a glowing rock face, its shine visible even in the brightness of the sun's power and the distance.

Shig rode up. "What's that, Zach? Looks beckoning."

Tiernan lowered his arm. "We call it Kingscrown Rock. Once you're closer, you can see its distinct crown-like shape. Combined with the perpetual glow, it earned its name from the reflective shine you'll sometimes catch within a king's crown."

"Why does it glow like that?" asked Firefly.

"No one knows. Unofficially, they're nicknamed the Fire Caves. My sis...family member once explored them. They described a wall of flame that blocked passages. Heat that could take your breath away. But yet, the cave walls themselves are as cool to the touch as anything else underground."

"Have you been there, Zach?" Shig had the face of someone wanting to do some side-adventure exploring.

Tiernan shook his head. "I have not. Rumor has it a metal flower grows at the peak of the crown. No one has ever had the courage to find it."

Firefly rode up next to Tiernan. "Shig. Come with me. I'm going to go scout for a crossing point to the south. Airvede, Zachary, head north. We'll meet ahead at that inlet and discuss the best place to cross."

Airvede and Tiernan nodded as Shig and Firefly rode south.

"Your sis-family, huh? Is that a word in Ancient Abrian you've yet to teach us?"

"Shut it." Tiernan sighed. *That was close.*

The four rode up to a crossing point Shig had recommended. Tiernan grumbled to himself, irritated he had never tried to ford the Lorelei or the Lake Conchobar run off. To his relief, Shig claimed to be an expert, explaining that crossing a river was just another day of the week in Watodo.

"See the break in the water?" Shig pointed. "That massive rock splits the flow just enough to create two shallow areas."

Tiernan wondered why no one had discovered this before. "What would happen if the waters coming down from Milston increased two-fold? Or even four-fold?"

"The rock wouldn't make a difference. The flow would overtake it."

Firefly reached over and clapped Shig on the shoulder. "I knew you'd be good for something."

Shig smiled, his eager and infectious grin making the rest of the group feel less trepidatious about the task ahead.

Tiernan's smile twisted a bit. "So how old are you, Shig? I don't think I've asked."

"Nineteen moons. What about the rest of you?"

"Twenty-one," answered Firefly.

Tiernan's eyebrows betrayed his surprise, expecting her to be older.

"What about you, Zach?" Shig asked.

Tiernan shifted. "I'll be twenty-six next month."

Airvede laughed. "I guess I'm the elder here."

"Oh yeah? How many moons?" asked Shig.

"Let's just say I'm old enough to have a son close to your age. He's younger by a few seasons."

Firefly stepped up. "If we want to hit Clericsfold by sundown, we should cross now. Shig, lead the way."

The younger man smiled and turned his horse toward the Lorelei River. "Oh, I should mention this. I've never crossed a river on horseback."

"Never?" asked Firefly.

"I thought that would be obvious. Remember, as members of the Ashigaru, we don't ride horses. That's one way to get kicked out of the Emperor's Court."

Firefly began to object, but then realized that horse or no horse, Shig's plan was a sound one. "Fine. Let's go."

Tiernan turned to Airvede and spoke to her in a near whisper. "Tell me how old you are and I'll answer a question that's not in that book."

Airvede laughed. "That's not a fair trade."

"Why not?"

She tapped her finger on her temple. "Because I have a suspicion, and I don't think I'm wrong, that you're going to tell us *everything*, anyway."

Shig led the group across the first shallow crossing within the Lorelei's flow, pointing to each place to avoid.

"Don't step there. Guide your horse around it. They'll lose their footing. Up here, we need to head north a bit. The water gets deeper in this middle section…"

Overhead, a circling avian watched the group with eyes aglow. It made an unintentional sound, and Firefly looked up in response.

"A marren! Everyone, be on guard." She pointed at the beast hovering in the sky.

"How long has it been following us, I wonder?" Airvede asked.

A few ticks later, they had a semblance of an answer. A wave of water came crashing over the rock. Its sound echoed down the riverbed, interrupting the group's walk and Shig's instructions.

"We need to move!" Shig pressed his thighs into his horse's side to increase the steed's movement.

The others followed his lead just as the wave overtook the rock.

Tiernan, bringing up the rear, eyed the coming onslaught. "It's Zoran. If the waters are this torrential, it means he has been watching us for a while. Somehow." Tiernan looked up at the marren. "We need to brace ourselves. Secure your persons."

The group checked their inventory, ensuring that everything they had would stay with them. A few moments later, the waves hit the group, soaking their clothes with icy cold water from the Abrian north. Tiernan shivered as he found himself now knee deep in a pool of water.

The impact spooked Airvede's horse. It began bucking, fearful of the waves and trying to escape. The White Mage placed her hands on its mane, a subtle glow emanating from her hands and into its head. "Breathe. You'll be okay."

As if on cue, the horse calmed. Tiernan couldn't tell, but thought he watched the horse make eye contact with its rider, almost in a connected sense of gratitude and understanding of the predicament.

"We have a problem. Look!" Shig pointed at the second half of the river ahead of them. "That wave filled the shallow side."

"You're telling me *this* is now the shallow section?" asked Firefly. When Shig didn't deny it, Firefly crossed her arms. "Well, that's wonderful." She looked up and down the river.

"We're going to freeze to death in this if we don't move now," said Tiernan. "This water is coming from Milston. The snowcapped mountains feed the river's anger during the seasons of Bloom and sometimes even into Flame. But never in Frost. Something or someone is sending water down earlier and faster than it should be moving this time of year."

With no other choice, Shig pointed ahead. "We'll be up to the horses' necks in water, but let's go."

"It's not ideal, but if you have to, use the reins to keep their mouths above water," said Firefly. "Horses are great swimmers, but just be aware."

Everyone pressed their legs into their steed's sides. Tiernan's heart hurt for the animals, though he felt pride for the way they carried their riders.

As they approached the final third of the Lorelei's width, Tiernan heard another crash. He looked north, where an even larger wave crested and raced toward them.

"We're almost there!" Shig pressed his horse harder and breathed a sigh of relief as its body emerged bit by bit from the river.

Tiernan swallowed, expecting the torrential waves to crush him. He almost cheered when he saw his horse's front shoulder emerging from the river.

"We can make it!" Shig was now at the western banks. He raised a fist to the air when his horse stepped up out of the river and onto dry ground. Firefly, just behind him, pressed her horse harder and felt the same sense of elation when she saw her steed's legs step onto the dirt.

The water around Airvede and Tiernan rose higher, covering the horse's shoulder that had just emerged from the water. Tiernan looked again at the coming onslaught, then back to Shig and Firefly. The two were on dry ground and waiting for their companions.

We're not going to make it.

Airvede's voice snapped him out of his thoughts. "Tiernan, move closer."

At first, his instinct was to deny his name. A tick later, he realized that at this point, it was irrelevant with Airvede. He moved his horse next to hers.

"*Now* you owe me."

"I'm thirty-eight seasons old. Hold on tight." She extended her hand and touched Tiernan's horse. "I hope this works." Airvede closed her eyes.

To Tiernan's surprise, both horses emerged from the water. Even more surprising, they had stopped walking altogether.

Instead, the horses levitated above the surface of the river just as the colossal wave overtook their position. The only part of their respective steeds that touched the raging waters were their hooves.

Using her powers, Airvede brought the pair to dry ground next to Shig and Firefly. The White Mage dug through her satchel and pulled out an ether, absorbing it right away.

"You could do that this entire time?" asked Shig.

"Are you dense, kid? Look at her. She's exhausted." Firefly moved her horse over next to the White Mage. "How are you feeling?"

Airvede took a deep breath and exhaled with a measured intent. "I've pushed myself harder on this journey than at any other point in my time as the White Mage. I don't want to do that one again."

Firefly moved her horse even closer and leaned in to give her companion a hug. Tiernan smiled, realizing in this moment that their small group was beginning to act like a family.

Family. That's what this is all about, isn't it? Four of us from separate walks of life, distant lands even, coming together as one.

He pointed. "I know it's hard to see, but there's a bridge up ahead. We can cross the Lake Conchobar run off there. We'll be on the southern path then, too. It'll make travel to Clericsfold much easier."

"Maybe we can get dry clothes there?" suggested Shig.

Firefly let go of Airvede. "I think we need to have our horses tended to when we arrive. That icy water couldn't have been good for them. Everyone ready?"

Shig turned his horse northwest toward the bridge. "I am. Hee-ya!"

Firefly did the same as Tiernan rode up to Airvede.

The former King gave her a slight bow. "Thanks for the save back there. Thirty-eight, huh? I wouldn't have guessed that."

Airvede threw her head back in the air with a delighted laugh. "I knew it! You're welcome, *Tiernan.*"

In the western skies, the light of the sun began to set over the mountains in a milky haze of orange, pink, and dulled white. A breeze flew in, wrapping the still wet adventurers in a chilly awareness of their predicament.

Tiernan saw the approaching gates of Clericsfold. He rode up to his companions and explained the unique layout of the city. "The southern path splits the community in two. The northern section is the majority of Clericsfold. Homes, shops, stables, the seat of their city government. The southern section is the primary orphanage in Abria."

"Orphans?" asked Airvede, feeling a connection to which only Tiernan was aware of in this moment.

Tiernan's face softened enough to let her know he understood. "Sometimes, accidents just happen. Mining incidents are common. With no one to take the children in, the different communities bring them here.

"Other times, the child has no known family. They're left here, abandoned. Regardless of the how, Clericsfold leadership takes the child in, giving them a dorm in the orphanage until someone adopts them or they age out."

Firefly's heart broke, and her voice put her emotions on full display. "Sounds like a system in need of an overhaul! Children should *always* be tended to and never neglected."

Tiernan smiled. "They are. I'm sorry if I made it sound unpleasant. While how they got here might be a tragedy, what happens after they arrive is special." He cleared his throat. "There was a man. Born well over four hundred years ago. He transformed this place from a simple dormitory to a full-fledged school and training grounds."

"You act like he's some kind of revered figured in your land. What was his name and who was he?" asked Shig.

Tiernan smiled and gave Airvede a sideways glance, knowing this would continue to reiterate his true identity. "You might have seen his statue back in the Valley. His name was Borun."

Chapter 34

The Legacy of Borun

Nightfall surrounded Tiernan and the others. The four brightest twinkling lights of the Abriacholae constellation served as a preview of what lie ahead. The four defenders, bright lights prepared to do whatever was necessary, would soon experience a showdown with the darkest evil imaginable.

Shig dismounted from his horse and walked up to the gates facing the group. Firefly followed behind, keeping her distance while giving Shig the opportunity to take control of the situation.

Tiernan slid off his horse as well and looked south toward the orphanage. *I'm here, Father. I wish you and Mom were here with me.*

Airvede walked up next to Tiernan. "Why does the path run through the center of town? It's as if you have to cross through Clericsfold to gain access to the western portions of Abria."

Tiernan put his hands on his hips. "Have you read the entire book yet?"

"No. I admit I've been skipping around."

"This is why the Statuo was such a big deal. If Kane's rebellion broke Clericsfold away, the southern path would have been under the control of a rival nation." He turned to face her as Shig talked with the guards. "Everything you need to know about Kane is in there. At least everything I know of him. The first Statuo stood to tear Abria apart. It's why Dad worked so hard to keep it together with the games."

Shig returned with Firefly. "They're opening the gates and are waking the stable hands. Terrible design. Who puts a primary road through a locked gate?"

Tiernan laughed. "This is how it's been since before I was born. You'd have to go back in time to find out."

The gates swung open wide. A group bolted through and rushed to the team.

One of them, a woman with curly blonde hair, spoke first. "How long were they in the icy waters? And how high did it get?"

Firefly put her hand on her horse. "About here. I know they can hold their own in the water, and it wasn't long. It's the temperature that has me worried. That water was freezing, and I noticed they were slower getting here than they had been since we left Lorelei."

The woman issued commands to the other three. Each grabbed a rein and guided the horses inside. As they did, a city guard ran out to the group and bowed while extending his arm toward the entrance.

"Welcome to Clericsfold. We'll get you set up in one of our inns. You say you came from Idlewind?"

Tiernan nodded. "We defeated the beast there, though at a significant cost. Gamelyon destroyed most of the old city, which is where the populace lived." He hesitated to say more.

Less tactful than his companion, Shig finished the story. "The ensuing battle turned their homes into an icy grave."

The guard turned his head sideways. "Your accent. Where are you from?"

Shig's face brightened, even in the darkness. "Tiko, a prefecture in Watodo. That's a far away Empire, in case you didn't know. I'm here to help free your land."

The man gave Shig an acknowledgement that implied he wanted to say more, but stopped. Instead, he led the group into the city of Clericsfold.

Tiernan looked around, struggling to understand how this community could have been the source of the first conflict almost a decade ago. Nothing about the buildings screamed division. Those who traveled by, including many Elves, seemed friendly with waves and nods of courtesy.

They passed a wooden home. "The Clericsfold Council would like to see you tomorrow," the guard said.

Airvede tapped him on the shoulder. "I understand your city is famous for the processing of 'folding' concoctions. My companions seem to think you would have the land's largest supply of ethers."

He nodded as they approached the inn. "The shops open at daybreak tomorrow. Look for one named Trask's Treasures. He'll have what you need. A few other kinds of potions, too. I'll send a runner with fresh, dry clothing for all of you, with a change or two for your travels if you'd like."

The group thanked the guard as they walked into the lobby of the inn.

Tiernan walked up to Firefly. "Since you're in charge, I'd like your permission to skip tomorrow's meeting. I think the three of you are more than capable of handling it. I have an errand I need to run." He bowed, deferring to her authority on this quest. "That is, if it's okay."

"I suppose you're only here as a guide, and you've already done more than enough. Yes, that'll be fine, Zachary. We'll handle the council and any questions they have. Will you be joining us when we head to Alwyn?"

"Of course. This is just something I have to do."

Airvede walked up and handed each of them their keys. "They said there is a bathhouse on the second floor with private stalls."

"When in the field, members of the Ashigaru tend to bathe in rivers. This is almost too much," Shig said.

Firefly pointed up. "If the water is warm up there, you might never want to go back to Watodo."

"That's unlikely," he said. "But I suppose we'll see. With that, I'm out of here. I'll see you all in the morning." Shig waved and bolted up the stairs.

Firefly leaned in and hugged Airvede. "Are you doing okay?"

"I am. Thanks for asking."

"Good," she said as she let go. "I'll see you in the morning. Goodnight, Zachary."

Firefly walked up the stairs toward her room just as the runner came through with bundles of clothing. They handed a pack to Tiernan and Airvede before heading up the stairs to the other rooms.

"Who knows you on the Clericsfold Council?" Airvede asked once they were alone.

"Several, including the mayor, Tomek. Had you realized this was the same reason I didn't go to Whispersong?"

"I assumed so. Was it for a vacation? Seemed like a lovely place."

"More like a recovery excursion." He tapped his satchel, thankful for the leather that kept his notebook dry. "It'll be in the next book. Long story short, after the big battle, I was beaten up. Badly. The Dark Elf, wait. Have you read about him?"

Airvede gave him a mournful look. "Yes."

Tiernan continued. "The Dark Elf sent me away. Teleported me to Whispersong. I spent a lot of time there recovering. Almost died."

Airvede took a few steps toward the stairs. She stopped and turned around. "What is something you didn't include in the *first* book?"

Tiernan laughed a little too loud, drawing the attention of a few guests in the inn's lounge. "I thought we were even."

"I changed my mind," she said as she walked back to him.

Tiernan leaned against a table. "I see. Well, obviously, there's everything I set aside for the second story, like what I just told you."

"And this adventure is a part of that."

He nodded. "Your story is as much a part of the legacy of my sister as when Farna fell. Zachary, the real Zachary that is, showed me your face along with the other two upstairs. I didn't include that in the book because it happened after I wrote the last page." He smirked. "And let's face it. It's kind of weird to tell another woman you saw their face in a vision. My heart belongs to my wife and her alone. It didn't seem…proper."

Tiernan walked over to a window and stared into the darkened streets of Clericsfold. Airvede stood alongside him.

"I could feel the love you have for her throughout the passages I've read. I understand *true love*, Tiernan. My husband, Eamon, and I have seen our fair share of problems. The Galvan Scourge was only one of them. I understand pain and loss. They hurt."

He closed his eyes, picturing the moment he was about to share with her. Tiernan's voice broke. "Have you ever seen a dragon?"

"Only in drawings. The two in your book are the first I've heard of during the New Era."

"There's at least a third out there. Except this dragon was far from the peaceful, friendly, even helpful persona of the first two. Of the one that saved Enid's life.

"For all the fear we had about Kane and Zoran, this beast did more damage than both of them combined. It tore Farna from the very foundation. Remember how Gamelyon breathed fire? This one breathed *boulders*. Farna is now a barren wasteland because of its attack."

He turned to face her as he wiped the tears that had fallen. "I feel as if we haven't seen the last of it either. There are so many pieces of the puzzle I'm missing. I have to see this journey through to the end. That's why I came with you. The thing is, it's like Rhys knew I was meant to come along. This is Enid's legacy. But what does that mean?"

She put her hand on his shoulder. "And when do you plan to tell the others your real name?"

Tiernan opened his mouth to speak, then shut it. Airvede stood for a moment longer, then left her companion alone with his thoughts.

As the sun's light and warmth filled the sky and Clericsfold awoke from its slumber, Tiernan moved through the streets with the hood of his robe raised. Ahead of him, he saw his destination growing closer.

He passed the outline of the southern path, still visible in the dirt despite its worn appearance. He continued south beyond it into a section of the city he knew he had never visited at any point during his life. Tiernan swallowed hard, not sure why he was undertaking this particular journey today.

He stood at the steps of the door leading to the orphanage. High above, in one of the towers, a large tokei had been built into the structure acting as a central timekeeper for the campus. The red-brown construction of the buildings throughout the orphanage itself reminded the former King of the brick buildings he saw in Milston.

Tiernan lifted his hand to knock.

Before he could, it opened. A man in a chair supported by wheels greeted him. "Come on in!" He backed himself up, using his arms to power his seat. He then spun around and yelled down the hall. "Minmi, we have a visitor!"

Tiernan followed this curious man down the hall of the primary building. Serving as a common area, Tiernan teared up as he saw a teenager with dark brown hair sitting next to one of his friends. *Is this what Dad looked like when he was here?*

"Minmi, where are you?" the man yelled. "I said we have a visitor!"

Tiernan increased his speed, trying to keep up with the pace of the wheeled man.

"Omi, I'm down here!" called a voice around the bend in the hall.

Tiernan, now knowing the wheeled man's name, debated what he should do. He paused and cast a glance back, wanting more than anything to stop and talk with the boy who reminded him of Davien. He sighed deep, then followed Omi into the next room.

There, a woman greeted them in a similar-styled wheeled seat.

"What's your name, my good fellow?" asked Omi. His countenance seemed bright and engaging, like someone who had woken up from the world's best night of sleep. Tiernan noticed his balding head with only a gray band around its sides. His striking blue eyes were soft and caring, like a fatherly presence with many seasons of experience.

"My name is Zachary. Who are you two?

Omi answered. "This is my wife, Minmi. I'm Omi."

Tiernan couldn't help but be enamored with their unique clothing and mode of transportation. Minmi's hairstyle, though well put together, was that of a mother who has worn the same updo for the past thirty years. Her outfit, like Omi's, was tidy and well kept, even if reflective of styling from many, many years ago.

"I've never seen something like those seats before. And where are you from?"

"Lyra," answered Omi.

"Lyra?" Tiernan guarded his next words carefully. "I think I heard the Elves running around are from that place! Did you know them?"

"We were born long after they left our Commonwealth. We're not that old!" Omi said with a chuckle. He patted on the wheels. "We've been bound to these though after an unknown ailment swept through our village."

Minmi piped in. "I had been after Omi to take a vacation for so long. Almost two centuries, in fact! So, he finally agreed to one and it almost cost us everything!"

Tiernan looked at Omi, waiting for the rest of the story.

"We arrived through the beaches south of here last year. Treacherous journey. Our ship broke up in the currents and we almost drowned. It was only because of the kindness of Isoshi we made it out alive."

Tiernan shook his head. "Who is Isoshi?"

"I am."

Tiernan turned around. Before him stood a man dressed in clothing that, if the former King didn't know better, he would have thought came straight out of Shig's wardrobe. This new arrival had his arms crossed and leaned against the frame between two rooms.

"Zachary, this is Isoshi. He's been running the orphanage here since. Hmm. What did you call it?" asked Omi.

"The first Statuo," answered Isoshi.

Tiernan extended his hand. "It's nice to meet you."

Isoshi grabbed it and shook it with respect. "Likewise, sir. Your royal heritage precedes you."

Tiernan paused and turned back to the couple. "Would you give us a moment alone?"

They obliged, using their arms to guide their wheeled seats out into a distant room. Tiernan gestured to a chair. They both sat facing each other.

"I'm sorry, but I don't know what you mean by royal heritage. Rhys is in charge; last I knew anyway."

Isoshi smiled. "I'm not of this Kingdom, but I've lived here long enough that I know who you are. Your trademark red hair? It's unmistakable, even if much shorter. You shouldn't have cut it.

"And besides, I saw the Mind Shield on your back. That's a dead giveaway. If you really wanted to hide your identity, you should have it under your robe."

Tiernan rubbed his eyes. "Alright. Enough games. Who are you? How do you know me?"

Isoshi extended his hand. "Watch." He made a fist, then rolled it to his left. Minmi and Omi returned, as if something had rewound their actions.

"If I let go, we'll take the place of our past selves. If I keep going further, there'll be two of us. Now watch." He rolled his fist in the opposite direction.

The couple disappeared, returning to the other room.

Isoshi lowered his hand, but kept his fist clenched. "I'm from Watodo."

"With clothing like that? Too obvious. Tell me something I didn't know if you want to impress me."

"Shig is my brother."

Tiernan laughed. "Okay. You win. I *didn't* see that one coming."

Isoshi released his hand to unfreeze time. "I arrived here, in Abria, on the night of a torrential storm. I was on a scouting mission for the Emperor. A giant oval mass of energy appeared in front of my group of Ashigaru. I fell through and landed north of here in the plains.

"I watched a battle unfold. Horseback riders trying to save what I later learned were their parents from a Dark Elf and a man named Kane."

"Stop." Tiernan's eyes grew wide. "Stop. You're telling me you were there that night?"

"I was. I disappeared into the darkness to remain hidden. A few months later, I woke up with this new power." Isoshi sat forward and looked Tiernan in the eye. "The first time I went back to the past, I watched the battle from a different viewpoint. I saw your father deflect the attack. The combination of the Soul Sword and the Dark Elf's power created the portal. I watched myself fall through and realized I couldn't change it."

Tiernan scrunched his face tight. "Omi said you had been running the place since the first Statuo. Did you go back in time even further?"

Isoshi sat back. "Backward, forward, and back again. I've seen the past and the future. I learned all I could about this land before I decided there was one man I needed to meet."

Tiernan swallowed. "Who?"

Isoshi stood up and walked over to a book on the shelf and flipped it open. Tiernan recognized it without even reading the spine.

"I know what that is."

Isoshi sat back down. "Then you already know who. Your grandfather's story inspired me. He was a great man. All that he did for the Valley. This orphanage." Isoshi closed the book. "Your family. It truly is an example of genuine strength. You should be proud."

Tiernan's jaw shifted, holding back his emotions. "I am."

"This orphanage. I visited it one time in the past, many centuries ago. I saw what it was like before him. Borun made it into what you see today. He gave these kids hope. Made it so they could have a job, and not just that, a career. Encouraged them to pursue whatever passion they had. It's inspiring."

By now, Tiernan was holding back tears. He took a breath. "And so, you're a teacher?"

"An Ashigaru foot soldier turned teacher. I decided the best way to honor the legacy of Borun was to come here and serve the school. I've been here for many years. I was sent to Abria for a reason. Who knows? Maybe one day I'll join the fight. For now, there's too much work to be done here."

Isoshi's face turned stern. "Listen. There's just one thing you have to do for me."

Tiernan narrowed his eyes. "Why do I get the impression I'm not going to like this?"

Isoshi bowed his head. "It's a solemn vow. We call it Ashigaru Chikai."

As Tiernan loaded up his new horse with supplies, he couldn't help but feel a tinge of sadness. Isoshi had remained at the school, his reasons understandable yet feeling wrong somehow. Tiernan cast a last peek toward the orphanage, reflecting on family, sacrifice, and loss. He pictured the brown-haired boy he passed, replacing his face with that of his late father.

A woman approached him. "I'm sorry."

Tiernan looked at her, confused. "Do I know you?"

"I doubt it. Your parents did. The last time I talked to either of them was on the morning of your sister's big race. My name is Teska. When I was much younger, I was a friend of Kane." Teska took a deep breath. "And Davien."

"You knew Dad?" Tiernan, already emotional from his encounter with Isoshi, couldn't fight the tears anymore.

She closed her eyes. "I misjudged Kane. I've *seen* Farna. I don't know what role he played in its downfall." She opened her eyes. "Back then, I was torn. My friendship with Kane lasted longer than the one with Davien. Once he moved away with Borun, I just naturally grew closer to Kane.

"Davien was a good man. So was your grandfather. I knew him before he adopted your dad. I can look back now and see how blinded I was to Kane's rhetoric.

"I know he had a hand in Borun's death, though I don't know how. I know he killed your parents alongside the Dark Elf. Whatever happened to the capital was him."

Teska swallowed. "Please. Forgive me for following him all those years ago."

Teska turned her back to Tiernan. "If I learned one thing from Borun's story, and yes, I read your book, it's that we need our family. I miss my friendship with your father and Kane from when we were kids. Your father taught me compassion—"

Tiernan didn't let her finish. He reached out and placed a hand on her shoulder to turn her around. He saw in her eyes a look of genuine sadness and regret.

Knowing Kane was the source of her anguish, he did the only thing he knew to do. Tiernan hugged her, tears streaming down his face.

Teska let her emotions take over with the tears flowing down her cheeks. "I'm *so sorry* for your loss, my King. All of it."

Tiernan began to sob. "I forgive you," he said as he gave the orphanage one final look and pictured his father running through the halls and into the arms of his eventual adoptive father, Borun.

Chapter 35

The Beauty of Life

Unsure of the reliability of their new horses, the four defenders of the land meandered through the Clericsfold countryside. They followed the southern road, though in the distance Tiernan could see the split where it turned northward and into what was called the western path.

There, they would head straight into the plains of Alwyn, entering the peninsula on their way to the coastline where the town itself sat. And it would be there, if Tiernan was right, that their next adversary awaited.

One he had hoped never to see again.

A gargantuan creature the former King did not know how they would defeat without the help of the Dragonborn Heroine.

Leviathan.

"At this pace, how long will it take us to get to Alwyn?" asked Shig.

Tiernan hated to break the news, but knew no one else here had the answer. "We'll have to camp out under the stars."

"Alright! It's been a while since I've had a chance to do that." Shig's grin, though usually infectious, led to another response in the rest of the group this time.

Curiosity.

Airvede broke the ice. "Shig, tell me about Watodo. What is it like? Are you in the army? Guards?"

"Defense force."

"Okay. So, you're a Paladin? What's that mean? Warrior? Knight? What's your role, Shig?" asked Firefly.

"The closest would be infantry. Foot soldiers. As I've said before, we're called the Ashigaru. My brother, Isoshi, enlisted first before I was even born. After he disappeared, I took the oath of enlistment. That was about two years ago. It's there I learned to be a fighter, saving hostages throughout Watodo from a group of rebels."

In the distance, Tiernan saw movement. "Heads up. Looks like more Kinswatch bandits."

Shig raised his head. "Let me handle these." He dismounted from his horse and rushed toward them. Before facing them, he stopped and took off his satchel.

"Here. Catch this, Zach." Shig tossed the bag toward Tiernan. "I want to make it fair. No weapons."

Shig ran toward them as the four bandits approached. Shig slid, swiping the legs out from under one. He jumped up and punched another in the face and then the abdomen.

"Does he know he still has his sanshin on his back?" asked Airvede.

Firefly laughed. "I don't know, but I think he'll be furious if one of them breaks it."

Tiernan watched Shig's movements, thinking back to some things Isoshi said about Watodo. Fighting styles. Sacrifice. An innate sense of honor.

Ashigaru Chikai.

Shig exemplified all of those and more. The Ashigaru Paladin made short work of all four, subduing them and pillaging their satchels. He brought the spoils back to his companions.

"Not much dinage, but plenty of potions." Shig tossed the potions to Airvede and pocketed the din for himself. He then put his foot into the stirrup and hopped back on the horse. "I wonder how many more of those we'll encounter?"

"I wonder how our original horses are doing," Firefly said, her mind elsewhere. "The stable hands seemed convinced they'll be fine, but it doesn't feel right to just leave them there."

Shig applied pressure to his steed's side. As he passed the unconscious bandits, he patted his horse's neck. "Tell me, Firefly. Why do you ride horses? In Lonlin, I mean," he said, pointing to Firefly. He pointed to the other two. "Same for the Isles and here in the Land of Enid. As warriors of each of your peoples, doesn't that make you feel weak? Dependent on another for your success?"

Airvede's face filled with humor. "I'm not a warrior, Shig. I'm a healer."

Shig shrugged. "Fine. What about you, Zach?"

Tiernan looked down at his horse. "I have a beloved horse. She's back home right now." He chuckled. "Besides, I'm just a scribe, remember?" Tiernan patted the satchel.

Shig gave Tiernan a look of doubt. "I know a lie when I see one. But okay. Firefly, I know you're a warrior. Heroine of Lonlin or something. And I can tell horseback riding is in your blood."

Firefly didn't hide it. "Horses and I are like the sun and the sky. You can't have one without the other."

Tiernan smiled. "Where's this going, Shig? Is that a part of your Watodian honor code as an Ashigaru?"

Shig gave him an odd look. "Others ride throughout Watodo. But those of us in the Ashigaru just believe we have two legs and that they're what's meant to carry us from place to place."

Firefly leaned forward. "So, you're telling me that with a country as big as Watodo, you'd walk from one side to the next rather than ride a horse while your countrymen pass you by on the back of a steed such as this beautiful animal I'm on right now?" Firefly rubbed her horse's mane. "Aren't you, girl?"

Shig smiled. "You make it sound so complex. Look." He pointed at a pair of passing seagulls. "Those creatures are far from the coastline. Did they hitch a ride with someone else, making them do the work for them? Of course not! They have wings and can soar high."

Tiernan rode closer to Shig, directing his steed to the Ashigaru Paladin's left. "What about when you visit lands like this? I don't ask this to be disrespectful, but do you find it offensive that we're riding a horse across the land?"

Shig thought about Tiernan's question. "The short answer is no. In Watodo, we believe in respecting one's personal decision. The Ashigaru might not ride, but since we're in your land, I'm obligated to respect your customs."

The group traveled in silence for a while, with the other three digesting Shig's comments as he took in the sights of the approaching Alwyn peninsula. Shig smiled, enjoying the increasing wildlife as they grew closer to the coastal region.

Tiernan was in a far less positive mood. Now visible, the others did not know the significance of the ruined structure in the distance to the northwest that used to be the city of Farna. Tiernan felt a sense of rage build within him as he saw snow-capped ruins where his home once stood.

"So, what else, Shig? Watodo sounds like a unique land. Did I hear you mention you're ruled by an Emperor?"

Firefly's question broke Tiernan's focus, bringing him back to reality. From his time in Abrian leadership, he already knew the answer but gave the Paladin a chance to explain.

"The Emperor is a royal position, a bloodline dating back before the New Era. Like the rest of you, we don't know what happened before then. What we do know is that at the start of recorded history, his family was on the throne, a position they secured when he defeated the Watatsumi. His victory meant that, from that day forward, the crown would remain within his family, passed down from generation to generation."

He pointed to the southern sky. "When the Snakehead appears at night, it reaffirms this eternal rule."

"Sounds like what we used to have here in Abria."

Everyone's eyes turned to Tiernan.

"Before King Rhys, we also had a royal bloodline."

"What happened to it?" asked Shig with genuine curiosity.

Tiernan motioned toward the ruins. "That way. See that structure in the distance atop that plateau?"

"I thought it was a bunch of rubble," Shig answered.

"It is now. That used to be our capital city. Farna."

Firefly couldn't hold back her surprise. "That's Farna?"

Tiernan's jaw twitched. "That's what's left of it. The city used to be a perpetual paradise. The royal family of Abria ruled there for centuries, dating back much like yours, Shig. To the start of the New Era."

"Did the King die there?" asked Firefly.

"In a manner of speaking. That's why you met Rhys in Lorelei."

"Instead of Tiernan?" asked Airvede with a knowing look of compassion evident on her face.

"This is Shig's story," Tiernan retorted.

Airvede got the hint and backed off.

Firefly, unaware of the context of the conversation between the other two, pressed on with Shig. "So, tell us more about the Emperor. Is he kind? Gentle? Harsh?"

Shig grinned with respect and admiration. "The Emperor is one of the kindest men you'll ever meet. Watch."

He jumped off his horse and ran toward a turtle on the ground. He moved it, taking it out of the path of the horses. "The Emperor taught us to respect life. Did any of you see him cross?"

The others shook their heads.

"Exactly. Close your eyes. Feel what's around you. This area is teeming with life. Everywhere. I can feel it in my bones."

The other three closed their eyes, though none of them felt what Shig described. After a moment, they reopened them as Shig climbed back on his horse.

"That turtle almost met his end. Those monsters back in the desert? They had their chance. I *still* feel bad for killing the giant, those spiders, Gamelyon. There was no other choice."

He rode ahead and stopped in front of the others. "That's the only time our code allows us to kill. To hunt another life for sport?" He shivered, revolted by the mere concept. "With Gamelyon, I did what I had to. In Watodo, life is *sacred*. It's a gift." He smiled. "And it's a gift I'm so honored to get to share with the three of you on this journey."

Shig turned his horse toward Alwyn. "What do you guys think? I'm feeling pretty good on this steed. I think we can pick up the pace. How far is Alwyn, Zach?"

"With a consistent canter, we could be there before sundown."

"With the Leviathan waiting for us," warned Airvede.

Tiernan swallowed. *Am I really doing this? Going back there, facing the beast that took my friend from me and broke my sister's heart.*

The former King's brow narrowed. "If we push these horses into a gallop, we could be there before golden hour." He felt a strange sense of determination set in. "Perfect time to slay the beast."

"If we have to," said Shig. "Will you trust me on this one, Zach? I have a hunch. It's just something I've been thinking about for a while. If I'm right, that is."

Tiernan wanted more than anything to have his revenge. He regarded Shig's words, then nodded.

"Okay. Only if we have to," he said in feigned agreement.

As expected, with their faster pace, Tiernan led the group into the outskirts of the city of Alwyn far before the sun lowered on the horizon. The former King felt even more accomplished, as this was despite two additional bandit ambushes and a lone diocene wandering the countryside.

"We made amazing time getting here," said Airvede.

Firefly motioned to Tiernan. "It's because of Zachary's guidance. We'd have been lost without him."

Tiernan, mindful of the city's usual atmosphere and its role as a vacation destination for the Kingdom, noticed something was wrong the moment he spotted Alwyn. Though never as busy as during their reception, Alwyn was almost always full of life. Today, much like Idlewind, the town was a proverbial ghost town.

Firefly was the first to point it out. "People do live here, right?"

Tiernan nodded. "It wouldn't surprise me if the residents of Alwyn evacuated or boarded themselves in their homes once Leviathan reappeared."

He stopped his horse and brought it in front of the group. "Last time anyone fought this beast was during a joint royal wedding. And that group had the advantage of the Dragonborn Heroine on their side. Firefly, do you still have the Fire Ring?"

She raised her hand, the Fire Ring proudly on her second finger.

"Airvede, what about your powers? So far, we've seen…"

Airvede ticked off each ability using her fingers. "Bind, Barrier, Heal, and an ability to levitate."

"Can you use this?" Firefly took off the Fire Ring and handed it to Airvede. The group could see her immediate distress and concern.

"Attack magic. I've never tried. I'm a *healer*." She swallowed, wondering how this might affect her reputation as a White Mage. She slid the ring on with a slow movement, one indicative of her personal apprehension to an offensive means of attack.

Without warning, a surge of power flowed through her. Airvede threw her head back and cried out.

"Airvede!" Firefly jumped off her horse and rushed to her friend's aid.

The White Mage waved her off and shook her head.

Tiernan rode up. "What do you feel?"

"This is different. I guess I was expecting a dark magic or something, but this is nothing like that. It's a sensation I'm not used to, I'll admit it. But I think I can use it just as much." She opened her palm as a ball of fire appeared. "Is this how it works?" Then, using her inner strength, she pushed the flame out of her hand and into the sky. It exploded and dissipated into the Alwyn expanse above the city.

As it did, a deafening rumble echoed throughout the town. Tiernan recognized it without needing to see where it came from.

"That's Leviathan," he said with a deep-seated, hateful grumble on his breath. Still on the north end of town, Tiernan gave his horse the sign to move forward by squeezing its sides with his heels.

Meter by meter, the group moved through the northern end of the community.

Firefly brought her horse to a stop. "We should get off of these and tie them up someplace safe. Shig,"

All four dismounted, with the younger man leading the horses to a distant sign post to secure them.

"I want to see the coastline." Firefly walked around the nearby buildings into the beach area. She continued moving east, taking in more and more of the Alwyn coast as she did. A few moments later, she returned. "I don't see it. Where is the creature?"

Another echoing bellow from Leviathan told them it was close.

Shig returned to them, twirling one of his daggers. "So, I have a question. I have a set of these, and they're great for throwing." He cocked his head sideways. "But I'd hate having to find a new set and I know we have a long journey ahead of us yet. Anyone have any ideas?"

The other three exchanged a look.

Airvede was the one to respond. "So, I might have *another* ability. It's something I haven't had much success with, but it's worth a try. Ready, Shig?"

He braced himself.

"Throw the dagger at that building down the alley."

Shig drew his arm back and released the weapon with a quick and powerful throw. It dug deep into the side of the home.

"Okay, now it's my turn." Airvede concentrated on the weapon. It vibrated, picking up momentum and shaking the exterior of the house.

"Those poor people." Tiernan lamented. The impact and vibrations were likely to have scared whoever lived there, plus they'd have to pay for damages.

"Whoops," Shig said as he, too, thought about the occupants of the home.

Meanwhile, Airvede's magic grabbed hold of the dagger's handle. With a quick motion, she pulled it toward the group.

Shig reached out and grabbed it. "Thanks. How'd you do that?"

"It's the same basic idea of binding two pieces of debris and crashing it against Gamelyon. Except I like to call this one Retrieve."

Tiernan smiled. "Did you come up with that name on your own?"

She shook her head. "I read about it back home. First time it's worked."

Leviathan roared again. Firefly looked around. At the edge of the residential district, she noticed an abandoned warehouse.

"What's that?"

Tiernan looked up. "It's a holding space. I think it goes deep underground too. It's how Alwyn stores grain and other supplies during shipping and receiving."

Firefly thought about his answer, then motioned for the group to follow her. Together, they walked through the residential streets of Alwyn toward the commercial district.

South of the warehouse, Tiernan spotted Gléineach Hall. Remembering his words from his earlier writing about Borun Mill, he tried hard to suppress the surge of emotions. *Rumors had spread in recent months that Tammith and Dagnall planned to turn it into some kind of wedding venue, like one for couples to get married in. Like the one Eislyn and I were married in.* The former King shook off the memory fragment and followed his companions.

Now in the open, Tiernan could see the entire Alwyn coastline. Reaffirming his grief, he saw the destruction of the docks. "Abria rebuilt those after the first attack in 920. Looks like King Rhys will have to do it again."

Firefly motioned ahead. "The door to the warehouse is open." She pulled out a red-tipped arrow from her quiver, and loaded it into her bow.

Airvede opened her palm with the Fire Ring as Shig gripped the handle of a dagger tight. Tiernan slid the Mind Shield on his left arm. With his right hand, he grabbed his new sword, having lost his first during the battle with Gamelyon.

Firefly crept up the stairs leading into the warehouse and fired the arrow into the darkened space. It exploded against the stone wall, illuminating the storage area.

Airvede tapped her companion on the shoulder. "I could have used this next time," she said, referring to the ball of fire in her hand.

Firefly smiled. "Sorry. Still getting used to this whole magic thing. Care to lead the way?"

Shig spoke up. "Why are we going into the creepy building in the first place? Aren't we here for Leviathan?"

"Look around, Shig. Do you see the sea serpent?' asked Firefly.

"Okay, but there are plenty of other buildings here. We haven't even tried to see if they're unlocked."

"Are you scared?" Tiernan asked. The question was genuine. The former King couldn't tell what was causing this reaction in the usually brave Paladin.

Shig shook his head. "We can *hear* Leviathan. We just cannot *see* it. That means it's here, somewhere, hidden to us."

Airvede closed her palm, extinguishing the flame. "He's right. There's some kind of magic here beyond anything we've encountered before. And this," she said, pointing back to the open hall, "feels intentional."

"You're saying someone wants us to go in there?" Firefly asked with a doubtful expression.

"Zoran." Tiernan threw his hands in the air. "It's the only answer that makes sense."

"Do you think he's here?" Airvede moved down the steps, wrinkling her forehead in worry.

"Maybe not here, but pulling the strings somehow." Tiernan slid his sword back into his sheath. "We do have one advantage if Zoran is somehow involved."

"What's that, Zach?"

Tiernan raised the Mind Shield. "I don't know how far you are into that book Rhys gave you. This shield isn't just a normal piece of armor. King Davien discovered three ancient relics. This is one of them."

"The Mind Shield?" Shig asked.

Firefly lowered her bow. "You've had it this entire time?"

"You've both been reading, I see. The Mind Shield prevents evil, in this case, Zoran and his minions, from sensing our movements. An enemy can still see us if it has eyes, unlike the diocene from the cave."

Firefly nodded in understanding. "It explains why the orc didn't know we were there until we were on top of it."

Tiernan paced, deep in thought and trying to decide their next move. Another roar from Leviathan caused him to stop. "Zoran wants us to go through this warehouse. It's too obvious. Our only source of light would be Airvede's Fire Ring. Aila, Catrin, the Snakehead, or whatever you want to call it," he said, smiling at the group while acknowledging their cultural differences, "knows what traps Zoran has set for us in there. What monsters lie in wait."

Leviathan roared again. The group turned to face the empty coastline.

Shig walked up and kneeled down to take a closer look at the Mind Shield. "Something to think about, Zach. This special shield of yours," he said as he grasped it from the side. "How wide of a range does it have?"

"I don't know, Shig. We know it's pretty big, but that's it. Why?"

Shig returned to an upright standing position. "Could it somehow be hiding Leviathan as well?"

Tiernan shook his head and shrugged his shoulders.

Shig paced, biting his lip. "That's my point. Have any of you heard of the Ryllix?"

"The what, Shig?" Firefly asked.

Airvede put her finger to her mouth, thinking. "I have not. What is the Ryllix?"

Shig looked at Tiernan, who had yet to answer.

The former King locked eyes with the Paladin without speaking. *What's he doing? Where is this going?*

"They're a timid, gentle species of gigantic sea serpents that live near the frozen waters of the north."

Tiernan's heart began to race. *He needs to stop. We're here to slay the beast. I* must *avenge my friend.*

"If this is a Ryllix, then the creature you call Leviathan is nothing more than a victim. That's why it's invisible. Your Mind Shield is stopping us from seeing it just as much as it can't see our presence." Shig smiled. "We're not here to defeat it.

"We're here to save it."

Chapter 36

Subverted Expectations

Tiernan covered the last section of the Mind Shield with a final scoop of sand. *This is stupid. That thing killed Wayland. Almost killed my wife and sister. Has now terrorized Alwyn twice over.*

He stood, grumbling as he hopped on the back of his horse. *What if someone finds the Mind Shield while we're gone?* Tiernan shook his head. Trusting Shig's hunch took more faith than the former King had at the moment. At the group's suggestion, and a practical order from Firefly, they decided the best place to bury the Shield was an approximate kilometer north of Alwyn itself. With any luck, this range would be far enough to reveal Leviathan.

A sickening feeling washed over him. Tiernan had a sense something horrible lurked around them. Resigned to what was ahead of them, he commanded his horse to return to the city.

After some time riding, he saw his companions along the outer edge of the first row of buildings. He slowed his horse as he approached them.

"Okay. It's done. I buried the Mind Shield. Now, how do we free—"

Tiernan couldn't finish the question before Leviathan roared again. Additional sounds followed, new ones, including thrashing and powerful dual streams of water Tiernan recognized as the one of the beast's attacks.

"That would be Leviathan," he said. "That spray you hear? It's coming from both sides of its head, some kind of water-based magic attack. The sound of crashing waves is more of the structures along the coastline falling victim to its anger."

"A telltale sign of a Ryllix in pain," Shig offered as an answer to their situation.

Tiernan threw his hands up in exasperation. "Okay then. How do you propose we free it from Zoran's control? Did you think that through, kid?"

"Zachary! Shig is only trying to help." Firefly gave Tiernan an irritated look, one stemming from his unwillingness to consider other possibilities.

In return, he dismissed her chastising by waving his hands at the group and turning his back to them.

Is this the time? They have to know this is personal. Tiernan raised his head to the sky, looking for an answer that would not come. *It's up to me. No one is going to tell me what to do.*

A Statuo.

Tiernan flipped around. "That thing *killed my best friend.* The closest person to a brother I ever had. My new brother-in-law. I watched that beast smack him with its tail and toss him into the Great Sea. I saw my friend, my closest and oldest friend, fly helplessly through the air until his body came to a hard smack against the water's surface."

Silence fell on the other three. Firefly began to make the connection, but kept quiet. Airvede maintained her composure, waiting to see what Tiernan would say next.

Tears streamed down Tiernan's cheeks. "Don't you understand? It was at his wedding reception. Our reception. A joint event between the four of us. His new bride and mine." Tiernan wiped away the tears from his face. "It was meant to be a joyous day. One of celebration, laughter. That beast took his life. My new wife and I watched as it tossed him into the ocean without a second thought, never to return."

Tiernan unloaded the emotions he had been holding back for this entire journey. "His wife. My *sister*. My beloved sister watched her new husband plummet to his death. Do you know the sound a Graelan makes when it hits water at that speed? I can still hear it in my nightmares.

"We searched for a week for his body. He was gone."

Tiernan fell to his knees, sobbing. He punched the ground, his warrior fierceness overtaking him. "Wayland. My friend since childhood. Gone, just like that." He looked up at his companions. "My sister took her anger out on the beast. The full strength of her Dragonborn powers, or so we thought." He paused in a moment of reflection, thinking about the battle in the caves below ground. "I didn't know how powerful she truly was until a few weeks later."

"You're *Tiernan*," said Shig. "Zach, Zachary, it's a, what?"

"A cover. The name of a friend. Someone who helped guide me a while back." Tiernan pushed himself to his feet. "It doesn't matter. We're here, facing Leviathan again, but this time without Enid to save the day. And you're telling me we're supposed to free it instead? How?"

Airvede watched as a form materialized behind Tiernan. "Ah," she said as she connected the dots.

"With this," the man answered. Tiernan didn't have to turn around to see who stood behind him. He already knew.

"The Power Ring, of course." Tiernan turned to face Zachary, assuming he had it all figured out. "That's why you - oh." He stopped talking when he realized the error of his assumption.

Zachary held the Mind Shield in one hand with the Power Ring extended in the other. "Well, you'll need both. But now, the Mind Shield more than ever."

Tiernan took his relic back from the old man. "Because I told them who I was for the first time."

Zachary pulled Tiernan into a quick embrace. "Only those at *peace* with their past, remember?" He stretched around Tiernan and handed the Power Ring to Airvede. "This is on loan. You'll need it too."

The real Zachary let go of the former King. "I'll meet you at the Alwyn Böchord as the Huntress makes her appearance." He gazed at the setting sun. "Better hurry. She'll be here soon." With that, he started walking toward the Archives.

Tiernan took a deep breath to steady his thoughts. Before he could say anything, he heard the Mind Shield speak again.

And now you can see what was right in front of you.

Tiernan turned to the coastline. There, he saw Leviathan come into focus, its masked appearance fading away.

He then looked at his companions and saw something new within each of them.

Airvede, a white, powerful energy surrounding her. Firefly, a yellow aura beaming from her body. And Shig, a green haze reflective of life and joy, emanating from the Paladin's body.

"Are you okay, Zach?"

Tiernan smiled. "Sticking with the nickname?"

Shig leaned in and threw an arm around his companion. "We can do this. You just need faith."

Firefly ran to the right side of Leviathan, dodging an attack that would have crushed her. The beast roared, letting all within hearing range know of its anger. It released dual streams of water from each side of its elongated head, creating deep lines along the beach. It directed the stream northward, finding a building that hadn't yet fallen to its rampage and toppling it like a child would knock over a toy.

Airvede levitated high into the air and around to the creature's back, extending her hands while closing her eyes. She opened her palms and brought them together. Leviathan twisted, feeling the attack of her Bind Magic. It began to charge the red oval on its body.

"Do you see that? It's about to release something!" yelled Shig. "I don't think it likes your bubble, Airvede." Shig ducked as Leviathan's tail swung toward him. The impact only missed him by half a meter as he rolled out of the way. His nimbleness helped save him from a similar fate as the departed Prince.

"Are all of you Ashigaru," Tiernan asked as he raised the Mind Shield to protect himself from an errant stream of water, "that quick on your feet?"

"It's a part of the training," Shig answered as he jumped up.

"So, what are we supposed to do here?" Firefly asked as she rolled in the sand to miss the water stream on the other side. "I don't want to hurt it, but it's not letting up."

"Try a series of fire arrows in front of it. See if the flame pushes it back," Airvede said as she swooped over to Firefly. She tossed her companion the Fire Ring as she returned to her position in the air above the creature's head. "Trust me. I have an idea."

Leviathan stopped its water stream attack and followed Airvede. The red oval in its chest grew brighter. Still bound by its torso, Leviathan's only option of attack was to move its tail and head. As the White Mage hovered above, the creature bellowed in anger.

Airvede landed on its head, steadying herself as the creature twisted left to right above her Bind Magic. She dropped to her knees and placed both palms on its head. The Power Ring's energy shone like a small sunrise atop of the horizon of Leviathan's head.

"Calm. Heal. We're here to help." Leviathan had no discernible eyes, though Tiernan could almost make out a relaxing of its facial muscles, at least where they would be assumed if it had them. The creature's tail fell dormant and the red glow in the oval dimmed to a darkened red, with almost no sign of power within it.

"Airvede, you did it!" exclaimed Shig.

She shook her head. "I know so much more now. I can feel the darkness within its mind. It knows I'm here, but it can't break free of the control it's under." She winced, tightening her forehead muscles. "The oval. It's the key."

Tiernan felt the Mind Shield nudge him within his thoughts to confirm. He looked down at the relic.

Before he could listen, Firefly let out a warning cry. "Airvede! Behind you!"

The White Mage looked up as a winged beast approached the shoreline at a rapid pace. It seemed to come out of nowhere, its wings flapping at an incredible rate.

Tiernan's jaw dropped as he recognized its familiar shape. "That's a dragon. Airvede, I've seen this before. Brace yourself." He looked at the other two. "Spread out!"

Shig and Tiernan ran to the left, while Firefly went to the right.

Because of their physical proximity, the Ashigaru Paladin elbowed the former King. "Do you recognize this one?"

Tiernan wished he could say yes. "No. This is new. This is now the fourth dragon to visit Abria. It's smaller too. A bronze one, three times as large, leveled Farna. A red one started out large but shrunk down to the size of a horse and saved my sister. Plus, a large white one took my grandfather for a ride."

"Bronze, red, white. Now blue. What's it mean?" Shig asked.

Tiernan frowned. "I've never seen a blue one before."

The blue dragon set its sights on Airvede. The White Mage worked in haste, trying hard to free Leviathan's mind before the new beast arrived.

At the last second, she dove off, using her levitating powers to soft-land on the ground. The dragon roared, angry that it missed her, but moved on just as fast with a new target in mind.

It breathed a stream of frost at Leviathan, creating an outline around the protective shield of the Bind Magic. The dragon roared and flew southbound, picking up momentum as it spun around. Then, at a speed rivaling the bronze dragon in Farna, it flew into the ice covering the orb on Leviathan's torso and shattered Airvede's magic with its head.

"It can do that?" Firefly asked as Leviathan bellowed once again.

Satisfied, the dragon rose high in the air and flew northbound. As it left, it made eye contact with Tiernan. He thought he saw satisfaction in its eyes.

It's heading to Farna.

Tiernan looked to the Mind Shield, thinking about the meaning of the briefest hint of a message about the red oval. As he pondered this, Leviathan released another stream of water magic toward him. This time, it directed both of its streams toward the former King. He raised the shield over his head and fell to the ground in as tight of a ball as he could.

Firefly lit the tips of several arrows and released them along the beach, where Leviathan rested just at the edge of the waters. It scared the creature enough that it retreated backward and ceased its torrential attack on Tiernan.

The four of them regrouped as Leviathan dipped below the water.

Airvede threw her hands up in the air in frustration. "I was close. The Power Ring alone isn't enough to free its mind."

"You need this." Tiernan raised the Mind Shield.

Shig shook his head. "She doesn't. You do. Don't you see, Zach? This is your chance to forgive it for what it did to Wayland."

Tiernan spun his head toward Shig, ready to rebuke him. After a moment of hesitation, he relented. "You're right. I heard this thing try to say something about the oval just as Airvede mentioned it. She can't do both."

Firefly pulled out another arrow. "The effect of my fire arrows is subsiding. I wonder why it retreated into the Great Sea?"

"It probably remembered when my sister brought it to its knees with a tremendous fire attack. I'd wager it's afraid of fire now."

Shig's eyes lit up. "You're right. These things thrive in the icy waters in the extreme north." He snapped his fingers. "That's it. Firefly, we need to direct it onto the coastline."

"With my arrows?"

"No. Not your arrows. Forget your bow. Use the Fire Ring. Get it out of the water and onto the coastline."

"What will that accomplish?" Tiernan asked.

"I can't use rings that way, Shig. I can only make arrows that have that kind of magic."

"Says who," countered Shig. "Says your doubt. You can do it, Firefly. I know you can."

"If we can get it out of the water, it might make it easier to subdue," suggested Airvede. "At least it can't retreat."

Tiernan raised his sword toward the bubbling waters. "Here it comes."

Just as he spoke, Leviathan roared out of the Great Sea.

Airvede rose above the ground. "Firefly, I have an idea." She pulled out an ether and absorbed it. "Grab on!" Airvede swooped down and wrapped her arms around Firefly. With the boost from the ether and increased power of the Power Ring, carrying another person was much easier for the White Mage.

"Distract it," Firefly said as Airvede took her along the coastline.

Shig pulled out a dagger — one he didn't care if he lost — and threw it at Leviathan as he ran in the opposite direction. Leviathan turned its head to follow him.

"Shig, watch out!" Tiernan ran after him and tackled his companion. He then turned around just in time, protecting the two of them from a water attack with the Mind Shield. Leviathan doubled down, intensified the attack, and pushed the men into the sand.

"It's angry," Shig said though an exhausted breath as he raised his face out of the sand.

"You think?" Tiernan pushed back, bracing himself and holding the line to protect Shig's body below.

Just as he thought he couldn't hold the defense any longer, the creature cried out. It dropped the water attack, straining its head to follow Airvede.

Firefly released another fire blast from her palm, followed by another and then another. Leviathan shifted its body meter by meter, falling back onto the beach.

Shig stood to his feet and raised his fists in the air while taking a small jump. "It's working! I knew you could do it, Firefly!"

Firefly continued to push enough so that Leviathan's body was now several dozen meters onto the sand. Airvede flew around it. Leviathan twisted in the sand with more difficulty than in the water. The White Mage lowered Firefly to the ground next to Tiernan and Shig and returned to the air.

Unsure which of them to target, Leviathan's head moved from Firefly to Airvede. The White Mage circled to the back of the beast again as her companion released another volley of fire.

Airvede hovered above its head. Leviathan charged its red oval, preparing to unleash some kind of magic onto Firefly. Just as it released the attack — an energy stream consisting of red magic fading to a pink hue in the middle of the beam — Tiernan jumped in front and pushed back.

As the Mind Shield absorbed and deflected the attack, Tiernan took offensive steps toward his adversary. He pulled out his sword. Shig watched with a great deal of sadness.

"Zach. We're here to…" He lowered his voice. "Tiernan. It's a victim as much as your family."

Airvede landed on its head and opened her palms. Leviathan's concentrated blast on Tiernan allowed her to remain steady on its head, almost as if the beast was unaware of her presence. She then leaned down and placed her palms on its head.

"Heal."

It roared and fell low to the ground, still releasing the stream of magic toward Tiernan. With its torso closer to the height of a Graelan, the former King saw his mark.

He raised his sword and charged at Leviathan with the Mind Shield, continuing to deflect its magic as he ran toward the creature. Shig watched in horror as his friend's blade was about to pierce the red oval.

At the last second, Tiernan dropped the weapon and used the full force of both hands on the back of the Mind Shield to make contact with the oval. It shattered like glass with a sound like the mightiest thunder echoing across the coastline.

From deep within, the now freed Ryllix released a sigh of relief. A pink mist emerged from where the oval had once been and dispersed into the sky.

The beast once known as Leviathan made a sound not unlike that of a cooing land creature. Airvede removed her hands and floated in front of it. It followed her movements as it backed up. It lowered its head to the sand in front of Tiernan, who watched things unfold in utter amazement.

She landed next to him. "It told me to tell you thank you."

Tiernan glanced at Airvede, then back at the creature's head. "You heard it speak?"

"Not in words. In emotions. It's grateful. And so very remorseful. It's devastated, not just for the lives it took here, but for the very personal loss it caused you."

Tears welled up in Tiernan's eyes. The Ryllix made the same sound again, then slid backward into the waters. It raised its head one last time. A much different sound echoed throughout the coastline this time.

One of thankfulness and sorrow. It turned around and dove into the depths of the Great Sea.

Chapter 37

The Blue Dragon

Tiernan walked through the open doors of the Alwyn Böchord. Inside, a fire burned bright along an open spot on the northern wall. The former King looked up and down the aisles, admiring the expansive Archives that, until this moment, he had never visited.

"You can learn a lot from the past." Zachary sat next to the fireplace in a large chair. Beside him, an empty chair beckoned Tiernan.

The King strolled along the outer row of shelves, catching various titles and volumes. He rolled his eyes as he saw close to a dozen copies of his manuscript. As he sat down next to Zachary, Tiernan noticed a glass of water on a side table. On top of it was a small loaf of bread.

"It's not Tammith's. How are the others?"

Tiernan took a drink. "Exhausted. Mayor Tibor secured them rooms at one of the inns." He tore off a piece of bread. Starving from the battle, Tiernan talked while chewing. "How did you know?"

"Know what?" he said with a sneaky grin.

So that's how it's going to be. "Don't play games, Zachary. Or is it Steve?"

"Steve is a boy whose life is only just beginning. He has many adventures ahead of him."

"So, it's true. When did you adopt the name Zachary?"

Zachary smiled. "Four hundred and ninety-three years ago. Your grandpa Borun was right. It is an unusual name. I once watched him parade around a room during a celebration. I think it was when they opened Borun Mill, now that I think about it. You were just a baby then.

"When I joined the Abrian Royal Guards during King Telford's war to seal Zoran, I knew it might raise questions. Zachary was a person I befriended many years before, and after he died, I adopted the name."

He raised an eyebrow. "Huh. Much like you did during this journey. Imagine that."

Tiernan swallowed another bite. "And the Power Ring allows one to travel into the past."

Zachary tore off a piece of bread for himself. "No. It amplifies whatever magic the person has. When you and your wife visited my family's home, I saw her magic. I wondered if I had any and began trying different things to activate it." He extended his hand and made a fist, turning it to the left.

Tiernan watched less with a surprised look and more in fascination as the missing pieces of bread returned and his glass on the table refilled. "I know someone else who can do that, too."

Zachary returned his hand to the starting position, bringing the duo back to the present. "When I realized I could do this, I wanted to understand love. You and your wife were our guests and the connection between the two of you was deeper than anything I could comprehend. I rewound time several times before beginning to make sense of it all.

"I've visited the time before the New Era. I've jumped around a lot and served under every King of this land at some point in history. If you want, I could tell you when you'll join them in the beyond, but I don't think that's wise."

"So, you know how this war ends?"

Zachary tore off his final bite and stood. "Yes. I've watched it from the shadows many times. I also learned the dangers of messing with time the hard way."

Tiernan watched Zachary's expression drift off, as if reliving a painful memory. "So, why did you interfere with me?"

Zachary looked down. "I didn't. Look."

Tiernan stood to look toward Zachary's extended finger. In the shadows, he saw another figure. They waved before cupping the Power Ring and disappearing.

"That was me. Let's see, I would have been around one hundred and twenty-five. Still going by Steve. During my travels, I saw myself interacting at different points throughout your journey. It helped me realize that, when the time was right, you would need me."

Tiernan walked up next to him. "So where will you go now?"

Zachary shook his head, a genuine look of uncertainty on his face. "I don't know. I can only tell you that I never saw myself again after this encounter. Maybe I'll die soon. Or maybe I just never crossed paths with myself." He walked toward the door.

"Hey, Zachary."

The old man turned back.

"Thanks."

Zachary bowed. "It's been an honor, my King. Oh." He motioned with his head toward the table. "One more thing. Your companion, Airvede? Give her the book on the table."

"Book? What book?" Tiernan whipped his head back to the table to see a bound volume that hadn't been there earlier.

"I found it not long after I met the first King of Abria, Farris. I had questions. He gave me that book, said it was one of the few things he had from what came before the New Era."

Tiernan's gaze was still fixated on the table. "Wait, Zachary. You've been there. What came before the New Era?" Tiernan's shoulders slumped. Before he turned back, he already knew what he'd see. *I shouldn't have taken my eyes off him.*

Sure enough, the room was empty. Zachary was gone, the book the only clue as to what came before.

To Tiernan, Shig appeared lost in thought. On the horse behind him, Airvede explained to Firefly the intricacies of how Zoran's magic worked from her connection with the Ryllix. Tiernan eavesdropped on the conversation while observing Shig's body language just as the group reentered the trail of the western path of Abria.

"So, is it like a kind of possession magic?" Firefly finally asked, still confused about the whole thing.

"Yes, and no. The Ryllix was aware of what was going on around it but had no power to stop it. Driving its every action was an unnatural need to destroy."

Firefly rubbed her chin. "That might explain why Zoran brought so many monsters from other lands to Enid. Diocenes and harachers came from Kinswatch. Marrens have always plagued us, as has the occasional orc.

"But the rest we never saw back home. Were the invaders already twisted toward darkness, or was this Zoran somehow involved in the invasion of Lonlin too?"

"The Ryllix was in so much mental anguish when I released it. The sea serpent didn't want to harm anyone. I wonder if the same is true for many of the other monsters here as well."

Tiernan, having heard most of the conversation, spoke up while letting his horse fall back next to them. "What's that pinkish mist? Is that Zoran?"

Airvede made a twisting motion with her hand as she answered. "In more ways than one. It's what weaves them to his bidding. It's also what allows him to physically see through their eyes. Zoran knew we were there the moment the Ryllix saw us. I'm sure that marren that tracked us by the Lorelei River played the same role. When I was linked to the Ryllix, I also saw through Zoran's eyes myself."

The group stopped except Shig, who continued on his journey northbound alone and lost in thought.

Tiernan turned his horse sideways. "You saw Zoran? What about Kane and Folas?"

Airvede shook her head. "Just Zoran. I know he is in that citadel-like structure in the north. The others could be anywhere. Even dead."

Shig raised his head to the empty air. He closed his eyes, hoping to let the sun's light brighten his mood. Despite its heat, he felt a chill inside.

"So what about Gamelyon?" He rotated his horse around to face the others. "I saw that pink mist emerge from its mouth as it died. Same for the diocene and other creatures in the desert. I had a hunch about the Ryllix because I've seen them before with my own eyes. Now, it makes me sick to think we could be ending other lives that could be spared."

Firefly rode up to Shig, leaned toward him, and put her hand on his forearm. "Hey kid. Stop. Listen, we can only work with what we know. We can't subdue every creature we encounter, hoping it *might* be kind to us after. And how would we free them? They don't have an oval jewel on their chests for us to break."

"But Gamelyon," he reminded her. "We didn't even give it a chance."

"What does your code say, Shig? You only kill when necessary. At the time, we did not have the Power Ring, only this." Tiernan raised the Mind Shield.

"Your friend could have given it to us earlier."

Tiernan rode over next to Shig. "Look at me, Shig. We only knew to save the Ryllix because of you. None of us here knew what Gamelyon was, and we still don't. You cannot beat yourself up over it." Tiernan looked west. "Trust me, I've done that for far too long."

Tiernan pointed toward the Abrian plateau. "It's this way to Farna. Or rather, what's left of it." He raised the Mind Shield, remembering its warning. "Our next battle will be there. The graves of those my Kingdom lost the day are begging for deliverance."

"From what?" asked Firefly.

"The blue dragon. Follow me. I'll tell you what happened to Farna on the way there."

Tiernan had never seen his home look so bleak, even when revisiting it after the downfall. On Firefly's order, they tied up their horses near a fence surrounding the Royal Cemetery.

Step by step, they climbed the rocky stair-like formations leading up to the top of the plateau. Tiernan looked down, hearing the crunch of his boots in the snow. He wondered where along this path Enid had run, trying her hardest to come in first during the closing race of the Statuo.

An icy, stiff wind blew past. The further they climbed, the snowfall increased fourfold, far more than should be expected during this time of year for the Plateau. A dozen steps later, Tiernan took in a deep gasp and understood why.

Before his eyes, the remnants of the Abrian Plateau had transformed into a frozen wasteland. The ruins of Farna, now a snow-capped, desolate scene of fallen boulders, collapsed walls, and broken timber, screamed back at the King. Even the extreme peaks of the Milston Mountains paled in comparison to what used to be a perpetual paradise.

Perched atop one of the shattered remnants of a tower, the blue dragon rested in silence with a watchful eye aimed at the group.

The graves of those buried under the rubble being defiled by this beast sent a surge of anger through the former King. His chest burned with hatred, knowing that the blue dragon they were about to face, though much smaller than the bronze one that originally destroyed the city, would be a formidable enemy.

"This was Farna."

Tiernan snapped out of his thoughts at Shig's words. The Paladin pulled out a dagger, demonstrating an unusual sense of unease at the devastation.

"Yes. I grew up here, was born here, met my wife here, and ruled here. This was my *home*, Shig."

The dragon, though still at a safe distance, rose and beat its wings. This created a windstorm of hail and ice directed at the group.

"And do you think we'll have to kill it?" Shig asked.

Airvede put her hands forward in a preemptive defense posture. "The dragon seemed intent on stopping our actions in Alwyn, Shig. Remember, it almost rammed me off the Ryllix. Something tells me this creature is aligned with Zoran, not controlled by him." She tapped the Power Ring. "Maybe it's this thing letting me know. To ease your fears."

Tiernan pulled out his sword. The earlier crunches of snow were replaced by something else. He looked down at his boots and realized that with each step, he walked through deeper and deeper piles of snow.

The dragon roared in the distance, raising its head and causing more snow and ice to fall on the ruins. Airvede stepped forward and cast a Barrier spell just as the earlier windstorm reached them.

The four stood on the safe side of Airvede's protective shield. Once the onslaught passed, she lowered the Barrier.

"We have one Fire Ring. Firefly, how many of those arrows do you have left?" asked Shig.

She flipped her quiver around and counted. With a swift twist, Firefly flung it to her back. "Fourteen."

Tiernan strategized in his mind. "Airvede, I think you will need the Fire Ring, at least until Firefly runs out of arrows. Shig and I can act as a diversion."

"Oh man, again?" Shig shook his head in a moment of self-chastising. "No, you're right. I'm the fastest, and Zach has that magic shield. The plan makes sense."

The group resumed their trek toward the ruins of Farna. Tiernan cast a quick westward glance in the direction of his wife and son's escape, thinking about them and hoping for their safety. He then returned his focus to the blue dragon.

Tiernan ran through the spot where the gates of Farna used to stand tall. He raised the Mind Shield, deflecting a hail of ice magic from the blue dragon.

It swooped down, trying to crush the former King within its open jaws. Tiernan batted its head away, causing it to snap hard to the right. The dragon recoiled, and Tiernan took advantage of its sideways momentum by sliding the Mind Shield off his arm. He used its pointed edge as a blade, jamming it into the neck of the dragon.

Dark navy blood trickled down. He pulled the relic out just as the dragon took flight. Behind it, Airvede hovered. She used her Barrier ability to catch one of the dragon's hind legs. She pulled her arms together in a snap, and Tiernan recoiled as he saw the trapped foot crush into a mangled mess of flesh and bone.

Now aware of how the Power Ring could boost her abilities, Airvede retreated backward. The dragon turned its head around and gave her a menacing stare before it flew higher in the sky than the White Mage could levitate.

Shig, standing on the opposite side of the battlefield, threw a series of three daggers at its body. Two of them dug themselves deep into the dragon's abdomen with the third hitting its wing and disappearing into the snowy battlefield. Using her Retrieve spell, Airvede pulled the two in its body out and sent them back to Shig for reuse.

Before it was out of range, Firefly released two of her fire arrows toward the opposite wing. They made contact, and its wing burst into flame as the dragon disappeared high into the mist of clouds and falling snow.

The four met up near the entrance of the former Castle Abria. Tiernan tried not to think about where he was standing, lest he let his anger take control again. Airvede floated to the ground while Shig spun a retrieved dagger in his hand, a trickle of blue blood on its blade dripping onto the ground.

"This seems easier than I expected it would be," said Shig.

"This is the smallest dragon I've encountered. Any idea where it went?" Tiernan scanned the sky, looking for a sign of the winged beast.

He didn't have to wonder for long. The dragon returned and perched on the tower from earlier, balancing itself on its good hind claw. It raised its head to the clouds and opened its mouth wide.

The dragon then emitted a circular blue wave of energy across the ruins. Tiernan and the others ducked, though it passed through them as it did the ruins and dilapidated structures within Farna.

The blue energy covered the entire Abrian peninsula. Without warning, it retracted, bringing all the snow and ice with it. Tiernan used the Mind Shield to protect him and Firefly as Airvede cast a Barrier to protect Shig and herself. The ice and snow bounced off both defenses as the elements continued on their way back to the dragon.

Tiernan looked down and saw hints of grass and dirt below his feet. Though far from the vibrancy of the old Farna, it felt good to see his home free from snow.

"Why? What purpose did that serve?" asked Firefly.

Airvede lowered the Barrier and reabsorbed the magic she had used to cast it. "Spite." The group turned to Airvede. "If there is one thing I've learned about Zoran from your book, it's that he hates Farna. Hates the royal family. This served no functional purpose other than to frustrate you, Tiernan."

The former King looked north toward the gaping hole where the magic had emerged several years ago. He followed the trail of destruction — the homes that fell in and the portions of Castle Abria that collapsed into the chasm — to his in-laws' tavern. He could make out a few remnants of the Drunken Alligator before it succumbed to the devastation as well. The blue dragon, now poised for attack, roared atop the ruins of the castle.

In his mind, he heard the screams of those crushed by the bronze dragon's boulders. Replayed the ramming of the walls and how that beast ripped them from their foundations.

Tiernan narrowed his eyes and walked forward. "You want me, don't you? I know you can hear me. You can see me through this dragon's eyes. I'm coming for you, Zoran. You can send as many dragons as you want. Bronze, blue, I don't care."

He dropped the sword. "So, why don't you face me head on? Are you afraid? I saw how Midir injured you. A mere Graelan with no relics or hidden powers almost ended your pathetic life."

Tiernan raised the Mind Shield. "You want me? Then come and get me." He shifted his stance, ready for the dragon's attack.

Instead, the creature turned its head left to right as if in communication with another. Malicious glee filled its eyes. Just as a Graelan would, it nodded in understanding or agreement. It gave the group one last deafening growl before closing its eyes. A bright, white-hot light began at its chest and enveloped it from head to toe.

Tiernan's instinct was to cover his eyes. He didn't care. He kept them open and watched the transformation with utter fascination.

When it was over, the blue dragon was no more. Instead, it had split into a glowing orb alongside two beings, both feminine in nature with long, flowing locks of hair.

Just like my old hair.

Their outfits had a mystical quality, draped around them in white fabrics accented with highlights of powder blue details. Each wore brown bottoms, though from the knee down, their legs appeared to be made of transparent ice and snow.

Like the dragon, both possessed a set of wings. Unlike the beast, their wings were as clear as glass. One of them, distinctive from its twin because of its mangled foot, held a long rose gold scepter almost the length of its body. The other held what Tiernan presumed to be a wand of a similar color, though with a transparent glass handle. The tip of the wand ended in what could best be described as a twisting snakehead.

They exchanged a look with each other as a third being formed from the orb. This was an archer with a rose gold bow and a similar style of clothing to the Ice Twins.

Tiernan picked up his sword as the others readied their weapons.

Shig walked up. "Nice job, Zach. I think you made Zoran angrier."

Chapter 38

Honor

The new archer jumped from pile of rubble to pile of rubble, bounding off the remnants of Castle Abria to take up an offensive posture against the group. The other two beings took to the skies and circled around them. After a few moments of observation, the one with the wand threw a powerful blast of ice magic toward Airvede, who deflected it with a Barrier.

Firefly readied an arrow. "Split up. Tiernan, Shig, deal with the other Ice Twin. Airvede, can you handle that one?"

"Of course," she said as she threw a blast of fire from the ring toward the Ice Twin across from her.

"Good. This," Firefly smiled, choosing a name for her opponent, "Frost Archer is mine!"

Tiernan watched as Firefly took off into the rubble, hiding within the collapsed structures. The Frost Archer looked from left to right, trying to find her position. Out of the rubble came one of Firefly's fire arrows. It hit the being in the chest and sent it flying backward into the streets.

"Shig! Duck!" Tiernan placed the Mind Shield in front of his friend, protecting Shig's body with the relic as the mangled twin came in for the kill. Its scepter appeared to be imbued with some kind of Frost Magic as well, though the ancient relic absorbed the attack. Enraged, the Ice Twin returned to the sky.

Behind them, Airvede cast her Bind Magic on the rubble. She brought the bound debris high into the air and smashed the masonry against the first Ice Twin. It knocked the winged being off course, taking it a few moments to recover. Airvede did it again, though this time the Ice Twin repelled the attack with a blast from its frost-enabled wand.

The Frost Archer ran from the streets where it fell and released an arrow at Shig and Tiernan. Tiernan tried to protect them again, but wasn't fast enough this time.

However, someone else was. Firefly deflected the Frost Archer's arrow with one of her own, sending it off course. She emerged from her hiding spot and rushed at the being, swiping at it with her bow.

The Frost Archer stumbled backward and uttered something in a language none of the Graelans understood. It raised its hand to the sky as the Ice Twin with the mangled foot picked up the Archer to transport it elsewhere in the ruins.

Firefly ran over to Shig and Tiernan. "The dragon was easier. We could coordinate our efforts."

"Maybe we still can," Tiernan suggested. "Shig, take this." Tiernan handed his companion the Mind Shield. "Zoran can see me through their eyes, anyway. Let's see if he falls for the bait."

"You're going to be the distraction for once? Thanks, Zach."

Tiernan smiled as he ran across the field toward the Drunken Alligator. He looked behind him to see Airvede engaged with the other Ice Twin. Despite her defensive-forward magic profile, she seemed to be holding her own in an offensive pattern.

Tiernan slid under the collapsed doorway of the Alligator. Though much of the tavern laid in ruins, he spotted the remains of the bar against the western wall. He navigated toward it, around the destroyed tables and drooping roof. He crouched low and found exactly what he hoped he would. Tiernan grabbed the items and returned to the battlefield.

By then, the second Ice Twin had returned to make strafing runs at Shig. Much as he had five years ago when Wayland helped to rescue Eislyn, Tiernan hoped the Mind Shield wouldn't find anything in the Paladin's past that would prevent the ancient relic from protecting him.

As Tiernan ran, he saw Firefly release a normal arrow at the Frost Archer. It pierced the being's arm, embedding itself deep into its left bicep. The Frost Archer pulled it out, blue blood running down its arm like the dragon before.

Before Tiernan made it back to the battle, Shig threw a dagger at the second Ice Twin. It impaled the creature deep in its chest, with the blade disappearing completely. The attack appeared to be fatal as this Ice Twin fell to the ground and did not get back up.

Horrified, the other Twin dropped its attack on Airvede and swooped over to its fallen half. Shig didn't see the winged being coming as it fired a blast from its wand at his exposed back.

Shig fell over, ice spreading across his back. He cried out in pain as the active Ice Twin retrieved its deceased half from the ground and carried it away. Tiernan rushed to his friend's side and placed his objects next to the Paladin.

Airvede glided over and landed next to him. She kneeled down and made a tight fist with her right hand wearing the Fire Ring. She placed her other hand with the Power Ring on his back. Fire traveled through her body from one hand to the next. It melted the ice and revealed the wound in Shig's back.

She motioned her head to her side. "I need another ether, and he'll need a potion. My satchel."

Tiernan quickly dug through it. He found the ether first and handed it to the White Mage.

"Press it into my palm." She let the fire effect dissipate from her right hand so Tiernan could press it in. Once absorbed, he resumed digging as she placed both hands on Shig's back. The skin around the wound closed. Airvede removed her right hand and reignited the Fire Ring, hoping to keep Shig's body warm until the potion could restore his strength.

A few ticks later, Tiernan found a small vial just as Shig coughed and as Airvede helped him to his feet.

The stunned and shaken Ashigaru Paladin sat on the ground. "Was I dead?"

Airvede laughed. "No. Nowhere close to it."

"Here. Drink this." Tiernan handed Shig the potion.

He flipped the lid off and swallowed the concoction. "How many more of these do you have? Because I feel weak." He looked at his friends, embarrassed at his forthcoming confession. "I, uh, I don't think I have the strength to fight."

Tiernan helped Shig scoot up against a fallen building. "It'll take some time for that potion to work through your body." The former King then put the Mind Shield in front of him. "Keep this in front of you. Stay behind it. The rubble protects your back, so your injury will be safe. Let us handle the Ice Twins. Rest up, my friend."

"Ice Twin. Singular. Tiernan, look." Airvede pointed toward a still-standing portion of the eastern wall.

The first Ice Twin eyed them, fueled by rage, as it now held both the scepter and wand in its right hand. Blue blood stained its white clothing as Shig's dagger, also dripping in the same color liquid, dangled from its right hand.

It spoke in the same foreign language as the Archer had before as the scepter and wand merged into a magical staff. It then threw the dagger high in the air. While it hovered, it raised the staff and enveloped the dagger in an ice-like effect.

It threw the frost-fueled dagger toward Shig, Tiernan, and Airvede. The White Mage cast a Barrier just in time, though the strength of the attack did not repel the weapon as expected.

Instead, the force of the Ice Twin's attack continued to push the weapon forward, aimed directly at Airvede's torso.

She turned. "Tiernan, go. Get Shig out of here."

He shook his head. "Shig is fine. I'll be back. Hold your ground." Tiernan ran back to the objects he brought from the Alligator and toward the direction of the rubble from where he saw Firefly's arrows emerging a few moments earlier.

There, he found her hidden behind a pile of stones and breathing hard.

"You okay?"

Firefly nodded. "Just needed a break."

"How many fire arrows do you have?"

"Four. Why?"

Tiernan raised the two objects in his hands. "See these bottles? Follow my movement. When you see my sign, send your best one toward them."

Firefly pulled out a fire arrow. "You want me to shoot a bottle?"

He smiled. "Yes. Do you trust me? I know what's in these."

"Fair enough."

Tiernan ran through the streets, using his knowledge of his hometown's layout to slip through the boulders and rubble without either the remaining Ice Twin or the Frost Archer seeing him. He came around the long way, sneaking up behind the winged being.

As Tiernan rounded a corner behind a portion of the wall, he saw the mangled body of the other Ice Twin, blue blood splattered near where its other half tore the dagger from his body.

Tiernan saw Firefly's gaze from the shadows. He raised the first bottle. From the darkness, he watched her load the arrow and pull it back, primed and ready for release.

Tiernan didn't dare speak. Instead, he threw the bottle toward the remaining Ice Twin. It saw the oncoming object, which distracted it enough that it released the magic that had been trying to push the dagger through Airvede's Barrier.

It tried to deflect the spinning bottle, though it was too late. Firefly released her arrow, which broke through the glass and ignited the liquid inside. The alcohol exploded in a spectacular display of fire, engulfing the Ice Twin and setting it ablaze. Pieces of glass pierced its body while the heat melted its icy wings. The flame scorched its clothing, charred its skin, and burned the staff.

Firefly then released a second fire arrow, which hit the creature square in the chest and exploded. The being plummeted to its death, landing on the ground on top of its other half in a fiery spectacle.

With her position now revealed, the Frost Archer released a volley of arrows at Firefly. Just in time, she ducked behind nearby rubble. Pinned down, she couldn't move as the Frost Archer moved in.

A moment later, it was over. Tiernan stood next to Airvede, who, with the power of the Fire Ring, had performed a similar trick with the second bottle.

The Frost Archer, now burned and in pain, tried to extinguish the flame spreading across its clothing using its hands. It dropped its bow and released the quiver from its back as the strap burned.

Firefly released another fire arrow at the distracted Frost Archer, making contact. The Frost Archer fell dead, joining the rest of the attackers in a smoldering defeat. She rushed over and removed the arrows from its quiver before it burned up.

Tiernan walked over to Shig and extended a hand to his friend. The Paladin grabbed it and stood.

"How are you feeling?" Tiernan asked.

"I'm sore, but I'll be okay." Shig looked around at the devastation. "You honored their deaths today."

Tiernan cast a somber expression toward the remains of Castle Abria, reflecting on Shig's words and picturing himself as a small boy running through the halls with his sister and best friend.

For a moment, he thought he could hear his mother's voice again, telling the three of them it was time for dinner.

Dusk fell across the Abrian Peninsula. As the group made their way down the now snow-free steps, Tiernan reflected on his journey so far. He knew that, even if his friends needed a place to rest and Oakshadow was far away, he had one last task to do here before they made their way north.

The others stood at the edge of the Royal Cemetery, giving the former King the privacy he requested. Shig assured Tiernan he would prepare the horses for the next leg of their journey.

Tiernan walked through the quiet rows of tombstones and grave markers. After a short while, he came upon an important one.

"King Farris. The First King of Abria. I never knew you. I know you're my grandpa's great-grandparents. What secrets do you know about what came before the New Era?" Tiernan furrowed his brow as he read the inscription next to the resting King. "My Beloved Wife, Riona."

Tiernan walked some more, finding lots of relatives he didn't know and what appeared to be honored castle attendants or servants from the past centuries. A ways up the row, he came to another royal tombstone.

"Telford and Netta. You fought Zoran, too. I guess Zachary even helped you with that at some point." He squatted down and read the dates on the inscription. "Grandpa even knew you before you died. How do I defeat Zoran?"

He returned to a standing position and put his hands on his hips. Knowing he wouldn't get any answers, Tiernan moved into the next row of tombs.

Starting here, the grave markers became more elaborate. Though Tiernan knew almost nothing about him, a rough sculpture stood upon a simple, square stone. Beside him was another square stone, though this one lacked a sculpture.

"Keelan. Grandpa's father. Yet another King." He moved closer and realized the top of the empty square appeared to be broken as he read the inscription. "Maeve, My Queen. Commander of the Royal Guards. Where is your statue, Maeve?" In that moment, Tiernan decided he would speak to Rhys about trying to fix this marker, especially if the Archives contains any paintings or images of the former Queen.

Next to Keelan was another grave. This one was much more elaborate, with a lifelike representation of the King resting below it.

"King Tiernan the First. Dad thought you deserved a statue. For the longest time, I didn't. You took my name away from me, forcing me to wear yours."

He smirked. "After going by another name for a while, I hate to admit it but I've grown used to it." He put his hand on the statue. "Rest easy."

Tiernan walked around to the next row and sat on the ground in front of a marker. He recited the inscription from memory.

"To my husband, my greatest love. Till we meet again." Overshadowing the former King stood the imposing presence of Wayland's memorial, a marker on its base etched with the words Enid intended to add but never saw completed for herself. Beside him, another grave occupied an even larger plot.

Tiernan buried his head in his hands as he spoke. "Sister." As the King at the time, Tiernan demanded her monument reflect her Dragonborn nature with wings stretching out to both sides, including one of them wrapped around that of her departed husband. In her hands, Enid's beloved axe was ready to strike any foe that might attack.

Tiernan lost track of time, unaware of how long he had sat here reminiscing. Once he felt he had stayed as long as he could, he sat up and pushed himself from the ground. "Goodbye, Way. I love you, Sis."

Tiernan then walked down the row to the central part of the cemetery. He took in the expertly carved monument, two figures standing side by side. He admired how accurately the sculptor had gotten the details. The hair pulled back into a knot. The beard. A crown carved atop each of their heads.

The look of love and joy on both faces.

"Mom. Dad. I know I've been away for a while. I don't have a lot of time to stay, either, but I just wanted to say I'm going to make this right. For all of you. Way, Enid, Grandpa, too. The next time I'm here will be to celebrate the end of this war.

"I love you." With that, he turned to leave the Royal Cemetery.

Chapter 39

The Oakshadow Raid

Shig rolled to avoid the deadly axe swing of an orc. Beside the dim-witted creature, an Elf fired a blast of Wind Magic at the hero, picking him up and tossing him like a sack of flour across the field.

Airvede extended her hand and caught him in her magic, lowering him to the ground. "Try to be more careful."

He threw up his hand in his signature wave as she returned her attention to the pair of giants terrorizing a small contingent of Abrian Royal Guards.

Firefly released a series of arrows toward a flame-based creature similar to the one they fought in the Windale Desert. These arrows, frozen with the power of a looted Frost Ring from a fallen Elf, dug themselves deep into her enemy.

It rushed at her, trying to end her before the arrows froze it from the inside out. As the ice spread, Tiernan ran up and sliced it from shoulder to hip at a diagonal. The creature fell into a heap and blew away into the breeze.

"What are those weird flame creatures?" he asked.

"I have no idea. I've never seen anything like it before. There's a land south of here called Infernus. Maybe they're from there?" Firefly switched rings, pulling out a Poison Ring and sliding it on her finger. She then squeezed the tips of several arrows to transform them into poisoned arrows. "Wish me luck."

Tiernan nodded as she ran off, releasing one of them against another orc. Though its skin was tough, the arrow nicked the skin enough for the toxin to enter its body. The creature let out a wail as it felt the poison spread.

Meanwhile, Tiernan turned his attention back to the orc and Elf closing in on Shig. The smaller man dodged another blast of Wind Magic and retaliated with a dagger. The Elf raised his hand to teleport away, but was too late. Shig's dagger found its mark, burying itself in the Elf's chest.

The orc noticed its companion fall and came up with another idea. It dropped its axe, picked up the deteriorating Elf, and threw him toward Shig as if it were a mere boulder. Shig dodged this too as the body of the Elf tumbled away into the field.

Shig retaliated with another dagger throw. This sliced the orc's arm and caused it to howl in pain.

Tiernan raised his sword and charged the creature, though like Firefly's attempt in the cave, the blade struggled to penetrate its skin. The furious orc shifted its focus from Shig to Tiernan. It grabbed the axe and swung at the former King. If not for the Mind Shield, Tiernan would have perished.

From across the field, Firefly released another poison arrow at this orc as well. Her expertise with the bow meant she could target its open cut on its arm from Shig's dagger.

"Shig, run!" Tiernan yelled as the orc chased after him.

Shig pulled his dagger out of the now deceased Elf and bolted toward Oakshadow, the original intended destination of the group. Rather than check-in and get some rest at an inn, they stumbled upon an ongoing battle between Zoran's minions and the city guards. In addition, Royal Guards patrolling this area had since joined the fight, leading to an all-out brawl.

A dozen meters south of the guards' position, another group of defenders from Oakshadow fought against multiple bandits. Shig caught up with them and tackled one rebel from behind, knocking them to the ground as the other insurgents looked down at their fallen companion.

This acted as enough of a distraction for the guard to impale several bandits with his spear. The one under Shig wiggled, trying to break free.

"Listen, my friend," the Paladin said between struggles. "Choose to live. These men will end you right here, right now. You can walk away if you stop."

The bandit got an arm free and sucker-punched Shig across the jaw.

"Ow." Shig looked down at the man, still mostly pinned under his body." He sighed. "That was the wrong choice." Shig whaled, subduing him with several intense blows.

He stood up and looked back at an approaching Royal Guard. "I knocked him out for you. You can put him in a prison before he wakes up."

The guard rushed over and, without hesitation, jammed his sword into the torso of the subdued bandit.

"Hey, that wasn't necessary," Shig said in protest.

The guard shook his head. "Our teams have been fighting groups like these all the way from Northwick and Milston to here. Lorelei is under siege just like Oakshadow. Rebel Elves, these ugly green creatures—"

"Orcs," Shig interjected.

"I don't care what they are. They've raided the northern towns. Killed many of our people, just like those vicious walking lizards—"

"Diocenes."

The guard gave Shig a look. "Stop. I don't know what the four of you have been doing, but things are a mess up here."

Shig started to explain before he caught the wandering gaze of a stalking green diocene emerging from the forest. "Watch out!" Shig threw a dagger toward the creature, impaling it between its already-blind eyes. It fell to the ground as two more emerged, along with a pair of avians he did not recognize.

Firefly did. "Those are marrens! Everyone watch yourselves!" She loaded her bow with another poison arrow, taking down one of them while the other circled above.

Tiernan stopped running. The poisoned orc had slowed down enough that it fell to its feet. As its body grew weak, it dropped the axe. The former King felt sadness for the creature and walked over to it, though far enough to remain safe from any errant attack it might attempt.

The orc made eye contact. Using what little energy it had left, its deep voice uttered two words that said more than a well-composed closing ceremonies speech from the Statuo.

"Help us."

Tiernan's eyes grew wide as it fell dead, succumbing to the effects of the Poison Magic from Firefly's arrow. He looked to the rest of the battlefield plaguing the entrance to Oakshadow. Hordes of creatures continued to emerge from the Rosewood Forest, including more giants, orcs, diocenes, marrens, the flame creatures, and a few others Tiernan didn't recognize.

The dying orc's words replayed in his mind. *How? How am I supposed to help you? Where's the red orb we can break on your chest like the Ryllix?*

Tiernan's answer came from the Mind Shield. *Reunite us.*

He looked down to the Mind Shield, then to Airvede wielding the Power Ring, and last to the Rosewood Forest.

Tiernan eyed the outline of the woods and saw what looked to be a definitive path inside of it. He bolted toward the battle to find his companions.

Shig stood back-to-back with the guard who had killed the bandit. Two more diocenes circled them as the rest of the battalion spread out to defend Oakshadow against new the onslaught of monsters. Shig pulled out a clean dagger.

"I think we need to rush them," the guard said.

"No. Be patient. These things can only sense us. The green ones like these can't see. If we're careful, they'll be easy to take down."

The guard shook his head. "We cannot wait. I'm going for it."

"No. Wait!" Shig felt the man leave his backside.

As the guard charged, the diocene in front of the Ashigaru Paladin charged, claws extended and mouth agape. Shig dove under it and rolled on his back, slicing the belly of the diocene with the blade. The creature bellowed and fell on top of Shig.

"Stop, it's a trap." Shig couldn't say anything else before the unthinkable happened. The remaining marren in the sky dive-bombed, grabbing the guard by the shoulders with its long talons digging into his shoulders.

Blood trickled out of his wounds as the marren raised him into the air. Frantic, the guard cried out. "Help me!"

Firefly turned when she heard his plea. She loaded an arrow and fired, but missed.

The marren rose even higher into the sky, above the tallest trees of the Rosewood Forest. The guard continued to cry for help as the marren's height surpassed even the nearby peaks of the western mountain range.

Satisfied, the marren released the man. Shig watched in horror from below the dead diocene as the guard fell at terminal velocity, impacting the ground along the northern path. The other diocene retreated into the Forest, having fulfilled its purpose as a distraction.

Tiernan pushed the dead monster off his companion.

Shig shook his head in frustration. "It was a decoy. The diocenes were a diversion to keep us occupied for the marren."

Firefly released several arrows into a nearby giant, toppling it with a fatal shot. She rushed over to the pair. "The marren knew one of you would get antsy. Once the guard moved, the diocene saw you as an easy target."

Airvede landed next to them. "How long can we hold them off? The number of monsters seems to be never-ending."

Tiernan pointed to her hand. "You have the Power Ring." He raised the Mind Shield. "I have this. We have to retrieve the Soul Sword. With the other relic, I think we can release these creatures from Zoran's control."

"Where is the Soul Sword, Z?"

Tiernan smirked at Shig's new shortened nickname for the former King, as it reminded him of the single-letter nickname his wife and family had grown accustomed to calling him. "I think it's in there. With Folas."

The four adventurers eliminated several more hostiles before leaving the rest to the city defenders and patrolling Royal Guards.

Tiernan hated abandoning them, but decided that if they didn't pursue this path, there wouldn't be an Oakshadow in the morning. As they took their first few steps into the Rosewood Forest, Tiernan swallowed hard. He had heard the Forest during the daytime was intimidating enough. In the middle of the night, it was downright foreboding.

Firefly stretched the string of her bow. Airvede used the power of her Fire Ring as a torch to light their way. Shig took up the rear, acting as the group's eyes for any ambushing monster attack from behind.

Airvede stepped on a branch, its sound echoing throughout the Forest. The other three froze, looking her way.

She pointed to her feet. "Sorry, I think I've gotten used to levitating. I haven't walked for a while. I'll be more careful."

"What are we looking for, Z?" Shig asked.

"There used to be an Elven settlement deep within the woods. Rumor has it the Dark Elf lives in here in the old encampment."

Tiernan stopped. "I need you three to understand this. Folas is *powerful*. We've all grown in our powers and abilities, but be prepared for anything. Understand?"

Silence. There was no response from the group. Tiernan put his hands backward, trying to feel for his companions.

Nothing. He spun around. The Rosewood Forest was gone, replaced by a green haze around him.

"Hello!"

Silence.

"I said, hello! Firefly! Airvede! Shig! Anyone?"

The only sound was the hollow echo of his voice.

Tiernan raised his sword, prepared to strike at whatever mind games Folas had decided to play with the group.

Chapter 40

Mind Games

Firefly ducked into a cave, unsure of how she ended up back in Lonlin after just crossing into the Rosewood Forest with her friends. Before she could call out their names, she heard the stalking sound of an enormous creature.

She slowed her breathing and, to the best of her ability, tried to ignore her heart about to beat out of her chest. With her mind clear and focused, she listened.

Not a diocene. Not even a giant or an orc. She strained her ears, trying to understand what she was about to face.

A vicious cawing revealed the answer. *A marren.* This confused her because the sound of the marren was louder and more threatening than anything she had heard from the species before, both here and back home in Lonlin. The thumping rivaled that of the orc that had chased her in the caves almost a week ago.

She remembered the poor guard from just a few moments earlier, plummeting to his death at the talons of a much smaller marren. *This creature shouldn't exist.* She dug through her satchel and pulled out a Wind Ring she had scavenged off a fallen attacker just before she entered the Forest. She slid it onto a finger on her right hand to test this new power.

She made a fist using the same hand. Then, she grabbed an arrow from her quiver and, rather than run her palm down it as she had so far, envisioned the power transferring from her to the item. She pulled it back tight on her string, raised up from behind the rock, and fired it outside through the cave entrance.

Firefly cheered inside. The transference worked. Not only did the Wind Ring increase her power, it sent the arrow flying at record speed and distance. She tried to estimate how many meters this distraction might have flown, but lost sight of it as it continued on its path.

Oh. Oh, that was a mistake. A gargantuan marren landed at the cave entrance. *That didn't distract it. It knows where I am now.* She slipped behind the rock again but peeked her head out just enough to watch its actions.

The marren lowered its head to look inside the cave, though it had to step back because there wasn't enough clearance to get a good view because of its overgrown size. The beast lowered its head again, looking for the source of the arrow.

Firefly wasn't quick enough. The two made eye contact before she could duck down. The marren roared as it found its prey.

Shig crawled through a ravine, staying low as arrows flew overhead. *This makes no sense. I was just in Abria. This isn't even Watodo. Where am I? How did I get here?*

An arrow just missed his head. Shig did his best to lower even further into the ditch. As he crawled over a hump in the ground, his body was exposed for a brief moment to his attackers.

A second oncoming arrow grazed his shoulder, slicing through his clothing and cutting a gash into his skin. He winced and crawled faster, though the pain in his left shoulder made it hard to move at his usual pace.

He entered a low spot in the ravine and saw one of his fellow Ashigaru flat on his back. At first, he didn't recognize the face or outfit.

As he crawled closer, it transformed into something familiar, his friend Tigamono. "Tiga!" Shig pulled himself forward on his hands and knees, feeling another arrow brush his arched backside.

Shig didn't care. Tiga needed his help, and he would not let some minor scrape keep him from doing the honorable thing.

Tiga did not respond to Shig's voice. As the Ashigaru Paladin drew closer, he discovered why.

A series of arrows had already ended his friend's life. Two had penetrated his heart. Another had grazed Tiga's temple and two more were lodged in his abdomen.

"Tiga, wake up. Please, no, my shin'yū." Shig smacked the ground, digging his fist into the mud. He pulled his hand out, wet soil lodged under his normally clean fingernails. He looked around his friend's body and saw dozens of Ashigaru lining the ravine further ahead.

"No. You can't *all* be gone. You can't." Shig backed up and felt his foot hit something. With a careful twist, he looked back at what he had hit.

More Ashigaru soldiers lined the trench, all dead from the exact same injuries as Tiga. Shig shook his head. "None of this can be real. They weren't there just a few seconds ago."

Shig closed his eyes. "This isn't real. This isn't real. This isn't real."

"But it is real, Brother."

Shig's eyes popped open. Now, his hands and feet were chained against the wall of a damp stone dungeon. The caked-on mud was gone from his fingers and his injuries missing. A musty smelled filled the air and, while a window allowed some light into the room, there were a half dozen torches lit in key points.

The flickering red, yellow, and orange flames cast a sinister glow on the man standing with his arms crossed.

"Isoshi? Thank the Emperor, Kyōdai, I found you after all this time!"

"Tell us, Shig. Which of your group is the weakest? Which of them deserves to die first?"

A chill ran down Shig's spine. "Isoshi?"

His brother walked up and raised a dagger. He put it against Shig's throat, the tip drawing a slight scrape of blood. "Is it the former Prince? Davien's son who would pretend to be King? Or maybe it's that floating White Mage of yours. She fancies herself to be more than she is."

A sickening, overwhelming cold sweat overtook Shig's body. "Isoshi, what is this?"

"Is it the archer? I don't like her. Reminds me of someone I once knew." Isoshi pulled the dagger away. "I know, though. It's you. The weakling little brother. The one always living in my shadow."

Isoshi turned his back to Shig and issued a command to the executioner, wearing a blackened hood and holding a sharpened kodachi blade. "Kill him. Make it hurt."

Airvede moved from person to person. Their faces, now mangled and in pain, showed the telltale signs of the only infection she knew of that could cause this much pain and deformity.

"The Galvan Scourge. But how?" She lifted her head and looked across the city streets. She appeared to be in Alwyn, which made no sense.

She levitated above one and recognized his face. "You're the mayor. Tibor, I think. How did this happen?"

It's me. I must be a carrier of the disease. And I passed it on to these poor people.

I am the Galvan Scourge.

She shook her head. "This is not right." She looked at the sky. "It was the middle of the night. Not the middle of the day."

Airvede spun around. Behind her were more bodies, now piled up three persons high. "None of this is real."

She snapped her fingers, and the scene changed to one far closer to her heart.

"The village of Clandagh. Eamon!" Airvede saw her home in the distance and rose above the ground to fly to it. Before she could, she fell back.

Moving toward her home at an incredible clip was a giant fireball. She caught a glimpse of her husband and two children through the window, laughing and playing, just as the flame engulfed her home. The destruction was absolute as the fireball hit the ground with a forceful impact, leveling her home, creating a burning crater, and killing her family in an instant.

Tears welled up in her eyes, though she pushed back at the sensation just as quick as it arrived. "This isn't real either. Whoever you are, this will not work."

The scene changed again. This time, she stood face to face with someone she did not recognize. It was a tall female Elf, one with skin like that of an ink well. Her clothing, draped in dark purple, pink, and gray, evoked a sense of control as well as elegance.

"What do you know of Ultimus?" the female Elf asked.

Airvede tipped her head to one side. "I'm sorry, I've never heard of Ultimus."

From the Elf's hand, a black ball the same tone as her skin formed. It emerged from her hand quickly, rushing toward the White Mage and attacking her in the stomach.

"Here. Have a taste." She made a *tsk* sound with her mouth. "Disappointing, though. You're a mage and you've never heard of Ultimus? Have you ignored the teachings of that book you have?"

"What book?" Airvede fought hard to talk through the pain.

"The one the old Time Master gave you. Have you even opened it?"

"I haven't," Airvede took a step forward. "I haven't had the time," she said through gritted teeth.

"Ridiculous. What kind of witch are you then if you haven't studied the secrets of what came before the New Era?"

"I'm not a witch. I'm a healer."

"Lies," the Elf said as she amplified the attack. "You carry the Power Ring. You're not as strong as she was, but you're just as annoying."

She. The Elf is referring to Enid. "What do you know of the Dragonborn?"

The Elf stopped her attack, giving Airvede a momentary reprieve from the pain. "Ah, now we're getting somewhere. So, have you met her?"

"Enid is dead."

The Elf raised her hand, another Ultimus attack on its way. "It's a shame. She might have been able to teach you how to save yourself from this."

She shrugged as Airvede raised the hand wearing the Power Ring.

"That won't save you, my dear."

Firefly ran through the cave as if she was being chased by the entire Kinswatch armada. Though the marren filled most of the cavern and would get stuck on outcroppings here and there, it still had enough momentum to continue moving forward. As it stomped, it knocked down boulders and debris from the cave ceiling.

Firefly looked back and saw the avian getting closer. She pulled out an arrow, focused on the Wind Ring, and turned to fire.

It flew by the marren's head, a mark she should not have missed even on her worst day.

The arrow hit the cave entrance and exploded in a high-pitched sound. A few ticks later, the ceiling started to crumble. Firefly sprinted toward the exit as the cave imploded around her, the marren growing ever closer.

The destruction of the cave caught up, passed overhead, and caused the rocks above Firefly to collapse. Some fell on her, pinning her leg and immobilizing her.

The marren raised its beak and cawed. It locked eyes with Firefly. She couldn't be sure, but was positive she saw something terrifying below them.

Exhilaration.

The marren wasn't just about to end her life. Instead, it was going to enjoy every moment of tearing her apart, piece by piece and limb by limb. It approached her with its mouth open, saliva dripping.

Tiernan walked in the direction he assumed to be north toward the Elven settlement.

"Is anyone there?" He was getting sick of the silence and hoped that someone, anyone, would respond soon.

He raised the Mind Shield. *Talk to me. You've been awful vocal lately. Now you're going to give me the silent treatment? Say something. Anything.*

Silence.

"Hello? Can anyone hear me?"

"I can, my love."

Through the haze, he thought he saw a familiar shape. He walked toward it, sword drawn but feeling a sense of calm.

"Eislyn?" Tiernan dropped the sword and slid the Mind Shield off his arm.

"I wouldn't do that. Pick them up. Now."

Tiernan squinted, trying to make out her features.

"T, just do it. There's no time to argue."

Tiernan squatted down and picked up the Mind Shield. He kept his gaze fixated on Eislyn as he attached it to his forearm. Tiernan grabbed the handle of the sword before returning to an upright position.

"Eislyn, what is going on? What is this?"

"Nivala. Welcome to the realm of dreams. Remember me telling you about it? Look." She pointed at a couple walking along the beach. "They're dreaming. Well, one of them is. I can't tell which—."

As fast as they had appeared, the couple walked toward what Tiernan thought resembled the Great Sea near Alwyn.

"Oh, see. Now they're gone." Her face, though blurry, filled with joy. "I've been hoping to contact you somehow. I've missed you so much." She ran to him and gave her husband a hug, though her hands passed through his body.

"Eislyn, where are you?"

She turned and pointed in a direction behind her with her thumb. "Beyond the mountains, beyond the desert, and beyond the wilderness on the other side. I'm not quite in Lyra, and I've learned so much. There's a whole world just waiting to be explored."

Tiernan's eyes grew wide. His voice stuttered as he asked the burning question on his mind. "Is our boy with you?"

She smiled. "Yes. T, he's getting so big. I remind him every day his daddy will come for him soon."

Tiernan shook his head. "How is this possible?"

"There's no time to explain. Absorption magic, remember?"

He made a face that said 'Ah' as she continued.

"You are trapped. I can feel your companions. They're *terrified*, T. And listen to me, my love.

"If they die in here, they die for good."

"How do you know that?"

She closed her eyes. "Again, I've learned a lot. I've been trying to make contact with you through your dreams. Whatever the Dark Elf is doing built the bridge I needed. I've seen what he can do through other Nivalan experiences. It's horrifying."

She opened her eyes. "You must stop him. If you don't, everyone we know, everyone throughout all of Grael, will perish."

Airvede bent over, her strength failing. She tried to use an open hand to dig through her satchel for an ether, but the female Dark Elf would have none of it. She used her free hand to hold Airvede motionless.

"I can't let you do that. You need to die first. Then, I can finish the others. I can't find the Brother of the Dragonborn. Strange, isn't it?"

Airvede's eyes widened as she realized the Elf was referring to Firefly, Shig, and Tiernan. "You won't win."

The female Elf laughed. "You can't even stand up straight and you hope to defeat me? Small-minded witch. This has been tiresome." The Elf created another ball of Ultimus in her hand, preparing to release it toward Airvede.

Before she could, Tiernan ran the Elf through with his sword. The female Dark Elf gasped as she saw the blade come through her chest.

"There you are, Brother of the Dragonborn. I wondered why I couldn't find you. And you brought a visitor. No matter."

The Elf snapped her fingers, teleporting away.

Tiernan rushed to the White Mage. "Airvede, are you okay?"

She started to grab an ether, then stopped. "Tiernan? Who is that?"

The former King smiled big, grinning from ear to ear. "Airvede, this is my wife. Eislyn. I hoped you might meet her someday."

Airvede floated over to Eislyn's form, forgoing her need for an ether. "He loves you. More than any other man I've ever known, perhaps besides my own husband, Eamon."

Eislyn smiled, looking past the White Mage's shoulder to her husband. "I know. Come, we need to save the others." She reached out her hand for both to grab.

Firefly braced for her death. She didn't understand how this was even possible, but after controlling magic herself, accepted some things in this land just didn't make sense.

The marren's saliva dripped onto her thigh. It stung like acid from a science experiment from her days at the Cykela Academy.

"This is not going to be fun," she lamented, as it raised its head one last time.

With a swift, deadly motion, the marren opened its beak and lowered its body, ready to tear into her.

Instead, the creature froze in place. It cawed out in anguish, ready to rip apart whatever held it back. Around the left side emerged Tiernan. Airvede arrived from the right, holding the marren in place with her Bind Magic.

"Hang in there, Firefly!" Tiernan yelled.

Firefly harrumphed. "About time the two of you showed up. Help me out of here."

Instead, a third person offered a hand. "You're not pinned down. Grab my hand. This is all in your mind."

Firefly couldn't make out the features of this new arrival as clearly as she would like, but paid the oddity no mind as she grabbed their hand. The rocks disappeared, and as if this had never happened, stood on her feet.

"T, get rid of that nightmare," Eislyn said.

"Yes, ma'am," he said. He ran his blade through the marren's torso. It disappeared into a haze of nothingness.

"Where did it go?" asked Firefly. "That thing about killed me." Panic set in. "Hey, where's Shig? Is he okay?"

Tiernan gestured to the woman in the room with the hazy appearance. "Firefly, this is my wife. Eislyn. I can explain later."

"And you're right, we have to help Shig. T, Airvede, grab my other hand."

The executioner moved toward Shig with a hateful smile. Though his head was covered in a black hood, the lower half of his face was visible, crooked and decaying teeth showing through a wide grin.

Isoshi stood by, relishing the moment. Without warning, his countenance changed.

"Hurry. End him. Now."

The executioner nodded and lumbered toward Shig.

"Isoshi, I don't know why you're doing this. Just know that I love you, no matter what."

"He's not your brother, Shig." Airvede appeared and threw several blasts of the Fire Ring at the executioner. It caught his clothing on fire as Firefly then released a series of arrows that brought the executioner to his knees.

"This is over." Tiernan appeared next to Isoshi, running his sword through the illusion's torso without hesitation.

Shig gasped in horror at the sight of his brother being impaled. Firefly fired an arrow into the head of the burning executioner, who disappeared into nothingness.

"This is far from over, Brother of the Dragonborn," Isoshi said as he disappeared.

"Tiernan! That was my kyōdai, my brother! Where did he go? Why did you do that?"

A woman, her face obscured as if she was being seen through a screen, walked up to Shig. "That was not your brother." She unlocked his chains with a snap of her fingers, letting the Paladin down from the shackles on the wall.

"How do you *know*? Tiernan, you may have just killed him."

"Shig, this is Nivala. The world of dreams." Tiernan walked over to his wife. "And this is my wife, Eislyn. I wish you could meet her under better circumstances."

Eislyn laughed. "If it's any consolation, T, I'm not here, anyway." She looked at the others. "I'm reaching out to you through what's called a Nivalan experience. How I can do this is a story my husband can tell you another day.

"You've been trapped. My connection with Tiernan is what allowed me to reach him. Whatever trap Folas had planned, I averted through our bond. Family is Strength, after all."

She turned to her husband as her form began to fade. "T, I can't keep this up much longer."

"Eislyn…"

She put her hands to his lips. "I. Love. You. You are mine and I am yours. This isn't the end to our story. Find me, Mr. Prince."

Tiernan rushed toward his wife, trying to grasp her form for a kiss, though to no avail. "I love you, Eislyn. Now more than ever. Tell our boy I'm coming for him."

"See you soon," she smiled. "I'm holding you to that promise."

Along with Eislyn's form, the room disappeared. Around them, sounds of nightlife returned. Tiernan looked down. His feet now touched solid ground, the familiar if uncomfortable texture of the Rosewood Forest confirming his return to the real world.

"We made it out?" asked Shig.

"I think my wife broke the Nivala when she left us."

A voice confirmed Tiernan's suspicion. "She may have broken my Nivalan nightmare, but your pain is just beginning."

The group turned as Folas held the Soul Sword high above his head, illuminating the deteriorating Elven encampment in its glow.

Chapter 41

His Sacrifice

The Soul Sword. The Mind Shield told me you had it. But for how long?" Tiernan stared down his adversary, recalling his previous two encounters with the Dark Elf. Flashes of his parents falling dead burned in his mind, followed by the snap that sent him to the plains of Whispersong in a wounded, near-death state.

Folas lowered the ancient relic. Tiernan followed the movement with his eyes as a look of sadness crossed the Dark Elf's face.

"Since I realized the error of my ways," Folas answered with a hint of truthfulness.

Airvede walked up and whispered to Tiernan. "Be careful. I've read your book. Remember who he is."

Despite her low volume, Folas heard the exchange. "What's done is done. Some things you don't come back from." With incredible speed and accuracy, he hurled a blast of Wind Magic toward Shig, tossing him across the encampment.

Firefly rushed over, kneeling down to check on him. "You okay?"

"Yeah," Shig said as she helped him to his feet. "Though I am tired of Elven magicians using that particular attack against me!"

Folas laughed. "If I wanted to kill you, I would have done so in the Nivalan nightmare."

Tiernan unsheathed his sword. "You tried to kill each one of us with your pathetic illusions. You want us to believe that now you're merciful?" He stepped forward. "After what you did to my family? Ridiculous."

Folas opened his palm and raised the Soul Sword in an attack position. "Aren't you even the least bit curious how those illusions worked?"

The group maintained a stoic, defensive stance.

"Humor me, Brother of the Dragonborn." Folas tossed the ancient relic back and forth.

It was Airvede who made the connection. "It's that, isn't it? The Soul Sword. But how?"

Tiernan raised his eyebrows. "The seat of who you are."

Folas grinned. "Your very soul. The things that mean the most to you. It's came in handy these past few years as I eliminated several traitors." He laughed. "Like Banix."

Tiernan's eyes narrowed. "What did you do to Banix?"

"What I had to. He took what belonged to me. This." He raised the weapon. "It took me a while to find him, no thanks to your shield. He needed some convincing, but once Banix confessed to his crime, I relieved him of the *guilt* he had been carrying." Folas gave them a sideways grin.

"Kane got what he deserved, too. I watched his fate from the shadows. Just after Farna fell and I reclaimed what was mine – oh yeah, that was me, by the way. That gust of wind that tore the sword from your hands? You're welcome.

"Afterward, I followed Kane around. I watched his painful, gut-wrenching demise with glee." He waved the Soul Sword in his hand. "With Zoran bringing in a fresh supply of monsters these past few years, I've been enjoying this kingdom of anarchy. I even let many of them run free here in the Darkwood Forest."

Tiernan took another step forward, his mind racing through a half dozen different strategies. "It's called the Rosewood Forest. And I can't believe you would subject your people to those creatures."

A small black ball formed in Folas' hand. "My people? I am the last Elf left in here." The magic in his palm intensified. "Leave this place and I'll let you live to see the downfall of this land. Cross me and, well." He cast a glance at the magic in his hand. "I haven't mastered Ultimus yet. But I can assure you, it's far more painful than you can imagine.

"Just ask Voron. Remember him? The Elf who tripped your sister during her big race." He harrumphed. "And your poor friend Banix. Let's not forget about him. Or the other Elven traitors I've had to eliminate since that day."

Rage filled Tiernan's eyes, though his mind told him what he had to do. "Let's go."

"Z?" asked Shig.

Tiernan shook his head at his companion. "Fine. You want to call it The Darkwood Forest? It's yours."

The other three exchanged a look of confusion and took a few steps backward. Shig kept his eyes glued on Folas, waiting for an attack.

Tiernan turned around and began walking away. With the lightest whisper possible, he said three words. "Dagger. Barrier. Poison." Then, with an audible voice, he reiterated what he had said earlier. "Come on, people. I said let's go. The Forest is his."

Shig put the dagger in his hand into his satchel and turned around to leave. With his back to Folas, he grabbed his favorite dagger, Haia, from his belt instead.

Airvede closed her eyes as she backed up. "Okay. Let's go." She turned around as well and focused her mind on casting a Barrier.

Firefly knew she had to act fast. Rather than make a fist with her right hand, she focused on the power of the Poison Ring. She lowered her bow and followed the rest of them, walking away from the Dark Elf.

Folas raised his eyebrows, first in suspicion, followed by disappointment. "That's it? No grand speech, no fight? You dishearten me, Brother of the Dragonborn."

With one final low whisper, Tiernan gave the attack order. "Now."

In perfect unison, the four defenders of Abria spun around. Airvede erected a large Barrier in front of the group just as Shig released Haia toward Folas. Firefly grabbed an arrow and loaded it in a flash, breathing a sigh of relief as she saw the swirling green mist on its tip and the trajectory following behind Shig's throw.

Tiernan raised the Mind Shield just as Shig's dagger stabbed Folas in the shoulder. Firefly's arrow hit the same general spot less than half a tick later.

"That's more like it." Folas reveled in the attack. "I'm going to enjoy this!"

He snapped his fingers and disappeared. Tiernan moved to the back of the group and raised the Mind Shield.

"Where did he go, Z?"

"Keep your eyes open, Shig. Folas has either cloaked or teleported. Be prepared for anything." A few ticks later, Tiernan felt the impact before he saw it. From across the encampment, a steady stream of Ultimus flowed into the Barrier just beyond Tiernan's body.

"Mind if I try something new?" Airvede asked.

"Go for it," Firefly said as she loaded and released another arrow.

Airvede closed her eyes and crossed her elbows. A sharp flash enveloped her and then disappeared. "It worked! Here." She did the same motion, then touched each of her companions.

"It's a *personal* Barrier. The book Zachary gave Tiernan called it Protect." She made an odd look. "I don't know how long it'll last. Watch yourself."

Folas laughed with a giddy madness. "So you have read the book!"

Ignoring him, Airvede took to the skies and threw blasts of Fire Magic toward Folas in rapid succession. The first missed him, hitting the ground by his feet. The second hit his arm attacking Tiernan with Ultimus.

Folas screamed in a twisted pleasure and snapped his fingers. The Soul Sword disappeared. Using both hands, he cast Wind Magic at the ground and used it to propel himself toward Airvede.

Firefly released a series of arrows his way, two of which hit his calf muscle.

Folas ignored the pain and the onslaught of fire from Airvede. He extended his hands and tackled her, falling toward the ground with Airvede under him.

Tiernan watched the exchange and bolted toward the two. "Shig. Do your thing!"

Shig ran across the field as well, releasing dagger after dagger toward Folas. The first one hit the same leg while the next two missed.

Airvede braced for the crash as she hit the ground hard. The impact knocked the air out of her lungs as they rolled along the dirt and into a dip. Pinned down, Airvede tried focusing on any kind of magic that would repel Folas.

"It's no use," he said, as if he could read her mind. "Your companions are too late to save you. Your magic can't stop me. And without *you*, none of what they do will matter." Folas snapped his fingers and brought the Soul Sword back to the battlefield. "Tell Enid I said hi."

Shig threw several more daggers at Folas' back. Tiernan raised his sword, intending to run Folas through. Firefly released additional arrows toward his exposed back.

With both hands on the handle, Folas raised the Soul Sword and plunged it through Airvede's chest. The White Mage recoiled from the attack as she felt the blade exit her body, knowing that he had ran her all the way through. She coughed as blood from her lungs spattered across Folas' face.

Satisfied, Folas pulled the ancient relic from her body and sprung to his feet. He turned to the advancing group. "Who's next?"

Tiernan yelled, swiping his sword at Folas who deflected it with the Soul Sword. Shig, now out of daggers, plunged his fist into the Dark Elf's abdomen in a series of rapid attacks. Folas released a blast of Wind Magic toward the smaller man, sending him backward and into the oncoming Firefly.

Tiernan brought his sword back up just as Folas brought the Soul Sword down. He deflected it with the Mind Shield.

With both of the relics making contact together, Tiernan heard a voice in his head.

I'm sorry. Someone must die.

Tiernan pushed the Mind Shield into Folas' chest like he had to other Elves during the underground battle. He extended his sword, slicing the Dark Elf on the side. Folas cackled at the pain before snapping his fingers and disappearing.

Tiernan heard Airvede cough. He looked back to Firefly, who was rushing over and tending to her friend.

Shig ran up next to Tiernan.

"Did he teleport again?"

"I don't know. Come on." Tiernan ran over to Airvede and kneeled down. "Protect. Did it not work for you?"

Airvede smiled as a small trickle of blood ran down from her mouth. "I only had enough left in me for three Protect spells, something I realized as I covered each of you in it." She grabbed the former King's tunic. "Tiernan, when this is over, find Eamon.

Tell him…" She coughed blood again. "Tell him I love him," she said as she let her hand fall to the ground.

Firefly gave Airvede a potion and helped her drink it. "I'll stay with her. Here, take my bow." She passed it to Shig and lifted her quiver from her back. "Go. I'm not leaving her side."

The men exchanged a sad, knowing look and turned back around, looking for Folas.

"Where is he?" asked Shig as he loaded an arrow into Firefly's bow. Under his breath, he whispered. "I've never used one of these before."

"It'll be fine. Remember, Shig. Folas can cloak and teleport." With that thought in their minds, Tiernan and Shig moved with their backs to each other, circling through the encampment as they walked.

They didn't have to wait much longer. Another blast of Ultimus hit Tiernan in the side. It hurt, though the Protect spell seemed to deflect any physical injury. Tiernan raised the Mind Shield toward the blast as Shig released an arrow.

Far less proficient with the bow than Firefly, Shig's attack was aimed for Folas' chest. It hit his knee. Folas sent another blast of wind toward his opponent, knocking the bow out of his hand and sending it flying.

"The two of you are beginning to bore me." Folas pulled out a Gravity Ring and used his fingers to slide it onto his thumb.

"A few years ago, I used this to end the life of a few guards in that old castle. Pity about the bronze dragon and what it did to the place." Folas smiled big. "Time to die."

Folas opened his hand and send a blast of Gravity Magic toward Shig. The Protect spell kept it at bay, though Shig felt himself unable to move.

Tiernan realized he had a choice: to protect Shig from Gravity or to protect himself from Ultimus. Without a second thought, the former King moved the Mind Shield in front of his companion to block the Gravity Magic.

"Shig, go. Get out of the Forest with Firefly. Take Airvede. Find a doctor in Oakshadow."

"No. That would be dishonorable. We leave here together!"

Folas amplified the Ultimus attack and stopped the Gravity blast. Tiernan saw a blip in front of him as the Protect spell failed. The full effect of Ultimus hit him in the side. Tiernan dropped the Mind Shield in excruciating pain.

"Get. Out. Of. Here."

Out of the corner of his eye, Tiernan saw Folas shift his stance and cease the assault. Both men looked up at the Dark Elf.

"I said it's time to die. You should have run while the Brother of the Dragonborn gave you the chance." Folas, with a maniacal smile and cackling cry of victory, sent the strongest attack of Gravity and Ultimus he had toward both men.

Tiernan closed his eyes. In the ticks before it hit him, he had two successive thoughts.

I'll see you soon, Sis.

I'm sorry I failed you, my love.

The time passed that the blast should have ended his life. Tiernan opened his eyes. Only centimeters from his body, the Ultimus attack hovered in stillness.

Shig looked down at the Gravity Magic, likewise hovering just out of reach of his torso. "Z, what's going on?"

From the shadows, a person emerged with their hand stretched out in a fist with the palm in the air. "I cannot hold this forever. Hello, Kyōdai."

Shig turned around to see the real Isoshi for the first time. "Isoshi!" Shig ran over to embrace him, but paused. "How do I know you're my real kyōdai?"

"When you were six, you fell into a well."

A sheepish grin crossed Shig's face. "Okay, okay. That's enough!" He bolted the rest of the way and wrapped his arms around Isoshi's neck. His brother moved his hand holding time still away from Shig while patting him hard on the back with the other.

"I would hug you back with both hands, but I cannot drop this."

Shig let go. "How long have you been here?"

Isoshi smiled. "A few years. Tiernan will have to fill you in."

Shig whipped his head back to Tiernan. "Z? You knew?"

Tiernan nodded, still in awe of the Ultimus Magic hovering in the air.

Isoshi explained. "He honored my wishes. I needed you to stay focused on the battle, and I knew your drive to find me one day would keep you alive."

Tiernan stepped forward. "Can you rewind this? Can you save Airvede?"

Isoshi first gave Tiernan, then Shig, a solemn look. "If there's one thing I've learned about time, it's that you cannot mess with it too much before it gets angry. A life ended here today. That cannot be undone, but maybe it can yet be rectified."

Isoshi motioned his hand toward Folas. "He knows I'm here. Even in this frozen state, the Dark Elf's rage is building. When I let go, the full force of his anger will be unleashed."

Tiernan turned back to Folas. He saw a glimmer in the Dark Elf's eye, a quick shifting of his gaze from Tiernan's original position to his new one.

Shig hugged his brother again. "It's so good to see you. How do we save Airvede?"

Isoshi embraced Shig. "The four of you are needed for the journey that lies ahead. The real Zachary taught me that."

Tiernan turned his head sideways. *He's met Zachary at some point.* He noticed Isoshi's hand beginning to twitch. *Oh, no. He's losing control of it.*

"Shig. This is my time."

"Your time for what, Kyōdai?"

Isoshi kissed his brother on his forehead. "Tiernan, you'll have one shot to end this. Do you understand?"

Tiernan nodded in somber understanding.

Isoshi squeezed Shig tighter. "When you get home to Watodo, tell mother and father how much I love them. Let our little sister and brother know how much they mean to me."

Shig's eyes opened. "Wait, what are you going to do? Isoshi, I don't like this."

The Time Master twisted his hand as those not locked in the current bubble retraced their steps. Folas' magic attacks reversed, then the Dark Elf disappeared. He reappeared near the fallen Airvede, his hands and motions repeating the battle with Tiernan, though the former King himself was not there to reenact them along with Folas.

Isoshi continued rewinding time until the fateful moment with the Dark Elf hovering over Airvede.

"No, stop. I know what you're doing. There has to be another way, Kyōdai. I just got you back!"

Isoshi cleared his throat. "Shigeharu Kaitoson, son of Kaito." His face softened. "Kyōdai of Isoshi Kaitoson. Please, help me move Airvede. This is the *only* way." Isoshi twisted his hand some more as Folas' past self raised the Soul Sword high in the air. "I cannot do this one handed."

"But why? Why can't we end him here and then no one has to die?"

Isoshi shook his head. "If I knew, I would tell you. All I know is the last time I tried to undo a pair of deaths, it ended in disaster." He looked at Tiernan, who now stood behind Folas. "I was able to rewind things enough to fix my mistake back then, though I could not save your parents. I tried. Believe me, I tried so hard. They died without purpose."

He turned to Shig. "Today, I will die *with* purpose. Protecting my little brother while ensuring Airvede does what she is meant to do. Remember, Kyōdai, if called to a strange land, we go. Whatever we're asked to do, whether it's to build a home for orphans or rescue prisoners, we do it in service to each other."

Tears flowed down Shig's face. "Ashigaru Chikai."

Isoshi smiled. "That's right. Ashigaru Chikai."

Shig ran next to his brother and gave him one final embrace. Isoshi's hand began to shake harder.

"It's time. Tiernan, you must run him through the exact moment I let go." With his free hand, Isoshi pulled Airvede out of the way as Shig used both of his hands to help move her to safety.

Once she was cleared, the brothers exchanged a final look.

"I love you, Kyōdai."

"Goodbye, Shig. I love you too, Kyōdai."

Isoshi laid in the spot where Airvede had just been. "For the glory of the Emperor."

Shig let out a cry through his tears. "For the glory of Watodo."

Tiernan pulled his sword back. *This feels wrong.* He watched Isoshi's hand, waiting for the moment. Isoshi nodded, and Tiernan began his powerful forward momentum.

Isoshi opened his palm. Folas' eyes grew wide as he thrust the Soul Sword through the wrong person. At the same time, he felt immeasurable pain as Tiernan's blade rammed through his body, tearing through his darkened heart and erupting through his chest.

Folas fell to his knees and tried to raise his hand to teleport. From far behind in her original position, Firefly released an arrow into Folas' arm, stopping his attempt at escape.

As he tried to raise his other hand, Airvede bound it using her magic. She stretched out her hands, forcing Folas' palms open and preventing any further attempts at magic. She then encased them in a Barrier in this position.

Folas coughed blood as he looked down at the blade sticking through his body. "For what it's worth, I regret ever meeting Kane that day." He twisted his head back to Tiernan on his left. "But I still hate you and all that you stand for, Brother of the Dragonborn."

Tempted to prolong the Dark Elf's suffering in retribution for his parents, Tiernan nodded and locked eyes with his opponent. A few ticks later, the former King's morality prevailed. His mouth tightened in pity and he pulled the sword out in the swiftest possible motion. Folas coughed again as it left his body, then fell to one side, his eyes wide in terror as the life started to slip from his body.

He blinked a few times, trying his best to keep his vision clear and refusing to let go.

Tiernan looked at Shig, who had since pulled the Soul Sword from his brother's body. He noticed how brightly it glowed in the Paladin's hand. His eyes moved from the relic to Isoshi's body. He let out a long, saddened exhale as the Time Master slipped into the beyond.

Tiernan looked back to Folas.

The Dark Elf blinked one more time, took a breath, and spoke. "Lyra."

Folas let the air pass from his lungs. His eyes turned motionless, locking on some unknown point in the distance. His mouth parted and his body relaxed.

He did not breathe in again.

Chapter 42

To Change the World

As dawn moved across the land, the four defenders — with Shig carrying the body of his brother — emerged from the Rosewood Forest. They could see an ongoing raging battle along the northern path.

Tiernan gripped the Soul Sword in one hand, though it lacked the glow from when Shig held it.

"Looks like this raid has been going on all morning," said Airvede. "Do we join in?"

Tiernan shook his head. "No. We can't fix everything, but we can at least help some. Shig."

The Ashigaru Paladin, fresh tears still along his cheeks, looked at the former King. Tiernan had the Soul Sword stretched toward Shig.

"What?"

"This is your moment."

"To do what? Bury my kyōdai?"

The White Mage pointed to the creatures. "No. To free their minds, Shig. Like I did with the Ryllix."

Shig took a deep breath, putting his feelings aside. "Alright. I'll try." He kneeled down and carefully placed his brother's head on the ground, then positioned the rest of his body with respect. "But how do you know I can do this?"

Tiernan passed the Soul Sword to Shig. The Ashigaru Paladin grabbed it and watched in amazement as it lit up in acceptance.

Shig eyed the blade, admiring its design. "Okay. This thing wants me to use it. But how?"

Airvede smiled. "Let's try this." She put the hand with the Power Ring forward.

Tiernan extended the Mind Shield, making contact with her ancient jewelry. Shig put the Soul Sword forward, touching the other two artifacts with the tip of his blade.

From the intersection of the three, a bright white blast of magic emerged and spread across the battlefield. As it carried forward, it passed through the various monsters, bandits, and Elven warriors engaged with the Royal Guards.

They fell to their knees, coughing and hacking. From each, a pink mist emerged. Once it left their bodies, the monsters looked around in confusion.

The diocenes took steps back, unsure of where they were. The bandits removed their hoods, looking frightened. Those brandishing weapons dropped them at the sign of the advancing guards.

The remaining orcs and giants exchanged looks. A group of the former bolted toward the plains in retreat. The giants raised their hands to each other in confusion, saw the guards, readied their weapons, and continued the advance. A lone haracher also joined the fight, rushing toward the soldiers. The Elves froze in place, unsure of what to do next.

"Should we help them?" Shig started to step toward the battle.

"No, Shig. Look. The guards have this under control." Airvede lowered her hand with the Power Ring. "It's as if removing the Zoran influence gave the guards the advantage they needed."

Tiernan moved his mouth, thinking. "There are raids in the other northern cities. If we head to Lakedon, then to Milston and

Northwick, we can do more good removing Zoran's magic than engaging in additional battles."

Firefly smiled. "He's right. So since the three of you have a relic each, and I'm in charge, according to Rhys, I say we head to Lakedon and eliminate Zoran's influence from the monsters there."

Shig looked back to where his brother's body rested. "I have something I need to do first."

Tiernan followed Shig's gaze and understood. "I know just the place."

Shig kneeled down next to the gravesite Minmi and Omi had suggested. Upon seeing it, he agreed right away, recognizing the similarities between the trees near Clericsfold and back home in Watodo.

"Your brother, your kyōdai, was an example to the orphans in the school," Omi said with his hand on Shig's shoulder. "It felt as if he belonged here."

"Just like we do," Minmi said to Tiernan. "I've learned a lot about Borun since I came here. His legacy lived on through Isoshi, and I promise you we'll keep it alive too."

Shig stood as a gentle breeze blew in. "It doesn't seem right to bury him here in a foreign land." He smiled at Tiernan. "But you're right, Z. This is like a small slice of Watodo."

Tiernan wrapped his arm around Shig's neck. "I've had my fair share of losses. I know what you're going through, kid. Isoshi's request to keep his presence from you didn't sit right with me. I didn't like it, but honored his wishes."

Shig, after a moment of reluctance, wrapped his arms around Tiernan's neck in return. "Ashigaru Chikai."

Firefly moved in. "What does that mean, Shig?"

"Chikai means vow. Ashigaru foot soldiers are true to their word." He let go of Tiernan. "When you give your word, there is no breaking it. Isoshi wanted me to know he put Tiernan in that kind of position." Shig looked up. "It's the same type of vow we take when we become an Ashigaru. All we do from that moment on is to bring honor to our family name and the Empire."

Tiernan snapped his fingers. "Speaking of names. Kaitoson. Is your father Kaito?"

Shig nodded. "Our surname comes from our father."

Surname. What an interesting idea. Tiernan Davienson? Tiernan let the thought linger in his mind for a bit, even wondering so far as to whether this idea could catch on across Abria.

Airvede smiled, the sun illuminating her fiery hair. "I hate to ruin the moment, but there are a lot of areas that need our help. Lakedon. Northwick. Milston."

Tiernan felt a nudge in his thoughts. He pulled the Mind Shield off his back and slid it onto his arm. A single word repeated on a constant loop.

Tera.

Tiernan shifted his gaze north. "The Cave of Tera. After we free the cities, we need to go there next."

The word changed. Like before, the thought repeated with a perpetual nudge the former King could not shake.

Now.

Tiernan narrowed his expression. The others noticed.

"What's wrong, Z?" Shig asked.

"I don't know why. But this thing," he said as he raised the Mind Shield, "is saying we have to go to the Cave of Tera right now."

The walls within the Cave of Tera were just as slick and foreboding as the last time Tiernan visited here. Unlike before, when the battalion creeped through the underground unsure of what to expect, this time Tiernan felt prepared for anything and charged through the passageways with confidence.

Firefly used her hand as a makeshift torch with the Fire Ring. In addition, all three ancient relics shone in a gleaming display of power, not enough to illuminate the entire passageway but adequate when combined with the luminosity of the ball of Fire Magic in Firefly's hand.

Shig spun the Soul Sword around in a circle. "What are we doing here, Z?"

Tiernan raised the Mind Shield, hoping for an answer. It remained silent despite his hope for guidance.

"I'm following what the relic told me to do. I don't know why or what could be more important than helping the cities."

Firefly turned back, as if she expected someone to be behind her. "If the Mind Shield thinks we need to be here, whatever it is must be vital to our success."

"Yes, but what could be more important than removing Zoran's influence?" Airvede asked.

Firefly shrugged. "What about those other two relics? Are they saying anything to either of you?"

Airvede and Shig's silence answered the question.

"Exactly. The Shield told Tiernan something awaits us in *here*. We do as it told us to. That's my decision as the leader." She chuckled. "Besides, I'm sure we'll recognize whatever it is as soon as we come upon it."

The group followed the same path as Tiernan and Enid's group from several years earlier, though at a much more expedited pace. Tiernan pulled out his tokei to check the time.

"We've been in here for five hours. Up ahead should be a major split."

"Which way should we go?" asked Firefly.

Tiernan shrugged. "When Enid and I explored these, it was to find the magic rumored to be below Castle Abria. So, we took the westbound split toward our home. There was a second one to the north. If there are others to the east or even looping back to the south, I wouldn't know."

"Why haven't you mapped these? It's one of the first things we did in Watodo. We've had complete maps of every cave and crevice since the beginning of recorded history."

Tiernan had to laugh. "You'd have to ask my predecessors. I wasn't King long enough for any of this to matter."

"There. Is that your split?" Airvede pointed ahead.

Firefly took point and used her hand with the Fire Ring to illuminate it.

Tiernan nodded. "Yes. Left and we'll end up under the remains of Farna." With those words, it dawned on him that much of Castle Abria fell into the chasm during the attack of the bronze dragon. The antechamber where the magic rested was likely inaccessible, which meant there was no reason to go that way.

He pushed the thought aside. "North leads into the unknown. You're right, Shig. One of the previous leaders of Abria should have mapped the underground."

Firefly's eyes lit up. "Airvede, you said you saw Zoran in the citadel."

"That's right."

"And that's north," Tiernan said. "But why? Why not let us deal with the cities first? What could be down here?"

Tiernan looked at the tokei again. By now, he estimated night had fallen outside. There was even the possibility it was the next morning. After a while, he quit checking the time.

At one point, Firefly suggested they rest. Using the tokei, they agreed to four hours, with each taking a watch. After each had a quick nap, they resumed their trek.

The path split several times, some to the east and others to the west. Tiernan planned to suggest to Rhys a complete survey of the Abrian underground, provided he survived this journey.

Firefly absorbed an ether. "That's four for me so far on this trip. How many do we have left?"

Airvede dug through her satchel. "Looks like six."

Shig gripped the Soul Sword. "I know this might sound crazy—"

Tiernan interrupted. "We now live in a world with time masters, magic rings, and shields that speak to us. Nothing is crazy."

Shig held the Soul Sword by its hilt with both hands. "It's not in my head, like a thought. More like an impression in my heart."

Tiernan jumped to his feet. "The seat of your innermost being, am I right?"

Shig looked up at Tiernan and nodded, while the other two looked at the former King for clarification.

Tiernan scratched his head. "In ancient Abrian, soul translates to the idea of seat. That's what Folas was talking about in the Rosewood Forest. Your soul, as in the very core of your inner being. The essence of who you are. It's communicating to Shig through all of the things that make our young friend here special."

Firefly stepped forward. "A kind, compassionate man who has the utmost respect for *life*. No wonder it chose you."

Shig's face turned red. "Thanks, Firefly. I've grown fond of you, too." He returned his gaze to the blade. "I think the relic wants me to know the battle is just ahead." Shig stood and pointed the sword north. "See that bend in the cave?"

Firefly extended her hand to light up the passage.

"Just past that. Something is there, waiting for us."

Firefly stepped up. "If that's true, it's time for an inventory and supply check. Shig, you have your daggers?"

He patted his satchel and belt. "All the ones I could find or Airvede retrieved for me. Including my girl, Haia."

The others gave him a confused look.

"Haia, my favorite? I retrieved her from Folas' body."

Firefly raised her eyebrows. "Her. Okay. The dagger is a her. Airvede, are you good?"

"I am. I have the Wind and Gravity Rings."

"And I have Fire, Frost, and Poison Rings." Firefly dug through her quiver. "I'm out of my fire arrows from Lonlin, but I think I can use the Fire Ring in its place." She flung it back around. "Tiernan?"

"I'm good. A sword and the Mind Shield. What about our potions?"

"Eight," Firefly responded. "That's two each. Let's try to save them."

Shig pulled his dagger out of his belt and slid the Soul Sword in Haia's place. He extended his hand into the middle of their group. "For the glory of Watodo."

Following his call to arms, Firefly put her hand on top of Shig's. "Long live Cykela."

Airvede put her hand on top of Firefly's, who smiled in return. "May the Moon always grace the Isles."

"I didn't know you had a saying like that," Firefly said.

"I'm full of surprises." Airvede looked at Tiernan.

The former King of Abria took in the faces of his companions. He placed his hand on top of Airvede's. "What else can I say? Family is Strength. The three of you honor my sister's legacy by being here and fighting in her place. Whatever is past that bend, it doesn't matter. We will be victorious."

Tiernan walked in front of the group, Mind Shield raised and poised for protection. Firefly had an arrow ready to load behind him, unsure which ring she would need. For now, the Fire Ring acted as a torch as it had throughout this underground journey.

Airvede had one hand out, ready to cast a Barrier. Her other hand was lit up with a ball of purple magic. She wasn't sure what the Gravity Ring would do once she released its energy, but decided its power must be immense if Folas had used it.

Shig brandished two weapons, the Soul Sword in one and his favorite dagger in the other. He had warned himself that he might lose Haia during this battle, but decided that detail was inconsequential if it meant freeing the land.

They cleared the bend in the path. Firefly extinguished the ball of fire in her hand as it was no longer needed. Before the group, a large antechamber was lit up, fires emerging from hidden recesses in the stone walls. Tiernan swallowed, wondering what required such a large space, never mind the need for fire.

Shig caught the first glimpse of the creature. "By the Emperor's crown. What is that thing?"

Tiernan froze in place, the others having a similar reaction. The former King thought he heard a voice speaking, though he couldn't be sure.

The creature's moving mouth grew more animated. "The Divider will build his empire upon my tomb. My tomb. The Divider. Empire. My tomb."

"What in the name of Aila?" Tiernan couldn't believe his eyes. Embedded into a massive rock formation, a structure three times the height of a Graelan with a proportional width, was a face. Its top came to a rounded peak, not unlike that of one with a bald head. The eyes were hollowed out with nothing more than giant holes where sockets should rest. The face had a nose, though like the eyes, the nostrils were an impression of a way to breathe rather than a functional space.

It had a mouth, however. One with sharpened teeth extending upward from the bottom row and likewise two long ones on either side. This mouth moved as it spoke, though the voice sounded similar to that of a Graelan if they were talking through a folded-up tunic.

Extending out from both sides of the head were two structures, almost an archway split into two, with the face occupying the middle. These separated from the body, creating a space Tiernan thought he could fit through if he were to move sideways. The structures continued downward until they reached the ground. Where they met the surface, broken rubble and jagged stones surrounded them.

The rock face appeared to be covered in markings. Dark terra cotta circles covered the hollowed-out eyes with the sharpened teeth a deep bronze color. On top, an odd symbol of deep navy and bright yellow intersected in a half-moon pattern. Embedded carvings similar to ancient Abrian, yet different, were etched into where cheeks would set.

"Upon my tomb. An immoveable force. The Divider. My tomb. An impenetrable rock. The Divider. Something to be reckoned with."

The Divider. This cannot be. Tiernan felt sick.

"Davien's Son. The prince who would be King. The failure who led his people to their graves. The child who could not defeat me."

"Kane." Tiernan gripped his sword tight and readied the Mind Shield.

Embedded into the base of the transformed Divider, Tiernan saw something else he had lost track of several years ago.

A shining red jewel about the size of a small book.

Chapter 43

The Legacy of the Dragonborn

Tiernan and the others spread out across the cavern. Firefly loaded her bow with arrows and slid the Fire Ring on her finger. Airvede flew from person to person, casting Protect on each of them before doing so for herself with the power from an additional ether. Shig ran to the far side of the cavern closest to Kane's new body.

"You brought friends. Your sister was not enough. What makes you think they are?"

Tiernan cringed at Kane's words. Before he could respond, two boulders shot up through the ground, each narrowly missing him. Their jagged tops looked like spikes meant to kill rather than a natural structure protruding from the ground.

"This is Kane?" asked Shig from across the room.

"Kane? A name I once wore." One of the boulders near Tiernan retracted. It burst through the ground near Shig, who rolled out of the way just in time.

"I am now Caudex. The immoveable force. An impenetrable rock."

Firefly readied her arrow. Tiernan caught her attention and shook his head. Airvede watched the exchange from her vantage point in the sky and landed next to Tiernan.

"What are you thinking?" she asked in a hushed tone.

"Shig! Daggers!" Tiernan yelled.

The Ashigaru threw a dagger at Caudex. He rolled out of the way again as another jagged boulder broke through the ground in an attack.

"Keep it up!" Tiernan pulled Airvede behind the structure Caudex had yet to retract as Shig threw a second dagger at the creature. "Get your Gravity Ring to Firefly. I don't think poison, ice, or fire will work against him in this form."

Airvede turned in Firefly's direction and took to the air. Tiernan rushed out from behind the boulder toward the creature that used to be Kane. He raised the Mind Shield.

"Do your best, Divider."

Caudex roared and retracted the other structure. From the ceiling of the cavern, it extended another pointed column, intent on stabbing Tiernan from above.

The former King used the Mind Shield and pushed back. It glowed as unknown power flowed throughout the ancient relic. The Mind Shield fought against Caudex as a blue halo effect enveloped it. It grew even brighter as Tiernan pushed, Graelan and relic fighting together against Caudex's strength.

The boulder shattered, exploding into a pile of rocks that landed around Tiernan. Caudex cried out in pain and anger, retracting the stump into the ground next to him.

Tiernan gloated. His plan had worked as intended. The focus on him allowed Shig to make his way closer to Caudex to retrieve his daggers. "Is that all you have in you?"

The left side of the archway coming out of Caudex came up out of the ground. Tiernan almost laughed at the sight of its broken end, shattered just like the attacking boulder from above.

The Ashigaru Paladin then made his way back around toward Tiernan's position.

Those are his arms. Or arm things. Tiernan waved the Mind Shield at Caudex. "This is more powerful than you realize."

The creature used its other arm to mend the broken one. Magic energies circled around the two appendages.

Shig ran up next to Tiernan. "Now what?" he asked as Caudex healed its broken arm.

"He's going to get angry. Give me the Soul Sword."

"You sure, Z? The thing acts like it wants me to use it."

Tiernan smiled. "Trust me, kid. Use Haia. And next time, let Airvede retrieve it for you with her magic. Don't risk yourself."

Shig handed Tiernan the relic as he ran off to the other side of the cavern. Tiernan spun around to Firefly and gave her a quick nod before returning to face Caudex.

"I heard you lost this." Tiernan raised the Soul Sword, taunting the thing that used to be Kane. "Your precious Soul Sword. Swiped from right under your nose. Folas, wasn't it? Your right-hand Elf."

Tiernan smirked. "I always thought you were his *servant*. That's how it worked, right? You did whatever Folas wanted?"

Caudex roared and dug both arms into the ground. Tiernan felt the ground rumbling below him and put the Mind Shield under his body. Both pointed columns shot up in the air, intending to impale Tiernan.

The Mind Shield acted as a barrier, propelling Tiernan into the sky. At the last second, Tiernan dove off the rising arms. Airvede used her magic to catch and lower him to the ground just as the sharpened edges of Caudex's arms dug into the ceiling.

It retracted them and burrowed through the ground. Tiernan was better prepared this time. He lowered the Mind Shield just as the rocks below began to rumble. Tiernan used the bounce of the impact to jump backward.

Tiernan raised the Soul Sword. "Is that the best you have, Kane? No wonder you needed Folas. It's a wonder your rebellion even got off the ground without him."

Caudex roared again. Tiernan smiled. The creature performed the same attack, though this time, Tiernan anticipated the location with greater accuracy. As the arms flew up out of the ground, Tiernan jumped out of the way without the Mind Shield's help.

On a hunch, he raised the Soul Sword and swung it toward the columns. The relic lit up and sliced through both of Caudex's arms. The weapon left a molten appearance where the blade cut through, almost as if the Soul Sword melted the structures.

Caudex cried out in anguish.

"Now, Firefly!" Tiernan yelled.

From across the cavern, she released three back-to-back arrows, each imbued with Gravity Magic. Two of the arrows hit the ceiling above Caudex. The other she aimed at the ground near the creature's mouth.

All three arrows exploded in a spectacular display of dark purple Gravity Magic, swirling around until the ground itself began to crumble. The ceiling collapsed, with rocks and dirt falling on top of Caudex. Below, the stone surrounding the jewel shattered, throwing it from its prison and off to the side near where Shig had collected his daggers earlier.

The crumbling ground gave way to a massive chasm, one that appeared to have no bottom. Caudex fell into the void, with the ceiling above continuing to tumble in until all effects of the Gravity Magic subsided.

The ground continued to implode on itself, with the crater growing even larger. Tiernan's eyes widened as he watched the jewel tumble. He bolted across the cavern, getting to it just as it fell into the growing chasm.

Tiernan dove, desperate to catch the book-sized object before it met its doom along with Caudex. His fingers glided along its top, but he was too late to grab it with his hands. It fell into the abyss.

A moment later, Tiernan fell with it.

Tiernan blinked. If he didn't know better, he would think he was floating among the stars themselves. Various colors of lights blinking in and out of existence floated amongst an inky midnight background. Hues of purple, red, yellow, and cream flashed around him.

He looked below his feet. Similar to the Nivalan experience, he appeared to be free-floating.

He felt a tap on his shoulder. He looked behind and saw his companions.

"How did you get here?" Tiernan asked.

Firefly answered first. "The cave continued to fall in on itself. Shig fell next, so Airvede and I jumped in."

"Well, I floated in behind them," Airvede corrected.

They looked around in confusion and wonder.

Shig asked what everyone was thinking. "So. Where are we?"

"I think it's like Nivala," Tiernan said as he pointed to the blinking lights. "So, like a dream, this may just be an illusion."

"You're wrong, Son of Davien. This is more real than you know."

The defenders turned toward the voice. Before them stood Kane in his Graelan form.

"This is one last gift from Zoran. The first gift was Caudex." He motioned around them. "Welcome to the heart of Ultimus itself, the place from where it originates, far beyond our world."

Kane grinned. "This is our last battleground. You want to play, Tiernan? Fine. Let's play. I'll end you like I ended your worthless excuse for a father and his loathsome woman."

Kane put his hands together and sent a blast of Ultimus toward the group. Airvede cast a Barrier at the last moment, deflecting the attack. Tiernan struggled to maintain his composure, doing his best to ignore the insults to his family.

"You cannot defeat this power. No one can. It's time to accept the truth," Kane said as he amplified the power. "This is where you die. Are you ready to know the pain your parents faced as they fell?"

Tiernan saw the Power Ring on Airvede's hand out of the corner of his eye. It glowed with brilliant power, increasing with each increment of Kane's attack. He glanced at the Soul Sword and Mind Shield, now both darkened like the midnight sky.

Her. A single word echoed in Tiernan's mind from his relic.

The former King looked to his other two companions. Shig had Haia ready in his right hand along with another in the other. Firefly, now wearing the Poison Ring, primed several arrows and stood by, ready to fire.

Airvede's face exuded confidence and power. She seemed unbothered by Kane's attack, the Power Ring appearing to amplify her natural defensive abilities.

This is my sister's legacy. The return of magic to Grael and the emergence of mages like Airvede who can change the world for the better. Tiernan took one last look at Kane. His adversary's face showed nothing but rage and contempt as he tried to break through Airvede's Barrier.

"Take these," he said to the White Mage. "This is your moment, Airvede." He whispered to her, hoping Shig would not hear. "This must be why Isoshi gave his life in place of yours."

The White Mage, repelling Kane's magic with her defensive field, looked at Tiernan in confusion. "Me?"

Tiernan extended them both her way. "Take them."

"No!" Kane yelled.

Shig raised his eyebrows. "That confirms it, I think. Airvede, do whatever Z says."

Airvede reached out as Tiernan slid the Mind Shield on her wrist. She gripped the Soul Sword in the same hand while her other hand continued to repel Kane's attack with a Barrier.

As soon as she held all three ancient relics, Airvede's entire body glowed in a blinding white light. Firefly shielded her eyes until she got used to the effect. Shig squinted, keeping his focus on Kane.

Tiernan basked in the glow. *Her power is similar to Enid's.*

Kane backed up. With one hand, he continued the Ultimus attack. With the other, he brought it back and threw it forward, releasing a strange bronze magic. As the beam approached the group, it transformed into boulders.

Boulders. Like the bronze dragon. Tiernan raised an eyebrow, trying to understand the connection.

"I've got this." Airvede twirled her hand, encasing the other three in an oval Barrier on all sides. She rose above them, using the Mind Shield to deflect every boulder. As she flew closer to Kane, the relic absorbed the magic before it had a chance to transform into stone.

"No! You enchantress!" He shifted his attack from the group on to her, one hand casting Ultimus and the other the bronze magic.

The Mind Shield, amplified by the other two relics, held its own. Airvede rammed Kane with it at full force. "I'm a healer. You'd do well to remember the difference."

Kane fell backward, groaning in pain as he floated on his back through the glowing star field.

With Kane's body out of the way, Tiernan saw the jewel a handful of meters behind where the Divider had just stood. "Airvede! Let us out!"

She blinked, lowering the Barrier. Shig and Firefly spread out left to right.

As Tiernan approached the jewel, he heard Kane cry out. "I am a caudex. An immoveable rock. I cannot be defeated!" Kane stood up and snapped his fingers, sending a blast of Ultimus across the star field and into the former King's abdomen. "When this world burns, when the Calamity is all that is left, I will be eternal."

The magic knocked Tiernan backward again, mere steps before he would have reached the jewel. He doubled over in pain, feeling the full force of the magic.

Firefly released her poison arrows at Kane, hitting him in the arm and chest. Shig threw Haia, hitting Kane on the other side.

With a wave of her hand, Airvede retrieved the dagger and sent it back to Shig. Then she flew at the Divider and batted him away once again using the Mind Shield. Kane fell from the combined attacks, the poison spreading through his body with a bloodied wound on the other side from Shig's dagger.

Airvede floated over to Tiernan. "The Protect Magic didn't work like I thought it would. I guess I'm still learning. Are you okay?"

"It hurts, but I'll be okay. Nothing your healing power can't fix later."

She smiled and put her hand with the Power Ring on his shoulder. "How about now instead of later?"

Tiernan felt the pain subside from the application of her healing ability. He stretched his restored arm in a circle and motioned ahead of the pair with his head. "The jewel."

Airvede looked back and saw the item free-floating in the star field. "Got it." She left Tiernan's side and hovered toward it with urgency.

"No!" Kane saw her attention shift. He sat up onto his knees, still wounded from the attacks, and released another blast of Ultimus.

Unprepared, Airvede felt the full force of the assault. She pushed through it as Kane sent a second stream of magic her way. It knocked Airvede out of the air. Firefly switched to the Fire Ring and sent two more arrows at Kane. Shig threw several daggers, each hitting various spots on the Divider's torso.

Airvede landed next to the jewel face down as she floated in the star field. Using her free hand, she reached out and touched the jewel, hoping to use her strength to pull it close.

Instead, the power of all three ancient relics spread across the battlefield in a majestic display of light. Their energies flowed from the White Mage's body into the jewel. Airvede raised her head up to witness the transference.

Just as had happened moments earlier, when Tiernan gave her the relics, the jewel glowed in an impressive white light. As it increased in its shimmer, Tiernan stood to his feet. He watched the object, still unsure of its significance, turn bright and then, even brighter.

A moment later, a blinding snap of light filled the entire area. Tiernan didn't have time to blink before the effect exploded and subsided.

Floating in the star field, a new warrior took the place of the jewel, lowering to the ground with their eyes closed and their arms across their chest. One who was empowered by some of the strongest magic Grael had ever known.

One whose innate abilities formed wings of fire as they lowered their hands, spreading them wide with the corresponding wingspan stretching far from side to side.

With her white-hot eyes, she turned to the former King. "Hello, Brother."

Tiernan's face lit up with sublime joy. "Enid!"

Kane cried out. "No. You *died*! I saw you!" He released blasts of Ultimus at her, trying to injure the Dragonborn.

Enid extended her hand and absorbed the attack. "Let's get out of here."

She closed her eyes and said a few words in a language Tiernan didn't understand. He blinked, as if teleported without the associated flash of light. Together, the five warriors reappeared in the cavern on the south edge of the still-growing chasm.

On the opposite side stood a still-Graelan Kane, raging with fury.

"I will not be denied!" He extended his arms back toward the ground. His body transformed, his face extending to the ground as his torso merged into it.

"Caudex," said Shig.

The creature began shaking the room. What was left of the ceiling rumbled, with pieces of it falling loose into the crevice.

"Let's get out of here," said Firefly.

Enid nodded. "The three of you go. May I?" she asked to Airvede.

The White Mage handed the Dragonborn all three relics without hesitation. "Good luck."

Enid smiled as she put the Power Ring back on. She held the Soul Sword and handed the Mind Shield to her brother.

"You ready?" he asked.

"You know it." Enid grabbed Tiernan by the waist as the twins flew into the collapsing cavern.

Caudex pulled an arm out of the ground and used it to send blasts of boulders toward them. Tiernan extended the Mind Shield toward the creature, deflecting attacks and sending the rocks left and right.

Enid extended the Soul Sword. It glowed in a blazing mix of her innate Fire Magic and the relic's natural illumination. The Power Ring on her hand and the Mind Shield on her brother's arm also lit up, with the same blue halo surrounding the Mind Shield and the Power Ring a mix of the other two. From the tip of the blade of the Soul Sword, a white light emerged and covered Caudex from top to bottom.

He put the arm back into the ground, trying to brace himself. "No. This cannot be." Caudex struggled as more of the cavern collapsed. Jagged extensions of his arms extended from the ceiling as he tried to impale Enid from above.

The Dragonborn flew around them. Caudex retracted his arms again and again, trying to no avail each time. Enid avoided every attempt on her life as if she was out for a leisurely stroll.

Then, the attacks stopped. The arms retracted from the ceiling and back into Caudex's body.

In what appeared to be a painful process fueled by the white beam from the Soul Sword, Caudex transformed back into Kane as the room continued to fall apart. "No." He threw his hands at the ground.

Nothing.

He threw them again, trying to initiate his prior transformation.

Kane remained in his Graelan form.

"Zoran. Help me. You trapped me down here. Made me into Caudex. An immoveable rock. A force to be reckoned with. Fix this!"

Silence, save for more portions of the ceiling falling in and piling up within the crevice.

Kane took one final look at the twins.

"I hate you and your entire family."

Enid backed up, carrying her brother to safety over the chasm. She lowered him to the ground as her wings disappeared and eyes returned to normal.

More of the ceiling fell in. Kane backed up, his hands touching the wall behind him. He gave the twins one final glance, eyes full of rage and revulsion, as the remnants of the ceiling began to fall on top of him.

Kane raised his hands to protect his face, but the implosion was faster and more forceful than any Graelan body could withstand. The falling ground from above crushed Kane as the twins observed his demise from a safe distance just outside of the cavern entrance, watching as his outstretched and bloodied fist relaxed into a lifeless pose.

Together, they stood side by side as additional portions of the Northern Plateau fell in, filling the chasm with debris and remnants of what was above. The destruction continued until the entire cavern was filled from end to end.

Once the rumbling subsided, Tiernan turned to his sister. "Enid!" He dropped the Mind Shield and wrapped his arms around her.

She let the Soul Sword fall to the ground as well, embracing her brother. She hugged him tight, though what she said next surprised him.

"No."

Tiernan opened his eyes. "No?"

"This." She looked him in the eye and pulled the hair at the base of his neck.

"Ouch."

"This better grow back." She then pulled the hair from his forming goatee.

"Ow!"

"And lose this. You look like a cat threw up on your face."

Tiernan laughed. "I missed you too, Sis." He hugged her again, feeling as if all that was wrong with the world was starting to be righted after so long.

Chapter 44

The Na'Goh

Tiernan let go of his sister's neck after what Enid thought was the longest hug in recorded history. She smiled once he let go, noticing the handful of tears welling up in his eyes. Enid leaned in to comfort him one more time with a sibling embrace.

The usually talkative Tiernan found himself at a loss for words. "How?"

Enid smiled. "How what, Brother?"

"I think you know, Sis."

Enid leaned down to pick up the Soul Sword. "We need to get this back to your companion. The one with the daggers. What's his name?"

"Shig. The archer is Firefly. The White Mage is Airvede."

"Here." Enid picked up the Mind Shield. "This one is yours."

Tiernan took the relic from her and slid it on his arm. "What about the ring? Is it for you or Airvede?"

She smiled and looked at the ring. "I don't know. I'm being honest, T. The Na'Goh weren't the easiest to understand."

"The Na-what?"

Enid put her arm around her brother's neck. "Come on, T. Let's go find your friends. I don't want to cover this twice." She looked around. "Besides, I think it's going to be a long walk back to the entrance. That cave in was the Northern Plateau, wasn't it?"

Shig flipped Haia in his hands as he waited in the passageway. He ran his finger along the blade, amazed that it showed no signs of damage or wear.

Firefly counted her arrows, relaxing in a sitting position and resting her back on the wall near Shig. "Great."

Airvede raised her eyebrows. "Problem?"

"Only seven left." She stood up. "Depending on where we go next, I may have to make a detour to a wooded area to harvest some myself if the merchants don't have supplies I can use."

Airvede looked down the cavern, using the Fire Ring as a light source. "I'm beginning to get worried."

Shig waved her off. "Z is tough. The rumbling has been done for a while now. And besides, he had *her* with him. The Dragonborn."

Firefly chuckled. "Did you finally finish his book?"

"Maybe not word for word, but I remember all that Tiernan wrote about her powers. The moment she reappeared, I knew we'd won."

Airvede smiled and pointed. "That's them." She waved as Tiernan and Enid approached the group.

Shig ran over to Tiernan and gave him a tap on the shoulder. "Good to see you, Z."

"Were you worried about me, kid?"

"Nah. I knew you had her with you." He bowed. "It's an honor to meet you."

Enid raised her eyebrows. "How does he know who I am, T?"

Airvede pulled out the book and handed it to Enid. "We all do. Everyone in your land does because of this."

Enid looked at the spine. "*The Tale of Tiernan*, huh? Who wrote this, Brother?"

Tiernan gave his sister a sheepish look. "I did. And I've been working on the second one. Here." He handed her his notebook. "You've been gone a while, Sis."

Enid flipped through the pages of the first book, then the second. "I think I'm going to want to read both sometime." She handed the book and the notepad back to their owners. "How long has it been?"

Tiernan swallowed. "Almost five years."

Enid froze in place. "Five *years*?" She swallowed. "I guess that's not too long of a time, relatively speaking. Grandpa Borun lived to be, what, over four hundred? It just didn't seem like it was that long."

"Where were you?" Tiernan asked. "You released the magic and then disappeared."

She gave him a sideways smile. "Perhaps we could walk and talk?" Enid gestured toward the passageway.

No one spoke right away. Firefly led the group southbound toward the entrance to the Cave of Tera. From behind, Airvede used her hand with the Fire Ring as their light source.

Enid shook her head in disappointment. "T, why didn't you bring a torch? You're making your poor friend back there do all the work."

"There didn't seem to be time, Sis. We had to bury…" He paused and sighed. "We had to bury Shig's brother. Right after, the Mind Shield made it sound as if we needed to come here right away. There was no time to find or buy torches."

The White Mage spoke up. "And I don't mind. When I take an ether, it rejuvenates my strength."

Enid harrumphed. "Graelans using ethers. A lot *has* changed. The relics told me I had to return the magic under the castle to the world. I guess it worked."

"You have no idea," Firefly said dryly.

"It's your legacy, Sis. Whatever power our enemies wanted for themselves, you kept from them. And right after you disappeared, it dispersed throughout the entire world. Firefly is from Lonlin and Airvede from The Isles. The magic changed both of them."

"What about you?" Enid asked Shig. "What did it give you?"

"Nothing. I'm just me. Though it gave my kyōdai — my brother, that is — the ability to manipulate time.

"Time," she responded. "The Na'Goh weren't clear about that. You said I've been gone five years?"

"Yes. And where were you?" Tiernan asked.

"I was with them. The Na'Goh."

"Who are the Na'Goh?" Airvede asked, her vocal intonation revealing her genuine curiosity.

"The dragons."

Tiernan pushed a boulder out of their way. "Another cave in. I wonder how widespread Kane's temper tantrum spread?"

Shig used his strength to slide another to one side. "This is the fourth one we've run across, but it's smaller than the last. Maybe that's a sign we won't see many more?"

Firefly used her hand with the Fire Ring as a light source. "The path ahead seems clear."

"I can take that back, if need be," said Airvede.

"I'm good. Give yourself a break from that Barrier move you did with the last cave in."

Enid smiled. "How did you learn to do that? It never would have crossed my mind."

"In Idlewind. I used a Barrier to expand an opening and later learned I could do the opposite to compress objects."

Enid nodded in appreciation. "It's impressive. I can see how it would be useful in battle."

"So, tell us more about the Na'Goh. The dragons." Tiernan hesitated to say more, not ready to tell his sister about Farna.

The group slipped past the boulders using the path Shig and Tiernan made and resumed walking.

After a few moments of silence, Enid continued with her story. "The Na'Goh are reclusive for a reason. They didn't tell me why, but I know one of their number played a hand in the fracturing of the world."

Tiernan looked at the others, who all shook their head. "Fracturing?" he asked.

Enid sent a blast of fire toward a boulder ahead, shattering it into pieces. "If I understood what they wanted me to know, for centuries leading up to the New Era, all of Grael was united, though even that wasn't clear. I'm not sure if it was the land just in our part of the world, like the Isles, Watodo, Lonlin, Abria, and so on, or everything else. We still had different kingdoms and empires, like we do now, but nothing separated the regions. It was one giant landmass with the Great Sea all around."

Shig elbowed Tiernan. "Imagine that. I could walk here and visit you all the time."

Tiernan laughed at the thought.

Enid watched with curiosity at the banter between the two. "Like I said, this was before the New Era. I don't know when, just that there was a dissension. They, the dragons, I mean, fought for centuries to contain the dissenters." She scrunched her face. "It's hard to remember. The Na'Goh wanted me to know things and not others. They were never clear about their reasonings or why some things were clear and others incredibly vague.

"So, while it was five years for you out here, it didn't seem that long to me. A few weeks, maybe? I truly don't know."

"Up ahead. Another cave in. I've got this one." Shig ran ahead. "Keep talking Enid! Maybe just a bit louder so I can hear."

"You got it, kid!" she said.

"I'm nineteen, D."

Enid mouthed 'D?' to her brother with a confused look on her face.

"He likes nicknames," Tiernan explained. Then, under his breath, he twisted his head toward the Paladin. "I call him kid most of the time, too, but I'm not sure what D stands for."

"D. For Dragonborn," Shig yelled back.

Enid raised her eyebrows again, not sure what to make of the younger man and his personality. "I see. Guess he heard you, T. Anyway, there were uprisings. The Na'Goh are the stewards of the planet. Each dragon has a special power. You can usually tell by the color of their skin. That was something they were very clear about. The red dragon that saved me was special."

"Fire. It explains your fire-based magic," Tiernan said with a nod.

"That's not all it had, but yes. Many can change forms. When it gave its life that I might live, it passed to me all that it possessed. Some have healing abilities, like the red dragon. A blue dragon—"

"We encountered one of those," Shig yelled. "At the ruins. It split into two winged women and a jumping archer."

Enid's face turned to confusion. "What ruins?"

Tiernan lowered his head. "Thanks, Shig."

The Ashigaru Paladin realized his mistake. "Oh no. Oh Z, I'm sorry."

Enid pressed the two of them as her blood ran cold. "I said 'what ruins?' Out with it now!"

Tiernan stopped walking and raised his head to the cave ceiling. "Our home, Sister. Farna. Castle Abria. The Drunken Alligator. Dad's workshop. Their home. Everyone is all gone. Destroyed by a bronze Na'Goh."

"Let me guess. One that could control the ground, the very rocks and dirt of Grael itself," Enid said. Tiernan's lack of denial confirmed her words. "It's returned then. That Na'Goh was a pivotal part of the uprising within their ranks."

She swallowed. "The dragon that destroyed our home is the same one that's responsible for breaking the unified land into what it is today."

Tiernan observed the others as they slept. Shig had his head against the wall of the cave. Next to him, Firefly dozed with her head on his shoulder. Their third companion, Airvede, rested comfortably on the ground despite lying flat on her back.

Enid's head rested on the wall with her arms around her knees. Tiernan turned around and stood between the group and the still-distant exit, Soul Sword in hand and ready to strike if anything came to attack them.

"Did you get any rest?" a voice behind him asked in a hushed tone. He flipped around to see his sister behind him. She whispered again. "Let's go up a ways. Let the others get a few more hours of shuteye."

Once they were out of earshot of the others, Enid spoke. "Tell me, T. What happened to Farna? You didn't elaborate much."

"It's hard to talk about, Sis. We came under a coordinated attack. Kane's rebels besieged every city in Abria. We thought we had them held off when the bronze dragon appeared. It ripped through the city like we would crush a sandcastle.

"When you released the magic, the effect created a gargantuan crater within the northern parts of Farna. We spent time rebuilding after, but the chasm was prohibitive to our reconstruction attempts. Despite 'round-the-tokei efforts, we were years from completion. But, in the end, it didn't matter, I guess. When that dragon arrived, it was all over. Much of Castle Abria fell into the hole. I'm sure it's still there now where we fought Folas and the others in that antechamber."

She narrowed her eyebrows. "We just stopped Kane. What happened to the Dark Elf, or is he still out there?

"No worries about that. Folas is dead. My friends back there made sure of that just before we came here. But our victory took a significant toll on them. Shig's brother sacrificed himself during the battle to save Airvede."

"And Zoran?"

Tiernan twisted his head back toward the cave. "Last we knew, he was in a citadel atop the Northern Plateau. Who knows, maybe he died in the implosion just now?"

"This dragon. Where is it now? How many died in the attack?"

"*Thousands*. We lost about a third of the populace. Eislyn's parents made it out. They helped Eislyn with leadership in my absence."

"Your absence?"

"That's a long story." He smiled. "You'll have to read my second book to find out about that."

Her eyes grew serious. "Eislyn. Where is she now?"

"Somewhere beyond the western mountains. She used her powers to teleport to safety."

"Powers? You mean Eislyn has them too?"

Tiernan nodded. "I guess I'm the odd one out. Even Way had something."

Enid's expression turned sad. "T, when the Na'Goh destroyed Farna, did it…?" She couldn't finish.

"His memorial is untouched. I saw it a few days ago. Same for Mom and Dad's." Tiernan didn't mention the statues, considering that all of them were finished some time after she vanished.

Pent-up emotions broke through Enid's normally reserved persona. She let tears fall to her cheeks and leaned against the wall in a moment of unprecedented vulnerability. "I miss him, T. I know it's been years for you, but to me, I just lost him a few weeks ago."

Tiernan pulled his sister in. She began bawling on his shoulder, pounding her fist into his already sore back.

Tiernan hugged her tighter, ignoring the pain. "I miss him too. Not a day goes by that I don't think about him. I could have used his friendship these past few years."

Through the tears and sobs, sounds Tiernan was sure would wake the others, Enid broke down. "When I released the magic, I thought I was going to die. And you know, I was okay with that because I saw him. I saw Way staring at me. I saw his big, goofy, bunny of a grin. I thought I would be with him in whatever comes next."

She let go and wiped her face. "Instead, the Na'Goh trapped me in that blasted jewel. Or the jewel was a doorway to their realm. I don't know. All I know is that I spent those few weeks in a strange place. It's hard to describe. It was like the place where you were fighting Kane, but different.

"I heard them talking to me, but not in audible voices. More like thoughts and impressions. I'd ask questions and thoughts would come to my mind with answers. I'd push back, and a confirming thought would come or a correcting one would take its place."

"It sounds horrible."

She wiped her face again and turned toward the entrance. "It was, and yet it wasn't. I learned a lot and nothing. Didn't have to eat at least," she said with a smile.

Her face took on a more serious appearance. "T, I think they know more about the fate of the world than they wanted me to realize." She turned back to him and, letting out even more tears, fell into her brother's arms, sobbing. "I thought I would be with *him*, T. Instead, it's like they kept me safe so I could, what? Appear at just the right time?"

Tiernan put his hands on the back of her head. "I wish I had the answers for you. I do." He kissed the top of her head. "Sister, when this is over, I promise you. We'll find them. We'll find where in Grael the Na'Goh live and we'll get the answers you deserve."

The twins embraced each other for a long while, happy to be reunited while sharing the emotions of their mutual losses.

Daybreak peeked through the open entrance to the Cave of Tera. Through it, Enid saw something she never thought she'd be so thankful to see.

Grass.

She ran up the rocky steps and into the open, feeling the warmth of the Graelian sun shining upon her face. Her blonde hair glistened in the light as she stretched her arms wide.

After a moment, she spoke. "It could be warmer."

Tiernan walked up next to her. "We're nearing the middle of Begynde. In a little over a month, we'll be twenty-six."

"You will be. Am I only twenty-one? Or does time not work that way?" she asked.

Airvede approached from behind. "You know, Enid, in three hundred years, these five years won't seem like that big of a gap."

"Yeah, you're still his twin. You've just been spared the effects of *horrific* aging. No offense, Z."

Enid used her thumb to point to Shig. "Is he always this way?" she asked of the women.

Tiernan threw his hands up in the air. "Thanks, Shig, for that reminder. And okay, fine. Everyone look at me right now."

The group turned to him. Enid raised her eyebrows.

"I'll lose the goatee and grow my hair back out," he said with a smirk toward his sister. "Is everyone happy?"

"So, what's next?" Firefly asked, though it was less of a question and more of a reminder of the need for expediency. "Remember, we left the northern cities under siege from Zoran's forces. There's still the need to deal with him, plus whatever role this bronze Na'Goh is playing." She motioned to the north. "Tiernan, you said Lakedon, Milston, and Northwick, right? I think we should take care of those first."

"Lorelei too," Tiernan mentioned. "Who knows, maybe even Lily of the Valley by now? If Zoran's forces have been advancing south, Tammith and the rest of that community might need our help."

Enid opened her eyes. "What do you mean? Zoran's forces?"

Tiernan took a deep breath. "Zoran has somehow been bringing monsters from a land known as Kinswatch and dropping them here. He then gives them a part of his essence, which allows him to control the beasts and 'see' through their eyes."

Tiernan didn't dare tell Enid about Leviathan. After her breakdown in the Cave of Tera, he decided that would be too painful for her to hear.

Someday.

"I wish I had my axe," Enid lamented.

"We recovered it after the battle. It was in the war room within Castle Abria when Farna fell."

Enid sighed. "Any axe will do. I'll make it work."

Chapter 45

2 Florin 925NE

Enid handed the dinage to a vendor. She raised the axe in the air as if to say thanks before turning around to leave. As she walked out into the streets, she took a look around at the scenery. Not far from where she stood, she saw a statue. Realizing she had never looked at it before, she walked up to read it.

She eyed the inscription on the placard below the likeness of the Elf. "Ready to go for a ride?"

"It's something Tolith once said to Grandpa Borun. On the day of our births when the white dragon, sorry, Na'Goh, appeared." Tiernan had his arms crossed and was leaning against a small, long-forgotten flowerbed.

"I don't think I remember Tolith. He died when we were so young."

Tiernan made a sound of acknowledgement. "How are you feeling today?"

Enid massaged her shoulder muscle and spun her arm in a circle. "Still sore. What did Firefly call those things? Orcs?"

"You should ask her about the one that chased us through a cave. That was an experience!" Tiernan handed her a piece of bread. "Hungry? It's Tammith's."

Enid grabbed the bite out of his hand. "Oh, T, and it's still warm. Have you figured out how she does it?"

He shook his head. "No. No one can. Maybe it's magic."

Enid chewed and talked at the same time. "No, from what you've told me, she's been able to do this since long before I released the magic. Where did you say she worked before she bought the Alligator?"

"One of the places here. I forget where. Tammith also told me she had a surprise for us. Asked me to bring you with me whenever you were done. Is the axe good enough?"

Enid looked at it, then shrugged. "It's an axe. It's not mine. Better than the ones we scavenged from that giant a few weeks ago. Now, gimme." She put her hand out, waiting for more bread.

"Oh fine. Take it." Tiernan handed her the loaf. Enid tossed the axe at him, which he barely caught in time. Its weight made him nearly fall to the ground. "Hey. This is heavier than it looks. Are you sure you can use this thing?"

Enid spun around. "It's perfect, except for it's not mine. You're just out of shape. When's the last time you did push-ups?"

"That's not fair. I've been busy."

Together, they walked through the rows of vendors, some open while others closed, of the Tolith Market.

"From what I hear, you've spent the past few years wandering the land, especially since you let Rhys run the place. Oh!" She stopped in her tracks and raised a finger to her brother's face. "He better change it."

"Change what?"

"The Land of Enid. Come on. *I'm right here*. This is *Abria*, Tiernan! No need for any sentimental name change, especially one that is based on an error."

He smiled. "I'll let him know. He seemed busy when we saw him a few days ago."

She finished her bite and tossed the loaf back to her brother. Enid then reached for the axe. "Give me that before you hurt yourself. I still can't believe we freed all four towns without a decent axe."

"We did okay in Oakshadow before you decided to show back up." Enid shot him a look. "Okay, sorry. Before the dragons decided to grace us with your humble presence."

Enid dropped the axe and tackled Tiernan, the rest of the loaf falling to the ground. She pinned him down, her knee on one arm, her left arm holding down the other and her right arm pushing into his chest.

He gasped for air. "I give! You win."

She released him and jumped to her feet. She extended her hand to help him back up. "Nice to see that animal gone from your face." She put her hand on his face and turned his head sideways. "The hair is going to take a while." Enid looked for the loaf, found it, and picked it up along with the axe.

Tiernan rubbed his chest. "There's Tammith. She's waiting on us, it looks like."

Tammith turned and said something to her staff inside of the Drunken Alligator. She closed the door and met the twins just outside of the entrance.

"I saw that little scuffle over there. Don't let him give you any lip, Enid. He deserves every punch you throw his way," she said with a grin. "Now, follow me."

Enid elbowed her brother. "What did you do to her?"

"I ordered water."

"Ah. The vow you took after Way…"

"Yeah." Tiernan sped up his pace to walk next to Tammith. "Where are we headed?"

She motioned for them to keep following her. "You'll see."

Tiernan fell back and shrugged.

Enid mouthed 'The Mill' and Tiernan's eyes lit up.

Expecting a preview of a wedding hall, Tiernan wondered what changes Tammith had made. Instead, his eyes widened once they crossed the fields.

Now operational, the giant water wheel of Borun Mill spun freely. Next to the entrance was a sign that made the twins feel overwhelmed with emotions neither knew how to articulate.

Tiernan read it out loud. "Welcome to Borun Mill. Tammith, what is this?"

She grinned. "Do you remember that crystal you and, what is her name, found for me?"

"Firefly."

"Yes. Firefly. The archer. The crystal you retrieved was worth more dinage than I'd make in thirty years running the Alligator. That's why I paid you so much for it. I traded it for the water wheel, along with eight times what I gave the two of you."

Tiernan ran to the side of the mill to watch the wheel in action. He yelled back to the other two over the sounds of the water. "So, what are you planning to do with it? Is this for show for the reception hall?"

Tammith motioned for Enid to follow. They joined Tiernan in admiring the power of the Lorelei River fueling the wheel.

"Actually, no. I'm looking for a family to partner with, someone who is good at running things and could help me get this operational as a mill. Just as Borun intended."

Enid smiled. "Tammith…"

"Stop," she replied. "Your grandfather's legacy made the Valley a strong, vibrant community, even despite this war. And as soon as that's done with, I'm going to need workers to get things moving again. Maybe the two of you could help me recruit employees."

Tiernan turned around and extended his hand. "You got it."

Tammith shook it. "Then it's a deal. Now, go free the rest of our land."

Firefly sliced at her arrows with her knife, whittling them into the proper thickness. The innkeeper had allowed her to set up shop in the main hall, understanding the importance of her task even if it created a substantial mess of shavings on his floor.

Airvede studied the book Zachary gave Tiernan before he left, trying to understand which magic she possessed and how to activate each power within her. At the moment, she was focused on teleportation, hoping it might give her an advantage in the battle against Zoran.

Shig plucked away on his sanshin. He found it comforting, thinking back on his short reunion with his brother a little over three weeks ago. So much had happened in the interim that the heartbroken Ashigaru didn't feel he had time to mourn his loss, at least with the reverence it deserved. With the looming remaining battles, Shig wasn't sure if he would have the opportunity soon either, wondering if it would take until he returned home to Watodo to find the time.

Enid and Tiernan walked in and spotted the three at their various tables. Airvede waved. Shig saw them, nodded, and continued playing. Firefly looked up, smiled, and continued her work.

"They're dedicated," said Enid.

"This has been an adventure, that's for sure."

"I can't wait to read about it in your next book," she said in a mocking voice.

"Uh huh." Tiernan proceeded to Firefly's table and noticed how clean each of her arrows looked.

"Only six more, and I'll have a full quiver."

"That should be more than enough," he responded.

"It sounds like this Zoran is pretty tough. Can't be too prepared," she said as she resumed her work.

Enid sat next to Shig, listening to his song. "What's the meaning?"

He stopped. "Meaning?"

"Of the words. There are words, right?"

Shig nodded. "There are. They're personal, if that's okay."

Enid nodded. "I understand. Maybe more than you realize."

"I read about your husband in Tiernan's book. Sounds like we all might owe our lives to him."

Enid narrowed her eyes. "What do you mean?"

Shig continued playing. "If he hadn't saved you, you wouldn't have been there to save us. We wouldn't have defeated Kane, and the way you helped us in the battles to the north over the past few weeks, we might have lost those, too."

Enid sat back in her seat. "I guess I never thought about it that way."

Shig continued. "Isn't it obvious? That's why the dragons did what they did. They kept you out of harm's way until the moment you were needed most."

"Did they?" She scrunched her mouth, thinking. "Why not bring me back before my home fell? All I did was remove Kane's ability to transform his body. His death was of his own doing."

Shig stopped. "You saw the Northern Plateau on the way to Milston."

Enid nodded. "Right. It had imploded."

"And the citadel where Airvede over there saw Zoran through the eyes of the Ryllix? It's gone. Crushed." He resumed his song. "I don't know about you, but that sounds like they knew what they were doing."

Enid looked toward the White Mage. "T told me about the Ryllix just last week. His hesitation was understandable. I'll be honest with you, kid. I'm not sure what I would have done in that situation." She turned her head sideways as she saw Airvede mumbling something to herself. "That being said, I'm grateful for you and the role you played there."

"By Clandagh, I've got it!" Airvede snapped her fingers. She disappeared in a flash typical of those empowered with teleportation.

"Hey, she did it guys!" said Shig. "Wonder where she went?"

Firefly made a slight cheering gesture. "If she can teleport, that means she can take us all to what remains of the Northern Plateau."

Tiernan nodded in agreement. "This war is almost over. We can find Zoran and finish this for good."

Airvede reappeared in her original spot. "We need to move. Now."

Each member of the team grabbed their gear and rushed outside. The twins shared a concerned look, with Tiernan knowing deep down there was only one thing that could cause this kind of reaction in the normally calm White Mage.

Once outside, Firefly looked around. "Okay, Airvede. What's the commotion? Where did you go and what's the big deal?"

"I went to the fields of Whispersong, where Shig and I travelled for his horse lessons."

"And what did you see?" asked Tiernan.

"A bronze Na'Goh heading west toward Clericsfold."

Shig's expression turned somber. "Toward my kyōdai's grave."

"I don't know if that's the intention, but we have to track the dragon," Airvede said.

Tiernan's mind raced. "The bridge near Clericsfold. Airvede, we all crossed the bridge after the Lorelei River flooded. Remember?"

Enid gave him a questioning look, which Tiernan waved off.

Airvede wasn't following. "Right. Yes, I remember that. What about it?"

"Grab our hands. Picture the bridge and take us there. Since you've seen it with your own eyes, you can take us there too." Tiernan said.

Airvede's face exuded her internal hesitation and self-doubt. "Tiernan, I just learned how to teleport *myself*. I don't know if I can teleport us all at once." She looked at Enid. "Can't you do it like you did in that weird void with Caudex?"

Enid put her hands on Airvede's shoulders. "That was a gift from the Na'Goh, just like the way I absorbed Kane's attack. A one-and-done kind of thing to help us break free of Ultimus.

"And, you're right. *You* can't. This magic is too new. But you can with my help. And Firefly. And yes, even those two bumbling losers as well."

"Hey!" Shig said in defense.

Tiernan nudged Shig. "She's right. They're the ones with powers. You and I are just here because of our good looks."

Shig laughed at the joke. "I know, but still."

Enid let a small smile cross her face. "You know I'm just teasing you, kid. Hold the Soul Sword tight. Let its power flow through you. Brother, concentrate on the Mind Shield. Here." Enid handed the Power Ring to Airvede. "Use this. I know this seems crazy. Maybe it's the Na'Goh in me, I don't know. I just know that we *can* do this. Everyone picture the bridge, grab Airvede's left hand, and focus."

Airvede slid the ring on a finger on her right hand. Once its power connected with the magic inside of her, she grabbed hold of the others' hands.

"Now, concentrate. Shig, T, use your relics. Firefly, feel it in your heart." Enid smiled. "Airvede, you can do this."

Everyone closed their eyes. Airvede raised her free hand with the others all holding tight to the other.

With a snap of the White Mage's hand, the five defenders disappeared.

Tiernan still didn't like the feeling of teleportation. As the world came back into view, he glanced around and did a head count. To his relief, everyone made it.

Shig stomped his feet. "Guys, we're on the bridge."

Firefly peered over the edge. "Airvede, you said you saw it heading west. Was it fast?"

"No. Nowhere near as fast as the blue dragon back in Alwyn. It seemed to fly with intention, but not in any hurry."

"So, it would be just over the plains between the Lorelei River and the eastern path." Tiernan pointed. "That way."

The group bolted in the direction of the bronze dragon's flight. As the defenders made their way north along the eastern path, each member did a quick inventory check. Firefly put on the Gravity Ring, intending to use it with her arrows to down the beast.

Shig pulled out both the Soul Sword and Haia, prepared for whatever might come his way. Airvede handed the Power Ring back to Enid. The White Mage then absorbed an ether and slid a Wind Ring on her hand.

Tiernan slid the Mind Shield onto his arm and pulled out his sword as his sister tossed the axe back and forth in her hands.

"Problems, Sis?"

"I guess you were right for once, Brother. The weight is off. It's not as balanced as my old one."

Tiernan's face lit up. "Did you just admit I was right?"

She shot him a look.

He waved her reaction off. "That settles it. We'll find your old one. Can you still do *the thing*?"

"You mean this?" She smiled as the axe head lit up like a smithing furnace, its head blazing in glass-like flame and causing the other three to turn their heads in admiration. "Or this thing?"

she asked as she sent a blast of her glass magic toward an errant rock, encasing it as she had done so many times in recent weeks.

"The first one. They've already seen the glass trick. Now you're just showing off," he said with a laugh.

As they moved north along the path, there was no sign of the dragon in the skies.

"Are you sure it came this way?" asked Enid.

"I am," Airvede answered. "Maybe it rose too high for us to see it, or maybe it changed course and headed east?"

"Sis, is there anything about this Na'Goh the others taught you?"

Enid shook her head. "Only what I've told you, T. I know it cracked the world. It led the uprising."

Shig stopped. "Hey, D."

"What, S?" Enid shrugged as the others looked her way. "Oh, come on. I can't call him a silly nickname too instead of just 'kid'? I've been thinking about it for weeks!"

"Shig is already short for his longer name. Shigeharu. S is redundant," Tiernan said with a grin.

"Oh, shut up, Brother."

Airvede raised her finger to the air while continuing to look for the dragon in the sky. "Actually, if I'm not mistaken, Shig has called Tiernan both Zach and Z. So, there is precedent for a shortened nickname and a single letter version. Don't let him deceive you, Enid."

Enid rolled her eyes and then pointed at the men. "See, exactly! Anyway, whatever, *Shig*. What's on your mind?"

Shig had the look of someone in pure bliss on his face, enjoying the banter between each member of the group. "So, D, you've mentioned an uprising within the dragons. Was the bronze dragon alone or were there others?"

Enid closed her eyes, trying to remember. "I got the impression there were more, but they weren't clear about that. You said you fought a blue one. I think that means there are more."

Shig kept scanning the sky as they moved further north. "So, could there be more than one bronze dragon? Maybe this one is good and the one that leveled your home is bad?"

Enid opened her eyes. "I'm sorry. I just don't know."

Airvede walked ahead of Shig, straining her eyes to see if she could see anything in the sky. "Maybe I should take flight?"

"Not a bad idea," said Enid. "I'll join you."

Both mages levitated, with Airvede using the Wind Ring to propel herself faster than usual. The power of the red dragon emerged from Enid, its wings spreading wide in their ghostly apparition.

As the two rose high, Shig walked over to Tiernan. "Is she always this way?"

"She's different. She's still my sister, but Enid has changed. When we lost her before, she was in her grief. It's still there, but she seems more confident in her abilities, too. Less afraid of them."

Firefly tapped each of them on a shoulder with her bow. "That, or she's had to put up with two childish boys for the past few weeks and has had enough."

Shig and Tiernan started to protest, then saw the playful look in Firefly's eyes. As the three of them watched from below, Enid and Airvede spread out, both hovering just above the trees and looking east to west and then north to south. Tiernan and the others couldn't hear them, though they saw Enid point in one direction. Airvede headed that way while Enid took off toward the Valley Woods.

Before either got too far, a blast of Wind Magic came out of nowhere and hit Airvede square in the chest. It caused her to lose her momentum, throwing her backward and toward the ground.

Enid heard the commotion and altered her course, flying just under Airvede's trajectory and catching her before she hit the ground.

Relieved that their friend was safe, Tiernan and the others turned in the direction of the attack.

Walking toward them along the other side of the Lake Conchobar run off was a lone figure. This unusual individual wore armor consisting of a royal navy and purple coloration, along with a helmet with opposing crescents adorned on it. Its hands were black with a stone-like appearance to them. The individual's face was bronze. Slightly taller than an average Graelan, it walked with a slow, methodical approach that exuded a sinister and otherworldly vibe.

Tiernan knew from a previous encounter the name of this new arrival. Nevertheless, he wanted to make certain his allies understood what they were about to face.

"That's Zoran."

Chapter 46

The Final Battle

Tiernan motioned for his comrades to move behind him. He pulled out his sword, with Firefly and Shig following his lead. Enid ignited the head of her axe and readied a blast of Fire Magic to level toward Zoran if needed. Airvede equipped herself, prepared to enact a Barrier in a moment's notice.

Zoran's face showed an array of emotions. Tiernan saw hints of rage and bitterness, along with a sense of apathy. Zoran snapped his fingers, appearing on their side of the Lake Conchobar run off.

"Thank you," Zoran said.

Tiernan angled his head and lowered his sword in confusion. "Thank you?"

"I was sure you would have figured it out by now. I thought Graelans were smarter than that." His apathy was on full display with his explanation. "I spread my power throughout the beasts and monsters you slayed. It was so I could track you, even though you carried that accursed shield. With each of their deaths, you returned a portion of my power to me, strengthening me for this very moment."

"Where is the bronze Na'Goh?" Airvede asked.

"The Na'Goh is where it belongs."

Tiernan raised his sword. "That's not an answer. I don't know what you're trying here. Remember, Telford defeated you centuries ago. Five years ago, a mere Graelan, Manus Midir, one without magic by the way, nearly ended your life with a simple sword. How do you expect to defeat us with two powerful mages on our side and all three relics?"

Zoran made no attempt to answer. Instead, he continued to deflect. "I propose a truce. Farna is gone. That's all I cared about. Let me go. I'll leave your little Kingdom to rebuild." Zoran smiled again. "Or not. It can rot and burn for all I care. Do what you will with the land. I'll even take the monsters you didn't kill with me. There are some still out there, after all."

Tiernan stepped forward. "Where will you go? To wreak havoc on another land?"

Enid moved next to her brother. "You lied to us just now. Five years ago, you wanted the magic. That was what your shapeshifting spy said. Not Farna. How can we trust anything you say?"

Zoran's eyes narrowed and filled with hate. "*You.* You should not be here, Dragonborn. The Na'Goh that gave its life so that you might live betrayed its people." Zoran's eyes then darkened, transforming into an inky black color similar to the Ultimus star field where they had battled Caudex. "That's a wrong I must right before I go."

Zoran growled, and in a swift motion, sent a blast of pink magic toward Enid. Quick to respond, Airvede extended her hands in front of the twins, erecting a Barrier that absorbed the attack.

"Do not think you can stop me so easily. Tell me where *she* is. This is your last warning. And leave those two," Zoran said, pointing to Airvede and Enid. "Give me what I want and I'll go."

Tiernan shook his head. "You keep changing the terms. First, you said you'll go in peace. Now you want the mages? And who is this she?"

A flash of memory flew through Enid's mind. Broken conversations of the Na'Goh, hints of what must not happen, and confusing phrases overwhelmed her consciousness. She fell to her knees, a response Zoran noted and seemed to relish.

Tiernan kneeled down. "Sister!"

Airvede erected another Barrier as the former King took care of the Dragonborn's distress.

"I asked you once. This is your last opportunity. *Where is she?*" Zoran bellowed again, his eyes returning to the inky darkness of the Ultimus battlefield.

Enid pulled herself back up by Tiernan's hand. "It's a word I kept hearing, T. The Na'Goh would say it followed by a repeating 'no,' almost with desperation."

"What word?" asked Firefly.

"Absorption. Sometimes with an image of a dragon. Gold, maybe bronze, I'm not sure."

Tiernan's heart sunk. "Absorption." He glared at Zoran through the transparent Barrier. "You want *Eislyn*. But why?"

Zoran roared loudly, his voice echoing across the plains.

"No," Tiernan said, finally understanding. "You don't want *her*. You need her *power*."

"To take back the magic from Graelans," Airvede said as she made the connection.

"The magic belongs to *me*," Zoran said as his body appeared to be contorting. He pointed to Airvede. "That one can take me to her in a blink of an eye now that she's learned the secret of teleportation. And that one," he said, pointing to Enid, "must not be allowed to continue."

Zoran raised his hands in the air, a new bronze magic filling both palms. His voice deepened into a chilling baritone with a reverberating echo. "Waiting all this time has been maddening, but it will be worth it. Worth it then to take back what was mine, and worth it now to see you all die."

Enid took a step forward. "You'll never find Eislyn." Her eyes lit up in a fury of rage at the mere thought of losing her sister-in-law. "This ends here. Today. Your reign of terror is over!"

"What do you know of my reign of terror, Dragonborn?" Zoran stepped forward, bellowed again, and extended his arms wide to each side. The bronze magic that had been in his palms moved through his body. His arms doubled in size along with his legs, which did the same before growing fourfold. He leaned forward as his fingers extended into claws.

Zoran's legs continued to expand as the bronze coloration from the Dark Emperor's face moved down along his body. His neck extended as his torso reorganized into a scaly pattern. Whatever semblance of clothing Zoran wore disappeared through the transformation, fading away as if it was nothing more than an illusion. The double crescent pattern on his head extended into two slicked-back horns. Wings protruded from his back, stretching far across the grassland.

Zoran's mouth and nose stretched into a snout. The last piece of the Dark Emperor to change was his eyes, glazing over from the inky Ultimus coloration a moment ago to a blinded solid bronze.

Zoran's body continued to transform until it now towered over the group in the form of a large bronze dragon. Shig's mouth fell open. Airvede and Firefly braced themselves, preparing to assault their attacker. Tiernan gripped his sword tight.

A final, distant connection to the realm of the Na'Goh spoke in Enid's mind.

Cracked the world.

Three simple words that put everything in perspective.

The beast that had been Zoran took flight, roaring as it ascended into the air. Movement of its giant wings created a windstorm like effect until it rose high enough for the effect to subside.

The Na'Goh released a flurry of boulders toward the group. Airvede cast a Barrier above them as Enid prepared her various magic attacks.

The Dragonborn raised her hands. "Airvede, let this through your Barrier."

"You got it!"

Enid sent waves of Fire Magic and her glass encasement toward the boulders, incinerating some and turning them into ash. The others fell in their glass tomb until the effect would wear off.

The dragon, sensing her defense, stopped the attack and turned northward, increasing in speed with each passing meter. It rose higher in the air, blinded but able to sense each member of the group through various means. Its nostrils sniffed, remembering the smell of the men. With its ears, it listened for changes in the air that would tell it where the mages moved in the air.

"It all makes sense now," Tiernan said. "Zoran wanted the magic for himself. Itself?" He looked at his sister, who shrugged.

"With that much magic, he would rule Grael. Which is why you had to release it back into the land," Airvede said to Enid. "That is your legacy."

"That's why the red dragon saved me." Enid's eyes grew wide. "To keep the magic away from Zoran."

"Whom Kane awakened because of his hatred toward Mom and Dad. The Na'Goh knew this would happen, Sis. Don't you guys see?" Tiernan looked at the group. "The Na'Goh need us to defeat the bronze dragon once and for all."

"Z. Look." Shig pointed toward the hovering beast as it circled back around.

"It's fond of this maneuver. It's a ramming attack. I saw it time and time again back in Farna. Everyone, spread out!"

"Spread out?" Enid said in incredulity. "You can't be serious."

"It knows where we were last at. As the bronze dragon, Zoran is blinded. Plus, it cannot sense our exact location because of the Mind Shield."

The group looked unconvinced. "You have to trust me here. This is exactly what it did in Farna."

Shig pointed. "It's coming back. I say with go with Z's strategy."

"Fine. It's settled. As Tiernan said, spread out," ordered Firefly.

The group bolted from the safety under Airvede's Barrier and moved apart. The bronze dragon, now on a ramming trajectory, lowered itself to the ground.

As it passed by Firefly, she ducked. She then turned around and released a Gravity Magic-fueled arrow at its leg. It exploded in a brilliant flash, with purple tendrils swirling around its hind left claw.

The bronze dragon roared, now knowing the position of the archer. Gravity pulled on its body as it felt the sting of another attack on its abdomen.

Tiernan saw Shig flat on his back, Soul Sword extended. It sliced into Zoran's body with the same molten effect as it had with Caudex in the caves.

In a fury, the bronze dragon rose into the air out of reach of the ancient relic. Bronze blood dripped along the northern path, dissolving any rocks it touched.

Airvede sent a Barrier toward the beast's other leg, encompassing it as she did with the blue dragon. Her magic missed and dispersed into the air.

Enid's eyes glazed over into a white-hot effect. Wings of fire extended from her body. She turned to her brother across the field. "Be right back."

Enid herself ascended into the air as the bronze dragon increased speed. It turned around, intent on another strafing run near where Shig had wounded it.

"Shig!" Tiernan motioned for the Ashigaru Paladin to join him. Shig jumped up and ran toward Tiernan. Both ducked down behind a nearby boulder.

In the air, the bronze dragon heard the direction of Tiernan's voice and planned its next move.

"Did you realize it, Tiernan?"

The unusual use of his real name startled the former King. "Realize what, my friend?"

"Caudex. What used to be Kane. The bronze dragon's attack. Cracked the world." Shig pointed. "Here he comes again." He took a breath. "All of Zoran's powers, whether as a Graelanoid or the bronze dragon, are rock based, including turning Kane into that abomination we fought below."

Tiernan nodded. "Everyone, duck!"

As they leaned down, the bronze dragon spread its wings wide, intent on knocking down any one of them. It sniffed the air, honing in on the exact position of the men.

Instead, a blast of fire magic startled the creature. It raised its head toward the attack, blaming itself for not paying attention to the Dragonborn. Another stream of fire hit it on its back and charred its scales.

The bronze dragon roared as it felt the full fury of the red Na'Goh bearing down on it. Enid opened her other palm as the beast looped back toward her. She sent another stream into its chest, scarring more of the bronze dragon in an ashen char.

It raised its claws, pulling boulders and pieces of the ground up. Tiernan and Shig rolled out of the way just in time as a giant piece of the land flew up from under their position.

Firefly released gravity arrows at various groupings of rock. Airvede encased some in Barriers, shrinking many of those encasements and crushing the ones she could. After this volley, she grabbed an ether and pressed it into her palm for a recharge.

Neither defender could stop all of them. The bronze dragon hurled a series of them toward Enid. The Dragonborn deflected and incinerated some while encasing a few in a glass prison, though several made it through her defense. As they passed into her wings of fire, the effect disappeared.

Enid fell toward the ground. Airvede propelled herself toward her at an incredible speed through the power of the Wind Ring, catching the Dragonborn similar to how she herself had been saved earlier.

"Thanks," Enid said.

"We're even."

Tiernan rushed to his sister's side as the bronze dragon ascended into the air. "Are you okay?"

"No."

Tiernan's eyes grew large. He motioned to Shig and Firefly to take point against the bronze dragon. "No? I've never known you to—"

"Save it, Brother. *That hurt.* Not the fall. When those rocks passed through the wings. I felt it like it was my own body."

Airvede put her hands on Enid's shoulders to heal her. A bright white magic enveloped them both just as Firefly sent several gravity arrows toward the bronze dragon.

The creature turned its attention from the direction of Enid toward Firefly. It pulled its wings back to increase speed.

Shig saw the attack coming, calculated the trajectory, and threw several daggers at the dragon. He then rushed Firefly, tackling her and pushing her out of the way.

Two of the daggers soared through its wings. Bronze blood dripped out of them, landing on the grass but causing no damage. As the dragon passed over the eastern path, the drips dissolved any rocks it touched.

"I had it," said Firefly as she stood up.

"No, you didn't," he said as she helped him to his feet. "You're welcome."

The two took a moment to regroup as the bronze dragon flew toward the Valley Woods. Using its other senses, it adjusted its plan of attack and turned around with its claws raised.

"Shig, move!" Firefly ran to the left while he to the right. Giant chunks of the ground traveled upward. At the same time, the bronze dragon breathed boulders toward their position.

"Look out!" Enid's eyes turned white-hot again as she attacked the boulders with her fire. She incinerated many, though some made it through and landed on the ground near Firefly's position.

Firefly peeked her head around the edge of a nearby boulder from the beast and waved Enid off. The Dragonborn stopped as Firefly hid and waited.

Airvede levitated over to Shig to check on his condition.

As she left, Tiernan rubbed his head. "How do we bring it down? Five years ago, we fought him as a Graelanoid. That was different. This is harder."

"It's not letting up. We are hurting it, just not fast enough," Enid said as her eyes returned to normal. "There it goes. Another strafing run. It's trying to wear us down. Sooner or later, it'll win unless we think of something."

Tiernan raised his sword. "Can you get me above him?"

Enid rubbed her shoulder on the side of a boulder where one had passed through her wings of fire earlier. "I think."

"I want to land on its back."

"Yeah, that's the spirit. Land on the angry beast." She shook her head as she let out a small chuckle. "It might work, though. This way, Brother." Enid motioned for Tiernan to follow her over to Shig.

The bronze dragon flew back toward them at a rapid pace. Firefly emerged from her hiding spot and released a series of arrows toward Zoran. Two hit a wing while the others found the creature's abdomen. After the flash subsided, Gravity Magic pulled it lower to the ground. Firefly fired one more from behind, hitting it on its foot.

The attack was enough to send the dragon rolling. It tumbled for a while, then stood on its feet and turned around to face Firefly at her last known position. It sent several more volleys of boulders in her direction, though she had already moved far enough away. Enraged, it roared in outrage as it realized she had escaped its fury.

Angered, the dragon took to the skies again, albeit with a slower momentum because of the Gravity Magic fighting hard against it. The Na'Goh turned southbound, preparing another ramming strike.

Firefly approached the group, a hint of sarcasm evident in her voice. "This is going well, I think. Why are the four of you all together? I thought Tiernan said to spread out."

"I needed to make sure Shig was okay," answered Airvede.

"Fair enough. What about you two?"

"We were just telling them about our plan," said Tiernan, now holding the Soul Sword along with the Mind Shield.

Firefly looked at Shig, who now held Tiernan's other sword. She sighed, though not out of frustration but growing exhaustion. "What do you need us to do?"

"Your arrows are slowing it down. Shig, I've seen you throw daggers. Incredible aim, by the way. Distract it with those and the sword. Airvede, keep these two safe, no matter what." Enid smiled. "We've got this. We just have to stay focused and stick together."

Firefly moved south to the west side of the path. Airvede moved the opposite way. Shig took up a central position, dead center of where the bronze dragon's current ramming trajectory would take the beast.

Enid and Tiernan bolted further to the north ahead of Shig. The Dragonborn's eyes turned white-hot again. Her wings of fire emerged, though not without a surge of pain coursing through her body.

Tiernan saw her face. "After this is over, you need to rest."

She shook her head. "I've been resting for five years. I'm fine." Enid wrapped her arms around her brother. When she made contact, all three relics lit up like the sun.

"We always wondered how Telford sealed Zoran centuries ago. I think that's our sign we're onto something," he said. "Family is Strength, Sis. Let's do this."

"I wish the Na'Goh had told me what's so special about these relics."

"Another time, maybe? Here he comes."

"I'm not doing that jewel thing again, so we'll have to ask them ourselves."

Ahead of the twins, Shig held his daggers. He pulled out Haia and kissed it. "Goodbye, gorgeous."

Firefly aimed several arrows at the approaching bronze dragon. Airvede extended her arms, preparing a Barrier.

The beast pulled its wings back, picking up as much speed as it could despite the Gravity Magic still working against it. It roared and released boulders toward the group.

As the bronze dragon passed Firefly, she released gravity arrows toward its abdomen. Airvede cast a Barrier, catching its already wounded wing in it.

Shig threw several daggers at its stomach, then, with one powerful, decisive swing, threw Haia at the dragon's throat. The Paladin fell backward again in an impressive move, one that was only possible because of his extreme Ashigaru training and resultant flexibility.

The gravity arrows exploded, slowing Zoran down. The Barrier extended around its wing, then shrunk quickly as Airvede pulled her hands together to crush it.

The daggers found their mark, wounding the beast's stomach. Haia dug deep into the throat of the bronze dragon, disappearing into its skin.

"Now, Sister!"

Enid took to the air just as it approached them at an impressive, albeit diminished, speed. She brought them down hard, landing on the creature's back.

With no hesitation, Enid released a rapid series of Fire Magic attacks onto its back. Tiernan raised the Soul Sword high, aiming it at the back of the bronze dragon much like he had with his sword into the ground that day in the Valley last year. With his warrior fierceness on full display, he plunged the Soul Sword into the bronze dragon.

Once embedded into the beast, the ancient relic grew brighter, blinding Tiernan and Enid. The two of them felt their bodies fall, as if the creature below them was falling itself. As their feet landed on its back, the Dragonborn tried to see through the light and realized the bronze dragon had fallen to and was skidding along the ground.

In addition, its body appeared to be going through a painful transformation process from the form of the bronze dragon back into a Graelanoid. As the light diminished, the twins both saw that the Soul Sword appeared to be causing these changes as the beast shifted and fought hard against the metamorphosis.

In short order, Tiernan and Enid found them standing over the wounded body of the Dark Emperor, with the Soul Sword buried deep in his lower back. Hoping to survive for another day, Zoran extended a hand out, preparing to snap himself away.

Enid stepped on his arm and sent a wave of her glass prison magic at his hand, encasing it in a locked position. The other three rushed over with Airvede surrounding his other hand in a tight Barrier. Firefly aimed several arrows at his head, while Shig readied Tiernan's sword and his last few daggers.

Tiernan put his hand on the Soul Sword's handle, pulling it out. "It's over, Zoran. Yield."

The Dark Emperor scoffed as bronze blood trickled down from the open wound. "I will never yield." Zoran breathed, a gurgling sound emanating from his chest with labored effort.

Tiernan turned back to face to his companions. "We'll use this," he said, raising the Soul Sword. "Telford sealed him away once. We can do it again."

"But how?" Enid asked. "It isn't like they left us instructions on how to make this thing do what we want it to do."

Zoran let himself smile, his eyes filling with satisfaction at their ignorance. He bellowed loud, using whatever powers remained within him to shatter Enid's glass casing on his hand. He jumped to his feet and lunged at Tiernan, intent on grabbing the Soul Sword.

"Tiernan!" Shig yelled as a warning.

The former King spun around with the Soul Sword extended. As Zoran rushed at them, Tiernan did the only thing he could do.

In an act of pure defense, he plunged the ancient relic through the upper half of Zoran's torso.

The Dark Emperor cried out in agony, raising his freed hand with a blast of Ultimus prepared to strike. Enid swung her axe, severing it. She then sent a short blast of her Fire Magic at his arm, cauterizing the wound.

Zoran fell to his knees with Tiernan keeping the Soul Sword at a sharp angle in his torso. The two locked eyes.

"I will not be denied," Zoran said defiantly. "And when I find her, I'll be sure to let her know you could not do what was necessary to protect her." He began to laugh, a sound that grew with intensity with each passing tick.

"Tiernan," Shig said.

Tiernan broke eye contact with Zoran to look at Shig.

The Ashigaru sighed, knowing what had to be done. "Protect your wife."

"And everyone else," said Firefly. "He's not going to stop."

Airvede maintained her stoic composure, though her eyes she said she, too, agreed with the decision.

Tiernan looked at his sister.

She met his gaze and gave him a subtle nod. "We're not just the Protectors of Abria, T, but of the entire world."

With her affirmation, he made up his mind. Tiernan kept his left hand on the Soul Sword. With the other, he reached for the sword in Shig's hand. "It doesn't have to be this way, Zoran."

The Dark Empire stopped laughing. "There's no way you can win here. If you let me go, I'll find her. If you try to seal me away, I'll break free." His eyes filled with satisfaction. "And if you kill me, it will be your first step toward darkness." He laughed. "Toward the heart of Ultimus." Zoran coughed bronze blood. "Admit it. You've lost."

Tiernan raised the second blade into the air, ready to end the Dark Emperor's life. His eyes caught something else at the last tick.

Zoran's back wound continued to bleed with visible bronze blood pooling on the ground behind him. *He's going to bleed out.* The former King locked eyes with the Dark Emperor.

"We only kill when we must. Choose to live." Tiernan gave Shig a quick glance, nodding at his friend. Tiernan then pulled the Soul Sword out of Zoran's chest. "What happens next is on you."

Zoran blinked several times. His earlier satisfaction gave way to rage. "No." He shook his head, rising to his feet in defiance. "No, you cannot—" He rushed toward them.

The group took a step back, with Zoran continuing to advance. He swung his remaining hand, still encased in Airvede's Barrier, at the group, trying in vain to attack them.

A tick later, he fell forward in agony, hitting the ground hard face-first. A coughing fit overtook his body.

Tiernan kneeled next to him. "Airvede can heal you before it's too late. I implore you again, Zoran. Choose to live."

Zoran raised his head from the grass. "I will never submit to the likes of you or any other Graelan." He let his face fall back to the ground. The Dark Emperor's chest rose a few more times, with each breath spaced further apart. After a prolonged break, Zoran took in one last gasp, then exhaled in a long, final sigh that carried with it the weight of what had just transpired.

The group stood in quiet reflection, waiting for some final act of rebellion or attempt of escape. When none came, Tiernan shook Zoran's body. After a few moments of waiting and not seeing any response, Tiernan motioned to Shig. The two men put their arms under one side and rolled Zoran onto his back.

They continued to observe his body in silence. Zoran's chest never rose again. No one knew what to say.

It was Shig who broke the tension. "We won," he said. He turned to Tiernan and the others in rapid succession. "Guys, we did it. We won!"

Airvede blinked, still processing what she had just witnessed. Firefly lowered her bow, on guard but beginning to feel at ease that she would not need them anymore today.

The twins exchanged a look of relief. Tiernan let out a small chuckle, the reality of their victory setting in.

Enid's eyes returned to normal. Her wings vanished, and she realized she'd been clenching her fist since Zoran fell. She let her hand relax and then took a deep breath.

"It's over, my love. We did it," Enid said, hoping she might somehow pass on their victory to her beloved Wayland in the beyond.

Chapter 47

Farewells

Tiernan put down the quill. For the past three days, he had been here in his chamber within Castle Midir. He ran his hands through his hair, hoping it might have grown a bit, though knowing it would not have changed since the day before, the day before that, and so on.

"It'll happen," he said with a smile. He picked up his notebook from the table and flipped through it, making sure he hadn't forgotten anything. "Oh. Right."

He grabbed the last sheet he had just written and tossed it into the fire. There, the words burned up, never to be read or shared with anyone. It dawned on him that, as he held the magic quill from Zachary, that this was the first page he had discarded between his two books.

He rewrote the section detailing their ultimate battle against Zoran. He opened his notebook and read Enid's words, acknowledging her departed husband.

Instead of including them in the manuscript this time, he wrote his own thoughts.

"The legacy of my sister lives on. Not just through her longing to one day be reunited in the beyond with her husband, my best friend, the lost Prince of this land. But in every one of you throughout the world who can now wield magic.

"We know there will be those of you who use it for nefarious reasons. To those who accidentally hurt others as they discovered their abilities, we mourn with you. No one likes change. It's difficult when

you're learning more about your place in the world, never mind when you've been thrown to the proverbial wolves with newfound abilities.

"We don't know what the future holds for our Kingdom. My Sister demanded Rhys change it back to Abria. I couldn't be sure because I witnessed the interaction from behind, but I'm sure her eyes glowed white-hot once again as a warning not to cross her.

"So, the Land of Enid is once again known as the Kingdom of Abria. There's rebuilding ahead. We must mourn the dead, giving them a proper burial now that we can breathe.

"There's the question of returning our friends to their native lands without risking their lives as they navigate the waters surrounding Abria. My sister and I will be leaving for Farna soon. What will happen after that? We don't know, other than I will see Eislyn and Edward again. Somehow.

"My name is Tiernan Davienson, son of Davien and Kyrie. The last thing I want to say is that these two memoirs are for you, the citizens of my beloved homeland. I suppose my tale and her legacy will soon become a part of the dusty Archives in Alwyn. One day, when we're long gone and reunited with our loved ones in the beyond, I hope you read this and learn our two stories were meant to teach a single lesson. It's one you should hold on to and cherish every day of your life.

"Family is Strength."

Tiernan placed the quill on the table. He yelled for a castle attendant, handing them this new manuscript named in honor of his sister and all she did for Abria.

Then Tiernan picked up the quill for the last time and stood, walking over to the mantel and letting it rest. He held his notebook in his hands and prepared to toss it in the fire.

Tiernan pushed the door open to the Drunken Alligator. He glanced around, picturing where he and Eislyn had once sat next to Wayland and Enid over five years ago. *The last Moon Rise before things fell apart.* He smiled, deciding to put aside feelings of sadness and instead embrace the joy that was slowly returning to Abria.

At the back of the tavern, he saw Shig sitting at a table with a maiden. Tiernan raised his hand in Shig's signature wave, something he had never done before.

Shig stood to his feet and bowed, a new gesture for the Ashigaru Paladin as well. He then sat back down to resume his story.

On the opposite side, Firefly sat with her feet propped up. Tiernan approached her as she moved forward. "Tiernan. Have a seat."

"Thanks," he said as he sat. "When are you guys leaving?"

"Tomorrow. Airvede is confident she can return us home. She's been practicing all day."

"Is she here right now?"

Firefly took a drink of her Dorian Ale. "No. We invited her, but she said this had to take priority. She's been moving from place to place throughout Abria, trying to hone her teleportation abilities. But on the bright side, I'm meeting her later tonight with your sister at some kind of impromptu music performance to celebrate the end of the war."

She smiled. "By the way. Your father was right. This is the stuff right here."

"Dorian Ale, huh?" Shig said from behind.

Tiernan turned around. "I thought you were busy back there with your lady friend."

Shig shook his head. "Nah. Just someone who wanted to hear the story." He patted Tiernan on the back. "Our story." With that, he walked over to the bar.

"So, where will you go next?" Tiernan asked. "Did saving our land inspire you to save others?"

"We'll see," Firefly said as she reached for a new pint from Shig. "Ah, thanks. Mine was getting warm."

"Of course," he said as he handed a Lorelian Mead to Tiernan. "The war is over, my friend. Is it time?"

Tiernan couldn't help but let a tear slip down his cheek. "You're right, it is," he said as he raised a glass to Shig and Firefly. "Thanks to you." The former King took a deep inhale, smelling the savory aroma coming off the mead.

"And Airvede and Enid, too," Firefly said with a smile.

Shig took a drink of his pint first. "Yup, it's like what I said the first time. This is the good stuff right here!"

"Everything is good to you, Shig!" Firefly raised her glass to him. "And that's why I'm going to miss you so much. We could use some of your infectious joy back home."

Shig smiled, touched by her words. "To friends."

The three of them clinked their glasses together.

"To family," Tiernan said with a smile as he took his first drink of Lorelian Mead since losing Wayland. "Rest easy, my Brother," he whispered to the beyond.

Tiernan found Enid sitting along the same alleyway where they had celebrated Moon Rise five years ago. His sister appeared lost in thought, staring at the Power Ring on her finger.

"Seems almost empty, doesn't it?" she said.

He leaned the Soul Sword against the wall of a building next to her. Tiernan then pulled the Mind Shield off his back and placed it next to the other ancient relic. "Not going to be that way tonight, though! Some kind of big celebration. How you holding up?" He pointed around. "Lorelei is actually a pretty busy place when it's not freezing cold out." He looked down at the ground. "No snow today, at least. Should make for an excellent performance."

"I want to go home. Not the Valley. Farna. That's where I'm going to build my home, T."

He put his hand on Enid's knee. "I know, Sis. I've thought about living in the Valley. Eislyn and I kept Grandpa's old place, and it will make it easier to help with the mill."

Enid lowered her head. "Maybe. That could work, I guess. Or maybe just until we rebuild Farna." She swallowed. "It was very kind of Clericsfold to donate such a large portion of their fields for the…" She struggled for the word. "…internments."

Tiernan shrugged his shoulders in agreement. "I know. It's crazy to think how much damage Kane did years ago with Clericsfold. And here they are today, that same community, freely giving so much of themselves so we can honor our dead."

She picked up her axe and admired its construction. "Daddy did what he had to preserve the realm. Remember when he brought us in as the Protectors? That shield was half your size." She let herself smile. "I think he pulled it off."

Tiernan felt uncomfortable, knowing this was the right time for the talk he had been dreading. "Listen, Enid. I know that you *disappeared* so soon after we lost them. Not long after we thought we lost you too, they finished the statues. Including Way's."

Enid put her hand on his shoulder. "Been saving that one, haven't you? Thanks, I'll check them out when I get over there in a few days. I'm going to leave as soon as the others head back to their homelands."

She then sat up and turned to face him, her eyes a subtle white-hot glow. "You didn't? Oh, Tiernan, for the love of Aila, please tell me you didn't?"

"I…did? I didn't? Going to be honest, I'm not sure what you're asking about, Sis."

She punched him in the chest with the full force of her fist. "You *did*, didn't you? I want it *gone*." She raised her head to the sky. "Oh, you probably even gave it wings, didn't you? Thought it would be majestic."

She pointed to herself. "Like I told Rhys, I'm. Right. Here. Alive and well," she said as she punctuated each word. "Tear it down or so help me, T…"

Tiernan rubbed his chest. "Oh. *That.* Yes. We'll take it down."

Enid noticed his hand movement as her eyes returned to normal. "I cannot believe how soft you've gotten in just five years. Drop and give me thirty."

"Now?"

Her eyes switched again to their white, fiery glow. "I said now, Tiernan."

Grumbling all the way, the former King got on his knees. He put his bare hands on the freezing cold ground, extended his legs into a plank position, and started doing pushups.

Tiernan peeked his head down the hallway of Castle Midir. A few meters outside of the throne room — an insignificant space that used to be nothing more than the mayor's office — his companions waited for him.

Enid walked alongside her brother. "How are your arms today?"

"Sore. But it was worth it. Going to start doing those each day again."

Shig turned around to see the twins coming their way. "Hey Z, D."

Airvede smiled. "I have good news. I tested teleporting with Firefly."

Tiernan raised his eyebrows. "Oh, yeah?"

Firefly explained, while pointing to Tiernan. "I took her to the cave Tiernan and I visited since Airvede had not seen it with her own eyes before. Through our connection, she was able to read my mind and see it for herself."

"It's like a form of telepathy. I can see through the eyes of another living being," Airvede said with a matter-of-fact wave of her hand.

Shig got excited. "Like you did in Alwyn with the Ryllix. So that's another power to add to your tally. I think I've lost count of them all!"

Airvede nodded. "Right. So, I know their lands are further than a cave up the way, but I'm confident I can make it work."

Firefly and Enid exchanged looks.

Tiernan saw them and scrunched his eyebrows. "What's wrong?"

"It just dawned on me," said Firefly. "After we meet with Rhys, we're leaving. Our group, the 'Defenders of Abria', will be no more. Disbanded."

She turned to Airvede. "I want you to know how much I'll miss you." Firefly gave her a hug. "I mean, I know you'll be taking me home," she said as she let go. "But this is it." Firefly looked at Shig. "The last time as…"

"Family," said Shig. "I'll be back here at some point. No doubt about it. My parents and siblings will want to come see where Isoshi rests. Maybe we could send messengers and you two could come back with us? Reunite the band, maybe even meet your families too?"

Tiernan felt himself getting emotional. "When the three of you arrived, I was still sorting through things." He paused for a moment. "A lot of things. You helped me work through them, even without realizing what you were doing at the time. I don't think I even realized it."

Enid smiled. "I only got to know you three for half as long as my brother did, but I enjoyed it. I wish we had more time together."

Airvede smiled. "Me too. I know I could learn a lot from you, but I need to get home to my family."

Tiernan laughed. "We keep using that word. Family." He put out his hand. "Family is Strength."

Shig put his hand on top. "For the glory of Watodo."

Airvede smiled and put hers in next. "May the Moon always grace the Isles."

Firefly joined in. "Long live Cykela."

Enid gave each of them a heartfelt expression of appreciation. "Thank you for freeing our land." She put her hand on top at last. "Until we meet again."

Tiernan led the group into Rhys' throne room. There, the former-Manus-turned-ruler of the land sat in his chair signing papers. With the sound of their arrival, he raised his head.

"Tiernan!" Rhys rushed over and hugged him. "Welcome back." He let go and shook the hand of the other three. "Your work in the northern cities was marvelous. And you," he said, looking at Shig, "the way you used that ancient relic to release Zoran's control over the monsters? That was a work of art! I wouldn't have believed it if I hadn't seen it for myself in Milston."

Shig gave Rhys a sheepish look back. "It wasn't all me. I had help."

"It was the combined strength of the relics, along with the Dragonborn's help," Airvede explained.

Rhys made eye contact with Enid. "Yes. Well, together you freed the Kingdom of Abria," he said with emphasis on the changed name. "We'll forever be in your debt."

Rhys snapped his fingers, and several castle attendants brought in their payment. "Please take these home with you. And let your leaders know we will honor our word with the trade deals for your services."

Airvede and Firefly gave each other a quiet stare. Shig looked back at them and nodded.

"We did not come here expecting a reward," Firefly said. "Nor will we accept this."

"We came here to help. The act itself was more than enough reward," Airvede continued.

"It was the only honorable thing to do," Shig finished.

"We just came to say goodbye. And to say if you ever need us again, don't hesitate to ask." With that, Firefly grabbed Shig and Airvede's hands.

"Are you two ready?" the White Mage asked.

"I am." Shig smiled at Tiernan. "Goodbye, Z. See you again someday."

"Farewell, my friend."

"Let's go then." Firefly also smiled at Tiernan. "Hey. I had fun. Thanks for everything, including our cave adventure. It was unforgettable."

"Be safe, Firefly," he said. "Watch out for orcs."

"Alright. Everyone close your eyes. Shig, we'll head to Watodo first." Airvede looked at Tiernan. "Tell your wife thank you."

Tiernan smiled big. "I will. I hope to meet Eamon someday myself."

Airvede took a deep breath, raised a hand, and snapped her fingers. In a flash, the self-proclaimed Defenders of Abria disappeared, returning to their homelands with the help of the White Mage.

Tiernan swallowed hard, realizing for the first time how much he was going to miss his companions.

Behind him, Rhys coughed. "There is one more thing, Tiernan Davienson."

"What's that?" Tiernan asked, his interest piqued at the unexpected use of his freshly declared surname.

Rhys snapped his fingers twice, and a different attendant walked in. This one carried an ornate purple pillow with a single gold crown on top of it.

"I think this is yours, my King."

Enid tried not to react, but couldn't help but let her eyes widen as she let out a slight gasp. She covered her mouth, waiting to see what would unfold next.

"King? Rhys, what are you talking about?"

The attendant handed Rhys the crown. He approached Tiernan with a solemn face. "I never signed the paperwork. On the day you stepped down, you left right away. The mayors and I had a conversation, and we decided we did not accept your abdication of the throne."

Rhys grinned big. "I merely kept it warm for you, much as my father did many years ago."

Tiernan turned around to his sister, now trying her best to keep her reaction calm and measured.

She shook her head. "I'm sorry, this is all you, Brother. Besides, you're clearly the older one."

Tiernan couldn't help but chuckle at her joke. He turned back to Rhys.

"Please, my King," Rhys said, "This thing is heavy."

Tiernan's chuckle turned into a full laugh. "No, it's not," he said as Rhys placed the crown on Tiernan's head. An almost imperceptible, though visible to all in the room, flash surrounded the King's neck.

A parting gift. I sped things up. Goodbye, my friend.

Tiernan felt his head. Brushing his shoulders were his long flowing locks of hair, now restored to their original length. Tiernan recognized the voice inside his head and smiled *Goodbye, Zachary. Thank you for everything.*

"Long live King Tiernan Davienson!" Rhys said.

Around the throne room, the attendants echoed the sentiment.

Tiernan turned around to Enid, words once again escaping him.

She grinned. "Nice trick with your hair. How'd you do that?"

"Zachary did. He's a Time Master or something, remember?" He grinned with the same boyish charm Enid hadn't seen for a long time. "Besides, you know what this means, don't you?"

"No. What's that, Brother?"

"Until we find Eislyn and bring her home, you're in charge of the Abrian Royal Guards."

Enid raised her hand to protest, but realized it was a futile objection. "Alright then. But only until we bring her home."

Tiernan leaned in and hugged her. The twins squeezed each other tight. A tear streamed down Tiernan's cheek, landing on Enid's neck.

"Oh, come on. Do you ever not cry, Brother?" she asked with a joyful laugh.

"Never," Tiernan responded.

A lone man moved throughout an open field. He used his rake, preparing the fields for the harvest. Though earlier than usual, the lack of snowfall since late Begynde made his father optimistic they could get a head start on the planting season.

Below him, he heard a *ting*. The sound was as if the metal tips of his tool had collided with something else on the ground.

He dropped the rake, letting it fall to the ground at his side. The man then dropped to his knees and ran his fingers through the grass, still slightly brown from the ongoing season of Frost.

After a moment of searching, he discovered the small object. He pulled it out of the dirt and wiped it off.

In his hand sat a small golden ring with accents of blue and fuchsia in an ornate pattern. The man shrugged and slid it on his fingers.

As soon as he did, he felt an immense sense of power flow throughout his body. It caused him to gasp as the surrounding scenery slowed down. Already aware of his ability to manipulate time for the past few years, this seemed to be an instinctive reaction between him and this piece of jewelry.

He eyed it with a cautious sense of uncertainty. He extended his hand as he had before, made a first, and twisted his arm. Rather than the usual slow rewinding of time, things moved at breakneck pace. The sun rose in the west, rising high to the sky. Satisfied, he then twisted his arms again in the other direction, watching the sunset, the moon rise, and the subsequent reappearance of the sun over the Valley Mountains to the east.

He raised his eyebrows in excitement, wondering how far things might go. On a hunch, he thought of a random date in the past.

"Mom and Dad's wedding."

Taking a deep breath, the man closed his eyes and put his hand on top of the Power Ring. In an instant, Steve — son of Ahern and Pernella, eventual guide to King Tiernan the 2nd, and the original name of the Time Master later named Zachary — disappeared.

Tiernan trekked up the steps of the Abrian Plateau next to his sister. The twins moved side by side, unsure how the other would react upon seeing Farna once again. Their trip across the land took a full week with unexpected layovers in Clericsfold for administrative loose ends.

For Tiernan, the arrival here meant the start of something new. With one chapter closed behind him, this would be a journey he would take with his twin, a mission to rebuild their home and the Kingdom's eventual capital.

For Enid, this was the first time she had seen Farna since she had left for the underground cave battle almost five years earlier.

Before they finished the summit, Enid grabbed her brother's arm. "Tiernan. Look."

"Hmm?" The King had been walking with his head down, partially out of a sense of respect for those who died here while also preparing himself for the sight of the devastation.

Instead of gazing upon Farna, Enid's attention was westbound. She pointed as he looked up.

"What in Grael?" Tiernan rushed to the top of the steps and stared in the same direction as her outstretched hand.

He scanned the horizon. To his surprise, there was no more western mountain range, at least near the Abrian Plateau. Instead, rubble and other remnants of what used to be there took its place. He wondered how far north this might be true, if places like Oakshadow and the Rosewood Forest might be open as well.

At the moment, this didn't matter. For the first time in recorded history, Abria had access to the rest of the continent.

"What do you think happened?" asked the King.

"I don't know. I could guess, but I'm sure I'd be wrong." She shook her head as she caught a glimpse of the destroyed Farna for the first time. Enid stood tall, unable to think of the words to say upon seeing the devastation that wrecked her home.

Tiernan ran his hands through his restored hair.

She saw the motion out of the corner of her eye. "We have a lot of work to do."

Tiernan looked back at the arriving caravan of supplies and workers. Many of them began unloading just at the edge of the Abrian Plateau.

"Look at all the timber, T. That's what Tammith had planned, isn't it?"

He smiled. "Gotta love that woman. No wonder she needs us to find employees for her operation. This is going to take workers from all over Abria."

Enid turned around to look at Farna one more time. "Family is Strength," she said, thinking about all the memories she had in the old city. Then, with a renewed sense of optimism, she wondered what new ones awaited her once the Kingdom finished the task at hand.

She looked back to talk to her brother. Out of the corner of her eye, she saw a bright flash far out in the ocean. How she saw it from this distance, she couldn't say. All she knew was that, in the very seat of all she was — her soul — the event was meant for her and her alone.

Because of her focus on the light show in the Great Sea, Enid missed the approaching gigantic flying shadow as it appeared on the horizon out of the west.

Tiernan saw it instead of the flash which had captured Enid's gaze. "Sister."

Enid continued to stare at the ocean.

"Sister!" Tiernan said again, this time shaking her arm.

Enid blinked. "What? Yes, I'm sorry T. What is it?" She turned around.

Tiernan pointed ahead. As the form lowered itself to the ground, it granted a calming sense of peace. Enid smiled, making the connection with what she just seen and what was about to happen.

Tiernan noticed her face and sighed. "I guess you and I are going for a ride before we start the rebuilding of Farna. Better send a messenger to Rhys and let him know."

Enid motioned ahead to her brother. "After you, *my King*," she said in a mocking tone.

"Wonder where it's going to take us?" he asked as they walked over to meet the enormous white dragon.

Chapter 48

Epilogue

The waves of the Great Sea bore down, fueling their power with an uncontrollable rage. Each crash acted as a reminder of the treacherous journey that lie ahead for any visitor who dared approach Abria.

After all, without the careful guide of an expert navigator, it would be easy to wreck, just as many had over the centuries when trying to access the fabled Kingdom.

The Great Sea's fury gradually subsided. Calmer waves and currents prevailed as travelers navigated further away from the Abrian coastline. As the solitary object drifted, the light of the powerful Graelian sun bounced off its shiny surface.

A seagull, not used to seeing anything this far between land masses, descended toward the object. When it made contact, the bird flew away, a hint of frostbite on its feet.

Over time, other creatures approached it. Some were drawn to the object like a moth to a flame, curious about its oblong shape and distinctive crystalline structure. Others felt encroached upon, as if the cobalt object was an invading monster intent on destroying its sovereignty.

The object itself was oblivious to this, instead content to wait. Wait until it was time to take the next step of its journey. Wait until its destiny could be fulfilled.

Once, it floated through a school of fish, freezing them as it passed by. Another time, it encountered a large whale, one common to the southern portions of Grael that had wandered off from its usual migration.

During one fateful day, it passed a more significant creature. This heartbroken beast, a lone Ryllix undertaking a long journey home to the icy waters of the north, paused. With reverence, it observed the object. Knowing there was nothing it could do, sadness and regret filled its heart.

The Ryllix hoped that one day it might all make sense.

As it swam away, its tail had an unintended side effect. With powerful momentum, it pushed the object along the last leg of its journey. Not long thereafter, the jewel made landfall on an island south of the Abrian Peninsula.

There, it sat undisturbed for a long time. Its shiny crystalline surface continued to reflect the light of the sun during the day. At night, the moon acted as its guard.

Various creatures watched it with genuine curiosity. Its blue hue was intoxicating, drawing them in though scaring them away with its ability to freeze anything upon contact.

Without warning, the object vibrated. Its jewel-like shape, a little over two meters in length and half a meter wide, shook so hard it dug itself into the sand. This left a large indention on the coastline.

At this lower latitude, the sun continued to shine with a burning intensity, though even its rays were no match for the increasing illumination of the large, blue jewel. The sound of its vibration echoed along the shoreline, turning into a shrill sound that caused all nearby animals and creatures to scurry away in abject terror.

Once its vibrancy reached peak, the jewel exploded in a blinding flash of light that was visible only to a specific individual who felt an innate, subconscious draw to be looking this way at this exact time.

Now transformed, a lone, ice cold Graelan warrior took its place.

With a gasp, the hero took a breath. Their eyes shot open. A single, solitary thought crossed their mind. The only name that mattered to them in this moment, or any moment for that matter.

"Enid!" yelled Prince Wayland.

Wayland will return
in
The Graelian Chronicles Book Three:
Kingdom of Sand and Water

Afterword

The story you just finished has been a collaborative effort. Thank you to my wife, Renee, for her tireless edits (including a major technical bug that erased several days' worth of work). In addition, thank you for your revisions to this cover. I love it just as much as the last one! To Mara, I love the map of Grael! To you and Liam, your feedback on your characters was invaluable. And finally, thanks to all three of you for helping to create Ancient Abrian.

What do I mean by "your characters" exactly? This story began as a tabletop homebrew board game. Though the final plot is *significantly* different from those early scenarios, some of the underlying ideas are still present. This includes Airvede, Firefly, and Shigeharu, who are stand-ins for Renee, Mara, and Liam. I played the role of Zachary/Tiernan as the narrator, appearing throughout the game and revealing clues about the land.

Together, *The Tale of Tiernan* and *The Legacy of Enid* conclude "Chapter One" of *The Graelian Chronicles*. Chapter Two will kick off with *Book Three: Kingdom of Sand and Water*.

There are other tales in the works, including a novella answering the question, "Who is Aila and why do they revere her so much?" That story has been alluded to several times and will be called *Song of Aila*. Plus, keep an eye out for more details on a coming title(s) that takes a deeper look at the Defender's backstories.

Thank you for joining me on this journey!

Family is Strength!
James Colson

Characters, Species, & Pronunciations

Tiernan Davienson (Teer-nin Day-vee-inn-sun)
Enid (Ee-nid)
Eislyn (Ash-lynn)
Wayland (Way-lind)
Firefly (Fire-fly)
Airvede (Air-vehd)
Shigeharu Kaitoson (Shig-uh-haru Kite-oh-sun)
Davien (Day-vee-inn)
Kyrie (Keer-ee-A)
Borun (Bow-run)
Freya (Fray-uh)
Eldar (El-dar)
Róisín (Ro-sheen)
Lugh (Lew)
Tammith (Tamm-ith)
Rhys (Reese)
Na'Goh (Nah-go)
Isoshi Kaitoson (Ih-so-she Kite-oh-sun)
Omi (Oh-mee)
Minmi (Min-mee)
Tibor (Tee-bore)
Midir (Meh-deer)
Kane (Cain)
Folas (Foal-lus)
Zoran (Zore-on)
Gamelyon (Guh-meel-yun)
Leviathan (Luh-vy-uh-thun)
Ryllix (Rill-ix)
Caudex (Caw-dex)
Marren (Marr-in)
Diocene (Dye-oh-seen)
Harachers (Har-uh-churs)

Cities, Towns, and Other Regions

Abria (Uh-bree-uh)
Farna (Far-nuh)
Alwyn (All-win)
Clericsfold
Idlewind
Whispersong
Lily of the Valley
Lorelei (Lore-uh-lie)
Northwick
Milston (Mill-stin)
Lakedon (Lake-dun)
Oakshadow
Rosewood Forest
Mystic Mornings
Fabled Wonders
Northern Plateau
Milston Mountains
Lake Conchobar (Cruh-hoor)
Valley Mountains
Valley Woods
Windale Desert
Kingscrown Rock
Kingscrown Bay
Abrian Plateau

The Isles: A series of islands
Lonlin: An island country of farmers
Lyra: A region on the same continent as Abria
Watodo: An empire proficient in mechanical tools
Kinswatch: A mysterious continent full of monsters
Infernus: The land of fire

The Abrian Calendar

338 days long | 26 hours per day | 7 days per week |
4 weeks per month | 12 months per year
2 festival days that fall outside of any specific week or month

Day 1: Moon Rise

Season of Frost
Begynde
Florin
Frostend

Season of Bloom
Windbloom
Daisymoon
Lysere

Day 170: Midfest

Season of Flame
Fawnmist
Flametide
Nove

Season of Ember
Origlow
Moonshadow
Darkember

Books by James Colson

The Graelian Chronicles
Book One: The Tale of Tiernan
Book Two: The Legacy of Enid
Book Three: Kingdom of Sand and Water – TBD
Book Four: Order of the Fourth – TBD

A Graelian Chronicles Novella
Firefly's Story / Airvede's Story / Shig's Story -- TBD
Song of Aila – coming 2026

Books by Renee Colson

Cookbooks
The Graelian Cookbook: Volume 1
The Graelian Cookbook: Volume 2

Books by Mara Colson

Spire: Hunted Kin – coming fall 2025

Books by Liam Colson

Cobra: Burnout – TBD

About the Author

James Colson is a proud husband and father. In 2024, he entered the world of self-publishing with *The Tale of Tiernan*, fulfilling a lifelong dream of becoming a published author.

In his free time, James enjoys spending time with his family, mountain biking, strength training, playing video games, and traveling.